THE SONGBIRD

Also by Valerie Wood

THE HUNGRY TIDE
ANNIE
CHILDREN OF THE TIDE
THE ROMANY GIRL
EMILY
GOING HOME
ROSA'S ISLAND
THE DOORSTEP GIRLS
FAR FROM HOME
THE KITCHEN MAID

For more information on Valerie Wood and her books, see her website at www.valeriewood.co.uk

THE SONGBIRD

Valerie Wood

BANTAM PRESS

LONDON • TORONTO • SYDNEY • AUCKLAND • JOHANNESBURG

TRANSWORLD PUBLISHERS
61–63 Uxbridge Road, London W5 5SA
a division of The Random House Group Ltd

RANDOM HOUSE AUSTRALIA (PTY) LTD
20 Alfred Street, Milsons Point, Sydney,
New South Wales 2061, Australia

RANDOM HOUSE NEW ZEALAND LTD
18 Poland Road, Glenfield, Auckland 10, New Zealand

RANDOM HOUSE SOUTH AFRICA (PTY) LTD
Isle of Houghton, Corner of Boundary and Carse O'Gowrie Roads,
Houghton 2198, South Africa

Published 2005 by Bantam Press
a division of Transworld Publishers

A catalogue record for this book is available from the British Library.
ISBN 978 0593 053829 (from Jan 07)
ISBN 0593 053826

Typeset in 11/13pt New Baskerville by
Falcon Oast Graphic Art Ltd.

Printed and bound in Great Britain by
Mackays of Chatham, Chatham, Kent

1 3 5 7 9 10 8 6 4 2

Papers used by Transworld Publishers are natural, recyclable products
made from wood grown in sustainable forests. The manufacturing processes
conform to the environmental regulations of the country of origin.

For my family with love

ACKNOWLEDGEMENTS

My thanks are due to Peter Burgess, theatre researcher, for information and advice on nineteenth-century Hull theatres, music halls and Jenny Lind.

My thanks and love to Peter, Catherine, Ruth and Alex for their support and encouragement.

Sources

David Piper, *The Companion Guide to London*, William Collins Sons & Co. Ltd, Glasgow, 1964

'Greensleeves', anon, attributed to Henry VIII
'A Red, Red Rose', Robert Burns, 1759–96
'A Whole New World', anon

CHAPTER ONE

'Mama!' Poppy untangled a wisp of red hair from her forehead and twirled it round her finger. 'Can I ask you something? Something secret?'

Mary Mazzini put down her mending and looked at her young daughter. 'You mean *tell* me something? If it's a secret?'

Poppy clasped her hands beneath her chin and swayed from side to side. 'No. I mean *ask* you something.'

'You can ask me anything at all.' Her mother smiled. 'You know that.'

'Yes, but this is especially special and I don't want anyone else to know. Not Pa, and especially not Tommy!'

'All right. What is it?' Mary took up her sewing again. Poppy sometimes took a long time to get to the point. She didn't like to miss anything out in case it was important.

Poppy came up closer to her mother and, breathing into her ear, asked, 'When will I be old enough to love somebody?'

Her mother pondered. Poppy constantly surprised her with a variety of questions, but this one surprised her more than most, and although she thought she knew what she meant, she answered in a vague manner and kept her eyes on her sewing. 'You love us already, don't you? Your pa and Tommy and me?'

'Oh, I don't mean us, our family,' Poppy said urgently. 'I mean somebody else! I mean somebody that I might want to marry one day.'

'I think, sweetheart, that at only ten years old, you're a little too young to consider that!' Mary gave a tender smile. What was the child thinking of? Or *who* was the child thinking of might be the better question.

'I know,' Poppy said earnestly. 'That's why I'm asking. When *will* I be old enough?'

'It's difficult to say really,' her mother replied in all seriousness, knowing that she mustn't laugh or make fun. 'It depends. It has nothing to do with how old a person is, it's a matter of meeting someone and knowing that you love him or her.'

'So could I have met somebody already? Am I old enough? Because I think I have. I do, I mean.' Poppy shook her mother's hand so that she had to put down her sewing and look at her.

'You might well be fond of someone,' her mother said gently. 'But love is a different matter and you are far too young,' she repeated, 'to even think of such a thing.' She leaned towards Poppy and kissed her cheek. 'Love is for grown-up people. Playing with toys and games is for children.'

Poppy frowned. 'Is Tommy old enough – or Charlie?' she added, as if in afterthought.

Ah, Mary thought. Charlie! He's the object of desire. Poor Charlie, how embarrassed he would be. 'Your brother is far too young, even though he thinks he's a man at fourteen, and so is Charlie. Boys don't fall in love until they're much older. Come now,' she said firmly, bringing the conversation to an end. 'Get the tablecloth out and set 'table. It's time for supper. Then go and call your pa in from the shop. He said he'd come to 'Mechanics with us tonight.'

Poppy and her mother went to the theatre or music hall nearly every Friday night. Tommy sometimes accompanied them, unless he thought there would be a lot of dancing, though he liked the singers and the comedians. If he wasn't too busy, Poppy's father, Joshua, would shut up his grocery and coffee shop in Savile Street, close by Hull's town dock, and join them until the last act when he would slip out of the theatre and hurry back, and he and Tommy would prepare coffee and put out the cakes and pastries, and open up again in time to catch the late night crowd who came streaming out of the Mechanics Music Hall, the Theatre Royal or the Assembly Rooms, which were all close by.

Then, as the crowds wended their way home, the performers arrived at the coffee shop: the singers, dancers, jugglers and comics, who, though tired and bereft of wigs and make-up, were not quite ready to fall into their rented beds, but needed to unwind and chat, which they could do at Joshua Mazzini's, for he was never in a hurry to close or go to his own bed. He was of Italian extraction and would have talked all night to anyone prepared to listen. They had all heard the story of his penniless grandfather, who had arrived in London from Italy looking for work, and was loaned a wooden cart by a fellow Italian, and advised to head north.

'There isa no worka here,' Joshua would mimic affectionately. 'That's what he was told. And so he walked. All 'way from London,' he would add in his own Hull dialect. 'All 'way to Hull, pushing his cart with his worldly belongings in it, and he finished up here.' He would look proudly round his shop, which on one side was shelved with groceries, with packets of this and that, sacks of flour, tins of biscuits, slabs of cheese and butter, while on the other side small tables were spread with checked cloths and a posy of flowers in the centre, with chairs with matching cushions, for, he said, folks will stay longer if they're comfortable. The coffee pot was constantly bubbling and spitting and there were always warm pastries, chocolate cake and sweet biscuits, for his wife, Mary, was an excellent baker. Joshua would open the shop door and the aroma would drift out, bringing the customers in.

Joshua advertised the local entertainment by putting posters in his window or on the shop counter, and for this he received two free tickets for a Monday, when the audience was sparse, and two for a Friday. Poppy, when she was allowed, would go to both performances, for she was entranced by the colour, the music, the dancing girls, the singers and the sheer magic of the theatre or music hall. She watched avidly as the dancers went through their routines, she memorized the songs, and when she came home she would put on her mother's shoes, drape a shawl round her shoulders and perform in front of the mirror in her attic bedroom above the shop.

That Friday night in April, Poppy hurried alongside her mother as they made their way to the Mechanics Music Hall in George Street. Mary Mazzini was, everyone agreed, the most elegant of women. She wore the simplest of fashion yet managed to look as if she had stepped out of a Paris *Journal des Modes.*

Tonight she was wearing a pale blue outfit with a long trailing skirt, the frilled bodice cut into a wasp waist to show off her petite figure, the leg-o'-mutton sleeves edged at the wrist with thick wide lace. Usually she wore a large hat but tonight she wore a small felt boater with a single feather. In one hand she carried a muff and held up her skirt, and with the other she restrained Poppy, who skipped along in her white ankle-length dress, blue wool coat and soft leather boots. On her head she wore a bonnet, tied beneath her chin with ribbons.

'I can't decide whether to be a dancer or a singer,' Poppy said. 'It would be nice to do both.' She took both dancing and singing lessons, not because her parents wished her to take up either of those professions, but because she had a sweet clear voice and a natural tendency to dance.

'Oh, not to go on the stage!' her mother declared. 'It's a very hard life. You've seen how exhausted the performers are when they come in for their supper? No, dear, just enjoy the pleasure of being able to do both. Besides, your papa wouldn't allow it. He wouldn't want you to go touring all over the country with strangers. He wouldn't like that at all!'

Poppy pouted. Her father spoiled her. She knew that well enough. Compared with her friends' parents, she realized how lucky she was with hers. She was indulged with pretty clothes, visits to theatres, music halls and concerts too. There were outings to the seaside, lessons in dancing and deportment with Miss Davina and singing and elocution with Miss Eloise. Yet her parents were protective of her; she had to be accompanied wherever she went, either by them or – reluctantly – by her brother Tommy, and was not allowed to go wandering round the town on her own as some of her friends did.

Mary Mazzini loved the theatre and music hall too. As a girl she had never been allowed to attend. Her parents were staunch chapelgoers and considered musical entertainment to be a ploy of the devil sent to entice young people into sinful ways. But Mary would sneak into the theatres on the pretence of doing something else worthwhile, and it was here that she had met Joshua, who had enough Italian blood running through his veins to enjoy music and singing, laughter and good food – all the things which she had been denied.

They fell in love and as she was twenty-one she told her parents she was going to marry him with or without their permission. One of the first things Joshua did on their marriage was to buy Mary a pianoforte from the music shop that stood across from them in Savile Street, Gough and Davy, who arranged for her to have lessons.

With a daughter of her own now, Mary had a better understanding of her parents' concerns for her, though not of their unjoyous outlook on life.

'I'll have to slow down, Poppy,' she said suddenly. 'I've got a stitch in my side.'

'We'll be late,' Poppy said anxiously, and looked back over her shoulder. 'And Pa will miss 'beginning of 'show. Oh, there he is! He's coming!' Her father had stayed behind to lock up as Tommy had gone out, but now he was hurrying along George Street to catch up with them. She beckoned to him to be quick. 'Shall I run on and save the seats?'

'No,' her mother said. 'Wait for your father. Don't pull,' she exclaimed, as a sharp pain ran up her arm. A wave of sickness and nausea swept over her. Whatever had caused that? She had had only a little supper of potted meat and toast with a small glass of red wine. The wine was too acid, she decided, that's all. It's nothing. It will go away. But the nausea increased, her arm ached and she felt very swimmy, and she put her hand to her mouth.

'Sorry.' Poppy looked up at her mother, alarmed at her tone of voice. 'You've gone ever so white! Papa,' she called as her father hurried towards them. 'Mama's not well. See how white she is!'

'I'm all right,' Mary said. 'I felt sick, but it's nothing. Let's go in. I'll feel better once I'm sitting down.'

Poppy was relieved. For a moment she had thought that they would have to go back home if her mother was unwell, and she really didn't want to miss the show.

The Mechanics Music Hall was the oldest music hall in the town. The building had once been a private house, owned by a local member of parliament and then by the Broadley clan, one of the distinguished families of Hull, who sold it to the Mechanics Institute, which had been founded in 1825 to provide education and useful instruction of members in the knowledge of science and art. On acquiring the property, the board built a large saloon at the rear which could hold twelve hundred people. In the front foyer, which was ornamented with fluted pilasters, stood a statue of the eminent Dr John Anderson, one of the founder members.

The saloon was now used as a music hall and had had many changes of activity, proprietors and names. In its heyday it had been the most popular entertainment venue in town, but as other theatres and halls opened their doors its spirit failed from time to time and trade lapsed. Now in the ownership of Boscoe and Downs and under the name of Boscoe's Empire Theatre of Varieties it was once again flourishing, but everyone still referred to it by the old name of the Mechanics.

Poppy wriggled in her seat to get comfortable, and in a moment the curtains rose and the performance began.

A magician came onto the stage for the first act. He was dressed in a colourful cloak adorned with stars and moons, which swirled around his feet as he moved about the stage. He produced balloons from his pointed hat, which drifted into the auditorium, and the children in the audience jumped up to catch them. He brought out rabbits from inside his wide sleeves and yards of coloured ribbon from his ears. Then he invited members of the audience to join him on the stage, whereupon he produced flowers from their hair, and a flock of doves, which flew round the participants and fluttered into the audience before returning to a straw casket which he closed with a flourish. He opened it a minute later, holding it aloft to reveal that it was empty, and took his bow to tumultuous applause.

'How does he do that?' Poppy turned to her mother, but her mother was bent low and didn't answer, and her father had his head close to hers and was asking her something. The next act started. He was billed as a character comedian and singer. He wore an odd-looking checked jacket and knickerbockers and told incomprehensible stories, which made the adults in the audience laugh, whilst Poppy fidgeted in her seat and wished he would finish, as the Terry Sisters, who were billed as delightful dancers and sweet singers, would be on next but one, after the juggler, and they were the ones she really wanted to see.

'Poppy!' Her father leaned towards her as the juggler threw

balls into the air. 'We have to leave. Your ma's not well. Pick up your coat.'

'Oh, Pa! The Terry Sisters are next! Can't I stay? I can come home on my own.'

Her father shook his head, but her mother placed her hand on his arm. 'She'll be all right,' she said in a low voice. 'Let her stay. Tommy can come back to fetch her.'

'Unless you want me to help you?' Poppy suddenly felt guilty about asking to stay when her mother wasn't well. 'I'll come if you like!'

But her mother was already rising from her seat as the juggler took his bow. 'No,' she said breathlessly. 'Stay until the end. But wait for Tommy outside.'

Poppy settled down again and gave a deep sigh of pleasure, then put her hand into her pocket and brought out a bon-bon, which she unwrapped and popped into her mouth just as the Terry Sisters danced across the stage. They were dressed identically in silver flounced dresses trimmed with fluffy white fur. Their skirts came down to their slim ankles and showed dainty silver shoes. On their heads they wore tall feathered headdresses adorned with silver beads, which glistened as they moved.

They were not very good singers, Poppy decided, as she sucked her bon-bon, but they were good dancers, moving in time to the music and tap-tap-tapping across the stage, their hips and arms synchronized, their white teeth gleaming in wide smiles.

I could do that, Poppy thought, as she watched their movements and routine. I'll practise when I get home. So absorbed was she that she momentarily forgot about her parents until the final curtain came down and she realized that she was alone. I know my way home, she thought, it's only round the corner. I don't need Tommy to collect me. But she was mindful that her father would be angry if she didn't wait for her brother, so she stood by the doors as the crowds surged out, talking and laughing and discussing the programme.

She waited for ten minutes and only a few stragglers were left and Tommy still hadn't come. Shall I go on my own? I'll probably meet him anyway. She looked down George Street towards the turning for Savile Street, but the entire crowd was heading that way, away from the theatre, and there was no sign of her sandy-haired brother coming towards her.

'Hello, Poppy!' She jumped as someone greeted her from behind.

'Charlie!' She gave him a quick smile. 'I'm – I'm waiting for Tommy. Have you seen him? Ma and Pa had to go home. Mama wasn't well. They said I'd to wait for him.'

'I know. I called for him, but he wasn't there. He must have gone to look at 'ships. I saw your pa. He asked me to come for you.'

Charlie looked down at her. He was older and taller than her brother, fair-haired with blue eyes, and he was the one she loved. She was sure it was love, for her mouth became dry whenever she saw him, and her stomach gave a flip. He was her brother's best friend. She saw him often and each time he had this effect on her. She would die if he found out, and her brother would tease her unmercifully if he discovered it. She was far too young for him, she knew, for Charlie Chandler was fifteen, nearly sixteen. His birthday was in June, whereas she had only had her tenth birthday in January. New Year's Day, 1880, she had been born. But it didn't matter, she decided as she gazed adoringly at him. When I'm a bit older, maybe when I'm twelve, I'll ask him if he'll wait for me.

CHAPTER TWO

Poppy put her hand out and bashfully Charlie took it, holding her fingers lightly. 'Your pa's sent for 'doctor,' he muttered in an embarrassed manner, and cleared his throat. 'Your ma isn't well.'

'I know. That's why they left 'theatre early. But they said I could stay,' she added, not wanting him to think her selfish for not leaving with them. 'I wanted to see 'Terry Sisters,' she added.

'Were they any good?' he asked, hurrying her across the road.

'They were lovely dancers, but they didn't sing very well. And they were a lot older than I thought they would be.' She pondered. The sisters had worn a lot of make-up. She could see it even from her seat upstairs. Their eyes were very dark and outlined in black and their lips were scarlet. 'They must have been about twenty at least,' she said.

'Gosh!' Charlie gave a dry laugh. 'As old as that!' Poppy looked up at him to see if he was amused by her comment, but his face was solemn and he looked straight ahead. 'There's Tommy,' he said, dropping her hand. 'Hey, Tom!' He raised his voice. 'I've been looking for you.'

Tommy looked from his friend to his sister. 'Where've you been? To 'Mechanics?'

'I came round to 'shop to see if you were coming out, but you weren't there. Your pa said he didn't know where you were and they wanted you to collect Poppy from 'Mechanics. So they asked me instead.'

'I could've come home on my own,' Poppy chipped in defiantly. 'I don't need collecting by anybody.'

'Ah, but Pa's little pet, aren't you?' Tommy grinned. 'He'd

think that somebody would run off with you! As if anybody would,' he said. 'They'd bring you back soon enough! But why were you there on your own anyway?'

'Mama's sick,' Poppy said. 'They had to leave 'show early. Charlie said that 'doctor's been sent for.'

'Oh! What's up?' Tommy asked. 'We'd better get off home then.'

'Where've you been?' Charlie asked him. 'I looked for you.'

Tommy glanced at Poppy. He shrugged. 'Just looking at 'ships in 'dock. There's two just come in.'

'Pa said don't get any ideas!' Poppy reminded him. 'You've got to help in the shop and with 'baking!'

'I know that, Miss Clever-clogs,' Tommy parried. Living in a port and surrounded by ships and seamen all his life, breathing the salty smell of the estuary, he had long wished to go to sea, but his father wanted him to work with him in the grocery and coffee shop.

'I'd better get off then,' Charlie said. 'It's half past nine. I've to be up early in 'morning. We've some orders to finish.' Charlie was apprenticed to his father who was a shoemaker in Scale Lane, in the old part of Hull. John Chandler was well known to the merchants and business people in the town. His boots and shoes were of the finest and softest leather and his reputation had spread as far as York. He was, however, a hard taskmaster and Charlie and he often crossed swords when youth and age disagreed. John Chandler spent most of his time in his workshop and even now would be working on orders, and probably fuming with exasperation because his son had taken time off.

There was a hansom cab waiting outside the shop, which had the name *Mazzini's* painted in bright red letters above the window. A smell of coffee drifted out from the door but their father wasn't there. Nan, a widow who cleaned daily, though didn't usually help in the grocery shop, was serving coffee and her daughter Mattie was clearing tables.

'Come on, Tommy. Give a hand,' Nan urged as they entered. She wiped her forehead with the back of her hand. 'I've been that busy. Your da's at 'back with your ma and 'doctor. Good job we called in. Just as well Mattie was with me or I shouldn't have been able to manage. As it is some folk wouldn't wait.'

Tommy put on a striped apron and went to serve the customers, apologizing to them for the delay. 'My mother's not well,' he explained. 'That's 'reason for 'hold-up. Very sorry,' and because he was a genial young lad with a pleasant manner they stopped their grumbling and ordered their supper.

'I'd better help as well,' Poppy said, taking off her coat, and started clearing the tables of dirty crockery. Then she looked up as two women came through the door and took in a startled breath. The Terry Sisters! They were smaller than they'd appeared on stage, she thought, and quite plain without their make-up and false eyelashes. And their hair was mousy brown, not black and gleaming as it had been under their headdresses. But it was them all right; they had a certain air about them that spoke of the stage.

'Can we have a pot o' coffee, darlin'?' one of them said to Poppy.

'And get a slice of cake, Ena,' added the other. 'And that table over there,' she said to Poppy, indicating a table for four. 'We've got some friends coming along in a minute.'

Poppy nodded obligingly. 'Walnut or ginger?' she asked. 'My mother makes the cakes. I've just been to 'Mechanics,' she added. 'I went specially to see you.'

'Did you, dearie?' said Ena, who was slightly shorter than her sister. 'And did you enjoy the show?'

'Yes, thank you,' Poppy said politely, and decided not to tell them that she didn't think their singing was very good. 'I liked the dancing best. I go for dancing lessons,' she said. 'And singing too.'

'Is that so?' Ena opened her bag and took out a cheroot, which she lit and put between her lips. She creased up her eyes as she drew on the cheroot. Poppy stared at her boldness, deciding that she was probably even older than she had first thought. Probably about twenty-five.

'And will you go on the stage?' Ena asked, blowing out a curl of smoke. 'Shall you be our rival?'

'I'm only ten,' Poppy explained. 'And my pa wouldn't want me to.' Then she grinned at the sisters. 'But I might try to persuade him!'

'Don't, darlin',' the other sister said. 'You stay at home and help your ma and pa in this nice coffee shop.' She looked round approvingly. 'Until some handsome and rich young man comes along and carries you orf. That's what I'd do, anyway,' she added with a sigh.

'No you wouldn't, Ronny,' Ena said as she sat down. 'You only say that at the end of a show.' She crossed her legs, showing a glimpse of trim ankles beneath her skirt. 'It's in our blood, you see,' she told Poppy. 'Our ma and pa were on the stage, so we know nothink else. Fetch us that coffee, there's a good girl,' she added. 'I'm fair gasping. And two slices of ginger cake.' She winked at Poppy. 'Got to keep our strength up.'

'A pot of coffee for the Terry Sisters,' Poppy sang out, 'and two pieces of ginger cake.'

'I'll take it, Poppy,' Tommy said. 'You'd better nip and see how Ma is.'

Poppy took in a breath. In the excitement of meeting the Terry Sisters, she'd forgotten that her mother had been unwell. She hurried through the door at the back of the shop and into their private rooms. She heard the murmur of men's voices and then the click of the door which led into the street, and her father turned from letting the doctor out.

'What did 'doctor say, Pa? About Mama? Is she all right?' She was suddenly worried. What would happen to them all if her mother was sick?

Her father patted her head. 'He said she's to rest for a bit. She's been overdoing it. So we'll have to look after her, won't we? Let her stay in bed in a morning instead of getting up so early.' Mary rose at five o'clock every morning in order to make bread, cakes and biscuits.

'So who'll do the baking then, Pa?'

'Tommy'll have to do more than he does,' her father said. 'Don't you worry your head about it. It'll only be until your ma's feeling better.' He looked down at her, and she thought he looked sad and worried. 'And when you're older you'll be able to help a bit more, won't you? Learn to bake like your ma does? She'll show you how.'

The idea of learning to bake didn't thrill her, but of course she would if it helped her mother. But did her father mean that she would have to work in the shop? The thought filled her with dismay. After being at the theatre tonight, meeting the Terry Sisters and seeing how they could transform themselves from being very ordinary-looking women into bright-eyed, cherry-cheeked, glittering, vivacious artistes had excited and stimulated her. I want to go on the stage, she yearned. That's what I want. Miss Davina used to be a dancer at the music hall. I'll ask her to teach me what to do. But I won't tell Mama or Pa just yet.

She went back into the shop and her father came too, telling Nan and Mattie that they could go home if they wanted to. 'Thanks, Nan,' he said. 'I appreciate your help. You too, Mattie.' He took some money from the cash drawer to give to Nan.

'That's all right, Mr Mazzini,' she said. 'I'll see you in 'morning. That table over yonder,' she added. 'Those stage folk. They'll be here a while yet. I think they've no homes to go to!'

'None that's comfortable anyway,' Joshua agreed. 'They'll be sharing 'em with bed bugs I shouldn't wonder.'

At the table with the Terry Sisters was the man who had been dressed in the check suit and told tall stories that Poppy didn't understand. He looked grey and tired and not as bouncy as he'd been on stage, and he had very little hair, whereas when he had been performing he had had curly ginger hair. Another man made up the foursome. He was tall and dark-haired and appeared to be laying down the law about something.

Poppy went across to them. 'Can I get you anything else?' she asked. 'Would you like more coffee, or chocolate?'

The tall man glanced at her and smiled. 'Shouldn't you be tucked up in bed, little girl?'

Poppy shook her head, her red curls tossing. 'I'm allowed to stay up late on a Friday.'

'She's been to see our show, Dan,' Ena told him. 'She's a dancer too, just like us!'

'Really?' The man swivelled round to look at Poppy. He nodded thoughtfully. 'How old are you?'

'Ten, eleven in January,' Poppy said. 'I can sing too. I go for singing lessons with Miss Eloise.'

'Miss Eloise?' Dan laughed and raised his eyebrows. 'Not *the* Miss Eloise.'

Poppy gazed at him. 'She's 'only one I know,' she said solemnly. 'She used to sing in concerts.'

'Don't tease her,' Ronny murmured. 'She's only a babe!'

'Let's see what you can do, then,' Dan said. 'Show us your speciality.'

'I'll have to ask my pa first,' Poppy said. 'I'm supposed to be helping. My mother isn't well. She has to rest.'

'All right,' Dan said. 'Is that your papa?' He glanced over to where Joshua was putting glasses into a cupboard. 'Tell him we'd like a bottle of red wine and ask him if he would join us in a glass; and that we'd like to watch you dance.'

'Pa,' Poppy said tremulously, and repeated the message.

Her father looked across at the group. People at the other tables were preparing to leave. The four from the theatre were the last customers. He nodded. He was tired. It had been a difficult evening. A glass of wine wouldn't go amiss; it would help him sleep, chase away his worries. 'Clear a space, then,' he said to Tommy, who was listening to the remarks. 'Then lock 'door. There'll be nobody else coming in tonight.'

'Can you dance without music?' Ronny asked Poppy, as she waited for her father to bring a bottle of wine and glasses.

'Yes,' she said. 'I can hear it in my head. But I'll sing first,' she told her. 'Whilst I've got plenty of breath. Then I'll dance.'

The Terry Sisters both smiled at that. 'You'll have to learn to do both and breathe at the same time if you go on the stage,' Ena said.

'She's not going on 'stage,' her father commented, coming to the table and pouring the wine into five glasses. 'Her ma wants her to sing and dance. She says it's an accomplishment.'

'And so it is,' Dan said. 'Everyone should have at least one. Some are lucky enough to have more than one.' He smiled at Poppy, who positioned herself the way Miss Eloise had taught her, and began to sing.

It was a simple ballad. A story of springtime and flowers and birds singing in the treetops, the music charming and lyrical for a young pure voice, and when she had finished the listeners broke into spontaneous applause, and her father drank his wine and nodded. Poppy gave a curtsy, and then began to dance. She hummed a tune in her head and tried to remember what she had been taught by Miss Davina. Keeping her head up and her shoulders back, and her arms and hands at a graceful angle, she tapped and pirouetted and swung her skirts. She also improvised on the dance steps she had seen performed by the Terry Sisters. Finally she swung round, put her forefinger under her chin and gave another deep curtsy.

The sisters clapped. The comedian yawned, but the tall man called Dan leaned towards her and said, 'Well done, young lady. Very well done. And what's your name?'

'Poppy Mazzini,' she said breathlessly.

'*Poppy Mazzini*! A lovely name for a young lady of talent.' He glanced at her father. 'A talent that ought not to be hidden away.'

Her father shook his head. 'We wouldn't want to lose her,' he stated. 'Like I said. She won't be going on 'stage.'

Poppy attended a private school, but now that her mother was unwell, instead of playing with her friends as she usually did after school was finished for the day, she had to help in the shop. Nothing too arduous, not like Tommy who was now baking the bread and cakes, whilst his father served the groceries, made tea or coffee, unpacked the provisions which came in daily and delivered orders to their customers. Poppy had to set the tables, clear away the dirty crockery and wash and dry it, but Tuesdays and Wednesdays were the days for her dancing and singing lessons. 'I can still go, Pa, can't I?' she begged him. 'Miss Davina will be expecting me.' She was allowed to attend the lessons alone as both Miss Davina and Miss Eloise had rooms in George Street, only minutes away from where she lived.

'Aye,' her father said. 'For 'time being anyway. Your ma wants you to keep going. But if we're busy when you get back you'll have to help.'

'Oh, I will,' she said eagerly. 'But I want to ask Miss Davina about some new steps that 'Terry Sisters did last week. I know I can do them.'

Her father smiled indulgently and patted her cheek, but added, 'Don't get fancy ideas, just because you've seen them two dancers. That life's not for you. It takes a different kind of person to perform on stage. It's not for folks like us.'

CHAPTER THREE

'One, two, three, turn. One two three skip. One two three *swirl.* Keep your head *up*! Smile. Step one two three, four five six, finger under chin – *and* curtsy! Well done, Poppy!' Miss Davina nodded approvingly. 'Now walk towards me, toes out, head up, shoulders down, tummy in, *derrière* nipped! Good! That's it for today, dear. See you next week.'

'Miss Davina! I went to see 'Terry Sisters last week. Can I show you the dance they did?'

Miss Davina looked at her watch. 'If it won't take long. I have another lesson in ten minutes.' She hadn't as it happened, but it didn't do to let her pupils know how much she relied on them.

Poppy performed as much as she remembered of the dance and improvised where she had forgotten, giving a provocative shrug of her shoulders and a twitch of her rear as she had seen the Terry Sisters do. Miss Davina raised her eyebrows. 'Well, Poppy, that's all very well for stage girls, but I don't think your mama would want you to learn that style of dancing.'

'But could you teach me if she didn't mind?'

'Oh, yes, of course I could. But you must ask her first.' Miss Davina, when she had been just Jane Davidson, had had aspirations to the stage and her parents had not considered it to be a demeaning occupation. But at ten, she had already inherited her mother's large build. No matter how she exercised, danced or starved herself, by twelve she was solid and heavy-limbed. At fourteen, as she auditioned for the theatre, she knew that it was hopeless, that no-one would want this tall, plain, buxom-chested, ample-hipped girl as a dancer. But yet she loved to dance and continued with her lessons, and when the teacher could teach her no more she turned herself to teaching and tried instead to inspire the children who came to her. None, she thought, would ever go onto the stage, for most were well-off tradesmen's children without ambition or talent, or if they had, then their parents would nip it in the bud as being an undesirable occupation for their daughters, as she thought that the Mazzinis would also.

'It's a pity,' she said to her friend, Miss Eloise, the following evening as they shared their weekly bottle of wine in Miss Eloise's rooms. 'Poppy is a beautiful dancer. She's not too tall, she's dainty and pretty, and has all the makings of a stage personality.'

'Not to mention those lovely red curls,' Eloise, formerly Ella Stanton, agreed. 'She would look good and she'll have the trim figure of her mother when she is older. But she also has a voice,' she added, and sighed. 'She could go far.'

She too had suffered disappointment. She was set for a career in the concert halls, but constant bouts of laryngitis had caused her to cancel appearances, and eventually ruined her voice. Fortunately her father had left her reasonably secure financially, so she had set up as a singing teacher for the children of aspiring parents who wanted their daughters to charm future suitors with their accomplishments.

'Just suppose.' Miss Davina tapped her mouth. 'Just suppose we train her – only to see what she can do,' she added. 'Not with any ulterior motive, you understand. But give her extra coaching, push her a little further than we would normally do. What do you think?'

It would be satisfying, they both agreed, to do something worthwhile. To prepare a child to her full potential. A life in the theatre and the music hall was becoming more acceptable in this last decade of the nineteenth century, though there were some who still considered it to be a degrading and immoral occupation for dissolute people. But Poppy had flair, grace and ability, they decided. She could, they thought, bring her own touch of class and style to the stage if she ever took matters into her own hands.

They opened another bottle of wine and gave a toast to Poppy's future, linked to their own, for wouldn't it add to their own esteem, Miss Eloise said, if they were known as the former teachers of a bright and shining star?

*

'Your voice is improving, Poppy,' her mother said. She was lying on the sofa in the parlour with a shawl over her and a pillow beneath her head. It was now September and her health hadn't improved. She still rose early to do the baking, but Tommy got up too to help her. He lifted the pans and the baking trays into and out of the oven. He kneaded the dough for the bread and carried the trays of finished cakes and pastries into the shop for their early customers whilst his father prepared orders, weighed flour into bags, stacked the shelves with tins and jars and saw to the delivery men who brought in sacks of potatoes and carrots from the market. Nan washed the floor and windows and then cleaned their private rooms.

Poppy had come home from school and her mother had heard her singing as she came through from the shop into the parlour. 'That sounds lovely,' she said. 'Is it something new?'

'Yes.' Poppy took off her coat and sat at her mother's side. 'Miss Eloise said we should try something different. Are you cold?' she asked, touching her mother's hand, which was thin and blue.

'I am cold,' she said. 'I don't seem to be able to get warm, except when I'm baking.'

It was a cosy parlour with pictures on the walls, and ornaments on the overmantel in front of the mirror. A bright fire burned in the tiled fireplace, and because the heavy curtains were partly closed to keep the room warmer, an oil lamp was lit in the centre of a round table, until later when Joshua would come in to light the gas chandelier.

'Pa said Tommy will have to take over the baking,' Poppy said, tucking the shawl closer round her mother. 'If you're not up to it.' She pressed her lips together. 'You are getting better, aren't you, Mama?' she asked anxiously.

'Not much,' her mother admitted. 'I don't seem to have much energy.' She gazed at Poppy and her eyes misted over. 'You'll help your pa if he needs you, won't you, Poppy? He'll rely on you and Tommy, though I know that Tommy wants to go to sea. He says he doesn't want to stop in the shop all his life.'

'You're not going to die, are you? I shan't bear it if you do.' Poppy started to cry. 'What will we do?' She began to sob. 'What will Pa do?'

Her mother sat up and put her arms about her. 'Hush, hush. I'm not thinking of dying for a long time. But everyone does, eventually.' She pushed back Poppy's red hair and kissed her forehead. 'We can't live for ever, you know.'

But I am tired, she thought. So very tired, and I don't like the way I feel; as if I'm living on borrowed time. But I must make an effort. For the sake of my son and daughter, I must fight this. And for Joshua too, but there will be some woman who'll come scurrying round if I'm not here. He's a handsome, prosperous man. But weak. He won't be able to manage on his own.

'Sing the song for me,' she prompted. 'From the beginning.'

Poppy wiped her eyes. 'All right.' She swallowed hard. 'Miss Eloise said the words were too old for me, but that the music would stretch my vocal cords.'

Her mother nodded. 'Then let's hear it.' She leaned back against her pillow again and closed her eyes as Poppy began. Poppy wasn't shy of performing in front of anyone; she concentrated always on the words and music, the meaning and feeling behind the words. But this particular song awakened in her something which she didn't quite understand. It was a song of love, full of pathos and longing.

Her mother opened her eyes in astonishment and watched Poppy, who had crossed her hands lightly across her chest and gazed into space as she sang. A tear trickled down Mary's cheek. On one of her stolen visits to the theatre when she was young, she had heard this selfsame melody. She had never thought to hear her own daughter sing it.

Poppy finished and gave a bow to her mother, who clasped her hands together and pressed them to her mouth. 'It's from an opera,' Poppy explained. 'Miss Eloise said it was one of her favourites when she was young. She used to sing it at concerts. It has an Italian name.'

Her mother nodded. ' "*La Sonnambula*",' she said. 'I remember it too. "The Sleepwalker".'

'Miss Eloise said it was made famous by Miss Jenny Lind and that she sang here in Hull at the old Theatre Royal when she was very young. When Miss Eloise was very young, I mean!'

'I believe she did,' her mother said. 'Though that was long before I was born.'

'Miss Eloise must be old then,' Poppy said. 'If she can remember her!'

'Mm,' her mother murmured. 'Not that old! Would you like a younger teacher?' she asked. 'One who knows more modish music?'

'No, thank you. I like Miss Eloise. She's teaching me how to breathe and she tells me of when she used to sing at concerts and how wonderful it was to hear the applause, and how to take a bow and all things like that.'

And filling your head with dreams, I don't doubt, Mary thought. But then what is life without a dream or two, even if they don't always come true? 'Would you like to be a singer?' she asked. 'Perhaps your pa wouldn't mind if you sang at concerts. In the town, I mean, like the Assembly Rooms or the Albion Lecture Hall. Not to travel.'

Poppy's grey eyes looked green as they widened. 'But then who would know me, Mama? I'd not be *the famous* Poppy Mazzini on the posters. You know, like they have on the walls of the Mechanics. I would have to travel.'

Mary watched her daughter's face fall as she said softly, 'Then it's impossible.'

The doctor came every three weeks to see Mary, then every two, and then every week as they came towards Christmas. Tommy was now doing all the baking and although he didn't have his mother's light touch at cakes, he made excellent bread and pastry. But though he was unhappy about his mother's increasing weakness, he felt trapped and didn't want to end his days in a grocer's shop like his father.

'It's a good business,' his father told him when Tommy had again done his grumbling. 'You should be pleased that your future is mapped out for you, as mine was.'

'But I want to make my own future, Pa,' Tommy insisted. 'I want to make my own mistakes and put them right.'

'Pah!' his father retorted. 'You don't know how lucky you are.'

There was nothing he could do. His mother was dying and it was only a matter of time. Tommy knew that and he wouldn't upset her last days by leaving home. Her heart was getting weaker and weaker. His father knew it; even Nan knew it. Only Poppy didn't and Tommy didn't think that she even guessed at how ill their mother was.

They closed the shop on Christmas Day and instead of making bread and cakes, Tommy and his father roasted a goose with all the trimmings of stuffing, roast potatoes and sausages, though not in such large quantities as usual for only Poppy had any appetite. Poppy cleaned sprouts and scrubbed parsnips and Nan, who with her daughter Mattie had been invited to eat with them, kept an eye on the Christmas pudding which was simmering gently in a pan, whilst Mary rested on the sofa in the parlour sipping an egg nog made with fresh eggs, honey and rum.

'Time you learned to bake, Poppy,' Tommy said, taking the goose out of the oven and carefully basting it. 'I'll teach you to bake Yorkshire teacakes, if you like.'

'Yes, all right,' Poppy agreed. She loved the rounds of bread, which were baked with currants, eaten warm and spread with thick yellow butter. 'Ma always used to make Yule cakes. Maybe next Christmas, when she's better, she'll make some.' Yule cakes were similar to teacakes but had extra fruit and candied peel, egg and spices.

Tommy glanced at his father, who looked at Nan, who put her head down to hide the tears which sprang to her eyes.

'Poppy,' her father said hoarsely. 'Go and set 'table in 'parlour. We'll eat in there, so your ma can stay where she is.'

Poppy looked up. Usually they ate in the kitchen, even at Christmas. It was warm in there with the range glowing and a table big enough for them all to sit comfortably. The table in the parlour was much smaller, though there was a good fire.

'We're eating in here, Ma,' she told her mother cheerfully. 'Pa said it would be better, and then you don't have to get up from the sofa. And we can look at the Christmas tree whilst we're eating. Shall I put your dinner on a tray?'

Her mother nodded. 'Only a little food, Poppy. Don't let Tommy pile up my plate. I won't be able to eat it.'

'You've got to eat, Ma,' Poppy said anxiously. 'You won't get better if you don't eat!'

I can't tell her today, her mother thought. Not on Christmas Day. And not on her birthday either. In another week or two, then I'll tell her, prepare her for the fact that I won't be getting better.

*

'It's been a very quiet birthday,' Poppy said to her mother a week later, just before she went upstairs to bed. 'But I saw the fireworks at midnight and heard the ships' sirens from the river and the docks.'

'Yes.' Her mother gave a gentle smile. 'I heard them too. Poppy,' she said softly. 'It's time for you to grow up. Time to help your pa and Tommy in the shop . . . and wait on 'customers in the coffee house. Will you do that?'

'Not go to school, do you mean?' Poppy hoped her mother didn't mean that. She liked school and she would miss seeing her friends if she didn't go. She thought of Mattie, Nan's daughter. She didn't go to school. But then Mattie was older than her. She was almost fourteen.

'No, we don't want you to finish at school. Not just yet, perhaps in another year . . . but you'll have to help before and . . . after school. It's only right that you should.' Mary was breathless with talking.

'Don't tire yourself, Ma,' Poppy said, leaning forward to give her mother a kiss. 'You should be in bed.'

'I'm just waiting for your pa to take me up. Poppy!' She clutched her hand, her resolve fading. Keeping the detail of her illness from her was not a choice any more. 'I – I might not be coming downstairs again. We didn't tell you before but – I won't get any better. My heart is very weak. It's an effort . . . even to talk. Every . . . step . . . every breath makes me . . . weaker.'

Poppy felt her heart hammering and her ears drumming. 'Then – then don't talk. We'll talk to you. Ma!' Her mouth trembled and she felt sick. What was her mother telling her? That she was going to die?

'Life . . . has to be . . . worth living, Poppy,' her mother murmured on a breath. 'Mine has been . . . a good one. I have been so very . . . lucky . . . having your father . . . and you and Tommy. I couldn't have wanted more.'

Poppy couldn't speak. It couldn't be true. They must bring the doctor in again. He must give her mother some more medicine to make her get better.

'Give me a kiss, darling,' her mother whispered. 'Don't be unhappy. You know that I love you. All of you. Keep singing, Poppy, my little songbird. Sing of love. Love makes everything worthwhile.'

CHAPTER FOUR

On Poppy's twelfth birthday, she thought dismally that it would always be a day of sadness. She would for ever remember last year when her mother had told her that she wouldn't get better. When she had woken the following morning, she had wondered if she had had a bad dream, and had raced into her parents' room. Her father was already up and her mother asleep. Poppy had gently touched her cheek and her mother had opened her eyes and smiled at her. 'I'm still here, Poppy,' she had said softly. 'Don't be afraid.'

She slipped away a month later, in the cold days of February. There was a fortnight of hard frost followed by blizzards and Poppy couldn't stop shivering. She hadn't wanted to go to school but her father had helped her into her coat, wrapped a warm scarf around her neck and ushered her off. 'It's what your ma would have wanted,' he told her. 'She said life must go on.'

But that was then and the life that was now wasn't the one that Poppy wanted. For a start, her father was employing a woman, Lena, to help in the shop and serve the tea and coffee to the customers. Lena had told him that she was a first-class cook and baker, but Joshua had said that they could manage for now, as Tommy was able to do all that. But neither Poppy nor Tommy liked her. She smiled and simpered at their father and couldn't do enough to please him, but although she was civil towards Poppy and Tommy they both felt an undercurrent of dislike directed towards them.

She was a big-bosomed woman with plump arms and a mass of brassy fair hair which she covered with a lace snood. Her clothes were too fashionable and fussy for shop work, and she spoke with a penetrating booming voice.

'Why her, Pa?' Tommy asked his father one day after he had had a heated discussion with Lena. 'You could have asked Nan to come into the shop more often, and she needs the money!'

'Nan is fine at what she does,' his father said. 'She keeps 'house and shop clean and she does 'laundry and ironing. She can't do any more. Lena can help out with 'baking if need be. She's all right,' he added. 'She's better for knowing.'

Tommy muttered something under his breath, for he was worldly wise, now that he had turned sixteen.

'And she knew your ma,' Joshua said. 'She was one of 'first to come and see if she could help after your mother died.'

Poppy frowned. She couldn't recall her mother ever mentioning Lena Rogers. She lived somewhere off Whitefriargate, Hull's main shopping street, but Poppy was convinced that she was new to Hull.

'She's a widow woman,' Joshua said. 'There's just her and her son. She needs to work too.'

'So why doesn't her son work?' Tommy grumbled. 'How old is he?'

'I don't know,' his father snapped. 'I didn't ask!'

Poppy was going to her dance class a few days later, after school. She came into the shop fastening up her jacket and looking for her father to tell him she wouldn't be late. 'Where's Pa?' she asked Lena. 'I'm just off.'

'Going gadding, eh?' Lena said with a cynical smile. 'You and your brother both!'

'What do you mean? Where's Tommy?'

'Gone out. Same as you're going to.'

'I'm going to my dancing class!' Poppy said. 'I go every Tuesday and every Wednesday I go for singing lessons.'

'Ooh, dancing and singing! What a lucky girl. Your poor pa struggling to keep you in such luxuries.'

Poppy had been taught never to answer back to adults, but she badly wanted to answer back now. She stared at Lena, then turned round and went to the door. 'You'll tell Pa where I've gone, won't you?' she said, glancing over her shoulder. 'Please,' she added. 'He worries otherwise.'

Lena shrugged and raised her eyebrows and Poppy just knew that she wouldn't, not unless her father asked.

She walked sullenly down the street, kicking any pebble that was in her path, and had turned into George Street when she realized that she had forgotten her dancing pumps. She turned about and hurried back towards the shop.

The doorbell rang as she went in and Lena looked up. She was in conversation with a heavily built youth of about eighteen, who was putting something into his pocket. Poppy saw his sudden furtive glance at Lena, and the way he bit his lip as if he'd been apprehended.

'I forgot my shoes,' Poppy murmured, hesitating.

'Better fetch them then, hadn't you?' Lena said acidly. 'Don't keep Miss Davina waiting.'

'Do you know her?' Poppy asked. She couldn't recall ever telling Lena her teacher's name.

'Of her,' Lena muttered, and the youth continued to stand there, his eyes shifting between Lena and Poppy.

Poppy stood her ground looking at them both, until Lena blurted, 'This is my son, Albert. He's just popped in with a message for me.'

'Oh!' Poppy said. 'Hello! I didn't realize you were grown up. I thought you'd be young, like me!'

'You're gone twelve, that is grown up,' Lena said sharply. 'Some folk start work when they're younger than you are.'

'I know,' Poppy replied. 'I'm very lucky. I've got friends who've started work already. So what do you do – Albert?' she asked. 'Where do you work?'

Albert hesitated for a second, then said, 'I'm looking for work at present.'

'He's in the shop trade,' Lena said. 'He's very good with figures, aren't you, Albert?'

'Yeah,' he said, folding his arms in front of him and looking at Poppy. 'I am. I just need the right opportunity.'

I don't like him, Poppy considered. I don't like him any more than I do his mother. She moved towards the door at the back of the shop. 'Have you lived in Hull for very long?' she asked. 'You don't sound like a Hull person. You haven't got 'Hull accent.'

Lena glared at her. 'Years,' she said. 'We've lived here for years, since before you were born I shouldn't wonder.' Her eyes narrowed. 'That's when I knew your ma. We went away to live but I couldn't settle.'

Poppy nodded and opened the door. 'Goodbye then,' she said to Albert. 'I expect we'll meet again.'

She dashed upstairs to her room and collected her shoes. They're up to something, she decided as she ran down again. I bet Lena's given him something from the shop and not charged him. I'll tell Tommy – I daren't tell Pa. I'm going to be late! Miss Davina will be cross. She hates unpunctuality. She says it's so important to always be on time.

When she went back into the shop, Albert had gone and Lena was flicking a duster over the shelves. 'That Nan isn't very good,' she said caustically. 'The dust is thick on these shelves. Don't suppose she ever moves anything!'

Poppy was too late for her lesson to stop and discuss Nan, but she knew that Lena was wrong. Nan was scrupulous in her cleaning; that was why her mother had employed her. She'd been with them for as long as Poppy could remember. She was thin and wiry and looked as if she had never had a decent meal in her life, and she probably hadn't for she had been left a seaman's widow when her daughter Mattie was only a baby. Since then she had scrimped and saved to keep her daughter in food and clothes and a roof over their heads. Summer or winter, Nan never wore anything other than a black dress and a grey shawl and worn down boots, but she never grumbled about her life and saw only those who were worse off than her, and never anyone who was better off or luckier.

'You're late, Poppy.' Miss Davina had had a terrible gnawing fear that Poppy wasn't coming for her lesson. The child had been distracted recently and unable to concentrate on her dance routine. She was relieved now to see her. 'Is anything amiss?'

'Not really.' The flurry of annoyance that Poppy had felt towards Lena had dissipated, leaving her downcast and sad and missing her mother. 'I was held up by someone, and I forgot my pumps and had to go back,' she admitted, aware that that was the real reason for her lateness, but if she hadn't gone back, she thought, then she wouldn't have seen Lena's odious son.

'Are you not very happy, Poppy?' Miss Davina asked. 'You seem preoccupied.'

Poppy looked down. No, she wasn't happy, but she couldn't say why. Miss Davina already knew about her mother. 'I'm all right,' she said in a small voice. 'It's just that nothing seems right any more.'

Her teacher nodded. 'It will take time for you to come to terms with the loss of your mother,' she said softly. 'It's not easy at the best of times,' she added. 'And it's worse when you're young. How old are you, Poppy?'

Poppy took a breath. Someone else was going to tell her that she was old enough to work. 'Nearly thirteen,' she sighed. 'And I know how lucky I am.'

'Do you?' Miss Davina was surprised. 'Not many people do. But . . .' She hesitated and pondered that it wasn't really anything to do with her, but she was quite fond of Poppy. The child had been coming to her for many years. 'I just wondered if you have an aunt, or perhaps a former friend of your mother's, whom you would feel comfortable talking to?'

Talking about what, Poppy thought? My mother? How I hate Lena? How Pa doesn't laugh much any more? That I don't want to work in the shop when I finish school?

'You are at a difficult age,' Miss Davina continued cautiously. 'Especially for females.' She coloured slightly. 'Erm, have you reached womanhood, Poppy? Sometimes the time of month makes a young woman feel out of sorts.'

Poppy lifted her head and gazed at her. What was she talking about? She shook her head. 'I don't know,' she said. 'I don't understand what you mean.'

'Ah!' Miss Davina was beginning to wish she hadn't begun this conversation, but now that she had she must continue. 'Women's bodies change,' she said nervously. 'You should speak to another woman, older than yourself. Is there anyone?'

Poppy blinked. 'Only Nan,' she said. 'She keeps house for us. My mother always liked her. She's got a daughter, Mattie.'

'Do you like Nan?'

'Oh, yes. I do. She's really kind.' Tears came to Poppy's eyes as she recalled how Nan had put her arms round her to comfort her after her mother died.

Miss Davina heaved a sigh. 'Then she's the one,' she said positively. 'Go and see her and tell her you'd like to know about growing up. Now, come along, change your shoes and let's get started.'

She was late getting home as Miss Davina had given her the full lesson, but Poppy's heart hadn't been in it and she kept making mistakes. She felt tired and lethargic and full of unease. Her father was standing in the shop doorway as she came down the street.

'Where've you been 'till this time? You shouldn't be out on your own!'

'I always go to my dance lesson on a Tuesday, Pa. I'm only a bit later than usual,' she said defensively. 'And I always go on my own.'

He grunted and ushered her inside. There were several people sitting at the tables. 'I'd forgotten that's where you'd be. You should have reminded me!'

'You weren't here. I told Lena,' she said. 'I asked her to tell you so that you didn't worry!'

'She must have forgotten,' he said. 'Tommy's only just come in as well. Go and slip off your things and come back in to help. I've had a rush on and nobody here to give me a hand.'

'Where's Lena?' Poppy looked round. Some of the tables needed clearing; they were littered with coffee cups and empty pots of chocolate.

'She had to go home. Something urgent cropped up. Just as I was getting busy as well. I could have done with her here.'

'I'm sorry, Pa,' she said when she came back a few minutes later. 'I didn't mean to worry you.' Her mouth trembled as she spoke, but she tried to smile at the customers as she went to clear the tables.

Tommy seemed disgruntled too as he buttered scones, cut up fruit cake and arranged slices of ham, aislet, dishes of potted meat, cheese and pickle on a serving dish. 'Where's the old harridan tonight?' he muttered to Poppy.

'Had to go home,' she murmured back. 'Something urgent.'

'Good! Let's hope she doesn't come back. She makes my skin creep.'

Poppy glanced across at her father as he was talking to

customers just leaving. 'I met her son today,' she confided. 'He's called Albert. He's older than you. I didn't like him. I think Lena gave him something. He was putting something into his pocket, anyway.'

'Huh!' Tommy grunted. 'If he's anything like his mother I don't want to meet him.'

They had a rush of grocery customers then, wanting flour, tea, potatoes and onions, for the shop stayed open until late. Joshua served them whilst Tommy made fresh coffee and supper for theatregoers coming from the Alhambra. Poppy cleared tables, washed cups and saucers, re-set the tables and took orders, and tried to listen to the conversations about the show. Finally her father said, 'Off you go, Poppy. It's ten o'clock; time you were in bed.'

'All right, Pa.' She reached up to kiss him good night.

He patted her cheek. 'I think we'll talk tomorrow, Poppy,' he said. 'About school. Maybe you needn't go back after 'summer holiday.'

'But,' she stammered. 'Can't I stay on a bit longer?' She didn't want to leave, not yet.

'You've seen how busy we get. But we'll talk about it.'

'I don't mind working after school,' she urged, 'except for Tuesdays and Wednesdays.'

'Ah!' He wagged a finger. 'You can't have it all ways.' Then he smiled at her. 'Go on, we'll talk about it later.'

Although there were several national schools in Hull, Poppy's father paid a fee for her to attend a select private school in Albion Street, a thoroughfare which was lined with elegant houses and the grandest building in the town, the Royal Institution, which contained a subscription library and museum, and where the Church Institute, formerly a private house, was open for both men and women to attend lectures in advancement and instruction.

A few days after her father's warning about leaving school, Poppy asked her teacher if she might be excused early. 'I have to go on an errand,' she pleaded, and as she was one of the brightest of the pupils and didn't take much time off, her teacher agreed.

Poppy scurried away from school and to avoid Savile Street,

where her father might see her, she took a longer route towards the old town where Nan and Mattie lived. She ran up Albion Street towards the Catholic church of St Charles and the Public Rooms in Kingston Square, where her mother sometimes used to take her to concerts, and cutting behind the Mechanics Institute, crossed the top end of George Street and headed towards the east end of the town dock where Tommy spent so much time. She huffed and took a breath and hoped that he was busy in the shop and hadn't skived off to look at the ships or talk to the seamen.

Although she had been born above the shop and had spent the whole of her life in the town, there were some areas where she wasn't allowed to go alone. Savile Street was a respectable street at the edge of what had once been the walled medieval town of Hull. There were other streets that were not so respectable: streets with poor court housing, built at the beginning of the century and now so dilapidated that only the very poor lived there. Some of these courts were situated behind shops which the affluent patronized and where the poor could only look and dream.

Poppy hesitated as she reached Lowgate. Charlie Chandler and his family lived and worked in a dark building down one of the lanes which ran between Lowgate and the old cobbled High Street. Scale Lane, I think it is, Poppy deliberated. She had been once with Tommy and seen Charlie's father with his head bent over a shoe on a wooden last. Another such lane, worthy only to be called a yard, darker and narrower, too narrow even for a handcart, was Stewart's Yard, where Nan and her daughter lived.

She turned into Scale Lane and hoped she might catch a glimpse of Charlie. He and Tommy were still friends but their respective fathers kept both of them busy. Poppy never mentioned Charlie's name to Tommy for fear of being teased. But she thought of him often and remembered how she had put her hand in his when he'd met her from the theatre. I was only a child then, she thought. I wouldn't dare to do that now; and that reminded her of why she was here, seeking Nan.

He was there! She saw Charlie sitting in the window, wearing a leather apron and with a bodkin in his hand. He looked up and she gave a tentative smile and waved her hand. His brow creased and with a swift movement he got up. Is he coming out, she wondered? Or has he only got up from his chair to do something else? Did he realize it was me?

The door opened as she passed and she looked up as he called her name. 'Poppy! Is it you? What're you doing down here?'

'Hello,' she said brightly. 'I'm going to see Nan. I have to talk to her about something. Do you know where Stewart's Yard is?'

'Yes!' He stepped down from the doorway. 'But it's no place for you.' He shook his head and she felt resentful as he added, 'Not on your own.'

'Nan lives there! And Mattie, and she's not that much older than me.'

'Yes, but they've always lived round here. They know it, you don't!'

She shrugged. 'Well, I have to go. She's always gone from 'shop when I get home from school.'

'Wait a minute and I'll come with you.' He turned back towards the door and she didn't know whether to be delighted that he was taking trouble over her, or peeved because he considered her a child and incapable of being out on her own.

'It's dark down there,' he said, appearing a moment later without his apron and with a jacket on. 'There are no street lamps in the courts.' There were gas lamps in Scale Lane but they were not yet lit, only the glow from the windows of the buildings breaking the gloom. Ahead of them, Poppy saw a spill of yellow light coming from the door and windows of the Manchester Arms and a group of men gathered there.

'You see!' Charlie said, taking her elbow and steering her to the other side of the lane. 'You'd need to avoid them.'

'They wouldn't bother me,' she said. 'Why would they want to? They're only having a drink.'

'Does your pa know that you're out?'

'Doesn't matter whether he does or not! I'm not a child, you know. I'm old enough to work!'

He looked down at her, and then he put his hand under her chin. 'Little Poppy's growing up at last.' He smiled. 'All 'more reason for taking care of you!'

She melted and gazed up at him. Was this what Miss Davina meant about reaching womanhood? She swallowed and felt a strange surging in her throat and chest, a fusion of joy and excitement. Her mother had told her that love was for grown-up people, but she had also said that it wasn't a question of age. Poppy could almost hear her mother's voice in her head. 'It's a matter of meeting someone and knowing you love them.'

I know that I love Charlie. She took a deep breath and felt a rush of hot tears fill her eyes. But what I don't know is how to make him love me.

CHAPTER FIVE

Charlie kept his hand on her elbow as they walked into the High Street. She felt firm fingers beneath her sleeve and could feel her heart thudding because of them. 'Do you still go dancing, Poppy?' he asked.

'Yes. Every week. I go for singing lessons too. We don't see you much now,' she added quickly, fearing that soon they would be at Nan's house and have to part company.

'I'm busy,' he said. 'My da keeps me at it. We've a lot of orders in. But I've almost finished my time. I'll soon be a fully fledged shoemaker.'

'So will you work for your father?' She glanced up at him and saw a grim expression on his face. 'Tommy still wants to go to sea. He told me he did.'

'I know. But he's tied to your father's shop, 'same as I am to mine.' His voice was irritable and sharp. 'But not for much longer. I'll make my last pair of shoes and I'll be off.'

'But . . .' She was horrified. That would mean that she might never see him again. 'Isn't that a waste? I mean, a waste of your apprenticeship? What will you do? Where will you go?'

There must have been something in her voice, some hint of desperation, for he turned and looked down at her. 'Will you miss me, Poppy, if I go away?' He smiled at her; she saw amusement and averted her head to hide her face. 'I'll set up on my own, away from here. I'll probably go to London. Start small, you know. But I shan't be a cobbler,' he added. 'Not mending boots and shoes that rightly belong on 'scrap heap.' He stretched his neck and squared his shoulders. 'No. I'll be shoemaker to 'famous. To royalty and nobility, to stars of 'theatre.' He nodded, a look of pride on his face. 'They'll all be clamouring for shoes by Charles Chandler.

'We're here.' He stopped abruptly and Poppy would have walked past the narrow opening to Stewart's Yard if he hadn't shown her. 'See how dark it is down here?' he said. 'That's why I came with you.'

'Yes,' she murmured. 'Thank you.' But I've still to come back this way, she pondered. There were quite a lot of people about: men pushing handcarts, women scurrying along with shawls about their heads, holding children by their hands. But they were moving purposefully as if they were familiar with the area, unlike Poppy who feared she might get lost within the alleyways and passages. They were close to the river Hull; just a few steps down the staith side and they would be able to see the water and the ships. Tommy came down here sometimes to watch the barges being unloaded or the ships making their way to the town dock.

Once this was Hull's main waterway, the mouth of the river whose source was up on the Wolds. For centuries it had served the whaling and fishing fleet, which had given the town its prosperity. Some old fishermen and boatmen still called it by its original name of the Old Harbour or Haven. Now the old town of Hull was almost an island, ringed by docks which led into the Humber estuary, whilst the newer town spread its tentacles to the north, east and west.

'I'd better wait for you,' Charlie was saying as they entered the yard. 'Will you be long?'

I can't let him listen! How can I talk to Nan when he's there? 'I shall be all right, thank you,' she said. 'I'll get Nan to set me to Lowgate.'

'What number is it?' Charles peered at a doorway.

'Four,' she said, beginning to wish she hadn't come. It was wet underfoot and there was a fetid smell. On one side of the narrow yard was a warehouse; on the other were small terraced houses. 'There don't seem to be any numbers.'

Someone called out to them and they looked up. A man was standing by an open loading door high up in the warehouse. 'Who do you want, mate?' he shouted.

'Nan Brewer,' Poppy called back before Charlie could answer. 'Do you know where she lives?'

'Second from bottom, left hand side. You can see 'light in 'window.'

They called back their thanks and continued down, and Charlie cursed as he trod on something slippery. Poppy knocked on the door and it immediately opened wide and Poppy wondered at that, for she would have wanted to know who was there before unlocking it.

'Hey, Poppy!' Mattie stood in the doorway; she had an old blanket wrapped about her shoulders and a shawl round her head. Her face was white and her eyes were red as if she'd been crying. 'Did you want Ma? She's not back from work yet. Hello, Charlie! My, we are honoured with such splendid company. Come on in. There's no fire cos I've onny just got in from work. Let me turn 'lamp up and we can look at each other.'

It's been a wasted journey, Poppy thought. And Pa will be starting to worry about me. 'What time will Nan be in?' she asked. 'I wanted to ask her something.'

'Any time now, I should think. But she has to go out again. We both have. We've got two jobs of work, you see. Well, Ma has three if we count 'washhouse and coming to your da's place.'

'I'll wait for a minute, then,' Poppy decided. 'Thank you for coming with me,' she said to Charlie. 'You can go if you want to.' Though she wanted him to stay. She'd be scared going back up the yard on her own.

'I'll be outside,' he said. 'I'll have a smoke.'

He left the small gloomy room, and Mattie raised her eyebrows. 'I'm surprised he even came in,' she said. 'Fancies himself as a bit of a gent, don't he?'

Poppy gazed at her. How could she say that? Didn't she see that he was very special? Different from most young men?

'How's that brother of yourn?' Mattie sat down and eased off her boots. 'Sit down,' she said. 'Make yourself at home.'

'I can't stay long.' Poppy sat on a wobbly wooden chair. 'I should be getting back. Pa will be worrying. I thought Nan would be in. Tommy's fine, thank you,' she added.

'What did you want to see Ma for?' Mattie asked curiously. She had an open freckled face, with fair hair like her mother's, and she stared at Poppy with a frank expression.

Poppy hesitated. Mattie would know, she thought. She works, so she's grown up I suppose. 'Erm, I wanted to know about, erm – reaching womanhood,' she muttered. 'My dance teacher, Miss Davina, said I should ask somebody if I hadn't reached it. And I don't know if I have or not.'

Mattie grinned. 'She meant your monthlies, didn't she? Some women don't like to say it.'

'I don't know. I don't know what she meant. She just asked if I'd reached womanhood and said to get somebody to tell me about growing up.'

'She meant your monthly bleed! Every female has it. Some start sooner, some later. I started mine when I was thirteen and I could wish that I hadn't.' Mattie pulled a face. 'Damned nuisance it is, I can tell you. Didn't your ma tell you about it?' she asked. 'Mine did, when I was twelve, so that I'd be prepared.'

Poppy shook her head and then listened carefully to Mattie as she explained. She was glad that Charlie was outside the door and not able to hear.

'Tell you what, Poppy,' Mattie said at last. 'I'll get Ma to fix you up with what you need, and then when it happens you can tell her. You don't need to tell your da or Tommy. Just say you've got a headache when it starts. You probably will have,' she added cheerfully, 'but you'll have to put up with that. It's just one of those things in a woman's life that we have to get on with.'

'Will it make my face white and my eyes red like yours, Mattie?' Poppy asked, thinking that if it did, she would wear some colour on her cheeks as the stage people did.

Mattie threw back her head and laughed. 'No! This is flour! I work in 'flour mill, don't I? And 'flour irritates my eyes and makes 'em sore. I try not to rub them but they really itch sometimes. I'd like to leave,' she said, 'and get work in a shop like your da's, but 'money's better in a mill and money is what we need, my ma and me.'

They heard voices outside. 'There's Ma now,' Mattie said. 'Do you want to stop and talk to her or shall you get off home?'

'I'll go,' Poppy said. 'But will you tell her why I came?' I'm glad that Mattie was here, she thought. I'd have been so embarrassed if Nan had had to tell me.

Mattie nodded. 'Mind how you go now. And . . .' She hesitated as the door started to open and she dropped her voice. 'Well, when you're a bit older, we'll talk again, about fellers, you know, and babbies and that.'

'Oh,' Poppy breathed. So there's more. 'Yes. Thank you, Mattie. Thank you very much.'

She said hello to Nan and said that she'd just come on an errand and that Mattie would tell her about it, then Charlie walked with her to the top of Scale Lane. 'You'll be all right now, won't you?' he said. 'I'd better get back or my father will start creating about me slacking.'

'Thank you very much, Charlie. I hope you don't get into trouble because of me.' She paused for a second before saying, 'Don't tell Tommy where I've been, will you? Please. He'll want to know why I went to see Nan and it's nothing to do with him.'

He gazed at her curiously. 'But you didn't speak to Nan, or hardly,' he said.

'No, but Mattie told me what I wanted to know.'

'Mattie! Ah, well.' His lips curled downwards. 'Mattie knows about most things,' he said. 'She's a fund of knowledge is Mattie. Knows more than her ma I shouldn't wonder.'

For a moment she thought he was scoffing and she was prepared to stand up for Mattie, but then he took her hand in his and gently squeezed it. 'Get off home then, Poppy.' He smiled down at her and she thought her heart would turn over. 'I'll see you again soon.'

As she walked into the shop, her father raised his hand and pointed a finger. 'Where've you been? You're late again! You'll have to stop this, Poppy. I'll not have you running round 'streets without me knowing where you are.'

Poppy glanced at Lena, who was standing with a smug expression on her face. 'I had to go somewhere,' she said. 'It was important.'

'You should have come to tell me first,' he said sharply. 'And what was important?'

'I can't tell you, Pa. I've been to see Nan.'

She heard Lena give a snort. Her father heard it too and it seemed to make him angrier. 'You've never been down 'High Street on your own?'

'It's quite safe,' she said. 'There were a lot of people about.'

'Come with me, young woman,' he said, and led her out of the back of the shop. 'Now,' he said when they reached their rooms. 'I don't want to discuss family affairs in front of Lena, but she must see how things are when you don't arrive home from school and Tommy clears off every afternoon. I shall have to take you out of school if this happens again, and I shall stop your dancing and your visits to 'theatre.'

We hardly ever go to the theatre now, she thought gloomily. Pa won't take the time off and he won't let me go on my own. She unwound her scarf and slipped her coat off.

'Are you listening to me, Poppy?'

'Yes.' She pressed her lips together and stared up at him. I could tell him I have a headache, she thought, like Mattie said. And in fact I have. 'I'm sorry, but I had to go to see Nan. I didn't know who else to ask.'

'Ask? Ask what? If there's anything you need to know you ask me!'

'About – about women's things.'

He opened his mouth and blew out a breath. 'W—' The words formed but he didn't speak them, only looked at her. Then he sat down, his bluster gone. 'Women's things?' he said in a whisper. 'Has my little girl come to that and no mother to talk to?'

He blinked rapidly and she thought he was going to cry, so she quickly reassured him. 'Not yet, Pa,' she said. 'But I soon will. That's why I had to ask.' She suddenly felt grown up and yet rather shy, and she understood now why Mattie said she shouldn't tell her father or her brother. 'You don't have to worry about it,' she said soothingly. 'It happens to all women!'

He gave a lopsided smile. 'I suppose it does.' He drew her towards him and patted her hand. 'Even more reason for me to worry about you,' he said. 'But there we are. You'll cope, I expect.'

She came home straight from school the next day and didn't loiter. She took off her coat and fastened an apron round her waist, prepared to help in the shop. Lena was behind the counter serving a customer and a sullen-looking Tommy was preparing supper food for the café.

'I want to speak to you, Poppy,' her father called to her from their parlour. 'I've something to discuss with you.'

She had a sinking feeling. She was convinced he was going to say she must finish school. But please don't make me give up my dancing or singing lessons, she prayed. Anything but that. She glanced towards Tommy but he didn't even look at her, and she went out of the shop.

'I've decided,' her father began. 'I've been thinking about things, and, well, I know it would be what your mother would have wanted.' He paused and gazed into space. 'She would have wanted you to stay on at school. She always said how important it was that girls should have 'same advantages as boys, and you and Tommy have been treated more or less 'same, except you've stayed on longer at school than he did.'

'Tommy didn't want to stay on. He didn't like school,' Poppy said.

'No, he didn't.' Her father sighed. 'I'm sure I don't know what he does like, but anyway . . . You can stay on at school for another year, and you can continue your dancing and singing as well.'

Poppy beamed. 'Oh, thank you, Pa,' she began, but her father had not finished.

'So what I propose is: Tommy can do 'baking as he does now. He's got a good hand at it – takes after his ma; Lena can look after 'coffee shop during the day until he's finished with 'baking; and her son, Albert, can help me in 'shop. He'll come in early to do deliveries, stack 'shelves, serve customers and so on. There's plenty for him to do, and that means you just have to help for an hour or so of an evening after school.'

'Albert!' she muttered. 'But we don't know him, Pa! How do you know if – if he can do the work?'

'His mother says he's good at figures and he's worked in a shop before. He used to be a manager somewhere out of town, but he came back to Hull to live with Lena when his father died.'

Poppy didn't know what to say. It's our fault, she thought, Tommy's and mine. If we'd been more willing we wouldn't have had to have Lena here, or that odious Albert. 'Just for a year then, Pa?' But even as she asked, she thought, I shan't want to be in the shop. She knew what she wanted. She wanted to perform. She wanted to sing and dance for her living. She wanted to see her name up on posters outside theatres and music halls. *Poppy Mazzini*, the celebrated shining star. She heaved a deep sigh. It would be impossible.

CHAPTER SIX

Albert was smarmily charming. To the customers who came to buy groceries, to the patrons of the coffee shop, to Joshua and to Poppy. But not to Tommy. Tommy had sized him up right from the beginning.

'You'll regret it, Pa,' he said to his father, late one evening as they were locking up. Albert and Lena had gone home. 'He's a braggart. I bet he's never worked in a shop before. I bet he's never even worked before!'

'So what do you suggest?' his father bellowed. 'You don't want to be here. Poppy wants to stay on at school. I've nobody else to help me now that your ma's gone. Just what am I supposed to do? Pack up 'shop? I can't manage it single-handed!'

Tommy was silent. His father was right, of course. They had to have help. 'Nan,' he said. 'She's helped out before. And Mattie. Mattie would be all right. She's very bright.' I might be happy to stay if Mattie was here, he thought.

'We need Nan to keep 'place clean and Mattie's a mill girl; she'll get better pay in 'mill than I can afford to give her.'

'So how come Lena and Albert can manage on what you pay them? And if he's so clever he could get a job anywhere!'

'I'm not going to discuss it,' Joshua said stubbornly. 'It's done. If he's not suitable, then he'll go. But I'm going to give him 'chance and that's 'end of 'matter.'

Lena increasingly took on more than was necessary. She moved tables and rearranged the stock on the shelves, 'so that I can reach more easily', she simpered at Joshua. 'You're so much taller than me,' she said playfully, and she left the dirty dishes and pans from the coffee shop for Poppy when she came home from school, saying that she hadn't had time to do them. Albert always appeared to be busy, checking stock or going out on deliveries and taking a long time over both.

Tommy became more and more sullen as he found himself always in the kitchen baking or preparing food, and when he came into the shop he barely spoke to either Lena or Albert, and not always to Poppy.

'Josh!' Lena called out one evening and Poppy and Tommy both looked up in astonishment. No-one, not even their mother, had ever called their father Josh; it was always Joshua. But he didn't seem to notice, merely turned towards Lena enquiringly.

'Someone called in for a penn'orth o' laudanum whilst you were out this afternoon,' Lena said. 'And we couldn't give it to her because we hadn't the key to the cupboard.'

'No.' Joshua fingered his waistcoat pocket. 'I keep that.'

'She said she needed it, so she went somewhere else.' Lena looked at him. 'I said you wouldn't be long, but she wouldn't wait.'

'Can't be helped,' he said abruptly.

'I suppose not,' she agreed. 'But not all grocers can be trusted to give the proper mix. Not like you,' she added.

Joshua was meticulous in mixing the laudanum which he sold in penny or sixpenny bottles, or if it was for a child in an elixir with a sweet syrup. He also kept opium grains in the cupboard for more severe illnesses. The cupboard was always kept locked and he had the only key.

Poppy worked in the shop during the school holidays and it was late one afternoon when Lena complained of a terrible headache. Joshua was out; he wanted to settle a grievance with one of his local suppliers, who he reckoned had sent a box of tea short in his order. He was going to send Albert, but it was a nice day and he fancied a walk, and he knew that if there was going to be any arguing, then he would get more satisfaction from the provender than his employee would.

'I think I'll have to go home.' Lena put her hand to her forehead. 'It's usually quiet at this time on a Monday, and I don't suppose Josh will be long. Do you think you can manage on your own, Albert?'

Poppy glared at her. Although she could sympathize with Lena over the headache, as she now knew what that meant, she was annoyed that she should ignore her and ask Albert if he could manage rather than her. She was also apprehensive about being left alone with Albert, for Tommy too had slipped out as soon as his father had left, and Albert sometimes came up too close to her, which made her uncomfortable.

'He's not on his own, is he?' she retorted. 'I'm here.'

'Oh, so you are, dear.' Lena didn't smile as she answered her. 'But we all know where you'd rather be, don't we? Tapping your toes or warbling your tonsils! Your father spoils you if you ask me!'

'Well, no-one is asking you and it's nothing to do with you what I do,' Poppy replied angrily. Where Lena was concerned she'd got over her conforming rule of not answering back.

'Not at the moment it hasn't,' Lena said smoothly, putting on an extravagant black and cream plumed hat. 'But just watch your step, my dear! And I don't mean dance step, which I would stop straight away if it were up to me. Wasting valuable money that could be better spent elsewhere!' She swept out of the door calling to Albert that she would see him later.

'Don't take too much notice of our Lena.' Albert came up to Poppy and put his arm round her shoulder. 'She gets these moods sometimes.'

Poppy didn't speak, but shrugged off his arm and moved away from him and smoothed out the tablecloths and rearranged the flowers on the tables. What did Lena mean, not at the moment? She wished someone would come in, but Lena was right, this was a quiet period. Although Monday mornings were busy with people buying groceries, in the afternoons they seemed to stay at home.

'Of course,' Albert came towards her again, trapping her behind one of the tables close to the window, 'if she and your da—'

'What?' Poppy stared at him, her lips apart. 'If she and my father what?'

'Well, you know! Get together.' He gazed at her from his little piggy eyes and grinned. 'They, erm, well, they seem to hit it off, don't they, and don't you think it's odd that they're both out at the same time? Lena hasn't really got a headache.' He sniggered. 'I reckon they've arranged to meet.'

Poppy was horrified. It wasn't true! Couldn't be true! Her father would never – it was only eighteen months since her mother had died; but she remembered her mother had said that life must go on. She had said that to Poppy's father. But surely he would never look at someone like Lena? Lena was harsh and brash and mean, a complete opposite to her mother.

'You're talking nonsense,' she said with a catch in her voice. 'My father would never—'

Albert spoke softly. 'He's a man. Of course he would,' he said. 'A man can't live without a woman around him, to look after him, keep him warm in bed at night.' He came up close again. 'And then you and me, Poppy – we'd see more of each other.' He reached out and drew her towards him. 'Course you're only a little lass, but you'll soon grow up, and we'd all be living here together, all cosy and nice.'

She lashed out at him, catching him on his cheek with her nails. 'Get your hands off me,' she said. 'I'll tell my father!'

'I'll tell him you misunderstood me,' he said, but nevertheless drew away from her and put his hand to his cheek. 'I'll say I was only being friendly towards you and you took it the wrong way.' He stared at her. 'I can make it worse for you, Poppy,' he said menacingly, 'and for your brother.' He leered at her. 'I know where he sneaks off to. He's always hanging round the ships. He goes on errands, but he comes home the long way round past the docks, to talk to the seamen.'

Poppy knew that Tommy did that, but she didn't think her father did. If Albert should tell him, he would be very angry.

'It's nothing to do with you. You only work for my father, and please get out of my way,' she said, pushing past him. 'I don't want to talk to you.'

But she was worried and lay sleepless at night, thinking of what life would be like if her father did marry Lena, who seemed to be insinuating herself into his life. She was bothered too about Tommy who was always morose and bad-tempered towards Albert, who in turn was affable and genial towards him, especially when their father was there, so that Tommy always seemed to be the instigator of any bad feeling.

Poppy told Tommy what Albert had said about his mother and their father and although Tommy scoffed, she saw that he was taken aback. 'If that should happen, Poppy,' he said, 'I'm off. I'll not stay where they are.'

'But what about me?' she protested. 'You can't leave me with those two!'

'You'll be all right,' Tommy said. 'You were always Pa's little darling, his sweet little girl!'

She wondered then if Tommy had been jealous of her. It was true that her father had spoiled her when she was little, but he didn't now, except for her dancing and singing lessons, and surely that wasn't spoiling? Shall I tell Tommy about Albert forever pawing at me, she pondered? But she didn't. She didn't know if he would believe her, but she was embarrassed and also felt a kind of shame.

'Miss Eloise! May I ask you something?' she said at her next singing lesson, and at her tutor's nod she hesitatingly asked, 'Would I make a singer? At concerts, I mean?'

'Professionally?' Miss Eloise arched her eyebrows. She had a very mobile face, her large eyes able to express emotion or passion, and her mouth formed to voice perfect diction and clear articulation.

'Yes! I just thought that – well, that I'd like to sing for a living. Or dance,' she added. 'My father wouldn't want me to go into music hall, but perhaps he wouldn't mind if I sang on 'concert stage.'

'On *the* concert stage, Poppy! Do not be sloppy in your speech. I realize that the Hull dialect leaves out the definite article and in general use it can be – *interesting*; but someone like you must know when to say *the* and when not to, depending on the company you are in!'

'Yes, Miss Eloise,' Poppy said. She had had this homily from her tutor several times and usually she did remember. 'So could I, do you think?'

'No, I think not,' Miss Eloise stated. 'You would have the stamina, I do not doubt, but I'm afraid you are too young and do not have the voice for the concert platform. I am not saying that you never will, but it would take years of practice to become proficient and to be perfectly candid with you, Poppy, I cannot think that your father would agree to it.'

She could not tell of the hatching and planning that she and Miss Davina had contrived for Poppy, but she consoled her by saying: 'Do not be downhearted. You would be perfect for the music hall or theatre stage as a ballad and descriptive vocalist. I understand you are also a very fine dancer, which would be to your advantage. All we have to do is convince your father.'

Poppy was very heartened by the compliment. Miss Davina and Miss Eloise must have been discussing me, she thought. She felt thrilled and excited and decided that she would talk to her father again on the subject of performing.

'Pa!' she said that night after they had locked up and there were only the two of them at home. Tommy had gone out to meet Charlie for a game of billiards.

'Why is that when you say *Pa* like that, I think you're going to wheedle something out of me?' Her father smiled indulgently. 'You're not a little bairn able to twist me round your finger any more!'

'I know that.' Poppy put the kettle over the fire to make a pot of cocoa, her father's bedtime drink. 'I wanted to ask you something.'

'A new skirt? A pair of dancing pumps?'

'No.' She smiled. 'I want you to take me to the Theatre Royal. It's ages since we went out to 'theatre or music hall,' she coaxed. 'And I saw a poster when I was coming back from my singing lesson, and I thought how nice it would be if we could go. Just you and me,' she added, as she stirred his drink and added milk. 'Lena and Tommy could run things if we went on a quiet night.' She avoided mentioning Albert's name whenever possible.

He sighed. 'I've not wanted to go since your ma died,' he said. 'It's not seemed right somehow to be enjoying myself when she's not beside me.'

Poppy sat opposite him and cradled her cup between her hands. 'I've felt the same,' she said softly. 'But I think that now we can. I don't think she'd mind.'

He glanced across at her. 'Oh, she wouldn't mind. It's me that does. I keep thinking of 'times when I was too busy to go with her. And now it's too late.'

'So, would you go with me, Pa? Ma would like it if you did.'

He gazed meditatively into the fire and didn't answer for a

moment. Then he took a breath. 'She would, wouldn't she? Aye, all right. Theatre Royal? It would make a change from 'Mechanics. What's on there?'

There were theatres, concert halls and public rooms for entertainment and music all over the town, catering for every taste. The Assembly and Public Rooms put on lectures and vocal concerts, and there were lantern lectures at the Royal Institution. The Mechanics Music Hall was probably the Mazzinis favourite, with the Alhambra in Porter Street and the Theatre Royal in Paragon Street running a close second. A new theatre for performances of opera and drama, the Grand Theatre and Opera House, was due to open in George Street fairly soon, such was the appetite of Hull residents for all things musical, entertaining or edifying.

'Next week there's Will Vane, the Banjo King,' Poppy said, knowing that he would enjoy that. 'There's a comedian, a baritone singer – you'd like him – and a ballad and descriptive vocalist,' she added last of all. 'Miss Agnes Cotton.'

'Mm,' he said. 'I wouldn't mind seeing Will Vane again, he's very good. Saw him a few years back; I thought he'd retired. All right. Next Monday, then. It'll be fairly quiet in 'shop. Tommy can look after things and we should be home by half past nine.'

Poppy jumped up and planted a kiss on the top of his head. 'Oh, thank you, Pa! Oh, I just can't wait!'

They heard a key rattle in the back door. 'Tommy!' Joshua said. 'He's early for a change.'

Tommy came into the kitchen followed by Charlie, and Poppy's heart skipped a beat. 'No billiards tonight,' Tommy said. 'They've had a flood at 'George and everybody's paddling around in the water.' He wagged his thumb over his shoulder. 'Charlie didn't want to get his feet wet.'

'Not bothered about my feet,' Charlie said. 'It was my boots I was bothered about. These are my best!'

'Quite right,' Joshua agreed. 'Good boots don't come cheap. How's your father doing?' he asked. 'Business good?'

'Fine. Fine.' Charlie gave Poppy a surreptitious wink, which made her blush. 'Keeping busy.'

'Make us a cup o' tea, Pops,' Tommy said. 'We're gasping, aren't we, Charlie?'

Poppy swung the kettle over the fire again as Charlie nodded and smiled at her. 'I will,' she said. 'Only don't call me Pops. My name's Poppy.'

Her brother pulled a face and invited Charlie to sit down and Poppy, self-conscious because Charlie was watching her, took two more cups and saucers out of the cupboard. 'Charlie wants to ask you something,' Tommy said airily.

'I can ask her myself, thanks,' Charlie admonished, and Joshua looked suspiciously at him.

'What?' he said. 'What do you want to ask her?'

'Could I make you a pair of shoes, Poppy?' Then he looked at her father. 'It'll be 'last pair for my apprenticeship.'

Poppy took a breath and felt her face flush scarlet. 'I—' She glanced at her father. 'I suppose—'

'I noticed – well, I always look at people's feet,' Charlie corrected himself. 'And I noticed when I last saw you.' His eyes caught hers and she hoped he wouldn't mention her visit to Nan's. 'Can't remember when it was,' he went on, 'but I noticed how neat they were.' He smiled again and once more her heart gave a flip. 'I'd be really grateful if I could.'

'Well, how about that, Poppy?' her father said jovially. 'Your very own handmade shoes! And your feet have probably stopped growing now so they'll last you. Shall I pay you for 'leather?' he asked Charlie.

'Oh no, sir,' Charlie said. 'I'll do that. It'll be a gift, if that's all right? We've just had some lovely soft calfskin delivered; it's red, which is why I thought of Poppy.'

He thought of me! Poppy could hardly contain her happiness. She was speechless and overwhelmed. *He thought of me and he's going to make me some shoes with his own hands.* 'Thank you,' she gasped and saw Tommy grin, so added primly, 'It's very kind of you.'

'It'll be my pleasure,' Charlie said. 'I'll have to measure your foot. If you could sit down?'

He knelt beside her as she sat back on the chair and Tommy, with an enforced sigh, said, 'I'd better make 'tea then!'

Charlie took her right foot in his hand and slipped off her shoe and placed his hand around her instep, then he did the same with the other, running his fingers across her toes and over her heels, measuring with his thumb. He nodded. 'I'll prepare 'leather tomorrow and then I'll have to come back to measure properly for 'cutting and stitching. They'll be completely hand sewn; I shan't use the machine on them. So what shall they be, Poppy? High-buttoned boots? Dancing slippers? Shoes?'

She pondered. When she was a child her mother had always dressed her in skirts to her ankles, with her petticoat showing, and this was also the desired length for school dress; but now that she was contemplating leaving school the following summer, she had thought she would wear her skirts long and trailing, as most grown-up women did. But it seemed a shame, she thought, that a special pair of shoes should be hidden beneath a skirt.

'Dancing shoes!' She made up her mind. 'Dancing shoes – not pumps! Dancing shoes with heels.' Her eyes sparkled and she laughed. Charlie, looking up at her, laughed too and squeezed her foot, which he was still holding and she thought she would burst with happiness.

CHAPTER SEVEN

Poppy and her father walked arm in arm to the Theatre Royal, which was only a five-minute walk away from Savile Street. She felt very grown up going out with her father. She had looked through her mother's wardrobe for something to wear, for she now felt that her own clothes were far too childish for the theatre, and had found an emerald-green skirt with a trailing flounced hem and a darker green jacket with a nipped-in waist and a high collar. They fitted her perfectly as her mother had always been slim and dainty. She had tried on her mother's hats too but decided that they wouldn't sit on her bouncy hair and that she wasn't yet old enough to wear them.

What will Pa say, she wondered as she came downstairs. Will he be upset if I wear my mother's clothes? But her father hadn't remembered them, and remarked how nice she looked.

'Colour suits you, Poppy. Looks good against your hair. Is it new? I didn't realize I gave you enough allowance to buy clothes!'

'You don't, Pa.' She pinned a ribbon in her hair. 'This was Ma's. She hardly ever wore it.'

'Well, you might as well make use of them. I expect your mother would have given them to you anyway.' He looked fondly at her. 'You look very grown up.' He buttoned up his jacket and put on his grey bowler. 'You've got 'look of her. And her style,' he added. 'There was nobody to touch Mary for style.'

She gave a small relieved sigh. So her father wouldn't be attracted to Lena then. She had no style at all.

There was quite a crowd waiting to go in when they reached the hall. People of Hull were keen on the music hall and the artistes were always sure of a large audience. They had to perform well, though, or they'd be booed off stage. This week saw the return of popular acts, hence the waiting crowd.

After they had taken their seats, Joshua looked over the programme. 'Seen some of these already. Will Vane's bound to be good. Trick cyclists – not fond of them; vocalists and dancers – should suit you, Poppy; and Miss Agnes Cotton, popular ballad singer and descriptive dancer – never seen her.'

'Nor I,' Poppy looked over his shoulder at the programme. Miss Cotton was the one she wanted to see. 'Do you remember the Terry Sisters who came back for supper after the performance at the Mechanics? They were good dancers, but didn't sing all that well.' She suddenly recalled, as she spoke, that that was the night her mother was first taken ill, and she wished she hadn't mentioned it. It was also the night she had danced and sung for the Terry Sisters and the man they called Dan.

'Mm.' Her father nodded, and looked round the auditorium to see if there was anyone there he recognized. 'I like to hear a good voice myself. I wonder if any of these will come back after the show? We won't linger,' he murmured as the curtain went up. 'Just in case we get a rush.'

The trick cyclists came on first, performing feats on various types of bicycles, including bone-shakers and penny-farthings, then monowheels, interweaving between each other, and finally ending with a great roar of noise which made everyone in the audience jump, as three men standing on each other's shoulders rode onto the stage with the fourth driving an engine-powered motor cycle.

'My word,' Joshua said, as he, along with the rest of the audience, vigorously applauded. 'That's 'future transport you're looking at, Poppy! Everybody who can afford it will have one, or a motor car. They're making them in Germany; it won't be long before they're here.'

Poppy thought the machines were very noisy and made a lot of smoke, though she'd seen pictures of motor cars and thought they looked rather exciting. But what's the point of them, she wondered, if, as they say, someone has to walk in front with a red flag?

The next act were the knockabouts: two men who pushed and tumbled, crashed and fell over each other, did the splits and turned cartwheels. Then came the comedian who told jokes about his dog and his wife, and then the baritone who sang music from opera. A short interval followed, before the curtain went up again to show Miss Cotton in a blue shepherdess dress and bonnet, a crook in her hand, singing a song about losing her sheep and her lover, the shepherd.

Poppy and her father exchanged glances, and he drooped his mouth humorously. 'She'll never find them if she sings like that,' he murmured and Poppy grinned.

I can do better than that and I can dance better, she thought as she watched the dancer pirouette around the stage. But how to persuade my father?

The final act was the Banjo King, Will Vane, who was given a tumultuous welcome. He entertained with his jolly songs and ditties and everyone joined in, including Poppy and her father. There was tremendous applause as he finished and Poppy reflected how satisfying it must be to receive such an ovation. It's what I want! It's what I want! I can do it, I know I can!

As they came out of the theatre, she saw Miss Davina and Miss Eloise in the crowd. 'Look, Pa,' she said. 'Over there. My singing and dancing teachers. Can I introduce you?'

'Aye, but let's not be too long. We might get busy. There's a good crowd tonight; we'll be busier than usual, I should say.' He let her lead him towards the two ladies.

'Miss Davina, Miss Eloise, this is my father. I don't think you have ever met.'

'Good evening, ladies.' Joshua gave a short bow and Poppy noticed how the teachers' cheeks went slightly pink. He's a nice-looking man, my father, Poppy mused. I suppose he would be considered very eligible.

'Good evening,' they answered in unison. Then Miss Eloise asked, 'Did you enjoy the show, Mr Mazzini? What did you think of the baritone? Splendid, wasn't he?'

'By Jove, but he was. A grand show all round. Didn't care for 'young vocalist myself, but I suppose she would appeal to you ladies?'

'On the contrary,' Miss Eloise demurred. 'Not to my taste.'

'Nor mine,' said Miss Davina. 'Not an accomplished dancer by any means.'

'And as for her singing,' Miss Eloise added, 'why, Poppy's voice is far superior.'

'Is that so? Well, what about that, eh, Poppy?' Her father beamed at her. 'There's praise indeed.'

'Yes,' Miss Davina agreed. 'And her dancing. If ever Poppy should decide to try her talents on the stage, she would be very well received.'

'Indeed she would.' Miss Eloise nodded in agreement.

'Well, well, well!' Joshua laughed. 'A talent to be sorely missed, eh?' He shook his head in amusement, then said, 'I'd never have a moment's peace if I thought she was traipsing round 'country with stage folk like these. Anyway, talking of which, we'd better be off before they all descend on Mazzini's coffee house for their supper. Come along, Poppy.' He put on his bowler, tapped it with his finger and said, 'Been a pleasure meeting you, ladies. Good night!'

They walked swiftly back towards Savile Street. Before they reached the shop, Joshua took Poppy's arm and tucked it into his. 'Don't think of 'stage, will you, Poppy? I meant what I said back there. Your fortune's here in Mazzini's, yours and Tommy's. We're not stage folk. That's a different kind of life from what we know. You've got to be born to it. Be content with what you've got.'

They reached the shop and Joshua pointed up at the door. 'Look. *Mazzini's.* This business was started by my grandfather – started from a handcart, he did – built up by my father and then me, and I hope – want it to be carried on by Tommy, and you too. There's a living here for the both of you.'

'But Pa!' She could have cried. The evening was ruined. 'I really would like to be a singer or a dancer. Could I not try it? Not yet, I don't mean, but maybe in a year or two, and if I'm no good or don't like it, then I'd come home.'

He put his hand on the door. There were people sitting at the tables and Albert and Lena were serving them whilst Tommy was making pots of coffee and chocolate. 'Look in there, Poppy,' he said. 'We're giving folks what they want. Everybody needs to eat and drink. We've got 'best of both worlds with 'grocer shop and coffee house. We cater for their every need.'

But what about my need, she wanted to say. Doesn't it matter what I want? But her father was opening the door and smiling and greeting his customers.

She worked in the shop every hour she could and tried to come to terms with the thought that this would be her life from now on. The only bright spots in her day were when Charlie came to measure her feet and show her the shoes in their various stages, but even that failed to lift her spirits completely for she wondered if she would ever wear them for dancing. She even told Miss Davina and Miss Eloise that she was stopping her lessons for the time being, much to their dismay.

Then Charlie came in one evening with a parcel under his arm. The coffee shop was quiet; Joshua was sitting behind the counter filling in an order form, and Lena was making herself busy tidying up and tut-tutting to herself. She had been complaining again that Nan was slacking in her cleaning. Albert was standing around looking bored and picking at his fingernails.

'Good evening, Mr Mazzini,' Charlie said. 'Are you well?'

'I'm all right,' he said. 'Business could be brisker. You?'

'Yes, fine, thank you. Would you mind if I had a word with Poppy? Is she about?' He held up the parcel and Lena and Albert both looked up.

'Aye, she's in 'back, I think. Go on through.' Joshua got up from his seat to open the door into the house for Charlie. 'Albert, you might as well get off. There's nothing much doing tonight by 'look of it.'

'Oh, I don't mind staying,' Albert fawned. 'I can walk Ma home when she's finished.'

The last customer in the café had just left and Joshua looked across at Lena. 'You might as well go then, Lena. I'll clear up.'

'Oh, are you sure, Josh?' she said sweetly. 'You put in so much time. Where's Tommy?' She gave a little frown as she pointedly implied that he should have been there to help his father.

'Gone to bed, I think. He's up early, you know.'

'But so are you!' she said. 'So are we all!'

Joshua didn't comment. Lena didn't know that he sometimes took an hour off in the afternoon and had a sleep. 'I'll lock up after you,' he said, closing up his books. 'It's gone ten. Time we were all in bed.'

Poppy was in front of the mirror, stretching her arms in the air when Charlie came through. She swayed from side to side, stretching her waist, neck and shoulders, and then she saw his reflection and turned. She blushed. 'Hello. I – didn't hear you.'

'Sorry.' He gazed at her. 'I didn't mean to disturb you. I know it's late. I, erm, I've brought your shoes. They're finished.'

'Oh!' she breathed. 'Thank you!'

'Is Tommy not about?' He seemed embarrassed, and she was certainly unnerved to think that she would have to try on the shoes when she was alone with him.

'He's just gone up to bed,' she said. 'Shall I fetch him?'

'No, it doesn't matter. I've come to see you, anyway. At least, to bring your shoes. Would you like to try them?'

'Oh, please!' She sat down and unbuttoned her shoes. 'I've been longing to see them.'

He sat opposite her and unwrapped the brown paper parcel. 'I imagine you're a very good dancer, Poppy,' he commented. 'You move very well.'

'Thank you,' she said shyly. 'I do try to practise every day, even though I'm not having lessons now.'

'Why's that?' he asked, gently lifting her foot.

She could barely speak. 'Because,' she whispered, 'Pa wants me to help in the business. And it seems a waste of lessons and money if I can't be a dancer or a singer.'

'Is that what you want to do?' he said, and slipped her foot into the shoe which was so soft and comfortable it was as if she wasn't wearing shoes at all.

She gazed at him with wide eyes. If only she could tell him. She was sure he would understand; but then a thought struck her. If she should go on the stage, then she wouldn't see him. If she stayed here with her father, then there was a chance that he might notice that she was growing up and come to care for her as much as she cared for him.

'There, we're all locked up.' Her father came into the room. 'It's been a quiet day. Nobody much about. So what's this then?' he asked. 'These the new shoes?'

Poppy stretched out her feet to show him. 'Aren't they beautiful?' she murmured. 'I shall keep them for ever.' She glanced shyly at Charlie. 'Thank you so very much.'

He nodded. 'I'm pleased with them, and my father is too. He says . . .' He hesitated. 'Well, I wasn't going to say anything just yet and I haven't told Tommy, but my father's agreed that I can go and work in London. He has some contacts there who might employ me. High-class shoemakers, you know.'

Poppy felt all the pleasure and happiness draining from her. 'When?' she whispered. 'When will you go?'

'That's a great shame,' her father interrupted. 'There's call here in Hull for a good shoemaker. What about your father's business? What will he do if you go away?'

'He says he'll take on another apprentice and then when I'm ready to come back I can take over 'business from him.'

As he spoke, he didn't look directly at Joshua, who pursed his lips and muttered something about 'you young people', and Poppy guessed – no, she knew – that once Charlie had left it was most unlikely that he would come back. She was devastated and felt as if her life was collapsing.

'It won't be yet.' Charlie glanced at Poppy, and she was sure that he knew she was hurting. 'My father has to write to his contacts and ask if they'd be willing to take me, and it might take some time. But I'll go.' He gazed at her as if he was pleading for her to understand. 'It's a big chance for me.'

Poppy felt her lips tremble. If Charlie left, then Tommy would leave too. They had been friends since they were very young and Tommy would be very disgruntled if he thought that Charlie was realizing his dream and he was being left behind.

And then what about me? Her eyes filled and tears trickled down her cheeks. I shall be left all alone with just Pa and Lena and the awful Albert.

'Right then, young feller! Time we were all off to bed. Poppy, will you lock up after Charlie?' Joshua made a move and Charlie stood up. 'Tell your da I'll drop by to see him and thank him personally for Poppy's shoes. It's most generous of him.'

'It's been grand working on them, Mr Mazzini,' Charlie said. 'A great pleasure. I hope you enjoy wearing them, Poppy.'

Poppy brushed her hand across her wet cheek. 'I will,' she said huskily. 'I'll treasure them always.'

She led the way to the side door, which led out to the street, turned the key and slid back the bolt. She stood against the wall for Charlie to come past. 'Thank you again, Charlie,' she whispered, swallowing away her tears. 'And – and I'm sorry that you'll be leaving.' She couldn't finish. He had told her before that he wanted to go to London. She should have been prepared.

She pressed her lips together to stop herself crying as he turned towards her, his hand on the door.

'You know that it's what I want to do, Poppy,' he said softly. 'It's what I *have* to do.' He lifted his hand and brushed away her tears. 'Don't be upset!'

'It's just that I'll miss you.' Her eyes misted over. So he did understand.

'I'll miss you too,' he said, and gently kissed her on the cheek. Then he drew back, taking in a breath, as if he was startled by his own action. He gazed at her for a moment, his eyes tender, then he leaned toward her and kissed her lips. 'Perhaps more than I should.'

When Poppy went back to school in the autumn, she was very conscious that this was her last year. Some of her friends had already left, having reached thirteen. She missed them as it was a small school and the new pupils were much younger than her. She had started her 'monthlies' as Mattie had called them and, with her emotions in turmoil, she had wept in Nan's arms when she had gone to her for advice.

'You'll be missing your ma, I know.' Nan had patted her as she comforted her. 'It's not an easy time for a young girl, but you'll get used to it. Accept it, for there's nowt else to do about it. It's all part of growing up and you'll want to do that, won't you? You'll not want to stop as a bairn for ever!'

'No,' Poppy sniffled. 'I don't. I want to be grown up.' I want to be able do what I like with my life, she thought. But at the same time I don't want to hurt Pa.

Miss Davina and Miss Eloise came looking for her and begged her to come back for lessons. 'You're an inspiration to our other pupils,' they implored. 'Please don't give up. Not unless your father says you have to,' they added.

So she started again in January after her thirteenth birthday, and found her enthusiasm coming back as the music filled her head and lifted her spirits. Her voice soared and her feet began to dance.

Albert and Tommy had a fight. They differed over something at the shop and Tommy suggested they take their argument outside. Albert had agreed, to Tommy's surprise for he hadn't thought Albert was built for fighting. Like Lena he was of heavy physique and moved slowly. Tommy was swift and lithe but before he had even taken his coat off and squared up, Albert had lashed out and caught him on the nose, causing it to bleed. Tommy was so incensed by the unfairness that he had pummelled Albert in his belly and given him a black eye. Albert took the rest of the day off.

Joshua was furious when Lena told him that Tommy had given Albert a beating for no reason, and stormed at Tommy. 'You should know better,' he bellowed. 'Albert is in our employ. What kind of way is that to treat an employee?'

'He had it coming,' Tommy groused, rubbing his sore nose. 'I've wanted to do that since he first came. He's a sneak. I don't trust him and I can't work with him.'

'Well, if he leaves, so will Lena,' his father said. 'She's told me so. And I depend on her now. She knows 'stock and 'customers. But Albert's willing to give you another chance. And Lena says she'll help out with 'baking to give you a bit more free time. She thinks you're probably overworked and can't manage all of 'baking by yourself and that's why you take it out on Albert.'

Tommy was aghast. The only time he could be away from Lena and her son was when he was in the kitchen. 'I don't want *her* help,' he said. 'I can manage. How do you know she can bake?'

'Because she told me so. She used to work for Conner's before they closed down.'

'That's handy, isn't it?' Tommy muttered. 'You can't ask for a reference cos old man Conner died.'

'That's enough!' his father barked. 'I can't be doing with this. You'll work with Lena and Albert, like it or lump it. When you're running things, you can say who works here, but until then it's my say-so and I say that they stay.'

Poppy had listened to their conversation with misgivings. Tommy, she knew, was at his wits' end as he battled with his hatred of Lena and Albert. They seemed to be always finding fault with him – the cakes had too little fruit, the scones too much baking powder – and they claimed that it was the customers who had complained, but only Lena and Albert had ever heard them.

Joshua left behind the key to the medication cupboard one morning when he went out to meet some suppliers and pay bills. 'You'd better keep it safe, Lena,' he said. 'You're in 'shop more than Tommy. But keep 'cupboard locked and hide 'key. Poppy, you're going to be late. Come on, I'll walk with you as far as George Street.'

As she left her father and walked on to school in Albion Street, Poppy took an envelope out of her pocket. It had come yesterday and she had read the contents several times. She hadn't shown it to her father, or told Tommy, but Lena had gazed at her curiously when the post came and she'd seen a letter addressed to Miss Poppy Mazzini.

'Got a young man, have you?' she'd asked in a sugary voice. 'Sending you love letters!' Poppy had ignored her, but she knew it would be only a matter of time before Lena 'accidentally' let the information slip in front of her father.

She opened it again. The letter had come as a complete surprise and the receiving of it was making her rethink her future. 'Dear Miss Mazzini,' she read. 'I don't know if you remember me but I came to your parents' coffee house two or three years ago when my clients were performing at the Mechanics Hall. You danced and sang for us and I said at the time that you could if you wished make a career on the stage.

'You will have grown into a young lady now and I wonder if you have given any thought to your future? If you have lent any consideration to a possible career on the stage, I would be interested to hear of it and could probably help you in that direction. From what I saw that day, you have considerable talent. This would be with your parents' permission, of course, as I realize that you are not of age, but many talented performers start when they are of tender years.'

The letter went on to give his credentials and the names of people he represented, and he signed himself Daniel Damone.

CHAPTER EIGHT

Tommy and Charlie walked from Scale Lane down to the High Street. Tommy had his hands clenched in his pockets. 'I never thought your father would agree to your leaving and find somebody willing to take you. But I suppose it's because you'll be going into 'same kind of business and will eventually come back? Fat chance of my pa letting me go to sea!'

'I won't come back! Well, not for years, anyway.' Charlie squared his shoulders, a habit he had when he wanted to assert himself. 'Why would I want to? There's nobody famous here. I'd just be stuck in that poky workshop day and night making shoes for merchants and their stuck-up wives. Where's 'excitement in that?'

Tommy nodded, his bottom lip stuck out in a pout. 'Well, it's not that I want to leave Hull. It's as good as any other town, I imagine. But I'm so close to 'sea and can't get 'chance to sail on it.'

'Can't think why you'd want to,' Charlie snorted. His future was now assured, he was convinced of it. 'But you could just leave if that's what you want. That's what I'd have done if my father hadn't agreed to me going.'

'I might do that,' Tommy said glumly. 'It's just that there's Poppy. I'd feel mean leaving her.'

'Ah, Poppy!' Charlie said softly. 'She was upset when I said I was leaving for London.'

'She's sweet on you, that's why.' Tommy glanced at his companion. 'Always has been, even when she was little. Didn't you know?'

Charlie nodded. 'I suppose I did,' he murmured and thought

of how he'd kissed her cheek and then her lips and found it very pleasant. 'She – she's becoming very attractive.'

'She's thirteen!' Tommy warned him. 'She's only a bairn.'

'I know, I know! I'm only saying! But another couple of years and there'll be a queue of fellows outside Mazzini's door.'

'That's as maybe,' Tommy growled, 'but in 'meantime keep your hands off. I know you and your philandering!'

They came to the King's Head inn, their choice of destination for the evening. It was already late, but Charlie had sent Tommy a note saying that his father had found him a position in London and he would be leaving the following week. Tommy had finished his chores and gone round to Scale Lane to see him at his father's workshop.

'I don't philander.' Charlie brushed back a lock of fair hair and straightened his cravat before they opened the door into the hostelry. 'I'm very particular about which females I consort with, and what's more I shall aim high when I go to London! Beautiful and rich women will fall over each other to be on my arm and wearing my shoes.' He grinned. 'Or even just rich will do.'

The King's Head inn was an ancient hostelry, one of the oldest in Hull. It was constructed of brick and timber, with shuttered windows and an overhanging top storey, where poets reputedly had stayed and composed odes to the strong Hull ale. As the two young men entered they were assailed by noise and laughter, for the inn was crowded with jostling men and women.

'I can't stay late,' Tommy said, 'and I'll only have one glass or I'll never get up in 'morning.' He elbowed his way to the counter. 'Mattie!' he called when he saw her and waved to her as she turned. He held up two fingers and she nodded.

'Didn't realize you worked here,' he said, as Mattie pushed her way through to them, holding two brimming tankards in one hand and a jug of ale in the other.

'I work wherever 'work is, Tommy.' She smiled. 'Me and my ma! Evening, Charlie. Don't usually see you two in here. Special night out, is it?'

'Came especially to see you, Mattie,' Charlie drawled.

'I'm flattered,' she said smoothly. 'Really honoured.' She gave him a coy glance, lowering her eyelashes. 'We'll have to put a plaque on 'wall. Charlie Chandler drank here.'

'You might one day, Mattie.' Charlie looked her up and down. 'When I'm famous.'

She gazed directly at him. 'And what'll you be famous for?'

'He's going to work in London,' Tommy said glumly. 'There'll be no talking to him once he's set up!'

'Dear dear,' Mattie said wryly. 'What a loss you'll be. How ever will we manage without you, Charlie?' She started to move back to the counter where men were clamouring to be served, and her mother Nan was frantically indicating for her to come and help. 'But you won't desert us, will you, Tommy? We can rely on you?'

'She's got a soft spot for you!' Charlie said caustically, when Mattie was out of earshot. He took a long draught of ale. 'You're on a winner there. If you dare risk it,' he added darkly.

'What do you mean? She's all right is Mattie. She's a good sort.'

'Course she is.' Charlie wondered why Mattie always managed to ruffle his ego. Was it because although she seemed so warm and seductive, she had always refused his offer of an evening out? 'I've to work for a living,' she would apologize in her slightly mocking manner. 'I've no rich papa to help me along.' He knew this was just an evasion and was slightly peeved when he heard her being more than friendly towards Tommy.

'Of course she's a good sort,' he repeated, giving a knowing grin. 'She's everybody's friend.'

Joshua Mazzini walked swiftly towards Scale Lane. He'd locked up the shop. Lena and Albert had gone home, Poppy had gone to bed and Tommy was out, but he had his own key to get in. Now Joshua was hurrying towards the shoemaker's shop before it too was locked up for the night, though he knew John Chandler to be a night owl, working until the early hours. A light was on in the workshop window and as he peered in he saw Charlie's father working on his bench by the light of an oil lamp.

He tapped on the window and the shoemaker looked up, then put down the shoe he was repairing and came to the door.

'Sorry to disturb you, John,' Joshua apologized. 'It seems as if there are not enough hours in 'day to do all I need to do.'

'Come on in.' John Chandler locked the door behind Joshua and sat down again at his bench. 'I'm trying to get this order ready for 'morning. Like you say, there's not enough hours in 'day. Sit down.' He indicated a chair covered in shoes and boots.

'Charlie not in?' Joshua gingerly lowered himself, trying not to sit on the footwear.

'Nah! He's out with your lad. Tommy called round about half hour ago.'

'Ah! That's where he is,' Joshua remarked. 'He'll be wanting to know how Charlie persuaded you to let him leave and go to London.'

The shoemaker looked at him from over his round wire-rimmed spectacles. 'He didn't persuade me. I decided to let him go.' He put down the shoe and folded his arms. 'He'd have gone anyway. I decided that if he was intent on leaving, then he'd be as well to finish his trade here and have some experience and good-will behind him. I'll not give him an allowance, mind. If he wants to go, then he's to stand on his own two feet.' He picked up the shoe again. 'I'll start another apprentice on. One who needs to work.'

Joshua nodded. 'Then Charlie'll come back when he's had enough of gallivanting in London?'

'No. He'll not come back. He'll imagine that I think he will; he's even suggested that he might. I suppose he reckons that'll pacify me.' John Chandler gave a cynical grunt. 'They think we know nowt, these young fellers. They don't know that we remember how it was with our own fathers. How we rebelled against doing what they wanted.'

'True.' Joshua sighed. 'I felt 'same with my father. But we did it. We knew how hard it would be if we went our own way.'

'Aye,' John agreed. 'But we've made some brass and our kith and kin think that life is easy. Well, Charlie for one will find out it isn't.' He paused. 'But he's not like me. He'll fight his way to 'top, and he'll not mind who he shoves out of 'road.'

Joshua frowned. 'Tommy's not like that.'

'No, I don't think he is. He's not made like Charlie.' John wagged a finger at his visitor. 'And if I were in your place, I'd let him go to sea the way he wants to do.' He pursed his lips and nodded. 'I reckon once he's done it and seen what it's like, he'll come home, marry a steady young woman and take over 'business from you. That's what I think, for what it's worth.' He sighed. 'But what would I know about owt!'

'Well, that's why I came,' Joshua said gloomily. 'I wanted your opinion. I don't want Tommy to feel resentful after Charlie's gone, so maybe I'll let him go.'

'Is business good? Can you afford to get some help if he leaves?'

'I've got staff already. They came a while after Mary died. Lena Rogers and her son. She used to be at Conner's bakery. That's why I took her on. She can do baking when – if – Tommy leaves.' He looked thoughtful. 'We seem to be busy, but I'm not making a deal of money. Paying out wages takes its toll on profit.'

'That's why we need our families working with us,' John Chandler said sagely. 'Well, at least you've got your daughter. She'll stop with you until she marries, I expect.' He grinned. 'Try to marry her off to a baker and keep it in 'family.'

Joshua got up to go. 'Poppy's set on going on 'stage. But I'll not have that. Not for my girl.'

Charlie came in as he was about to leave and Joshua wished him luck in his new venture. Charlie thanked him and told him that he'd just left Tommy, who was on his way home.

'Good night, then,' Joshua said. 'I'll catch him up. And thanks for that, John. I might do as you suggest.'

He hurried down Scale Lane, across the junction of Lowgate and down Silver Street and Whitefriargate, the fashionable shopping streets of Hull, and caught up with Tommy who was leaning on Monument Bridge, gazing into the waters of Prince's Dock. Above him on its towering monument the statue of Wilberforce, the most famous of Hull's sons, surveyed the town.

'By, you don't half walk at a pace,' Joshua puffed. 'I can't have been more'n a minute or two behind you.'

'Where've you been?' Tommy turned to look at his father. 'I thought you'd gone to bed.'

'I've been to chat with John Chandler. We don't often get 'opportunity to talk, so I went round. I knew he'd be up.'

'Charlie says he works all 'hours God sends.' Tommy turned back to look down into the water which ran between Prince's Dock and Queen's Dock and into the Humber Dock. 'He never takes any time off. What sort of life is that, eh?'

'I agree,' his father murmured. 'But sometimes we get so bowed down with trying to earn a living that we forget how to do anything else. I had your ma to remind me when she was here, but now that she's not—' He stopped for a second and cleared his throat. 'She enjoyed life,' he continued. 'She liked 'theatre and music halls, singing and dancing. Poppy's like her in that respect.'

Tommy silently nodded. He missed his mother more than he had ever admitted to anyone.

'She was restricted by her parents, you know,' his father went on. 'They were joyless people. Never laughed. Always looked on 'black side. Walked on 'straight and narrow all their lives.'

He took a deep breath and sighed it out. 'We, your ma and me, when we first married, we always said we'd do 'best we could for our children if we had any. We'd set 'em on 'right path, make them feel secure, and we hoped that they'd follow in our footsteps. But if they didn't, well—' He too looked out across the dock as he searched for the right words.

'What I'm trying to say, Tommy, is – well, if you really want to go to sea, then you can. And if it doesn't work out, then you can come back any time you want and there'll be no recriminations – no I told you so.'

Tommy looked at him. He didn't speak for a moment, and then he said huskily, 'You mean it, Pa? But – what about 'bakery? What about 'coffee house?'

'Lena can do 'baking. She says she's good, and what she can't do I'll have brought in; there's plenty of small bakers who'd be glad of 'extra custom. And Poppy will be leaving school soon. She can look after 'coffee house. She's good with people, knows how to chat to them. She'll maybe even help with 'baking.'

'And what about Albert? Will you keep him on?'

Joshua nodded thoughtfully. 'I'll have to if Lena is tied up in 'kitchen. We'll need an extra pair of hands.'

'Are you sure you'll be able to manage?' Tommy was having doubts now, even though there was an exultant excitement growing inside him.

Joshua glanced at him. 'I'll worry about that,' he said. 'Do you want to go or don't you?'

Tommy put his arm round his father's shoulder and hugged him. 'Oh, I do,' he said. 'I really do!'

CHAPTER NINE

Poppy wept when Tommy told her his news the next day, after she returned from school. 'I know it's what you want to do,' she cried. 'But I shall be left with those two horrible, *horrible* people!'

'Pa will be here,' Tommy said. 'He won't let them bully you.' He knew very well that Poppy wouldn't be bullied. She was quite capable of standing up for herself, and he wasn't going to be put off. When his father had caught up with him on Monument Bridge he had already decided that he was going to sea and had even considered leaving home without discussing it with his pa. He had made enquiries at the docks and had heard of a cargo ship that was departing shortly and needed deck hands.

'And anyway,' she sniffled, 'who'll take you? You've no experience of sailing on ships. You only know baking.'

'I don't need to know about sailing.' Tommy pulled woollen jumpers and thick cord trousers out of a cupboard. 'The owners don't have to take on proper seamen any more. Engines are so reliable they hardly ever use sails.'

'You'll come back smelling of fish,' she groused.

'No, I won't. I'm not going fishing.' He sat next to her on his bed. 'Poppy! I'm going! I'm applying to one of Wilson's cargo ships that's in 'dock now. It was built here, Earle's I think, so it'll be a reliable one. It's got massive boilers and engines and carries about six hundred tons of cargo. It carries sail but doesn't need it, only if 'boiler or 'engine breaks down.'

'Who told you about it?' She was sulky.

'I'm always down there, talking to 'seamen. One of them told me about this one. She's doing 'Rotterdam run as soon as she's finished repairs.'

'So you'll soon be home again?' she said hopefully. 'If it's only going to Rotterdam?'

He fished a canvas bag from under the bed. 'No. It'll be going on somewhere else, I expect. I don't know, do I? I haven't been taken on yet.'

'You might not like it,' she said finally. 'I bet you'll be sick!'

'Probably.' He grinned. 'And as for not liking it, how will I know if I don't try it?' He put his hand on her shoulder. 'Your time will come one day, Pops. Be sure that it will.'

She shook her head. She was so miserable that she didn't even admonish him for calling her Pops. 'Only if I run away,' she said. 'Pa won't ever tell *me* that I can go on the stage.'

She hadn't told anyone about the letter from Dan Damone, nor had she answered it. She had tucked it away amongst her petticoats where no-one would find it. She couldn't tell her father or Tommy. She had toyed with the idea of telling Miss Davina or Miss Eloise, but they would be duty bound to advise her to discuss it with her father. She'd considered telling Nan, but Nan was loyal to her father and besides, she was like a mother hen. She would worry about her, for sure.

She gave a deep sigh and put her chin in her hands. Mattie! The thought suddenly struck her. Mattie. She's sensible and she's not that much older than me. She would understand. I could ask her what she thinks I should do.

She got up from Tommy's bed and gave him what she considered to be a brave smile. 'I wish you luck, Tommy. I hope you enjoy your life. Just think of me sometimes, washing the dishes and fighting off Albert's advances.'

'What! What do you mean?' Tommy stared. 'He doesn't try anything, does he? You must tell Pa if he does!' He recalled what Charlie had said about Poppy's being attractive. He hadn't seen it himself. She had red hair for a start, redder than his, which was sandy-coloured and he hated it. He preferred girls with dark hair, although Mattie was fair and he'd always found her attractive, in a comely kind of way.

Poppy shrugged. 'I'm sharpening my nails,' she said nonchalantly. 'Just in case.'

'Poppy!' Tommy turned to her. 'You mustn't talk like that. If you're at all worried about Albert, I'll tell Pa if you daren't, or are embarrassed about it.'

'It's not that I daren't,' she asserted. 'But if Albert leaves, then Lena will go as well, and Pa says he needs her; though I'm sure there are plenty of other women could do the baking just as well as her.' She scowled. 'She's wheedling herself into his life. Or trying to.' And if she does, she thought, then I shall run away. I shan't stay, whether Pa wants me to or not.

Tommy was only seventeen and had little experience of young women. He thought of Poppy only as his little sister, and as she had always been merry and adventurous, singing songs and telling tales, he didn't attach too much credence to what she was saying about Albert. They both disliked him, it was true, but surely he would never take advantage of her, not here under their father's roof? He didn't want to think about it. The idea made his skin creep, but also he wanted to go away with a clear conscience. He didn't want to be worrying whether or not Poppy would be all right.

'Pa wouldn't look at another woman,' he said, pushing clothes into his bag. 'Not after Ma. You're exaggerating, as usual.'

'Why are you packing now?' Poppy ignored what he was saying. 'You said you haven't been taken on yet.'

'Just in case,' Tommy said. 'I need to be prepared to say I can leave immediately. There.' He fastened up the bag. 'I shan't need to take as much as Charlie will when he goes on Saturday.'

'On Saturday?' Poppy took a breath. 'Which Saturday?'

'Day after tomorrow,' he replied casually, disturbed by her stricken face. 'Thought you knew.'

'I didn't know it was to be so soon,' she said huskily and swallowed hard. 'Will he – will he come to say goodbye, do you think?'

Tommy glanced at her. She had gone quite pale. 'I don't know. Maybe. I'll drop round later to tell him my news. I'll ask him to call, shall I? Tell him you'd like to see him before he leaves?'

'Yes,' she gulped. 'I mean, no. It doesn't matter. He'll be busy, I expect, getting packed and everything.'

They heard a banging on the stairs. It was Lena. 'Is anybody there?' she shouted. 'I could do with some help down here!'

Poppy opened the door and stared down at Lena. 'I'm coming,' she muttered.

'About time,' Lena grumbled. 'I'm rushed off my feet in here.'

'Where's Pa?' Poppy asked as she went downstairs. 'I thought he was here.'

'Had to go out,' Lena said abruptly.

Poppy greeted a woman who was waiting to be served, and asked Lena, 'Where's Albert?'

'Gone.' Lena put her hand out for money from a woman buying two ounces of tea and dropped it in the cash box. 'He's a bit off colour, so I sent him home.'

'Thank you, Mrs Jackson.' Poppy smiled at the woman she had served with flour and oats, as she left the shop. 'See you again.'

'You will, honey,' Mrs Jackson said. 'It's good to see your pretty face.' She looked pointedly at Lena's severe expression. 'Not everybody's able to raise a smile.'

Lena grunted as the customer went out. 'It's all very well smiling when you've nothing else to do. You'll have to do more, young woman, when that brother of yours clears off on his ship.'

'I didn't know that you knew.' Poppy was peeved to think that Lena had heard the news before her.

'Your pa had to tell me, hadn't he? I shall be the one doing most of the work.' She looked at Poppy. 'I'm to take on the baking, so that skivvy Nan will have to look to her laurels with the cleaning. I'll not have a dirty kitchen.'

'It's not dirty!' Poppy objected. 'It's cleaned every day.'

'It might be clean enough for your brother and that Nan.' Lena looked scathingly at Poppy. 'But not for me. I said to your father, if I'm to be in charge of the baking, then I'll have things done the way I like it.' Then she gave her a thin smile. 'We'll get on well enough, I don't doubt, Poppy, as long as we understand each other. Especially when I move in; it'll be a lot easier then, won't it? I shall be on hand to organize everything.'

'Move in? Move in where?' Poppy was flabbergasted.

'Why, here, of course! I can't be expected to start so early if I'm not living in. I'll be using Tommy's room as he won't be needing it.'

Poppy stared open-mouthed. 'Has Pa agreed to it? Did he say that you could?'

'Well, I suggested it. It would make it easier all round, now wouldn't it? Course,' she sighed, 'I realize there won't be room for Albert – not at the moment, anyway. But he can eat here with us and just go home to sleep.'

I can't believe what she's saying. Poppy licked her dry lips. How could Pa agree to it without discussing it with me?

More customers came in so there was no chance of further talk, but in any case she felt so sick and miserable that she couldn't have spoken of it. Tommy came through and said he was going out. He addressed himself to Poppy not Lena, and she guessed that he was going to see Charlie.

Her father came back and asked where Albert was. 'I've sent him home, Josh,' Lena said, an anxious frown on her forehead. 'He must have eaten something that's upset him.'

'Huh,' Joshua said grumpily. 'He never said anything to me. You wouldn't think to look at him that he'd a delicate constitution.' Poppy realized that Albert must have left after her father had gone out.

'Oh, he hasn't,' Lena was quick to reply. 'Constitution of an ox usually, but maybe he ate some bad meat or drank out of a dirty glass. He'll be back in the morning.'

That evening after they had locked up for the night, Poppy, Tommy and her father sat by the range in the kitchen. They rarely lit the fire in the parlour during the week for they hadn't time to sit in there, but the kitchen was cosy since the fire was always kept in to heat the ovens and for boiling the kettle or cooking meat and vegetables.

'I've got 'job, Pa,' Tommy said quietly, although he couldn't keep the exultation out of his voice. 'They said I can sail with them on Monday.' He glanced at Poppy for her reaction but she simply nodded her head.

'Well, we'll see how you get on,' his father said. 'I told you that if you don't like it, then you can come home again. There's always a place here for you.'

'Except that Lena's having his room,' Poppy said bitterly. 'Will she be willing to move out?'

Her father shifted uncomfortably. 'I didn't say for sure that she can,' he said. 'She suggested it as she'll have to be here early, and it sounded like a good idea. But I didn't agree for sure,' he repeated. 'I said I'd give it some thought.'

'My room!' Tommy said in astonishment. 'That means I'll have to store my things somewhere! I don't want her poking about amongst them.'

'I don't know what you two have got against Lena,' their father said sharply. 'She works hard, she's willing to do all of 'baking and yet still you don't like her!'

'What about Albert?' Tommy glanced anxiously at Poppy and then his father. 'It won't do to have him here, not with – not with Poppy!'

'I don't need you to remind me of what's right and what isn't!' Joshua said irritably. 'Of course he won't stay. We haven't room for him for one thing. But I just said, nothing's been decided yet. We'll see how things work out.'

But Pa doesn't realize that Lena has already decided what she's going to do, Poppy thought as she rose to go up to bed. *She's* worked it out already.

'Poppy!' Tommy whispered at her bedroom door later. 'Charlie said he'll be on Monument Bridge tomorrow night at about eight o'clock, if you want to say cheerio. I told him you could probably get away about that time.'

'I might,' she said casually, opening the door a crack. 'I want to go and see Nan about something anyway, so I'll come back along there.'

That decided her. She would go and talk to Mattie before she went off to work. Nan was just an excuse.

'Ah!' Tommy said, before she closed the door. 'If you see Mattie, will you tell her I'm leaving? I, er . . . or I can tell Nan in 'morning, I suppose, when she comes in.'

'You could tell Mattie yourself, of course,' Poppy gibed. 'I expect you didn't think of that!' She closed her door.

The following evening she told her father she was going to see Nan. He no longer told her that she mustn't go into the High Street on her own. He simply warned her to be careful and be back before dark. She hoped she had timed it right to see Mattie and then be in time to meet Charlie. She was wearing one of her mother's cream skirts; it had a kick pleat on the hem, which tossed around her ankles as she walked, and she had teamed it with an emerald-green shirt tucked into the waistband.

'You look lovely, Poppy,' Mattie said admiringly. 'You going to meet somebody?'

'I've come to see you, Mattie,' she hedged. 'I want to discuss something.'

'Shan't have to be long,' Mattie said. 'I'm due at work in half an hour and I've got to get cleaned up. Still, if you don't mind me getting washed while you talk?'

'No, of course not.' Poppy sat down, realizing that Mattie had only just come in from the flour mill. She worked long hours and she had flour on her face and hair as she had when Poppy had come the last time. 'I want your advice.'

'From me?' Mattie laughed, and started to strip off her shirt and skirt. She stood in her thin cotton shift, and Poppy thought that it was a pity they were not nearer in size, for she would have passed on some of her clothes. But Mattie, although no taller than her, had well-rounded breasts and hips, whereas Poppy was still slender.

'Do you know that Tommy is going to sea?' she asked, as Mattie splashed cold water from a bucket over her face. 'Pa said he could go if he wanted to. He's been taken on a ship that's leaving on Monday.'

Mattie turned to her, water running down her face and streaking the flour into runnels of white paste. 'Tommy! No! I didn't know.' Her expression, usually so cheerful, was downcast. 'On Monday?' She stood for a moment, her lips parted, and then she turned back to her ablutions, cupping water into her hands and splashing it over her face. When she looked up again, she had assumed her usual bright demeanour. 'That's nice for him. It's what he wants to do, is it? Doesn't want to stay here in Hull?' She picked up a piece of cotton towelling and scrubbed her face dry. 'It's not because Charlie's leaving, is it?'

'I don't think so,' Poppy said miserably. 'He's always wanted to go to sea and Charlie has always wanted to go to London. The thing is, Mattie . . .' She hesitated, wondering if she should say anything about herself after all. 'I shall miss him.'

'I expect you will,' Mattie said kindly. 'So will I, as a matter of fact.'

'Will you? Do you like him? Tommy, I mean?'

'I thought that's who we were talking about.' Mattie frowned. 'It is, isn't it?'

'Oh, yes, of course I meant Tommy! Though I'll miss Charlie too,' she confessed. 'He's going away on Saturday – tomorrow – and the thing is,' she repeated, 'I'll be left on my own.'

'You've got your pa!' Mattie said. 'I know it's difficult for you without your ma, but your pa – well, he idolizes you, doesn't he? And you'll be busy, you'll be leaving school soon, and you've got your singing and dancing and you'll help in 'shop.'

Poppy nodded. The way Mattie put it, it sounded like an ideal life, and for Mattie it probably would be. But not for me, she thought. I have other ambitions, but I realize now that I can't tell Mattie. She'd only try to talk me out of them anyway.

'I'd better go,' she said. 'Thank you for listening to me, Mattie. I won't hold you up any longer.'

'Is that it, then?' Mattie seemed surprised. 'I don't seem to have done much.'

'I just needed to talk, that's all.' Poppy forced herself to smile.

'Any time.' Mattie slipped on another skirt and shirt, and reached for a hairbrush. 'You can come and talk any time you want.'

Poppy walked back along the High Street and cut down Scale Lane. Charlie's father was seated in the window as usual, his back bent over his bench. She crossed Lowgate, avoiding the surge of carts and waggons, and as she passed down Silver Street she glanced at the display of gold and silver in the shop windows. In the fashion shops of Whitefriargate she looked at her reflection rather than the objects displayed. People were still shopping or strolling and the evening was pleasant and still light. Ahead of her was the Monument Bridge, crowded with people looking over into the water, but she couldn't yet see Charlie and she hoped that he hadn't forgotten that he'd said he would meet her.

Charlie stood beneath the Wilberforce monument, positioning himself so that he could look across towards Savile Street, in the direction from which he thought Poppy would come. He took a turn round the base of the monument, gazing at the rippling water and the barges and ships which were moored in the dock. Then he cast his eyes down Whitefriargate, the way he had just come, and saw her.

He had tried to analyse his feelings towards Poppy as he'd walked here, arriving early so that he could watch her coming towards him and judge how he felt about her. She had always been just his friend's little sister, but the last few times he had seen her he had felt differently towards her. He had noticed how attractive she had become, and although he had laughed when Tommy warned him off, he had thought of her often. She had become more womanly, more desirable to his senses. She had disturbed him since that first kiss, which he would quite like to repeat. But he was going away. There will be other women, he told himself. Women, not schoolgirls, which is what Poppy still is. Tommy said she has a crush on me, and it's always flattering to a man's vanity when a woman, or a girl, admires him.

He watched her now as she came towards the bridge, unaware yet of his presence. Most of the other women around were dressed in dark clothing, their dull skirts trailing on the ground, but Poppy was like a bright flower in a garden. So apt, her name, he thought. She's lovely. Her cream skirt flounced around her ankles as she walked, tall and straight-backed, her chin slightly tilted, and her hair gleaming like burnished copper above her emerald shirt.

Some youths leaning on the bridge caught a glimpse of her over their shoulders and turned round completely, their backs and elbows resting on the iron rail, so that they could watch her. Charlie saw their lips lift in smiles of admiration and so that they wouldn't call out to her, he walked towards her.

'Poppy,' he said. 'Here you are!'

'Yes,' she said a little breathlessly. 'Am I late?'

''No.' He took her arm. 'But it wouldn't matter if you were.' He smiled down at her. 'You look lovely,' he said softly. 'Really, really lovely.'

'Do I?' she whispered, gazing at him. And he knew then, with a certainty that sent his senses reeling and his heart racing, that she loved him.

CHAPTER TEN

'Shall we take a walk?' Charlie asked.

Poppy hesitated for only a second. She hadn't been long at Mattie's and she had hurried there and back. Her father wouldn't expect her just yet. 'All right,' she said. 'As long as I'm home before dark.'

Those few words emphasized that she was still young enough to be in her father's care, and that he was nineteen. 'Let's walk along 'dock side,' he said. 'Towards the pier.'

'Yes,' she agreed. 'That'll be lovely.'

They walked in silence along the side of Prince's Dock, both of them looking at the ships as if they were the most interesting vessels they had ever seen, but when they reached the junction of Humber Dock Poppy said, 'We'd better not go any further. It's too far to the pier. Pa will be anxious if I'm late.'

'What a good girl you are, Poppy,' he teased. 'Worrying about your pa worrying over you!'

He drew her towards the railings at the side of the water and they watched a tugboat easing its way towards the lock. He put his arm round her shoulders. 'I'll miss you, you know, Poppy. I'll think about you while I'm away.'

'Will you?' Her mouth trembled and she pressed her lips together. She looked up at him, her eyes filming with tears. 'I'll miss you too, Charlie, and do you know why?'

A little awkwardly he patted her cheek and shook his head. 'We've known each other a long time, that's why. It's just unfortunate that I'm going away at 'same time as Tommy. You'll feel a little lost, I expect, because of things changing, but you'll soon get used to us not being here.'

'No,' she breathed. 'I won't. I'll miss you, because I love you and I can't bear to think that you won't be here!'

He took in a breath. 'Poppy! You're much too young to love anyone!'

'I'm not,' she whispered. 'When I was ten, I asked my mother when would I be old enough to love someone; and she said . . .' Her mother's words were hazy but she thought she remembered the gist of them. 'She said, it wasn't a question of how old someone was, but of meeting someone and knowing that you love them. And I've known since then that I love you.'

Charlie gazed at her, her grey-green eyes swimming with tears, and he wanted to put his arms round her and tell her that he loved her too; but he wouldn't, for he didn't know if it was true. He felt a great fondness for her, but she was innocent and vulnerable, and she was also Tommy's sister. Had she been older and bolder, it would have been different; he wouldn't have hesitated to show his love, whether or not it was steadfast or enduring.

'Perhaps I am young.' A tear trickled down her cheek as she spoke, and he brushed it away with his finger. 'But I'm growing up all the time. And when I'm eighteen, you'll be twenty-four, and there won't be such a difference between us.'

'Poppy!' He drew her towards him. 'We don't know what's going to happen in the time between now and then. You'll probably have found someone else that you love even more than you think you love me, and besides, I have to go away,' he said softly, but firmly. 'I want to make my mark in 'world. I can't do that if I've a wife to look after.'

She stared up at him, her lips parted. 'I'm not asking you to marry me, Charlie!' she said huskily. 'I'm only asking you to love me, even if it's just a little.'

His tension eased and he gave an imperceptible sigh. 'Well, that's easy enough, Poppy. How could anyone not love you? You're beautiful and talented and clever – everything about you says that I should love you.'

He bent and kissed her on her lips, and then once again, cradling her face in his hands. She blinked away glistening tears from her lashes. 'So do you?' she whispered.

'Of course I do,' he whispered back.

'And will you wait for me?' she asked. 'Until I'm old enough to know about love?'

When Charlie left on the Saturday and Tommy on the Monday, Poppy felt isolated and alone. 'Come on, Poppy,' her father said on the following Friday, 'let's take a couple of hours off and go to a concert. There's one on at 'Assembly Rooms. It'll cheer us both up. Lena and Albert can manage and we'll be back ten minutes after 'show is over.'

Reluctantly she agreed. The coffee shop would be quiet until the theatres came out, and the grocery only had a few customers who were popping in for something they had forgotten. Most groceries were sold early in the morning or at midday. She would be glad to go out, for she found the presence of Lena and Albert suffocating. Albert seemed to be always watching her and Lena had taken over the kitchen, moving the table and chairs and re-arranging the store cupboard where flour, butter, sugar and dried fruit were kept for baking.

Poppy resented her being there; it was as if she was eradicating her mother's presence. Tommy had left everything as it was when he had taken over the baking, not seeing fit to change anything, but Lena tutted and complained, and poor Nan took the brunt of her fault-finding with a patient compliance.

'I don't know how you put up with it,' Poppy had said to her one day, when Lena, who had fussed about finding mice droppings in the cupboard, was out of earshot. 'I'd just walk out.'

Nan sighed. 'I expect you would, Poppy, but I need to work and I like working for your father. He's fair, he pays me on time and he always says thank you when I've finished. Besides,' she said quietly, 'your ma was good to me. I'd think I was letting her down if I left.'

'Oh, Nan!' Poppy put her arms round her. 'I'd hate it if you left. I'd run away too.'

'No you wouldn't,' Nan said. 'You wouldn't go off and leave your pa with those two, would you?'

Poppy had considered. I just might, she thought, if things get worse.

The Assembly Rooms catered for a different kind of taste from the Theatre Royal, or the Mechanics Hall. No talking dogs, comedians or ventriloquists. The programme began with a ballad singer, followed by a violinist, and then roles from *La Traviata* were memorably sung by a German baritone and an Italian soprano.

Joshua looked at the programme during the interval. 'Anthony Marino in the second half,' he murmured. 'Concert pianist. Mm, we're in for a real treat tonight. You'll wish you'd kept up with your piano lessons, Poppy!'

The curtain rose to show a grand piano centre stage, and a young man in a black frock coat walked on, took a bow and seated himself at the keyboard. Poppy felt her spirits rise, and she knew her father had been right to suggest they came out. Anthony Marino, whose dark hair hung to his white high collar and flopped over his forehead as he bent his head, had a slight smile hovering on his lips as he began to play.

'Chopin!' her father whispered, as he read the programme. '*Grande valse brillante.* Opus 18.'

Poppy nodded. Her feet were beginning to move as if of their own accord and she longed to get up and waltz. When he came to the end of the composition, with barely a pause the pianist began the 'Minute' Waltz and she felt as if she was lifted from her seat and dancing as her body moved in time to the music.

'He's wonderful, isn't he?' she whispered to her father, as Anthony Marino came to the end of the piece and stood to accept their applause.

The pianist bowed and then suddenly gave a big smile. 'You are out of breath now, aren't you, with all that waltzing?' he said, his voice humorous and Poppy thought with the slightest trace of a Mediterranean accent. The audience murmured appreciatively and clapped, and then laughed as he added, 'So now you can take a rest whilst I play Mozart's Rondo *alla Turca*,' which he played so swiftly and merrily that Poppy really did feel breathless and happy.

Marino acknowledged the applause with a bow and sat down again. The mood changed as with a toss of his head, closing his eyes for a second and taking a deep breath, he began Beethoven's 'Moonlight' Sonata. A hush, a stillness, fell over the auditorium as he played the serene and peaceful notes.

When it came to a close, and before anyone roused themselves to applaud, he half turned in his seat and said quietly, as he gently ran his fingers along the keys, 'If you will allow me, the final piece of music which I will play tonight is my own composition. I hope you will enjoy it.'

Poppy sat back. How wonderful, she thought, to have such talent; to be able to compose your own music. She closed her eyes and let the melody wash over her. It was light and seductive, stirring and sensual, haunting and bittersweet, and she found herself crying. How can music make me cry, she thought as she reached for her handkerchief. There were no sad words, yet the music held a sensation of heartbreak and loss. She blew her nose, and as the pianist stood up to take his final bow from an appreciative audience, she saw that her father too was wiping his eyes.

'Never heard of him before,' Joshua said, and for once was not in a hurry to leave. 'But he's good. We'll hear a lot more of him, shouldn't wonder.'

Poppy took the programme from her father to read about Anthony Marino. 'I thought he was wonderful. I wish he'd write a song for me.'

'I thought of your mother whilst he was playing.' Her father gave a sigh. 'I don't know why his music brought back so many memories, but it did.'

They walked back from the concert hall arm in arm and passed the Mechanics as the manager was pinning a poster to the board outside. 'Good evening, Mr Mazzini, Miss Poppy,' he said. 'How are you both?'

'Grand, thank you,' Joshua said. 'We've just been to a concert at 'Assembly Rooms. Marvellous, it was, especially the pianist!' Then he glanced at his pocket watch. 'Have you had a good show? Your customers will be calling on us on their way home, I hope. What's coming next, then?' He read the words on the poster. 'An entertainment competition!'

'We are trying to encourage local talent,' the manager said, 'and of course bring more people into the theatre. We've a good deal of competition from 'Alhambra, and now that there's 'new Grand Theatre we've got to do something a bit different.'

Poppy stared at the poster and her heart started to hammer. 'What kind of talent, Mr Johnson? Comedy or—'

'Anything.' He smiled at her. 'Singing. Dancing. Comics. Fancy trying it?' he asked.

Poppy looked at her father. 'Yes, I do. If Pa will let me.'

'No harm in it, Mr Mazzini,' Mr Johnson coaxed. 'We need as many contestants as possible. There'll be auditions, of course. Dan Damone, the agent, is going to be judge.'

Poppy stifled a gasp. 'Could I, Pa? Please!'

Her father took her arm to hurry her on. 'If it puts a smile back on your face, then yes, you can.'

She felt such joy that she even ignored the grumbles of Lena and the presence of Albert. She sang and practised her dance steps in her room, and when she went for her dancing and singing lessons the following week, she couldn't wait to tell Miss Eloise and Miss Davina.

They were both thrilled and agreed to give her extra coaching and said they would put an act together for her. The auditions were to be in a week's time, which meant she must practise every day.

'What nonsense!' Lena groused when she heard, though she was careful not to be so blunt when Joshua was around. 'What a waste of time. Not that it's anything to do with me, of course.'

'That's right, Lena,' Poppy said sweetly. 'It isn't.'

The evening of the audition coincided with Poppy's last day at school. She had said goodbye to her teachers and fellow pupils and felt a mixture of emotions, excitement and trepidation. 'You're on the threshold of womanhood, Poppy,' Miss Miller, one of her teachers, had said. 'And very fortunate indeed to have your father's support and a ready-made business to enter. So many young women would be glad of such a settled life.'

Poppy looked at her. She was in her thirties, unmarried, and always wore a passive expression. Rarely did she smile and Poppy wondered if she had ever felt happiness or indeed any kind of emotion.

'I realize how lucky I am, Miss Miller,' she replied, and because she knew it was expected of her, added, 'I'll always try to be grateful for it.'

As she was about to turn away, the teacher said, 'Will you be entering for the auditions at the Mechanics, Poppy? I hear that you sing and dance.'

'Yes.' Poppy was astonished that she knew. 'My father says that I can.'

Miss Miller gave a sudden smile. 'If you get through, I shall come and see you.'

'Thank you, miss,' Poppy said. 'That's really kind. There'll be a lot of entrants, I expect.'

'Good luck,' the teacher said and Poppy felt that she meant it.

She was nervous as she dressed for the audition; not of performing, but of meeting Dan Damone again. She wondered whether he would recognize her, and if he did, would he be annoyed that she hadn't answered his letter?

I'll have to explain that I wasn't able to make a decision, she thought as she brushed her hair, and, looking in the mirror, she pinned a silk flower which had been her mother's into her unruly red curls. 'Wish me luck, Ma,' she whispered. 'I wish you were here to see me.' She felt a lump in her throat as she wondered whether perhaps her mother was watching over her. Would she be encouraging her or warning her that this was a wrong step?

'I have to do this,' she said softly. 'I'm not a little girl any more. I have to make my own decisions, but I'd like your approval.' As she gazed into the mirror, she thought she could see her mother's eyes within her own. Her mother had had grey eyes with soft lights in them and long lashes which she darkened with soot. Poppy smiled as she remembered her mother whispering not to tell her pa. 'This is a woman's secret,' she'd said, and laughed. 'We don't have to tell our husbands what we do to make ourselves beautiful.'

Poppy put a little colour on her lips and on her cheekbones, then stepped into the gown she had found in her mother's wardrobe. It was cream silk with a beaded chiffon petticoat worn to be shown, and a flowing skirt which she knew would sway as she danced. The bodice was softly draped and embroidered with silver beads which caught the light, shining and scintillating. Her mother had worn dull, sombre clothes when she was young, as her parents had decreed, but this gown had been bought when she was newly married and reflected her escape from the rigid confinement of her youth.

Last of all, Poppy took the shoes that Charlie had made her, out of the tissue paper in which they were carefully wrapped, and slipped them into her bag. 'These will bring me luck, Charlie,' she murmured. 'I know they will.'

Her father looked up as she came downstairs, and his lips parted. 'Why, you look just like your ma, Poppy! Beautiful,' he said hoarsely. He blinked a few times, and then said, 'I'm going to call you a cab. Can't have you walking to 'theatre when you look so grand.'

'I don't mind walking, Pa,' she said. 'But will you walk with me? You needn't stay if you don't want to. The auditions will take hours, I expect. But I'd like you to come with me.'

'Course I will.' He took off his apron and put on his jacket and called to Lena in the shop that he wouldn't be long, and they stepped out into the street.

There were many admiring glances as they walked towards the Mechanics Music Hall and women turned to look at her, and some, who knew the Mazzinis, called to her how fine she looked, whilst working men and gentlemen touched their caps and hats.

'See how heads turn, Poppy.' Her father grinned proudly. 'You've brightened up their day!'

She took a deep breath. Was she at the start of something? Was this going to be a turning point in her life? She smiled up at her father. 'Thank you for letting me enter, Pa. I'm so excited.'

He looked down at her and she saw something in his eyes: pride, warmth and affection, and something that she couldn't quite define but was almost an awareness of loss.

'I don't know what might come of this, Poppy,' he said, as they reached the stage door. 'That fellow, Dan Damone, who's coming to do 'audition. He's the one who watched you dance, isn't he?'

'Yes,' she said, her eyes on his face, amazed that he had remembered. 'He came for supper that night with the Terry Sisters.'

'Aye, he did.' He stood at the door. 'And he said that you could make a career on 'stage.'

Poppy nodded. Was he going to say again that she couldn't? Because if so, she might as well go home now, without singing a note or dancing a step.

'Well, what I want to say is that it would be a hard life and not one that I would wish my only daughter to take.' He pressed his lips hard together and her heart sank. 'But,' he went on, 'if it means that you'd be unhappy and unfulfilled, then I wouldn't want to deprive you of 'chance of finding out for yourself what kind of life it was.

'So, what I'm saying is 'same as I said to Tommy. If it's really what you want, then I'll not stand in your way.' He gave her a trembling smile and she reached up to hug him. 'So off you go and show them what you're made of!'

CHAPTER ELEVEN

There were other hopeful entrants waiting in the wings. Acrobats, singers, dancers, men who could whistle through their teeth, clowns already in costume, two young boys in oversize evening suits with violins tucked under their arms, and innumerable others all anxious to show off their talents.

The stage curtains were still closed as Mr Johnson tried to make some kind of order of the participants. 'Could we have the comedy people in a group over here, please? Musicians over there, singers and dancers to the side of the stage. Thank you. Keep away from the curtain please!' he told a small girl with dark hair who was wearing dancing pumps.

Poppy sat on a nearby chair and took off her outdoor shoes and slipped on her dancing shoes. They felt soft and comfortable and she did a pirouette, stretching her toes and calves. She noticed some of the other dancers watching her. There seemed to be more dancers than any other kind of performer, and so she made an instant decision. She would dance, but she would concentrate on her singing. Miss Eloise had coached her in two songs and she now decided which one she would sing; it was a light romantic melody, a song of love, but one in which she could also express herself in movement.

The curtain opened and she saw Dan Damone sitting in the front row with another man. He signalled them to start and a comic came to the front of the stage and gave his name and began his patter. He gave quick-fire jokes until Dan Damone called, 'Thank you. Next!' The comic looked startled at being asked to finish, and the next person, an acrobat, ran onto the stage, almost knocking him over. He turned somersaults and handsprings until he too was discharged. 'But I haven't finished,' he complained. 'There's a lot more I can do,' but he was hauled off by the manager to be replaced by the young violinists, who sawed and squawked on their instruments until everyone's teeth were on edge.

An hour went by and various hopefuls were asked to wait and others were told they hadn't been successful. Then it was the turn of the dancers and singers. 'We'll have the singers first,' Mr Damone called out. 'Then we'll break for fifteen minutes and see the dancers after that.'

Poppy hoped that she would be amongst the first of the singers, for she was sure that the agent was getting bored. She saw him yawning from time to time and the man beside him was asleep.

Mr Johnson signalled to her. 'You're next, Poppy,' he said. 'Give your name before you start.'

She'd seen the other performers lumber onto the stage, give their names and then awkwardly begin their acts. She didn't. Lightly, with springing steps, she ran to centre stage, raised her right hand and swept it to one side, did the same with her left, then with both arms and fingers outstretched in a graceful movement gave a low bow, rose up and announced, 'Poppy Mazzini, for your entertainment,' swirled round and began to sing.

She saw Dan Damone sit up in his seat and nudge the man next to him. She smiled as she sang. It was a popular, sweet little tune, one she liked and one which people could whistle or hum to. As she came almost to the end, she incorporated dainty dance movements so that her skirts floated about her, and finished with a deep curtsy to the floor, her hands clasped and her head bent.

'Bravo,' the man sitting next to Dan Damone called out. 'Excellent!'

She rose to her feet, gave a bow and started to back away. 'One moment,' Mr Damone called out. 'We've met, haven't we?'

She came to the front of the stage. 'Yes, a few years ago.'

He nodded. 'I remember. Come down here. We'll take a break now,' he said to the manager. 'Ten minutes only. Tell those who don't want to wait they can leave.'

Poppy made her way down the steps into the auditorium. Both

men stood up as she approached. Dan Damone took her hand and shook it. 'I remember you, Poppy. You were in your father's coffee house and danced for me. I wrote to you,' he added.

'Yes,' Poppy said shyly. 'I'm sorry I didn't reply. I would have done, but I didn't know what answer to give.'

'Your parents wouldn't approve of you taking a stage career?' He perused her thoughtfully, his eyes keen and scrutinizing. 'Is that it?'

'My mother died,' she said. 'My father, well, he doesn't want to lose me. And he would worry about me.'

'That's understandable,' the other man said. He was short and balding and held an unlit cigar in his hand. He put the cigar in his mouth and held out his right hand. 'Ben Thompson's my name, if you don't know it. I own theatres and music halls in the north. Always looking for fresh talent.' He looked her up and down. 'You could do well. Good voice. Nice presence. Neat dancer.'

For some reason which she couldn't fathom, she didn't like him, but she politely shook his hand and sat down as they suggested.

'So! Your father? Is he here?' Dan Damone asked. 'Could we talk to him? I gather that you'd like to be on the stage or you wouldn't be here.'

'I would,' she said. 'I really would. But my father would need to be sure that I'd be all right, be safe, you know.'

He nodded. 'Lots of young women start in the theatre and music hall when they're younger than you. What are you, fourteen? Fifteen?'

'Thirteen,' she said. 'I'll be fourteen in January.'

'We'd have to dress her up a bit, Dan.' Ben Thompson chewed on his cigar. 'She'd pass for eighteen easy then. If she gets through this audition, which she will, I'll take her for Bradford, then Wakefield.'

'Hold on. Hold on!' Dan Damone interrupted abruptly. 'She's got to show us she can do more than she's done today. Poppy,' he said, 'you've done well today, passed with flying colours, and if your father agrees you'll be able to do your act here at the Mechanics for a week. You'll be paid for performing, and if we like what you do, then we'll offer a contract.' He turned to

Ben Thompson and looked directly at him. 'It's got to be done right. Fair and square. I've my reputation to think of.'

Poppy looked from one to another. It was happening too fast! Would her father agree? Would she have to work for Ben Thompson? Who would pay for her train fare or lodgings?

Dan Damone was speaking to her. 'First things first. Will your father agree to your performing next week? If he won't there's no point in continuing.'

She nodded. 'Yes, I'm sure he will.' She felt a sudden fluttering and breathlessness, as if she was being turned inside out. She swallowed. 'Shall I do the same song all the week or different ones?'

'Full repertoire so that we know what you can do,' he said. 'Learn as many songs as you can, for if your father agrees and we take you, then we'll be on the road the following week. No dithering, will you won't you,' he said firmly. 'There's plenty of others who'll be glad to come.

'Right,' he called out. 'Let's get on. Break over. Next.'

If she had expected any special treatment because he had met her before, she would have been disappointed, for Dan Damone turned to watch the other acts, and Poppy slipped out of the building to make her way home. On the way, she called in to see Miss Eloise and found Miss Davina there as well.

They were delighted with her news and said they would prepare her, though Miss Davina said, 'I don't think I can advise you any more, Poppy. If you're going to perform next week, then do what you've been taught, and if you wish to improvise then that is what you must do. I think,' she said reluctantly, 'that perhaps you should concentrate on your singing. That's what people who go to the music hall like to hear. Everyone likes a good melody, something they can hum on the way home.'

Miss Eloise gave her some song sheets to take with her so that she could practise and both said they would come to see her at the Mechanics the following week.

Her father looked up from serving a customer as she opened the door into the shop. He gave her a little wink and a smile and signalled for her to go through into the house. Lena and Albert were both in the shop, Lena cleaning the windows by the tables, making a great show of huffing on the glass and polishing vigorously. Albert was weighing up oats into bags and Poppy noticed that his little finger was touching the scales.

Her father followed her into the kitchen and closed the separating door. 'Well?' he said. 'How did you get on? Did they like you?'

'Yes!' she said excitedly. 'Dan Damone remembered me. He wrote to me, Pa,' she added. 'Not long ago, but I didn't answer his letter.'

'Wrote to you?' Joshua frowned. 'Why did he do that? Why didn't you tell me?'

'He asked if I'd given any consideration to being a performer,' she confessed. 'Now that I'm older. He said I had talent. And I didn't reply because I didn't know what to say. I didn't think that you'd let me go.'

'He wrote to you!' Joshua said incredulously. 'That means that he thinks you'd do well. Why would he bother otherwise?' He sat down hard in a chair and put his chin in his hands. 'You know, don't you, Poppy, that performing on stage is considered indecent by some folk? They think that only those with loose or improper morals would do such a thing!'

He looked up at her as she stood there. 'I'm sorry to have to talk in such a way to you, but you have to be aware of it. There are men who – well, men who hang about a stage door. They bring flowers and presents and invite young ladies out to dine, and their intentions are not – honourable.' His face flushed as he spoke. 'If your mother was here, she could have explained it to you. You're almost a woman, and yet you're still just a girl and I could be very fearful for you.'

She bent down and kissed his cheek. 'I know what you mean, Pa. But I'm not easily led.' Besides, she thought, I love Charlie. I wouldn't want anyone else to take me out, or buy me flowers. 'Mr Damone said that he would see my performances next week,' she said, 'and if I'm any good, then he'd talk to you about a contract. So you could ask him then about how safe I'd be.'

As she spoke she was consumed by anticipation and excitement. Was it really happening? Was she really on her way to becoming a performer?

'Pa,' she said, 'if I did go away, would you employ Mattie? She works so very hard in the flour mill and she works in the evenings as well, in one of the inns.'

'If she already has two jobs why would she want to work for me?'

'She's honest,' Poppy said. 'She'd never cheat you, and I know she'd be pleased if you could see your way to offering her some work.'

'Honest? What do you mean?' Joshua stood up, frowning. 'Are you implying that somebody here isn't?'

'I don't trust Albert,' she said, but didn't tell him about his finger on the scales.

'Oh!' Her father flapped his hand, dismissing her fears. 'I don't know what you've got against him. He's very useful to me. He can lift boxes and take out orders. Mattie couldn't do that. Don't you worry about me,' he said. 'I'll manage all right.'

For the next few days, Poppy rose early each morning, even before Nan arrived to do the cleaning. She took out the flour and fats, mixing bowls and tins and helped Lena with the baking when she came down from Tommy's room, which she had now appropriated. Lena was not an early riser and Poppy suspected that she tumbled straight out of bed and into her clothes without getting washed, for she was flushed and sweaty and her hands were hot, which Poppy knew, for her mother had told her, was not good for kneading bread, which required cool hands.

Albert came in at half past six. He was sour and uncommunicative. Not that Poppy wanted to talk to him, but when she asked him to help her bring in the trays of fresh bread, cakes and scones, he merely grunted. Her father, on the other hand, was energetic and talkative in the morning as he filled the shelves and checked his stock, and would sing refrains from music hall songs. Poppy would join in, and they would laugh when customers made comments about the singing duo.

When she had spare time during the day, in the lull between customers, she would escape to her attic room and practise her lyrics and dance steps, opening the window and letting her voice soar. People passing by would look up and smile and, when they next saw her, wished her good luck for the following week's performance. Already word had gone out that Poppy Mazzini was going to appear at the Mechanics Music Hall and was on her way to stardom.

CHAPTER TWELVE

Poppy dressed carefully, putting extra petticoats beneath the red skirt she had bought especially with money her father had given her. She brushed her hair and arranged her curls around her cheeks, for tonight she was going to appear winsome and charming and play on her youth and innocence. She had chosen a popular medley of songs that the musicians, who played regularly at the venue, would know.

The doors were opened to the public at six o'clock in time for them to buy their drinks at the bar and claim their favourite seats. Today being Monday was bound to be quiet, though many of the older citizens preferred Monday above all other evenings as they could sit in comfort without being hassled by the rowdier patrons at the end of the week.

Poppy was intentionally early. It was barely five o'clock, but she wanted to rehearse her routine on the stage, and the musicians were there to go over the pieces of music she had chosen.

But there was someone on the stage already, a comic, dressed in a large suit and bowler hat, who was shouting out his patter to an empty auditorium. He stopped when he saw Poppy and fumbled his lines. 'I've lost 'thread of what I was saying now,' he grumbled. 'I came in 'specially so I could practise.'

A violinist with his instrument case under his arm had just walked in the door. He laughed at the comment. 'You'll get a few interruptions on Friday and Saturday night,' he said. 'So you'd better practise a bit more!' He turned to Poppy. 'You the singer that was here for 'audition?'

'Yes,' she said. 'I came in good time too, so that I could rehearse.'

'Right.' He nodded. ''Pianist will be here in a minute. I've just seen him up 'street. Have you brought some music?'

'Yes.' She showed him the sheaf of songbooks. She was beginning to feel nervous. 'I've marked the two I'm going to sing.'

'Been given two slots, have you? They must think you're all right.' He looked over the music. 'That's fine. We can manage those.' He looked up at the stage, where the comic was still muttering his patter under his breath, his lips hardly moving. 'Right then, Jack,' the musician called to him. 'We need 'stage now. You can go to 'back of 'stalls and practise. 'Patrons won't be coming in just yet.'

The comic glared at Poppy, then at the musician. 'Me name's Billy,' he mumbled. 'Billy Toke. 'Chap with a joke.'

Poppy smiled. That was the funniest thing he had said so far. 'Sorry, Mr Toke,' she said. 'But I need the stage and the music.'

'You didn't have music for 'audition,' he grumbled as he climbed down the steps.

'No.' She eased out a breath. 'But this is the real thing, isn't it? I really want to get it right.'

He stopped in front of her. 'Not going professional, are you?' and when she said she was hoping to, he replied, 'I suppose your da will help you out wi' finances? I tried it for a bit, but I barely made enough for food and lodgings.'

'So why are you here now?' Poppy took off her coat and outdoor shoes and slipped on her dancing shoes.

He shrugged. 'Can't stop! I just like performing. I enter these competitions and hope that somebody will come along and offer me a good contract; one that'd allow me to eat now and again.'

The pianist had arrived and was running his fingers along the keys. The violinist nodded to Poppy and she ran up the steps to the stage and began.

She didn't notice Dan Damone and Ben Thompson come into the theatre and stand at the rear of the stalls and she went through one song with the musicians without stopping. Then, after consulting with them, she began the second.

'She needs spicing up a bit,' Ben Thompson muttered, chewing on his cigar. 'This little girl thing is all well and good for a Monday night in Hull, but it won't do for my places up north on a Saturday night. She could be another Marie Lloyd if she put her mind to it.'

Dan Damone didn't answer. He thought he knew why Poppy Mazzini was putting on her sweet demure act. She was a Hull girl, a theatregoer. She had probably seen the queue of elderly ladies outside the theatre on a Monday night, and knew what they would like. He'd see how she performed the rest of the week. One thing a performer should know was how to judge an audience, and if Poppy Mazzini was aware of that already at thirteen years old, then he'd be happy to offer her a contract; but as her agent, he would decide on the towns and music halls where she would sing, and, he thought, it won't be in Ben Thompson's seedy flea caves and smoky concert halls.

On the Tuesday night, Poppy included more dancing. She sang a witty ditty, then tied a kerchief on her head, carried a scarf in her hand and danced a lively mazurka, the music in triple time which taxed the musicians but set the audience clapping their hands and calling for more. On Wednesday and Thursday she sang popular melodies and on Friday night she danced and sang to a waltz from sheet music that Miss Eloise had given her. She held up her arms to an imaginary partner and hummed, 'La la, la la, la la-ah, hold me close forever more. La la, la la, la la-ah.' She danced dreamily round the stage; the music was soft, her handkerchief skirt drifted about her ankles, and there was a hush in the auditorium. She thought of Charlie. Did he really love her, as she loved him? 'Do you love me as I love you?' she sang, 'Will you be forever true?' With her arms held high, she clasped her hands together as if she was circling her partner's neck. She swayed her body in time to the music, humming the melody, then stepping back a pace she opened her arms, held up her head and with arms spread wide swept around the stage as if searching for someone.

'You said we must say adieu,' she sang, and came to the front of the stage, her hands held out imploringly to the audience.

> 'Sweet memories are all I have left of you.
> Of sunny hours, shady bowers and secret kisses.
> Of vows of love and hopes we whispered.
> But now you say you must depart
> And have taken with you my tender heart.
> Gone on the silent breath of night.'

She gave a low bow, keeping her head down for a moment and breathing deeply. Then, as she rose, she was stunned by the sound of the audience applauding and whistling. She bowed again. 'Thank you,' she mouthed. 'Thank you.'

From the corner of her eye she could see stagehands in the wings and the next performer clapping. She smiled at the audience, bowing once more before backing away, and as she did so she saw a woman stand up in one of the front rows. 'Don't you worry your pretty head about him, darlin',' the woman called out. 'He's not worth it. Plenty more fish in 'sea.' The people sitting near her laughed, then told her to sit down, and continued applauding and shouting for more, but Poppy backed away, bowing her head and disappearing into the wings.

'Well done, Poppy!' Dan Damone stood behind the acrobat who was on next. 'Wonderful. You're going to be a shining star. No doubt about it.' He smiled. 'All we have to do now is persuade your father to part with you.'

She was given a rousing round of applause as the whole troupe came on the stage at the end of the show and felt flushed and exhilarated as the audience called out her name. Would Pa agree to her wishes? Was she being selfish in leaving him? As she changed into her outdoor clothes in the dressing room she shared with the other female performers, some of whom didn't speak to her and kept their heads turned away, she heard her name being called. 'Poppy Mazzini! Poppy Mazzini! Gen'leman for you!'

'Huh,' said one of the dancers. 'Started already and her only just out of baby clouts. Watch out,' she said as Poppy passed her. 'He'll have his hand up your skirt. That's what happens if you become a professional.'

Poppy glanced at her. She was a dancer and singer too, older than Poppy, but her nose had been pushed out of joint by Poppy's success. 'It won't happen to me,' she replied. 'I won't allow it.'

'That's what everybody says, but I know different.'

'Has it happened to you?' Poppy asked.

'Fat chance!' a young clog dancer called out. 'She's never been propositioned in her life! Take no notice,' the girl went on. 'She doesn't know. All she does is these competitions. Nobody has ever offered her anything, nor's likely to.'

Poppy left them squabbling and went towards the door. What if it was someone bringing her flowers, as her father had warned? Suppose someone followed her home? But, silly, she told herself. I can run home, it's not far.

There was someone waiting with flowers. It was her father, looking pleased and proud, and behind him were Nan and Mattie, both wreathed in smiles and offering congratulations.

'You were wonderful!' Her father swung her into his arms and gave her a great bear hug. 'Just wonderful. How proud your ma would have been!'

At his words, Poppy burst into tears. She had expended so much emotion in her singing and dancing and thinking of Charlie that now, at the mention of her mother's name, it all became too much to bear. 'I won't leave you, Pa,' she sobbed. 'How could I? It isn't fair.'

'We'll go now,' Nan said, and Mattie hovered behind her. They both gave her a kiss. 'We've to get back to work and you and your pa have a lot to think over,' Nan said. 'You've got great talent.'

'Yes,' Mattie whispered to her. 'Don't let it go to waste. Your pa'll be all right. We'll see that he is.' She squeezed Poppy's arm. 'You go and look for fame and fortune. You deserve it.'

As they left the hall, Dan Damone appeared. 'Mr Mazzini,' he said, 'may I call on you later? At your coffee house? There's something I'd like to discuss. And Poppy,' he went on, 'I need to talk about tomorrow night. It's the last night of the show and I'd like you to be top of the bill.

'Just one other thing, Mr Mazzini,' he added, as Poppy took in a sudden breath. "There were people in the theatre tonight who might make offers for Poppy before I can get to you. Could I ask you to sign nothing until I've spoken to you?'

'Why should I trust you above anyone else?' Joshua said shrewdly.

'Because Poppy needs to be nurtured,' Damone answered. 'She has a talent beyond her years. We don't want her burning out by over-playing her.'

Joshua nodded. 'I see. However, I must find out first what Poppy wants. She's my prime concern. But yes,' he added. 'We'll wait for you.

'Is it really what you want, Poppy?' he asked as they walked home, Joshua looking at his pocket watch and hurrying his steps. 'It won't always be as easy as it's been here this week. Folks know you round here; you've had plenty of support. Going to other towns where they've never heard of you, they might be more critical.'

'I'm not bothered about that, Pa,' she said quietly. 'I'm more bothered about leaving you on your own, especially now that you haven't got Tommy to help you.'

'Just supposing you were a few years older,' he murmured. 'Say eighteen or so and someone wanted to marry you. Would you say to your suitor, I can't marry you cos my pa will be lonely?'

She gave a little smile and tucked her arm into his. 'That would be different,' she said. 'If I was getting married, I'd probably live near you.' Then her smile faded. Though I only want to marry Charlie, she thought, and he won't come back here. 'Are you trying to persuade me to sign up with Mr Damone?' she joked. 'Wanting rid of me after all?'

'You know that's not true, Poppy,' he said seriously. 'I only want what's best for you and for you to be happy.'

They were busy in the coffee house and Poppy put on her apron and served the customers. 'Give us a song, Poppy,' one of the regulars said. 'Just so's we can boast that we heard you first before you were famous.'

She laughed. 'Only if you join in, Mr Thomas. What shall I sing?'

'One of them popular numbers,' he said. 'Nothing soppy.'

'No,' said his wife. 'Sing that one you sang tonight, about 'lass whose lover left her. Fair broke my heart that did. It was as if it had happened to you and I know it can't have, cos you're far too young and lovely for anyone to have loved you and left you.'

'I can't sing that, Mrs Thomas,' Poppy replied lightly. 'Not now. Everybody would be weeping and going home and then what would my pa say?'

'Sing one of Marie Lloyd's songs,' someone else called. 'Something lively.'

'All right.' Poppy laughed. She knew all of the popular music hall star's songs, or most of them, but she knew she hadn't got Marie Lloyd's cheeky manner or turn of phrase. She sang, putting on cockney airs and intonations and giving her listeners a wink and saucy smile, and as she was strutting around the room Ben Thompson came in. He took off his top hat and sat down at a vacant table.

'I'd like to sign her up,' he whispered to Joshua when he came to bring him coffee. 'She can start next Monday at my free-and-easy in Bradford. Twice a night for the whole season. A pound a week and no agent to pay.' He took a sheet of paper from his pocket. 'If you just sign here,' he said, through clenched teeth as he chomped on his cigar. 'You are her guardian, I take it? Then she's on her way to stardom. I'll make her into the next Marie Lloyd!'

'I don't think so.' Joshua took the paper from him. 'I'll need to read it first. Leave it with me and I'll let you know.'

The cigar dropped from Ben Thompson's open mouth. 'Can't do that,' he blustered. 'I'm only here for tonight. I've got a big show on tomorrow. It's now or never!'

'Then it's never.' Joshua gave him back his contract. 'I'm not willing to sign away my daughter's rights without reading the terms first. I don't even know who you are!'

'Don't you? I'm astonished! Everybody knows Ben Thompson. Here.' He fumbled in his waistcoat pocket. 'There's my card.' He quickly drank down his coffee. 'Let me know if you change your mind.' And with that he was gone, out of the door, leaving Joshua staring after him.

'Would you believe that?' he said to Poppy as she finished her song. 'He didn't even pay for his coffee!'

CHAPTER THIRTEEN

Joshua carefully read the contract that Dan Damone had brought with him. It didn't make promises, apart from those which said he would endeavour to find suitable engagements with reputable managers and proprietors of theatres and music hall, and would take 10 per cent of any fee.

'Seems fair enough,' he said.

'Read it through, Mr Mazzini, and let me know tomorrow.' Dan Damone looked at Poppy, reading over her father's shoulder. 'I'm not promising that it will be easy,' he said. 'There'll be days when you'll wish you'd never come into this business. Nights when the halls are empty of patrons, and you can't sleep because the beds are lumpy and the landlady is a harridan. I'll try to put you with people who can show you the ropes, and keep an eye out for you. But this is a hard life. Everybody is seeking stardom, and you won't always get applause like you've had this week.'

'Isn't that what I said, Poppy?' her father commented. 'My very words.'

Poppy nodded. She felt frightened and apprehensive, but also exhilarated, so filled with pent-up joy and excitement that she felt she could fly.

'If you do decide to sign,' Dan Damone went on, 'I might have an engagement for you the week after next. There's a hall in Brighton with a vacancy for a singer. I've other auditions next week, but if they're not suitable, well . . .' He left the suggestion floating in the air.

Brighton! Poppy gulped. That was miles away. She glanced at

her father, who was pursing his lips. 'Well, we'll see,' he said. 'We'll let you know tomorrow.'

He walked to the door with Dan Damone. All the other customers had left, as had Albert, and Lena had said she was going up to bed. 'I, erm, there's something I need to ask you, Mr Damone,' he said, opening the door as the agent called good-night to Poppy.

'Call me Dan,' he replied. 'Everybody does.'

'Well, it's like this. Poppy's only thirteen. I, erm, she's got no mother to advise her.' Joshua looked anxious. 'I wouldn't want her to get into any kind of trouble – you know – with young men, I mean. I know how they hang around stage doors, waiting.'

Dan grinned. 'Not often, they don't. Only for the stars, or young women with a reputation, and most performers only want to go to their own beds after they've finished a stint on the stage. It's darned hard work, you know!'

'Yes, but, well, we don't know you, Mr Damone. We live a quiet life here, and I don't know what kind of reputation you have. Meaning no offence,' he added. 'But I'm giving Poppy into your care.'

Dan nodded thoughtfully, and folded his arms across his chest as they stood on the doorstep. 'Yes, it's a big responsibility,' he answered. 'And not one I take lightly. But when I obtain an engagement for my clients, I don't go with them. They make their own way there and have to take the consequences.' He gazed across the street as if considering. 'But I'll tell you this, Mr Mazzini. I can't do anything about Poppy falling for some young buck, but there is no cause for worry as far as I'm concerned.' He turned his head so that he was looking at Joshua from wistful blue eyes. 'I am a celibate man. Your daughter need have no fear of me.'

He seems an honest sort of fellow, Joshua pondered as he closed the door behind him. But do I believe him?

Poppy was sitting at one of the tables with her chin in her hands and her expression animated. 'I really like Mr Damone,' she said eagerly. 'I feel as if I can trust him. Can I go, Pa? I'd really like to.'

Her father gazed at her. What a huge responsibility to look after a daughter. How to protect her? Who to ask for advice? I suppose, he mused, there comes a time when she has to look out for herself, and that time is now.

He sat down opposite her. 'Are you absolutely sure, Poppy? You know that you'll meet people who are . . . well, not like us. They'll have different values, different ways of looking at life, not just 'ordinary run of 'mill like we're used to.'

'That's what makes it so exciting, Pa.' Poppy hunched up her shoulders. 'But I promise you that if I'm unhappy or don't get work, then I'll write to you for advice.' She didn't say she would come home, but that is what he hoped she meant.

Joshua got up and went behind the grocery counter, bringing back a bottle of ink and a pen. He sat down again and drew the contract towards him. He read through it. 'Quite sure?' he asked quietly, and when she nodded, he signed his name.

They both turned as the door to the house creaked. Lena was standing there in her flowing pink nightrobe with her hair hanging down her back. 'I've just made you some cocoa, Josh.' She simpered. 'I know you like a cup afore bed.'

Poppy stared. How dare she appear like that in front of her father? Though Lena's robe covered her nightgown, the buttons at the top were undone, showing the tops of her ample breasts. Lena gave her a little self-satisfied smile. 'I expect you'll want to be off to bed, won't you, dear?' she said. 'You've had a busy evening!'

She's been listening! Poppy was angry. And she'll be glad that I'm going because she'll be alone here with Pa! But that won't do! Everybody will think— What will they think? That she and Pa— It doesn't bear thinking about. Suppose she puts Pa in a compromising position? Is she too old to say she's been caught with a child?

As she stared at Lena she felt herself flushing at such thoughts. But Pa wouldn't . . . surely he wouldn't? Why, she looks like a witch with her scraggy hair hanging down her back and her long nose all shiny! Nothing like Mama, who was so sweet and pretty and who Pa loved. She wanted to cry now, and only a minute ago she had been so happy.

'I don't want to go to bed!' she stated. 'I'm not in the least tired and my father and I are having a discussion.' She rose from the chair and went towards her. 'I'll bring Pa's cocoa in here, seeing as you've made it, and then you can go to bed. You look tired,' she said nastily. 'You need your beauty sleep.'

'Poppy!' her father said severely when she came back with the pot of cocoa and Lena had stomped upstairs. 'Don't go upsetting her. I need her here. If she leaves I'm left without a baker.'

'She won't leave, Pa.' Poppy pouted and folded her arms. 'But she'll be glad when I do. She'll have you all to herself now that Tommy's gone and I'm going. People will talk, you know,' she added, turning her face away from him.

Her father grinned. 'Not about me, they won't! Only about her. That's an advantage that men have over women. But I might bring Albert to live in to stop tongues wagging.'

Poppy opened her mouth in horror. 'Not in my room! Not in my room! I don't want him in there with his smelly feet and his sticky fingers going over my things!'

'No!' her father declared. 'I'll bring 'truckle bed down, and he can sleep in 'kitchen. If he's a mind to, that is. He might not want to.' He shook his head admonishingly. 'You can't have everything your own way, Poppy! I've a business to run. A business that one day will be yours and Tommy's. I can't let it run down just because you don't like Lena and Albert.'

Her father was right, she knew that. But she wept into her pillow that night, tears of frustration, joy and excitement, all rolled into one with the worry of how her father would manage without her.

Saturday night was the busiest night for the music hall and especially when there were so many local people appearing. There was huge support for home-grown talent and most of the performers had brought along friends, relatives, friends of relatives, and relatives of friends to give them a cheer and encouragement. As Poppy walked along George Street there were queues already forming and good-natured banter working along the line.

'Good luck, lass,' someone shouted, and one or two others added their good wishes. When she arrived at the door she saw that a new poster had been put up, displaying a list of the performers with her name at the very top.

She tried to hide her smile, but failed. She was so thrilled and excited. I just hope that Pa will come. He said he'd come later if he could, and oh, how I wish that my mother could have seen me and shared this moment.

Her act was to be at the end of the show, so she stood at the back of the stalls during the first half to watch everyone else, the dancers, the jugglers, the comics; all the people she had been with throughout the week, who had shared their successes and failures and supported each other. She understood the comic's jokes now, and had seen how the magician did his tricks. The acrobat still amazed her for her body was like India rubber, and in a quiet moment one night after a show she had shown Poppy how to turn a somersault.

'Come on, Poppy.' Dan Damone's voice came from behind her. 'Come backstage and get changed. It doesn't do to let the public see you before your act.' He smiled at her. 'We have to try to maintain the magic, build up the excitement of the audience at the thought of seeing Poppy Mazzini.'

She gazed at him. 'But they know me.' She laughed. 'They've known me since I was born!'

'You're no longer the daughter of a grocer,' he said. 'You are now Poppy Mazzini, a star of the music hall. At least,' he said solemnly, 'you will be, unless you've changed your mind?'

'I haven't.' She handed him the contract. 'I won't. Do you really think I'll be a star?' she asked, her eyes shining.

'There's every possibility.' He lifted her chin with his finger and turned her head this way and that. 'You have the looks. You have the talent. You have youth on your side. Do you have the determination?' He shook his head. 'I can't tell you that, Poppy. Only you can know. Come on!' He took her hand and led her towards the side entrance and the rear of the stage. 'Get changed,' he said, as they reached the dressing room door. 'And when you come out I want you to have forgotten everything about your childhood, your school and your father's coffee house. You are Poppy Mazzini, a music hall performer, singing and dancing to a new audience, not to friends you have known all your life. Can you do that?'

She took a deep breath. 'Yes,' she said. 'I can.'

CHAPTER FOURTEEN

The theatre was packed and the Saturday night audience was in a jolly mood, joining in with the singing or heckling the comic whenever he made a joke. Poppy could hear the racket from the dressing room and it only increased her nervousness. The young acrobat, Stella, was the only one left in the dressing room with her for she was to be the penultimate act, followed by Poppy. She was small and petite and wore a huge woolly jumper over her costume and thick socks on her feet.

'Are you nervous?' Stella asked. 'I am. Although I know I'll be all right once I'm on stage. Is it true what they're saying, that you've signed a contract with Mr Damone?'

'Yes, but how did you know?' Poppy was astonished that anyone should have found out. 'I haven't told anyone.'

'Somebody saw you hand him what looked like a contract. Doesn't matter, does it?'

'No, not really, it's just that I haven't got used to the idea myself yet.' She brushed a little colour onto her cheeks and then admitted, 'I'm anxious about it, I suppose.'

'You'll be great,' Stella said. 'You've got 'aura of stardom already.' She grinned. 'I heard 'stage manager say that. I'd like to turn professional,' she added, 'but I might have to join a circus rather than 'music hall.'

'Would your parents let you?' Poppy asked. 'My pa is very worried about me, even though I'm nearly fourteen.'

'I'm seventeen,' Stella said, her cheeks dimpling. 'Everybody thinks I'm about twelve. When I was twelve they thought I was seven! It has its advantages.' She winked. 'I only pay half price for seats in 'theatre or 'music hall or for a train ticket, but I also get asked where's my ma!'

They heard a round of applause and Stella jumped up and started to peel off her jumper and socks. 'I'm next,' she said. 'Keep your fingers crossed for me.'

'I will,' Poppy said. 'I'll come out and watch you from the wings.' She took a deep breath, 'And then it's me!'

She picked up a shawl to put round her shoulders so that she wouldn't be cold whilst she was waiting, having noted how Stella had kept warm with her jumper and socks, and followed her towards the stage. The applause had died away and the compère was announcing the next act. Stella somersaulted her way onto the stage, performing back flips and cartwheels and all manner of gyrations with her supple body.

Poppy rubbed her hands briskly together as she watched. She wasn't cold but the action helped to relieve her nervousness. Why am I nervous tonight? I've been fine on the other nights. Is it because this is the last time I'm going to be here? Before I go away to find success or failure elsewhere? She remembered what Dan Damone had said about forgetting she was a grocer's daughter. I'm Poppy Mazzini, she intoned under her breath. I'm Poppy Mazzini. Top of the bill. Top of the bill.

She swallowed hard as Stella bounced off the stage, then somersaulted back again to take another round of applause. She bowed and backed away and, on reaching the wings, grinned at Poppy. 'You won't be able to do a thing wrong tonight,' she said. 'They're really out to enjoy themselves. Listen!'

The musicians were tuning up, playing a few notes from the melodies Poppy had chosen, and the audience were chanting. '*Popp*-y! *Popp*-y! *Popp*-y!'

She took in another breath. The compère was announcing a star in the making. 'Tonight – she is making her final appearance as an amateur performer; tomorrow – who knows? Please welcome – the star of the show, Hull's own, our very own – *Popp*-y *Mazz-ini*!'

Riotous applause broke out and, giving it just a second longer, Poppy ran out onto the stage and gave a low sweeping bow. As she rose, she looked out into the audience to the first few rows that she could see beyond the stage lights. Her father was sitting in the middle of the first row, flanked by Nan and Mattie. Miss Davina and Miss Eloise were both there, as were some of their other pupils. Mr and Mrs Chandler, Charlie's parents, sat at the end of the row next to Miss Miller, her schoolteacher, and another teacher. Lena and Albert were on the second row and she recognized several of her father's customers from the shop. She smiled. Pa's closed the shop, she thought, before again recalling Dan Damone's words. She swirled round, lifted her arms and began to sing.

She had been given three numbers and started with a medley of popular songs so that the audience could join in. Then she broke into the mazurka, which set everyone clapping their hands in time to the music, and as she polkaed her way to the front of the stage and stood momentarily with her hands clasped, someone called out, 'Sing "Will You Be Forever True", Poppy.' 'Yes,' someone else called. 'Sing "Forever True".' '"Forever True",' the call rang out from different areas of the hall and Poppy smiled and bowed. That was the one she had intended singing anyway.

She held up her arms and beckoned with her hands as if inviting the audience to dance, and began to waltz. 'La la, la la, la la-ah, hold me close forever more. La la, la la, la la-ah.' This will be my song, she mused as she sang and danced. This is how I hope they will remember me at the Mechanics Music Hall.

As she finished with a wide stretch of her arms, tumultuous applause broke out. Her father and all those in the first few rows rose to their feet and she saw Mattie put her fingers to her lips and whistle. Then everyone else stood up, clapping and stamping their feet, and from the wings Mr Boscoe himself, the owner of the theatre, came onto the stage carrying an enormous bouquet of flowers.

'We'd better have a party,' her father said when he came backstage. He wiped his eyes and hugged her. 'Tell everybody to come back to Mazzini's – all these grand folk who have entertained us tonight. What talent,' he snuffled. 'What talent! Right under our noses, here in Hull.'

All the performers and Dan Damone came back to the coffee house, as did Mr and Mrs Chandler, Miss Davina, Miss Eloise, and Miss Miller, and Nan and Mattie who helped a grumpy Lena to serve coffee, chocolate and cakes to everyone. Albert had gone home, and Poppy was glad for she didn't want him near her on this most wonderful night.

'I can't not let her go,' Joshua told Dan Damone. 'Not after tonight. She has talent. I saw it for myself.'

'It will be hard for her,' Dan told him. 'Sometimes audiences don't come or there are bad reviews, or maybe she won't feel like singing or dancing.' He nodded thoughtfully. 'But we'll see. Poppy's been protected; she's always had you to look after her. Now she'll be on her own. She won't be able to run home to her papa.' Then he smiled. 'But yes, she has talent. She could go far. I saw that right from the beginning.'

Poppy slept late the next morning and awoke to hear Lena clattering pans below. She quickly washed, dressed and hurried downstairs, though she wondered why Lena was up so early when they didn't open the shop until nine o'clock on a Sunday morning, and they didn't make bread either. 'Sorry, Lena,' she apologized. 'You should have given me a shout!'

Lena grunted. 'Huh. Not up to me,' she said. 'I didn't think you'd be down at all now that you're a star! Good thing our Albert is here to give me a hand.'

'Does that mean you won't be able to manage if I leave?' Poppy asked astutely, ignoring her sarcasm.

Lena glanced swiftly at her. 'Wh— I thought it was all arranged? Yes, I can manage. Your pa and me will soon get into the way of doing things together.' She gave an unctuous smile as she said it. 'And Albert can lift the heavy pans.'

'Well, I wouldn't be able to do that anyway,' Poppy said, putting on a clean apron and noticing that Lena's was greasy from yesterday's baking. 'Tommy always did that for Ma, or Pa did.'

'Yes, well Tommy's not here either, is he? And your pa is busy looking after the shop. But never mind, I'm sure we'll manage without either of you.' Lena pushed a stray lock of hair under her cap with a floury finger. 'I wonder if you and your brother realize how lucky you are to have such a lenient father? There's not many that would let their sons and daughters go gallivanting all over the place.'

Poppy swallowed. She didn't know why Lena made her feel so cross and uneasy and she felt sure she had got up early that morning and clattered about just to wake her. 'We do realize it,' she said quietly, recognizing that what Lena said was true. 'But Pa believes in letting us run our own lives and making our own mistakes. We'll make them, I expect,' she said. 'But we know he's here whenever we need him.'

Lena raised her eyebrows and turned down her mouth in a cynical manner. 'Let's hope he is,' she murmured. 'Let's just hope that he is.'

On leaving on Saturday night, Dan Damone had said he was catching a train for London first thing Sunday morning and that he would write to her as soon as he heard anything from Brighton. 'Be ready to leave immediately,' he had said. 'Have your trunk packed with all that you need for a long stay.'

The shop and coffee house closed early on a Sunday. Lena went out for a walk, and Poppy, glad to have her father to herself, asked him if he would bring the metal trunk from his bedroom into hers. It hadn't been opened in a long time, and as they lifted the lid a scent of lavender rose from the contents, which were wrapped in brown paper. In it were baby clothes, cotton night-gowns and dresses which had belonged to her and Tommy. There was a sailor suit and knickerbockers from when Tommy was small, and a pretty cotton dress and bonnet, trimmed with ribbon, which had been Poppy's when she was a toddler. There were clothes belonging to her mother too, which she had worn when she was newly married.

'I remember this.' Her father lifted out a white broderie anglaise bodice with leg-o'-mutton sleeves. 'Your ma used to wear it with a black skirt and a string of pearls. And this,' he said, bringing out a pale green silk afternoon dress with porcelain buttons. He held it against Poppy's red hair. 'You should wear this,' he said. 'Colour would suit you.'

Some of her mother's clothes fitted her and were hardly worn, so she put them on one side, and the children's clothes she repacked in a box and put them under her bed. 'You won't let Lena or Albert touch them, will you, Pa?' she said plaintively.

'I'll lock 'door and put a padlock on it,' he said placatingly. 'Though why you think they would want to come in, I don't understand. What about Nan? Can she come in to clean or is she banned as well?'

'Nan's all right. I know she won't go nosing around.' She pressed her lips together. 'Sorry,' she said. 'I know I'm being unreasonable. It's just that . . .' She sighed. 'Well, when I come back I want everything to be exactly as it is now.'

He smiled pensively and stroked her hair. 'But it won't be, Poppy,' he said quietly. 'And you'll be different too.'

There was nothing in the post from Dan Damone all the week, and when the Friday post came and still there was nothing, Poppy was filled with disappointment. 'They must have taken someone else on in Brighton,' she said dismally to Mattie when she met her out in the street during the afternoon. 'Mr Damone said they wanted a singer by next week, by which I suppose he meant Monday, so it's too late now.'

'There'll be other places,' Mattie said, 'or there might be all kinds of reasons why he hasn't written. Maybe you'll hear tomorrow,' she added. 'Don't give up hope.'

'But it will still be too late,' Poppy groaned. 'I couldn't get to London and then Brighton for Monday.'

'I'll come and see you off when you do go,' Mattie promised. 'I think you're ever so brave travelling alone.'

'I'm not brave at all,' Poppy replied. 'I feel sick when I think about it. I've to change trains twice, and Pa has made me promise that I'll only travel in a ladies-only carriage.'

Saturday morning a letter came. 'Dear Poppy,' Dan Damone wrote. 'I travelled straight to Brighton to enquire about the booking on your behalf, only to find that there had been a small fire in the hall and next week's performances have been cancelled. The management are hoping to have everything ready for opening the following Monday and are willing to take you, act unseen, on my recommendation, for the first week. If you'll travel down to my office next Wednesday or Thursday, I'll give you all the details and that will give you enough time to get to Brighton and arrange lodgings. In haste, Dan Damone.'

'Oh, Pa,' she whispered. 'It's come. I'm to go to Brighton.' And as she well knew, Brighton was at the ends of the earth.

She'd never been to London and whenever she had travelled by train to the seaside, as sometimes they used to, her parents had always been with her. But she hadn't been out of Hull since her mother's death.

Charlie's in London, she thought as yet again she checked the contents of the trunk. How wonderful it would be if he could meet me. But I haven't got his address. Should I, dare I, ask Mr Chandler for it? She decided that she dared. Charlie is Tommy's friend too, she mused, and it would be natural for us to write to him. She had been cast down that she hadn't received a letter from Charlie since he went away, but then, she sighed, men don't write letters very often. They had received only one communication from Tommy and that was a brief note saying that he had arrived in Rotterdam and had been sick for the whole of the voyage.

She called on the Chandlers the next day and Mrs Chandler, who was a dour woman and hardly ever seemed to smile, gave her Charlie's address. She archly asked Poppy to remind him that he had parents who would be glad to hear from him sometime. 'Though I don't know why I worry,' she said. 'Your father's letting you go to London and you're onny a young girl!'

Poppy hastily wrote to Charlie telling him that she would be arriving in London late afternoon on Wednesday and gave him the approximate time of arrival. 'I don't expect you to be there, of course,' she wrote, 'but I can be contacted via my agent, Dan Damone of St Martin's Lane, which I understand is near Covent Garden.'

She read the letter through and felt a singular pang of pride and excitement at the words 'my agent'.

'I shall be appearing in Brighton,' she added, 'on the first step of my stage career. I do hope that we might meet. Your friend, Poppy.'

There, it's done, she breathed as she dropped the letter into the postbox. Am I being forward? But he knows that I love him for I've told him so already, so it can't do any harm. Then she pondered. But I will be so upset if he doesn't come, or at least write to me.

Her father had ordered a horse cab to pick them up early on Wednesday morning and take them to the Paragon railway station. She said goodbye to Nan who was there early every morning to clean before Lena started the baking. Nan hugged her and told her to take good care of herself and to let them know how she was getting on. Poppy felt quite emotional. She would miss Nan, who had always been kind to her, and especially since her mother had died.

Lena just nodded as she said goodbye, busying herself with flour and baking tins, and Albert, in the shop, stared and then said, 'London, eh? Better watch yourself. Lot of foreigners in London.'

'Are there?' she said. 'Have you been, Albert?'

'As a matter of fact, yes, I have. Lena and me—'

'Albert!' Lena called to him through the open door. 'Can you come here and help me? Don't stand there gossiping; she'll miss the train!'

The cab arrived and Joshua helped the driver heave the trunk in, then he and Poppy climbed in for the short drive to the railway station, which was bustling with travellers even though it was still so early.

'Poppy! Poppy!' Mattie called to her from the concourse. 'Good luck!'

'Mattie! Shouldn't you be at work?' Poppy was thrilled to see her.

'Aye, I should be, but I told 'foreman I had to see someone important onto 'train, and when he asked me who it was and I said Poppy Mazzini, she's going to be a star, he said in that case all right, but don't be too long!'

'Well, cabby's waiting, Mattie,' Joshua said. 'So you can ride part of 'way back with me.'

They walked through the barrier, following the uniformed porter who was trundling Poppy's trunk on a trolley. 'Just 'young lady, is it, sir?' The porter touched his hat as Joshua tipped him a threepenny bit. 'Come into this carriage, miss. These other two ladies are travelling to London.'

Poppy leaned out of the carriage window. There were two very genteel-looking elderly women already seated, and although she was glad not to be travelling alone, they didn't appear to be the kind who would approve of her chosen career. She pressed her lips together, then took a deep breath. 'This is it, then!' she said nervously.

'Have you brought some dinner with you, Poppy?' Mattie asked. 'It'll be late before you get there, won't it?'

Poppy nodded. 'Yes, I've packed up some bread and beef, and a piece of cake, and I'll be able to get a drink from one of the station trolleys when we stop.'

'We should have bought you a magazine or a newspaper,' Joshua said. He seemed to be as nervous as she was.

She nodded. 'I'll buy one from W. H. Smith's news stalls when I change trains, Pa. Don't worry about me,' she said. 'I'll be all right, really I will.'

Joshua took a handkerchief out of his coat pocket and blew his nose. 'Aye, I know. I know.'

There was a screeching whistle of steam and the booming shout of the guard warning, 'Mind the doors! Stand back! Mind the doors please!'

'She's off!' Her father leaned forward to give her one last hug and Mattie waved vigorously as the guard signalled with his green flag. 'Take care, Poppy. Send me a note or a telegram when you get to Brighton!'

'I will, Pa.' Poppy's eyes flooded with tears. 'Take care of yourself. You too, Mattie.'

She waved until the train curved away from the station and her last glance was of Mattie taking her father's arm, and of them walking away. That's it, then, she thought. Now I really am on my own.

CHAPTER FIFTEEN

A porter at King's Cross station, his boots polished and the buttons on his heavy worsted jacket gleaming, took her trunk from the luggage van and loaded it onto a trolley. 'Do you need a cab, miss?' He pushed his peaked cap to the back of his head and scratched his sweaty forehead. 'Or is somebody meeting you?'

'No,' she said, worriedly wondering what she would do if Mr Damone had gone home and his office was shut. Rather unwisely, she had thought that when she arrived he would direct her to lodgings for tonight, but it was getting late. 'I need to get to St Martin's Lane.'

'Righty-ho,' he said. 'We'll see if we can hail a cab, though it's busy this time of night.' He turned to her and grinned. 'Going to St Martin's? You on the stage then? That's where the theatres are.'

'Oh, are they? I didn't know. Yes.' She was flustered. 'Or, at least, I'm going to be. I'm going to Brighton. To a music hall. I'm a singer.'

'Are you now?' he chatted as he pushed the trolley. 'Love a bit of a singsong myself. Our Marie, she's my favourite. She's a darlin'. Saw George Robey in Islington not so long since. He's on the up and up is George.'

She swallowed, feeling proud and exhilarated to be associated with such famous names. 'I've never seen them,' she said. 'I don't think they've ever been to Hull which is where I come from.'

'Long way from 'ome then, miss!' The porter pushed his way through the crowd, calling out, 'Mind your backs if you please.

Mind your backs, sorry sir, beg pardon, ma'am,' and Poppy hurried after him, overwhelmed by the mass of people and fearful of losing sight of her luggage. They reached the exit and the porter put up his hand to signal to the driver of a four-wheel growler, but someone else dashed towards it and climbed aboard. Poppy felt she had never seen so many vehicles at any one time. There were gigs and dogcarts, and a welter of hire vehicles, as well as private carriages. There was a smell of horses and dung, a cacophony of cracking whips and shouts from the cabbies, whilst across the busy road people were dashing to catch waiting horse-buses.

'Poppy! Poppy!'

She turned in astonishment at hearing her name.

'Poppy! Over here!'

She looked round. There were so many people milling about, but there, with his hand held up above a crowd of travellers, and waving to her, she saw Charlie.

'Got a lift after all, 'ave you, miss?' The porter took stock of Charlie as he came towards her. 'Know 'im, do you? Can't be too careful, you know!'

'Oh, yes,' she said, her voice breaking in delight. 'He's my brother's best friend.'

'Shall I leave you, then, miss? Otherwise we'll be some time, trying to get a cab.'

'Poppy!' Charlie greeted her. 'Yes, thank you, porter. I'll look after her.'

'Thank you so much.' Poppy took out a coin to give the porter. 'You've been very kind.'

He touched his cap. 'Thank you, miss. I'll look out for you on the stage. Good luck!' He dashed off, whistling, towards the trains.

'Poppy!' Charlie said again. 'How nice to see you.'

'It's lovely to see you, Charlie. It's good of you to come and meet me.' She cast her eyes up to his face. He looked different. He had grown a neat moustache, which made him look older. His hair was longer too, and parted down the centre; he was, she thought, even more handsome than before. In his hand he carried a bowler hat.

'I work not far from here,' he told her, 'so I came as soon as I was finished.' He took hold of her hand and gazed at her. 'It's good to see you, Poppy. You look so – grown up, even after only a few short weeks.'

She blushed; it was just what she wanted to hear. 'I was hoping that we could meet,' she said, 'though I didn't really expect—'

'Let's see if we can get a cab,' he said. 'Where are you off to? To see your agent?'

'Yes, in St Martin's Lane. Do you know it?'

'Fairly well,' he said airily. 'The theatres are in that area, and variety houses and tavern concert rooms too. There's such a lot to do in London, Poppy. So much entertainment, but one needs a large pocket book to pay for everything.'

He's very confident, she mused as Charlie put up his arm and whistled for a cab. He even speaks differently. 'How is your work?' she asked diffidently as Charlie kept on trying to attract the drivers' attention.

'Mmm? Oh, it's fine, for the moment – here's one! Good fellow,' he said to the cabby who clattered his cab towards them. 'Give me a hand with this, will you?' and the driver, with only a little help from Charlie, hoisted her trunk aboard and they climbed in. 'St Martin's Lane, if you please.

'That's a very large trunk,' he commented, dusting off his hands. 'You must be planning to stay a while?'

'I have my stage costumes in there as well as my ordinary clothes. And Nan insisted I brought my own sheets, in case the ones in the lodgings weren't clean.'

'How droll.' He laughed. 'Typically provincial!'

'She was only thinking of me!' Poppy said in Nan's defence. 'She was bothered about bed bugs!'

There had been a good deal of demolition in the area round St Martin's Lane, as the capital, unable to accommodate the mass of population and horse-drawn traffic which had proliferated in the last decade of the nineteenth century, turned itself topsy-turvy, chopped and widened in an attempt to modernize the London thoroughfares. The Lane itself was narrow, with ancient shopfronts, inns and coffee houses, taverns and theatres, and old courts and alleyways leading off it, providing domestic housing within the Regency exterior.

Poppy could feel excitement growing as she peered out of the cab window, though the springs were sagging and she was jolted around. Charlie smiled indulgently. 'I found it most interesting when I first came here,' he said, as Poppy made several gasping sounds as she noticed music shops and clubs, and windows full of paintings.

She turned to him. 'But is it not still? You've not been here very long, only a few weeks!'

He shrugged. 'I've found my way around,' he said smoothly. 'Yes, I like it here. I'll not go back to Hull. London is 'capital of the world, you know.'

He's so knowledgeable and experienced, Poppy thought, even though he's only just come to London. It's as if the air has rubbed onto him like a second skin. But I hope he doesn't forget those who cared for him. 'When your mother gave me your address,' she said, 'she asked me to say they'd like a letter from you.'

'Oh, yes. I must write,' he murmured. 'I've been so busy, you know, settling in and so on. Oh, here we are.' He leaned forward as the cab came to a halt at a shopfront. 'This must be it.'

Dan Damone. Agent was engraved on the glass, and in the window were framed photographs of music hall performers, and yellowing theatre programmes. Charlie helped Poppy out but she turned to the cab driver. 'Would you wait a moment, please, whilst I find out if anyone is there?'

'The door's locked,' Charlie said, and put his forehead against the glass to look through. He put his hand up to shield the reflection. 'I can see a light at the back.' He knocked loudly. 'There's someone in there.'

Poppy peered through. 'It's a woman,' she said. 'Knock again.'

A woman in a black skirt and blouse, with her hair tied neatly in a chignon, came towards the door. 'We're closed,' she called. 'Mr Damone isn't in. Come back in the morning.'

Poppy took in a breath. 'But he's expecting me. Poppy Mazzini! He said for me to come today.'

'Well, he's not here,' the woman replied. 'You're too late. Come in the morning.'

'But I've nowhere to stay!' Poppy could have cried. How could things go so wrong so soon?

'This isn't an hotel!' The woman glared at her through the

glass door. 'Plenty of lodging places hereabouts. Come again in the morning.'

'Excuse me, sir!' the cab driver called down. 'If you're looking for a place to stay, I know of a lodging 'ouse just up the road. My sister-in-law runs it. I can take you if you like?'

Poppy looked up at Charlie. 'I don't know what to do,' she said. 'Do you think it will be all right?'

Charlie pursed his lips, then called up to the driver. 'Is it respectable?'

'Yes sir, it is. Will you be wanting it just for the one night?'

'It's only for me!' Poppy interrupted quickly. How dreadful. The cabby thought it was for her and Charlie!

The driver touched his hat. 'Beg pardon, miss. But I can still take you if you want. Might not be what you're used to, but . . .'

Beggars can't be choosers, she pondered and looked again at Charlie.

'I could take you back to my lodgings, I suppose, but—' he started.

'No!' she said. 'Thank you. It wouldn't be right.' Whatever would Pa think, she thought? He'd be mortified.

'I was going to say that it was a long way to come back in the morning,' he finished. He chewed on his lip for a second, then suggested, 'Let's go and look at this place, and if it's all right you can leave your trunk and I'll take you out for supper; show you the sights.'

She agreed and they climbed back into the cab, which took them less than half a mile before stopping outside a rundown clothing shop. 'Oh! Is this it?' Poppy murmured dismally. 'It doesn't look very clean!'

'It's only for one night,' Charlie said. 'Let's take a look.'

The cabbie hammered on the door, and as a bolt rattled inside he called out, 'It's Jack, Fanny. Got a customer for you.'

A woman with matted grey hair opened the door a crack and peered out. She narrowed her eyes at Poppy and Charlie. 'Two customers by the look of it!'

'Just for me,' Poppy said, feeling hot and embarrassed. 'May I look at the rooms, please?'

The woman shrugged and opened the door wider. 'No visitors allowed after ten,' she said, looking up at Charlie. 'Not unless you're staying and paying. This is a respectable house!'

'Just for the young lady,' Charlie repeated. 'I won't be staying.'

The woman grunted and with swaying hips led Poppy up the uncarpeted stairs. 'A shilling,' she said. 'Including breakfast. Payment in advance. You'll not get better than that anywhere round here. Rooms are at a premium on account of its being theatre province. I've had famous people stay at my diggings and never a grumble.'

Poppy looked round the small room with its narrow bed. It smelt damp but seemed reasonably clean, though she was thankful that she had brought her own sheets. 'Could I have a fire?' she asked. 'It feels cold. If I can, I'll take it.'

The woman, Fanny, eyed her. 'Are you an actress? Or on the music halls?'

'Yes,' Poppy said. 'I'm a singer. And I must keep warm. The cold affects my voice,' she lied.

'All right,' the landlady agreed. 'I'll get the girl to light a fire and no extra. How old are you? Fifteen, sixteen?'

'Yes,' Poppy lied again as she wondered if the woman would take her if she thought she was younger. 'Nearly.' She unfastened her purse. 'A shilling, you said? Could I have a key? My friend is taking me out to supper but I won't be late. I'm tired after my journey.'

'I don't provide keys.' Fanny led the way downstairs again. 'But I'll be up. I like to know who's coming in and out.'

The cab driver carried Poppy's trunk upstairs, she paid him and gave him a tip and he drove off.

'Come on,' Charlie said. 'We'll take a walk, and then see if we can catch an omnibus. We'll do a bit of sightseeing before dark, then have supper.'

'Charlie,' she said, stepping out of the lodging house door, 'it's really kind of you, but if you don't mind I'd like supper first. I'm hungry and tired and I'd rather go straight back to the lodgings and get to bed.'

'Would you? Oh!' He seemed a little put out. 'That's a shame.'

'I'm sorry,' she said in a small voice. 'But it's been a tiring day. All the travelling, you know!'

'Of course.' He was at once solicitous. 'I'm forgetting that you're not used to travelling. In London, of course, people are moving about all the time, getting on and off omnibuses, taking the underground train and so forth.'

'Oh, the Underground! I'd like to see that. I don't know if I dare travel on it, though. But not tonight, I don't mean. Perhaps some other time.'

'It's a great way of getting around,' Charlie enthused, 'and not dark or smelly as you might expect. I use it quite often.'

Once again, Poppy gazed at him wide-eyed. How experienced he was already; would she ever get used to this hustle of people and the clatter and rumble of traffic? She lifted the hem of her skirt as they crossed the road. There was horse dung everywhere and she wrinkled her nose. The street sweeper had obviously not been out today.

Charlie laughed as he saw her disapproval. 'Young lads come and clear it up every night, then they sell it to gardeners,' he said. 'Apparently it's very good for roses!'

Quite by chance they came across a small Italian restaurant, Trattoria Mario, just off St Martin's Lane. Charlie was dubious about it, but Poppy looked through the window and saw the gleaming white tiles and the bright cloths on the tables. 'Let's try it,' she said. 'It's small but it's very neat and clean, and oh, the smell!'

On a Sunday evening when Mazzini's was closed, Poppy's father sometimes cooked an Italian meal for them from recipes handed down from his family. He cooked veal or beef in Chianti, or ravioli which he made with flour and eggs then cut into squares and filled with spinach and ricotta cheese. Now the smell coming from the restaurant as they went inside made her feel quite homesick for her father. '*Buon giorno, signor. Buon giorno, signorina.*' Mario, plump, short, with dark curly hair, greeted them. There were only five tables, and two of them were occupied.

Poppy replied in the little Italian that she knew, and he smiled and said, 'You are Italian, *si*?' and led them to a table.

'My father's family,' she said, sitting down as he held back a chair. 'So I have a drop of Italian blood. But not very much. *Non parlo Italiano!*' she explained.

'And your red hair comes from your mama, *si*?'

'*Si.*' She laughed, her mood lightening, and glanced at Charlie, who was moodily picking up the menu.

'You not want that.' Mario took it from him. 'That is for the English. I bring you proper Italian food. From Tuscany, yes? You are a little tired, I think, signorina? You have had a journey?' At Poppy's acknowledgement he went on, 'I bring you *pappa al pomodoro, si*? And then *crostini di fegatini*. That is good for you, not too heavy in the evening before you sleep.'

'Thank you.' Poppy smiled. 'That sounds delicious.'

'I'd like a steak,' Charlie said briskly. 'Then I know what I'm eating.'

'He only suggested tomato and bread soup,' Poppy whispered as Mario dashed away towards the kitchen. '*Zuppa*, and then chicken livers on toast. My father told my mother about the soup, and she used to make it for Tommy and me when we were little.' She was silent for a moment, then gave a deep sigh. 'I don't know what I'm doing here,' she said sadly, and choked back tears. 'I should be at home with Pa.'

Charlie reached across and patted her hand, then gently squeezed her fingers. 'You're in a game of chance,' he said. 'Seeking fame and fortune, just like me. You'd never find it in a backwater like Hull.'

She looked miserably at him. 'But I've left Pa behind and all those I care for, like Nan and Mattie, and I don't even know where Tommy is! Have you heard from him, Charlie?'

'No, but then he doesn't know where I am. We left about the same time, remember?' He lifted her fingers to his lips and kissed them. 'Don't worry, Poppy. Things will work out all right, and I'm so pleased to see you again.'

She felt her heart beating fast and she flushed at him kissing her fingers in such a public place. He really must love me, she thought. He wouldn't do that otherwise. She took a breath. If only he would say it.

Mario brought Poppy's soup and placed a plate bearing a small pancake filled with mushrooms and dressed with tomatoes in front of Charlie. 'What's this?' Charlie asked abruptly. 'I asked for steak.'

'*Si. Si.* Your steak he is coming,' Mario said. 'This is – eh – gratis – and for the young lady a glass of red wine.' He took a wine glass from his tray and placed it in front of her. 'You like, yes? It make you sleep good.'

Poppy raised her eyebrows. She didn't normally drink wine, though she had tried it with water. She took a sip. 'Thank you.' She smiled at Mario. 'It's good.'

'I can't stand mushrooms!' Charlie grumbled, pushing the pancake around his plate.

'Just eat the pancake, then,' Poppy whispered, not wanting to offend Mario. 'I suppose he didn't want to leave you waiting without food whilst he's cooking your steak.' She wondered about Charlie. Why was he so grumpy? Was it because she was getting the attention and knew a little Italian, when he did not?

As they were eating their main course, and Charlie was reluctantly conceding that the steak was tender, Mario came to their table. 'Everything is good, yes?' He nodded his head as he spoke and his curls bounced. 'You live here in London?' he asked. 'I not see you before.'

'I live in London,' Charlie told him. 'On the Pentonville Road.'

'And I'm passing through,' Poppy said. 'I'm going to Brighton tomorrow.'

'So where you stay?' Mario asked. 'In hotel?'

She told him where she was staying and he pulled a face. 'Not good for young lady on her own.' He turned to Charlie. 'You must see her to the door. It is not safe for her.'

'Well of course,' Charlie said huffily. 'Of course I will!'

'Next time you come to London,' Mario said to Poppy. 'You stay 'ere.' He pointed above his head. 'I have good room upstairs and you eat 'ere, good food. You come for breakfast in the morning and I show you. My wife she is 'ere. You see it is nice place.'

'Oh, thank you,' Poppy said, and thought it would be very comforting to have somewhere like this to return to if she should have to stay in London again.

She insisted that she should pay half of the bill, as Charlie fumbled in his pocket book at the end of the meal. She realized that he was probably not earning much money yet, and her father had given her sufficient to tide her over for the first few weeks.

As they left the restaurant, Mario kissed her hand. '*Buona notte.* You come back again,' he said. 'You come for breakfast. We open at seven o'clock.'

She said she would and said goodbye as Charlie held the door for her. She felt grown up and confident, her homesickness dissipated by the food and wine.

'Of course you won't go, will you?' Charlie said as they neared the lodging house. 'For breakfast, I mean?'

'Yes!' She looked up at him. 'I said that I would! I'm sure his breakfast will be better than anything they'll cook here.' She was starting to dread the thought of being in a strange bed. I hope there aren't cockroaches. She shivered. Or bed bugs.

Charlie shrugged and his mouth turned down. 'Not 'best place I've eaten at,' he said. 'Can't say I care for Italian food all that much. Well, here we are.' They reached the lodging house door. 'Delivered safe and sound. Such insolence for that fellow to suggest I'd let you come back alone!'

'I think he meant well, Charlie,' she said quietly. 'He must know the area.'

Charlie took hold of both her hands. 'Never mind him,' he said softly. 'It's just so good to see you, Poppy.' He kissed her hands. 'So good.'

She swallowed. Was this dangerous territory? The unaccustomed wine had made her feel light-headed. She moistened her lips. 'It's nice to see you too, Charlie,' she whispered.

He leaned forward and kissed her mouth. 'Do you still love me, Poppy? Or have you fallen in love with someone else since I left?'

'Oh, no,' she breathed. 'I'll never do that. I'll always love you. I told you that.' She looked up into his eyes and thought she saw pleasure, but indulgence too. He still thinks me too young, she realized. And I'm not.

'Good night, Poppy.' He smiled. 'Send me your address in Brighton and I'll try to come down. I can get the train.'

She nodded, and reached for the knocker on the door. She watched him walk away and sighed. He never said he loved me in return.

CHAPTER SIXTEEN

The bed was hard and lumpy and Poppy was glad of her own sheets for the ones on the bed were grey and stained. She lay very still, trying to keep warm, for although the landlady had lit the fire it burned low and smokily. She slept only fitfully and woke the following morning feeling tired and aching. Perhaps this is a taste of how my life will be, she thought, sleeping in strange beds in seedy neighbourhoods.

She put on warmer clothing when she dressed, for a wind had sprung up and leaves and rubbish were blowing along the street outside. 'I won't have breakfast, thank you,' she said to the landlady when she went downstairs. 'I'm going for a walk.' She refrained from telling her that she was going elsewhere to eat. There was a smell of fatty sausages and burnt toast coming from the kitchen at the bottom of the hall.

'I don't knock anything off for meals not taken,' Fanny grunted. 'And you'll have to move out by ten.'

'That's all right,' Poppy said. 'I'll be back before then to collect my trunk.' She had repacked her sheets and towel, and locked the trunk so that she was ready to go as soon as she had breakfasted and hailed a cab.

Mario greeted her cordially and introduced her to his wife, Rosina. 'You have some of my olive bread and coffee?' she said. 'And an omelette?'

'Just the bread and coffee please.' Poppy warmed to her. 'I could smell the coffee as I came down the street. My father has a grocer shop and coffee house,' she told them. 'And my mother used to make the bread for the shop.'

'And now she does not?' Rosina asked.

'She died,' Poppy explained. 'Someone else does it for us.'

'Aah!' Rosina made sympathetic tutting noises. 'You are so young to lose your mama!'

'I was eleven,' Poppy said. 'I'll be fourteen in January.'

'And now, why you in London?' she asked. 'Why you not home with your papa?'

'I'm going to be a singer,' she said. 'In the music hall. I'm going to see my agent, Dan Damone, this morning.' She hesitated. 'I have to get my trunk to his office. Where could I hire a cab?' There had been very few hire vehicles in the street, mostly waggons or private gigs.

'We fetch it for you,' Mario said. 'I have a cart. When you finish your breakfast we fetch it here. I know Dan; he's good man. You go see him, then come back here for your trunk.'

Poppy could have cried with relief. It was all very well coming to London, but getting about with a massive trunk seemed impossible.

After she had finished breakfast, with Mario pushing the hand-cart, they walked back to the lodging house. She told him her father's story of his grandfather pushing a cart all the way from London to Hull.

'It is true,' he said seriously, not understanding the humour of the tale. 'There isa no worka here at that time. My own grand-father he say the same. Now is better, *si*? Though not for everyone.'

After depositing her trunk at Mario's and inspecting the room upstairs, which was clean and neat with a patchwork quilt on the bed and a breeze blowing through the open window, Poppy walked along to Dan Damone's office and knocked on the door. The same woman opened the door. 'Yes?' she enquired.

'I – I came last night,' Poppy said. 'Poppy Mazzini. Mr Damone is expecting me.'

'He's busy just now.' The woman looked in a large diary on her desk. 'He hasn't got you down. I'll make you an appointment for tomorrow.'

'Tomorrow is too late,' Poppy told her, and sat down on a wooden chair, one in a line of others. 'I'll wait until he's free.'

The woman looked down her nose at Poppy. 'You might have

to wait for a considerable time, and he doesn't see anyone without an appointment!'

Poppy stared stubbornly at her. I'll remember you when I'm famous, she thought. 'I'll wait,' she said.

She waited for about half an hour and cast her gaze round the office. There were posters on the wall and pictures of music hall artistes who had appeared at various venues across the country. She stifled a yawn and looked at the woman at the desk. She was busy writing in a ledger, though she glanced up at Poppy from time to time.

Presently the inner door opened and Dan Damone put his head out. 'Is there any coffee, Dora? I'm parched.'

Poppy stood up and greeted him. 'Hello, Mr Damone.'

'Poppy!' He came towards her and shook her hand. 'How are you? When did you arrive?' He looked towards the woman at the desk. 'Better make that two coffees please, Dora. Come along in, Poppy.' He led the way into his inner office, which was furnished with a large wooden desk, which was covered with papers, two comfortable chairs, and a fire burning in the grate.

'I didn't realize you were here. Have you been waiting long?' he asked anxiously, dropping his voice. 'Dora doesn't always tell me.'

'Half an hour,' she said. 'She told me that you wouldn't see me without an appointment, even though I told her you were expecting me.'

'I'm sorry,' he apologized. 'She's not very good with people, especially stage people; she thinks they're all ne'er-do-wells, but she's wonderful with figures and my diary, remembering who's been paid and who hasn't, which is why I keep her.

'Now,' he said. 'Are you ready for your stage career? You've got your act worked out? Brighton will be quite different from your home town. The audience want to be entertained. They like to feel happy, so do your polka dance and a few jolly ditties. There are still some holidaymakers there, so you'll need to put on a good show that they'll remember, and tell others about when they get home. It's all word of mouth. Quite a few Londoners go to Brighton; it's a good run on the train. They walk by the sea, take a look at the pier – which still isn't finished – have an ice cream sundae, see a show and then come home.'

Poppy licked her lips. Was she ready? She wasn't sure. 'I'll do my best, Mr Damone,' she said. 'But I'm very nervous.'

'Sure to be nervous, but that's a good sign, and call me Dan, everyone does. Don't they, Dora?' he asked as the dour-looking woman came in with coffee cups on a tray.

'Yes, Mr Damone,' she replied crisply. 'They do.'

He gave a wry grin. 'Any biscuits?'

She sighed and returned a moment later with a plate of biscuits.

'Everybody but Dora,' he said, when she had left and closed the door behind her. 'And she would rather I called her Miss Battle, but I don't!'

She's well named, Poppy thought as she sipped her coffee. It was black and bitter and not as nice as the coffee she had had for breakfast with Mario and Rosina. 'So shall I go to Brighton today?' she asked. 'I've left my trunk at the Trattoria Mario.'

'Ah!' he said. 'The best Italian food in town. Did you stay there?'

'No.' She told him where she had stayed. 'But I'll stay with them if I should come back to London.' She suddenly felt grown up, making decisions of her own. 'So, do I go to Brighton today?' she repeated.

He nodded, fished in a drawer for writing paper and proceeded to write down a name and address. 'Yes. You'll need to find diggings and settle in before Monday. This is who you should ask for. Bradshaw's is only a small hall, not far from the pier, seats about five hundred,' he said, his dark head bent over the paper. 'It's round the back of the Alhambra. Very popular and gets some good artists. There you are.' He handed her the address, then wrote again on another piece of paper and passed it to her. 'Try these diggings – they take theatricals. I don't know the train times but they're fairly regular.'

He got up from his chair and went to the door. 'Dora! Do you have the train timetable for Brighton?' He nodded and came back into the room. 'She'll give the train times to you on the way out. Well, good luck.' He held out his hand, her interview over.

'Thank you.' She stood up and took a breath and looked down at the papers in her hand. There were so many things she had wanted to ask him, but she couldn't now think of a single one.

'Will you be all right?' It was as if he was just remembering that this was her first venture into the theatre world. 'Drop me a line if you're worried about anything, and I'll try to come down and see you at the end of the week. If they like you, they'll offer you a contract and I'll negotiate that. All right?'

She nodded, her lips pressed tightly together. 'Yes. Thank you very much.' She walked to the door. So this was it. Anything she did now, she did alone. No Pa to advise her or hold her hand, no brother to ask for an opinion. She was alone in a strange city, and a new world was approaching. She took a deep breath, then put up her chin. She smiled a brave smile and saw him watching her with a small frown wrinkling his eyebrows. 'Goodbye!'

Mario had sent a young boy to find a hansom cab to take her to the station. She had had to wait only fifteen minutes for a train, the journey was fast and she was now in another hansom, bowling along the streets of Brighton, on her way to one of the lodging houses Dan had told her of. 'Will you wait a moment, please?' she asked the driver as he pulled up outside a row of terraced houses alongside a narrow court. 'I have to ask if they have any rooms.'

He nodded and took a pipe out of his pocket whilst she hurried along to find the right address. They were full, the landlady told her. She'd just let the last room. 'Try Mrs Johnson,' she said, and Poppy looked at her list and saw that was one of the names Dan had given her.

'I know it,' the driver said, when she went back. 'She keeps a clean house though she's a bit stingy with food.' He tamped out his pipe and put it in his pocket and Poppy noticed that there were brown burn marks on the cloth. 'That's what I've been told, at any rate.'

Poppy shivered. It was a cold blustery day and a sharp wind was blowing off the sea. They passed the Alhambra and she took note of where it was, as Dan had said the hall she was playing in was at the back of it. The driver drew up again outside a neat house with a clean front step, a red door, lace curtains at the window and a sign which said *Vacancies.*

She stepped down and said, 'I won't be long,' and worried about how much the driver was going to charge her for waiting.

Mrs Johnson said she had a room free and asked who had recommended her. When Poppy said Dan Damone, she opened the door and asked her in. 'My trunk's in the cab,' Poppy said. 'I'll get the driver to bring it in.'

'You're new to this life, hain't you?' the landlady said. 'Don't you want to see the room first?'

'I'm sure it will be all right,' Poppy answered. 'If Mr Damone says so.' She gave the landlady a smile. And if it isn't, she thought, then I'll move.

'How long for?' Mrs Johnson asked. 'Cos I 'ave my regulars.'

'The rest of this week and next,' Poppy said, anxious now that Mrs Johnson might change her mind. But she didn't and the driver brought in the trunk and once again she gave a tip on top of the amount she was charged. He touched his hat. 'Thank you, miss. Where're you appearing?'

When she told him, he nodded. 'We go there regular, my missus and me. We'll watch out for you. Singer are you? Or dancer?'

'Both,' she said. 'But mainly singing.'

'Sing some of Marie's songs,' he advised. 'Everybody likes them.'

She nodded. I don't think so, she thought. I couldn't compete with Marie Lloyd, and besides that's not my style. I'm a romantic singer. I like to sing of love. I can feel it in my heart.

'Fancy a cuppa tea, dearie?' Mrs Johnson called up to her as she started to unpack her trunk. 'I've just made a pot.'

Poppy ran downstairs to the parlour. Her bedroom was small, with a narrow bed and a washstand with a jug and bowl, a long cupboard for hanging clothes and a single chair. But it's adequate, she decided.

'There's no 'ot water hupstairs, you realize,' Mrs Johnson said as she poured the tea. 'But I'll fill your jug with 'ot every morning. If you want more you'll have to come down and get it yourself from the kitchen. There's a proper flush lavatory out the back, though.' She handed Poppy a cup of very weak tea. 'You're very young.' It sounded like an accusation. ' 'Ave you been on the boards before?'

On the boards, Poppy wondered? 'On the stage? Yes,' she said. 'But only at home, in Hull. This is my first professional work.'

'Mm.' Mrs Johnson settled back in her chair. 'Right then. Let me tell you the rules of the 'ouse. I'll let you have a key to the door, as you'll be late back from the the-ayter. No young men to visit. Other visitors such as relations by prior harrangement. Breakfast to be finished by 'alf past eight. No dinner, I don't cook dinner, and supper if you want it will be hextra. You can bring your own tea and coffee if you like,' she added, 'and 'ave use of the kettle at no hextra charge.' She nodded benignly. 'I like my guests to feel at 'ome.'

'Thank you, Mrs Johnson.' Poppy felt a giggle running round her chest. 'I'm sure I'll be very comfortable.'

After she had hung up her clothes and shaken the creases out of her skirts, she took out her red shoes and stuffed them with brown paper to keep them in shape. She put them lovingly against her cheek and thought of Charlie. How debonair he had seemed as he had pointed out the landmarks of London, though he wasn't so confident when he was dining with her at Mario's. I'll write to him, she thought, before putting on her coat to go outside, and tell him not to call here, or if he does, to tell Mrs Johnson he's my cousin!

The sea air was very fresh and the breeze blew her hair round her face. As Dan Damone had said, there were still holidaymakers in Brighton, although the season was drawing to a close. She could tell the visitors from the locals by their free and easy manner. The children were dressed in their best: sailor suits for the boys and pretty pastels and bonnets for the girls. Many of the women wore large hats with feathers, which blew dementedly in the wind, whilst the men strolled nonchalantly in striped trousers, waistcoats and straw boaters, scarves slung around their necks.

As Dan had said, Brighton Palace Pier, which was replacing the old Chain Pier, was not even half finished, but there was a flapping poster which proclaimed that eventually it would contain a music hall and entertainment venues. Poppy wandered down the seafront, admired the four-storey houses in the Royal Crescent, and the old balconied terraced houses, and then went in search of Bradshaw's.

She found the hall, as Dan had said, tucked away in a side street, behind the Alhambra. Her first impression was that it was shabby and needed a lick of paint. Inside it was dim, for there were no lamps lit, but as she entered the auditorium she saw a wide stage, gilt ornamentation and plush red seats to seat at least five hundred, and smelt the reek of smoke and ale.

'Is anyone there?' she called. 'Hello!'

'Hello!' A man's voice answered back. 'Who is it?'

'Poppy Mazzini. I've come to see Mr Bradshaw.'

A man carrying a saw appeared at the back of the stage. He wiped his arm across his forehead. 'He's not here. I'm only the carpenter.' Someone started banging behind him. 'Can you shut it for a minute, Fred?' The noise stopped and he walked to the front of the stage, which, as Poppy saw when she came closer, was littered with pieces of wood, hammers and a saw bench. 'He'll be back later this afternoon.'

But it's late afternoon now, Poppy thought, sighing. And I'm hungry. She realized that she hadn't eaten anything since breakfast with Mario and Rosina. 'I'll come back,' she said. 'What time do you think?'

The man shrugged. 'Six? Maybe seven. Don't know. He's doing a band call in the morning if you want to come back then. I'll tell him you've been if you like. Polly did you say?'

'Poppy,' she called back. 'Poppy Mazzini. Mr Damone arranged for me to come.'

The man shrugged again. 'I'm just the carpenter,' he repeated. 'We've to be finished by Monday,' and he turned back to whatever he had been doing.

She remembered then that Dan had told her there had been a fire in the hall, hence the workmen and the smell of smoke. So now what do I do until tomorrow morning?

The first thing, she decided as she stood outside the hall, was to eat. I'm so hungry! She had a good appetite and no matter what she ate she stayed slender, which, although unfashionable, meant that she could dance without any effort at all, and sing at the same time. Ever since the Terry Sisters had told her she must do both and still breathe, she had practised breathing exercises according to Miss Eloise's instructions.

She glanced back at the door and saw a poster regretting the closure of the theatre due to fire, and announcing that the date of opening was to be Monday. Top of the bill was a comic, Bill

Baloney, which she thought was a very silly name, and underneath, returning by popular request of Brighton audiences, were the Terry Sisters.

Oh, how wonderful! She hugged herself with glee. Someone I know! Or at least have met. She ran her finger quickly down the list of performers looking for her name, and saw right at the bottom: *Ballad and descriptive vocalist. Miss Polly Massini.* 'Oh, no,' she cried out loud in frustration, her joy at having her name on a programme vanishing. 'They've got my name wrong!'

'That's not unusual,' a man's voice behind her said. 'Everybody gets mine wrong!'

Poppy turned round, tears welling in her eyes. She looked into brown eyes fringed with the darkest, longest lashes she had ever seen on a man. She blinked and put her fingers into her pocket for a handkerchief. I know him! How do I know him?

The young man in front of her with a teasing smile on his lips was tall and slim and had long dark hair which flopped over his forehead and collar. 'Show me,' he said. 'Show me how your name should be and we'll see if we can't change it.'

She pressed her lips together anxiously and pointed to the bottom of the poster. 'It should be Poppy Mazzini.'

He scrutinized the name. 'Well, Miss Mazzini. I think that will be easy enough to change.' He turned to her. He was in his mid-twenties, she thought, and very amiable and good-mannered. 'I'll bring a black pencil when I return and alter the ls to ps and the ss to zs, and there we will have Poppy Mazzini.' He glanced at the poster again. 'And what about my name? Have they spelt it right this time?' He too ran his finger down the list. 'Ah, yes, here we are.' He stopped halfway down and Poppy knew then why she had recognized him. 'Anthony Marino.' He gave a small bow to Poppy. 'I'm very pleased to make your acquaintance, Miss Mazzini.'

CHAPTER SEVENTEEN

'How do you do,' Poppy said shyly, and wished that she hadn't been so foolish as to cry. She delicately wiped her nose with her handkerchief. 'I know who you are,' she said. 'You're Anthony Marino, the pianist. I came to hear you play at the Assembly Rooms in Hull.'

He seemed astonished. 'Did you? And you remembered me?'

'Oh, yes,' she said enthusiastically. 'I thought you were wonderful! Your music made me cry. I think my pa cried too.'

'Oh! Oh, dear.' He frowned. 'That wasn't my intention, I assure you. I want to make people happy, not sad!'

'It didn't make me sad,' she explained. 'It made me feel . . . well, just feel, really. The music touched me, somehow, especially your own music.' She gave him a shy smile, wondering if he would think her silly and childish. 'I wished at the time that you'd write a song for me.'

He gave her a wide beaming grin. 'Well, perhaps I might one day. What kind of songs do you sing?' The carpenter coming through the doors with a ladder over his shoulder interrupted her reply. 'I say,' Anthony Marino called to him. 'Is Jack Bradshaw in, by any chance?'

'No he ain't,' the man said, 'and I'm going to put a notice up to say so, for if I've been asked once today, I've been asked half a dozen times. There'll be a band call in the morning.'

'Thank you,' Anthony replied politely. 'I'm sorry to have troubled you.'

The carpenter nodded, then looked at him in recognition. 'Ain't you that fellow what plays the joanna? My old lady loves to hear you play. Makes her cry, she says. She'll want to come and see you, I expect.'

Poppy laughed as he went off whistling. 'There you are,' she said. 'So it's not just me!'

Anthony Marino shook his head disbelievingly. 'Do people like to cry, do you think?' he asked. 'Maybe they do. I hadn't thought of that before.'

'I don't think they like to,' Poppy said. 'But sometimes they have to.' She gave a shiver. A strong breeze was rushing up the street as if being drawn up a funnel. 'It's nice to meet you, Mr Marino,' she said. 'Perhaps we'll meet again tomorrow at rehearsal?'

'I'm sure we will,' he said, 'though it won't be a full rehearsal. The other performers won't arrive until Sunday night. But I promise to bring a pencil with me so that we can change your name,' he added. 'Such a lovely name. We would want people to remember it.'

She said goodbye and went off in the direction of the Alhambra and the seafront, looking for somewhere she could have her supper. Although Mrs Johnson had said she could have supper there, Poppy didn't want to go back to the lodging house yet as the evening, she was sure, would loom long and lonely.

She found a small café, empty of customers, where she ordered a meat and potato pie. When it came, the pastry was soggy and the meat unchewable. She picked around the potatoes, which were hard, then pushed the plate to one side and ordered a steamed pudding and a cup of coffee. But the pudding was leaden and although the coffee was hot it was very weak.

She sat cradling the cup in her hands as she looked out of the window and watched the waves lashing on the shore. She felt terribly homesick and as she thought of home and her father, she reminded herself that she must write immediately and tell him that she had arrived safely in Brighton.

Her pen and ink were in her trunk back at Mrs Johnson's, so she paid the bill to the rather surly woman who had served her and left. The wind was blowing wild and sharp sand spattered her face. By the time she had walked back to her diggings she was frozen through and feeling thoroughly miserable.

'Mrs Johnson, could I possibly have hot water for a bath?' she asked when she went in. She'd realized there was no separate bathroom in the house when she'd seen a tin hip-bath hanging from a nail on the wall near the lavatory.

'Oh, no, dear. Not tonight.' Mrs Johnson was sitting beside her parlour fire and seemed quite taken aback by Poppy's request. 'Sunday you can have 'ot water for bathing, after the other guests have gone and afore new ones arrive, or else you can go to the public baths, which is what some of my guests do. Next year, landlord says I can 'ave one o' them newfangled geysers and then I'll turn one of the little bedrooms into a proper bathroom. You can have a kettle of 'ot water if you like,' she finished, relenting.

Gas geysers were hardly newfangled, Poppy thought, as she carried the steaming kettle upstairs to her room. At home they had had one over the bath for years, and her father had talked of having hot water piped upstairs to replace it. She put cold water into the earthenware bowl so that it wouldn't crack, poured in the hot, then took the kettle down again, refilled it from the tap over the sink and put it back on the hook over the fire. 'I can see you're used to doing things for yourself,' Mrs Johnson pronounced. 'You've not had servants to run after you?'

'You're quite right, I haven't,' Poppy replied, though she thought of Nan who did the washing and made sure there were always clean towels for when they had their baths. 'I'll say good night now, Mrs Johnson. I shall go to bed when I've finished unpacking.'

Mrs Johnson nodded. 'Good night then. I'm expecting another guest to come in after the the-ayter. 'e'll want supper, I expect. 'e usually does.'

Poppy undressed and washed in the meagre amount of water, put on her nightgown and her robe, then, wrapping herself in a blanket off the bed, sat by the low fire to write to her father.

'Dearest Pa,' she wrote. 'I'm missing you more than I can say. I'm in Brighton now and have lodgings with a Mrs Johnson.' She put in the address and told him of her meeting with Dan Damone, and then added that Charlie had met her at King's Cross railway station and escorted her to her first lodgings in London. 'Even though it was a very long way from his own,' she added, lest he should think the worst. 'It wasn't a nice place,' she wrote, 'but we' – she bit her lip. Should I have put I? No, that would be deceitful – 'had a very good supper in an Italian café,' she continued. 'And the people there said I could stay with them when I'm next in London.

'I feel very homesick,' she went on, 'and Brighton is quite different from Hull. But I'm sure I'll be all right once I start at the theatre on Monday. One very nice thing that has happened,' she told him, 'is that I've met Anthony Marino, the pianist, who we heard at the Assembly Rooms. He'll be playing in Bradshaw's too, so I feel very proud to be appearing with him. He's very pleasant and kind,' she continued, 'as well as being accomplished.'

She finished the letter by saying she would go to bed early and look forward to exploring Brighton the next day. She folded the letter into an envelope, and put it by her door so that she wouldn't forget to post it the next morning. Then, keeping the blanket wrapped round her for comfort as well as warmth, she climbed into bed.

But she didn't sleep. She tossed and turned and heard sleeting rain and wind rattling against the window. She got up once and looked out into the small yard below and saw rubbish bowling around. A metal bucket blown over by the wind was rolling and clanging about the yard. She was just drifting off into a doze when she heard the front door bang and a male voice booming and laughing, and then Mrs Johnson's higher-pitched one joining in, dropping aitches left, right and centre, and adding them in between.

Poppy sighed. In her room in the eaves at home, she had often heard the din and hullabaloo of carousing people as they passed the shop. But they were familiar sounds and she had always felt secure knowing that her father and Tommy were below. But these were unfamiliar voices in a strange house in an unknown town. 'It'll be all right tomorrow, I expect,' she murmured sleepily, and snuggled further under the covers. 'Once I'm used to being away from home.' But she couldn't control the few tears that slipped down her cheeks or the sense of loneliness that overcame her.

The guests ate breakfast in the parlour. A folding table had been opened out and a white cloth put upon it and set for three. Poppy was the first down and she had almost finished her breakfast, which was porridge and a kipper, when the door opened and a man in a striped dressing robe and nightcap appeared. He was thickset, though not very tall, and his jowly chin had not yet been shaved. 'Morning,' he muttered. 'Didn't think anybody else'd be down.'

'Good morning,' Poppy replied, embarrassed to see a strange man in his night attire. She wondered if he was the one making the noise last night. 'I thought we had to have breakfast finished by half past eight.'

The man gazed at her from bleary eyes. 'That's what she says, but take no notice. I didn't get in until midnight. I can't be expected to get up for half past eight.' He put his head back and bellowed towards the kitchen. 'Coffee, if you please, Ma!'

Mrs Johnson scurried in with a pot of coffee and poured it for him as he sat at the table opposite Poppy. She noticed that it was stronger than the one she had been given.

'How are you this morning, Mr Harding? Have you met our new young guest?' Mrs Johnson fussed around him, bringing him fresh toast and marmalade, which she hadn't offered to Poppy. 'She's going to appear at Mr Bradshaw's when it opens on Monday.'

'Is she?' the man muttered. 'Well good luck to you. Hope you get some money out of him!' He gazed at Poppy over the rim of his coffee cup. 'What are you? Dancer? Singer? They're ten a penny, you know. All you young girls think you can make an easy living on the stage. Don't realize just how hard it is.'

Poppy looked back at him. Who was he to speak so rudely? Was he so famous that he thought he could speak in such a manner to someone just starting out? 'My name is Poppy Mazzini. I'm a singer and dancer. May I ask who you are?' she asked politely but pointedly.

'This is Tate Harding!' Mrs Johnson said in a surprised tone of voice, as if Poppy should have known. 'He's a very well-known comedian, playing at the Alhambra!'

Tate Harding's mouth turned down, but before he could comment Poppy said, 'I beg your pardon, Mr Harding. I'm afraid I haven't heard of you, but perhaps you're better known in the south of England than the north, which is where I come from.'

She watched as a slow flush came to his already red face. 'Only been north once,' he muttered. 'Went to Bradford. They didn't understand my humour. I said I'd never go again. Riotous lot!'

Poppy nodded her head. 'I believe they know what they like in Bradford,' she said in an innocent manner, and thought of Ben Thompson's offer for her to perform at his free-and-easy in Bradford, which Dan had warned her against. I think Mr Tate Harding was probably booed off the stage. That's why he won't go back. 'We have very well-known performers who come to Hull,' she told him. 'Will Vane, Norah Conner, Anthony Marino; he's playing at Bradshaw's next week,' she added, anxious to show that she wasn't just an inexperienced young girl, even if she knew that she really was. 'And the Terry Sisters.'

Tate Harding humphed, but didn't answer. He took a last gulp of coffee and scraped back his chair. 'Going back to bed for an hour, Mrs J. Don't be clattering about upstairs until I'm down again.' He left the room and didn't even acknowledge Poppy.

'He's got a sore 'ead this morning,' Mrs Johnson said as she cleared away his breakfast things. ''ad a drop too much last night.'

'He's a very rude man.' Poppy was cross and offended. 'There was no need for him to be so unpleasant. He doesn't even know me!'

Mrs Johnson sat down and put her elbows on the table. 'It's dog eat dog out there, young lady. You'll find there's some who'll stab you in the back as soon as look at you, if they think you're taking their spotlight. Then there's others who'll give you an 'elping 'and. I know,' she said, nodding her head. 'I've seen it all. And Tate Harding is no better or worse than any of 'em.'

Poppy swallowed and considered. She'd only known her home town where everyone knew and supported her. She couldn't expect the same in a strange place. She would be judged only on her performance, not because she was the local grocer's daughter. 'Does he always stay here?' she asked.

'Always, when he's in Brighton. I'm the honly one who'll put up with 'im.' Mrs Johnson settled herself comfortably with her arms across her chest. 'He came to stay with me when I first started in this business and 'e always paid prompt. He was the one who told me I should ask for money hup front, because he said that there were some who'd disappear at the end of the week without paying.'

The door opened again and a very small elderly lady with grey hair and a stoop looked round it. 'Has he gone?' she whispered. 'Is it safe to come in?'

'Yes, come in, Miss Jenkinson.' Mrs Johnson got up from the table and smoothed the tablecloth. Miss Jenkinson took the remaining set place and touched the ornate silver brooch which clasped the silk scarf round her neck.

'He makes me very nervous,' she confided to Poppy. 'Mr Harding, I mean. I'm so sorry,' she said. 'Have we met?'

'No,' Poppy said. 'I'm Poppy Mazzini. I only arrived last night.'

'Ah,' Miss Jenkinson said in a soft vague voice. 'I see! Then you won't have met Mr Harding before?' She fussed again with her scarf and then patted her hair which was tied in a bun at the nape of her neck. 'I'm always pleased when his time is up, but he's had a season at the Alhambra so we've had him for quite a long time this year.'

Mrs Johnson came in with a pot of tea and a plate of thin bread and butter, which she placed in front of Miss Jenkinson. 'Miss Jenkinson is a permanent guest,' she explained to Poppy, 'so she knows all of my regulars.'

'I'm the pianist, you see.' Miss Jenkinson stirred the pot vigorously and then picked up the strainer and carefully poured the tea into her cup. 'At Bradshaw's. I'm the oldest musician there. I was there even before Mr Bradshaw took over the theatre. So living here suits me very well.' She took a tiny bite of bread, then wiped her mouth with a napkin. 'Mrs Johnson looks after me admirably.'

Poppy felt her spirits sink. That must mean that Miss Jenkinson would be playing for her next week and she surely was too old to play with any vigour. What about the mazurka? What about the waltz? And most important, would she be able to accompany her singing?

'Will you—' Poppy cleared her throat. 'Will you be playing at Bradshaw's next week?' she asked. 'I'm appearing there.'

'Are you, my dear? Yes, I will. Well, how very nice.' Miss Jenkinson gazed at her from bright beady eyes. 'What will you be doing? You look like a dancer, so slender and light.'

Poppy warmed to her in spite of her misgivings over her talents as a pianist. 'Yes, I do dance. But I'm a singer.'

'Really!' Miss Jenkinson sat back and surveyed Poppy. 'And what did you say your name was?'

'Poppy. Poppy Mazzini.' She pronounced it clearly so that there was no mistaking the consonants.

'Oh! That means that Mr Bradshaw has made a mistake. He's put Polly on the bill.' The old lady shook her head. 'He's a little deaf, I fear. He gets names wrong so often: either that or he's careless! Poor dear Anthony was always telling him how to spell his name. The artistes don't like it, you know, if their names are wrong.'

'Anthony Marino, do you mean?' Poppy asked. 'The pianist?'

'You know of him, do you?' Miss Jenkinson again patted the side of her mouth with the napkin. She had now taken two bites from her bread and butter. 'Oh, yes.' She smiled and nodded. 'I've known him since he was a boy. I gave him his very first piano lesson! He was four,' she added. 'A wonderful musician. He could go even further than he has if he put his mind to it. I told his parents so, but he is contented with his present life, I think.'

Poppy considered. If Miss Jenkinson taught Anthony Marino, then perhaps she is a good pianist after all. 'Will you be playing at the rehearsal today?' she asked. 'I have to go to the hall to meet Mr Bradshaw.'

'No, Monday morning, when the other performers arrive. They all travel on a Sunday, you know, after they have finished their week elsewhere.'

'Of course,' Poppy said, having forgotten that players were often booked weekly.

'But go to the theatre by all means,' Miss Jenkinson advised. 'Get to know the stage. If they've finished it, that is. We had a fire,' she explained, 'otherwise I wouldn't be sitting here enjoying myself and eating this enormous breakfast.

'Mrs Johnson!' she called, and rang a little brass bell on the table, which Poppy hadn't noticed before. 'I can't eat another thing,' she told the landlady. She waved a finger at her. 'I've told you before not to give me too much!'

Poppy looked at the unfinished bread and butter and wished she dared ask if she could have it. She was still hungry; the porridge had been thin and the kipper very bony. 'If you will excuse me,' she said, rising from the table, 'I think I shall take a walk before going to the theatre.'

'Quite right,' Miss Jenkinson agreed. 'You must keep fit. But wrap up warm, my dear. Keep a scarf round your neck. You mustn't risk getting a sore throat or a chill. Not if you're a singer!'

Poppy smiled and said that she would take her advice. She ran upstairs and put on her coat and did as Miss Jenkinson suggested and wrapped a scarf round her neck. Suddenly she was happy and felt like singing. Miss Jenkinson hadn't questioned her age or her ability, nor had she said that she was one of many, as Mr Harding had implied.

She looked in the spotted mirror over the washstand and smiled at her reflection. 'I'm a singer,' she chanted. 'I'm a singer!'

CHAPTER EIGHTEEN

'Let's see what you can do, young lady. Just a verse so I can hear your voice, and then a twirl round the stage.' Jack Bradshaw was an overweight brusque man with a shaggy moustache and a nasal twang to his voice that Poppy found hard to understand. She sang a few notes and moved around the stage and he nodded. 'Right, that'll do. Damone says you're all right and he's generally got good judgement. You can play next week and if the audience like you we'll talk about a contract for what's left of this season.'

Poppy gathered up her coat and was preparing to leave when he added, 'Come in first thing Monday, Miss Massini. The musicians will be here at nine o clock.'

'Excuse me, Mr Bradshaw,' she said timidly. 'My name is Poppy Mazzini, not Polly Massini as you've put on the posters. You must have misheard Mr Damone.'

'What?' He stared at her. 'How do you spell that?'

She told him and he grunted that it was too late to change the posters for they were all over the town.

She was too nervous to argue and as she approached the door it swung open and Anthony Marino entered. He touched his wide-brimmed hat, a black felt trilby. 'Good morning, Miss Mazzini.' He smiled and held open the door for her, then he pointed a finger towards the poster outside and raised his eyebrows. 'You'll see that I've changed it!'

'Thank you,' she murmured. 'But Mr Bradshaw says that the posters are all over town and that it's too late to change them.'

He gazed at her for a moment. 'Oh!' he said. 'That is unfortunate.' He took off his hat and ran his fingers through his long hair. 'Look here, are you in a hurry?' As she shook her head, he said, 'Well, if you can hang on until I've had a word with Bradshaw, I have an idea.'

She looked up at him, wondering what he was going to suggest. But she went back inside and waited at the back of the stalls, gazing around the auditorium and scanning the gallery, trying to imagine the empty plush seats filled with people and feeling an apprehensive flutter of excitement in the pit of her stomach.

Anthony Marino came back up the aisle towards her. He moved swiftly and lithely and he grinned as he approached. 'I've congratulated Bradshaw on getting my name right, and told him that yours is wrong and what we are going to do about it.'

'What are we going to do about it?' she asked as he took her arm and ushered her out of the theatre.

'We shall search out those offending posters and change every one of them!'

'Oh!' She was astonished that he should take the trouble. 'But where are they?' She glanced at the one by the door of the theatre and saw that he had indeed changed it with thick black pencil, so that now her name stood out.

'All over town, as he said. But I have a notion where most of them will be. Bradshaw uses the shops, and gives them a free pass for a Monday afternoon, or he has them put on lamp posts along the seafront.' He smiled down at her. 'Cheer up, we'll find them. Or most of them, anyway.'

'You're really kind, Mr Marino,' she said, swallowing hard. 'I'm very grateful. I don't know why it's so important, but it is.'

'It's very important,' he said gravely. 'It's your name; therefore it has to be right. And speaking of which, could we drop the Mr Marino? It makes me feel old and I'm not! Please call me Anthony. And may I call you Poppy?'

'Yes please.' She laughed. 'I'd like that. Everybody at home calls me Poppy. I'm not used to being Miss Mazzini.'

'You'll find that most people will call you Miss Mazzini. That's how you'll be billed, as *Miss Poppy Mazzini*. Unless they get it wrong,' he joked, and added: 'Tell them if they do. Make sure that they know how to spell it and that you'll be angry if they don't get it right.'

'I don't think I dare,' she said. 'Everybody's older than me!'

He took her arm again as a gusty gritty wind propelled them along. 'That is probably true. But I started as a professional pianist when I was twelve, although I'd been playing in concerts when I was even younger than that, and people do indulge you if they think you have talent.'

'So, if you were playing in concert halls when you were young,' she asked, 'how is it you're playing in a music hall now? I mean, Bradshaw's is all right, but it's not terribly grand, is it? Not even like the Hull Assembly Rooms.'

He hesitated for a moment, and then explained. 'I want to write and play my own music,' he said. 'Playing in big concert halls, I'm expected to play Chopin or Beethoven, Mozart and the rest. Don't misunderstand me,' he said emphatically. 'They are the greatest composers of piano music ever, and I could never aspire to their stature, and even in variety halls I do, of course, play other people's music. The audience want popular tunes that they can sing to, but I can also include and try out my own compositions.'

'Ah, which is what you did at the Assembly Rooms.' She smiled. 'When you made me cry!'

'Come on,' he said, changing the subject. 'Let's have a cup of coffee and we'll discuss our strategy for finding the Polly posters!' Then he hesitated. 'Unless you had other plans?'

'None,' she said. 'I was wondering how to fill the time between now and Monday.'

He steered her into a coffee shop in one of the narrow cobbled lanes, where he was greeted like a lost son by the owner who shook his hand vigorously, but then stepped back in dismay as Anthony playfully grimaced and shook his fingers as if in pain. 'Always, I forget,' the owner said. 'I will ruin your playing! Ah, you must have coffee and biscuits to recover!'

Anthony laughed and introduced Poppy to him. 'This is Orlando. He's a friend of my parents.'

'Mazzini?' Orlando said. 'You are Italian too, yes? So, we are all Italians together?'

Poppy explained about her father and his forebears and how they came to be in Hull. 'We keep a grocery and coffee shop. But I don't have much Italian blood in me,' she confessed. 'We're Hull people.'

'You need only a *leetle* drop.' Orlando raised his hands. 'It is enough!'

'My parents have a restaurant too,' Anthony said. 'They're close to the theatre world, off St Martin's Lane.'

She gazed at him in astonishment. 'Not Mario?' she gasped. 'And Rosina?'

'Yes! Have you met them?' he asked incredulously. 'How amazing!'

Poppy explained about Dan Damone and the office being closed and how they had found Mario's by chance after booking in at the lodging house.

'You weren't alone?' Anthony asked, a frown wrinkling his brow.

'No,' she said. 'A friend who works in London – that is, a friend of my brother's – he came to meet me.' She blushed slightly as she spoke of Charlie. 'He's a shoemaker. He escorted me.' She sipped the coffee that Orlando had brought, to cover her embarrassment. 'Your father said I could stay with them the next time I'm in London.'

Anthony grinned. 'He would. There is always an open door at Mario's. I must have just missed you,' he said thoughtfully. 'I was there too for a short visit. Dan is my agent as well.'

When they had finished their coffee they left Orlando's and went looking for Bradshaw's posters. Anthony knew the shops where they were often displayed and asked the shopkeepers if he could alter them as there had been a printing error. 'This is Miss Poppy Mazzini,' he said, introducing Poppy. 'And Brighton has been chosen as the place for her premier professional performance!'

Eyebrows were raised and mouths shaped into round Os as this news was given and several shop owners said they would come along to see her and bring their friends. 'We know you, of course, Mr Marino,' some of them said. 'We always look forward to hearing you play.'

'So there we are, Poppy,' Anthony said as they left a confectioner's shop. 'We shall be sure of an audience on Monday at least!'

'Look, there's another.' Poppy pointed to a lamp post with a poster on it. They dashed across and Anthony carefully altered the name of Polly Massini to Poppy Mazzini.

'Well, at least I shall never forget your name,' he commented. 'It is etched into my mind for ever. Nor will I ever forget how to spell it!'

'I've really enjoyed this morning,' Poppy told him. 'I don't know what I would have done with myself if you hadn't been here, not knowing anyone or knowing where to go. I've always had someone with me,' she confessed. 'My father always wanted to know where I was, and my brother Tommy always looked out for me. I've been pampered and spoiled, I suppose, and now I have to manage on my own.'

He nodded and perused her with his dark eyes. 'You seem quite self-assured to me. You're probably feeling a little homesick, are you? After all, you're starting on a brand new career in a strange place far from home.'

At his words, to her horror, she started to cry. 'Yes,' she snuffled. 'I miss my pa, and I miss my ma. I should never have left.'

He patted her shoulder. 'You'll be all right, Poppy. Don't worry. After Monday you'll feel differently. Once you see the audience file into the theatre and hear the music strike up, you'll get that frisson of excitement and everything will be all right.' He handed her a clean white handkerchief. 'Come on. Dry your tears. You're a performer and everyone gets down at some time.' He peered at her anxiously. 'How old are you? Sixteen?'

She blew her nose noisily and shook her head. 'Thirteen and three-quarters,' she said in a muffled voice. 'And I want to go home!'

'Oh!' he said, staring at her. 'It is rather scary the first time on your own: although,' he added, 'some start much earlier. Marie Lloyd and Vesta Tilley were very young children when they went on stage, although both were from music hall families, which makes a difference, I suppose.' He frowned, then asked, 'Couldn't someone have come with you for your first week?'

She explained that there was no-one, that her mother was dead and her only brother had gone to sea. 'I thought I was so clever, you see. Doing it by myself. But it's different now I'm away from home. I know Hull and I know the people and they know me.' Tears began to fall again. 'And here I'm a stranger.'

He led her towards a steamy little café where he ordered tea and toast for them both, and sat silently watching her as she recovered and drank her tea and ate first her toast, and then his. 'Nothing wrong with your appetite, anyway!' he said solemnly.

She gave a little giggle and then blew her nose again. 'My mother used to say she could always tell if I was sickening for something as it was the only time I came off my food!'

'That's better.' Anthony smiled, then said softly, 'You must miss her a lot.'

'I do,' Poppy said and gave a deep sigh. 'But I wonder if I would be here if my mother were alive. She always said that my father wouldn't agree to my having a stage career, and yet he did.'

'You persuaded him?' he said. 'Twisted him round your little finger as daughters are apt to do?'

She nodded. 'I suppose so.'

'Look,' he said suddenly. 'I have to go.'

She immediately felt guilty at taking up his time until he went on to say, 'I asked Bradshaw if I could go into the theatre and rehearse for an hour or two. But if you're not doing anything tomorrow, why don't we have a stroll round Brighton? Perhaps go and have a look at the Royal Pavilion if it's open, or some of the gardens?'

'I'd like that,' she said. 'But I don't want to be a bother to you if you have other things to do.'

'I haven't,' he assured her. 'And perhaps later we could have a meal at Orlando's? Real food, I mean, and not lodging house stodge.'

'Oh, lovely,' she said, feeling much better. 'And that reminds me. I met Miss Jenkinson at my lodgings. She said she gave you your first piano lesson!'

His face wreathed into a grin. 'Dear old Jenky. She did indeed. I must take her out to tea whilst I'm here in Brighton. She lived round the corner from us in London and taught me when I was about four. She was quite famous herself when she was young, apparently.' He nodded at Poppy's surprised expression. 'She toured all the big concert halls and theatres. Then she fell in love with someone and gave up performing at his insistence, and then the bounder jilted her two days before their wedding. She never played a performance again, but only taught, and then later she moved to Brighton and played in the theatre orchestras.'

'Goodness,' Poppy murmured. 'And I was worrying whether or not she would be good enough to play for me! I thought she was too old. I didn't look beyond her age or appearance.'

'That's what we do when we're young,' Anthony answered. 'At least that's what my father says. Antonio, he says,' he put on an Italian accent, 'you musta looka further than ze skin.'

Poppy laughed. 'Oh, you've cheered me up so much, Anthony. I'm so *very* grateful to you. I think I'll go back to my diggings and write another letter to my father and tell him how I'm looking forward to Monday.'

But she didn't write to her father that day, but wrote instead to Charlie to tell him where she was appearing and saying how nice it would be if he could come and see her. 'I begin my career on Monday,' she said, 'and I'm very excited but also very nervous.' She didn't tell him about Anthony Marino, for she didn't think he would have heard of him, nor did she want him to think that she had a male friend, which, she gnawed on the end of her pen as she meditated, I think he will become.

The next day, she met Anthony and they walked to the Royal Pavilion, once the lavish and bizarre establishment of George IV when he was Prince Regent, and subsequently used by other members of the royal household. Then, when the railway came to Brighton, and made it into a popular seaside venue for the London masses, the pavilion was sold to Brighton town.

'How wonderful!' Poppy exclaimed as they approached the Steine Front and saw the domes and elegant pinnacles, the rotunda, and the Indian and Chinese influences on the once simple farmhouse which had been transformed into an exotic palace. 'It's like a magical eastern palace set by the English sea!'

'I've never visited it before,' Anthony said, as they gazed at elaborate ornate ceilings and candelabra; at Indian silks, cabinets and ottomans, the Chinese interiors and delicate porcelain, and the Japanese lacquered furniture. 'I've been often to Brighton but there's never enough time between performances for sight-seeing. You'll find the same, Poppy, once you're under way with your career: all you'll see of a town is the railway station, the inside of a theatre and your lodging house, where you'll fall exhausted into bed every night.'

As they left at the end of the afternoon and walked back

towards the town, she thanked him for taking her. 'My pleasure,' he said. 'Thank you! I've often wanted to visit, and having a companion with me made it all the more enjoyable. Now, shall we eat? Then I'm for an early night. Tomorrow is a busy day and for you a most exciting one. Your very first professional performance.' He glanced at her, his eyes crinkling. 'Your first step on the way to stardom!'

They ate supper at Orlando's restaurant and Orlando wished her luck for the following day, promising that he would try to come and see the show some time during the week. Anthony gave her a letter, which he asked her to give to Miss Jenkinson, and walked with her to Mrs Johnson's. Then he said goodbye and set off back the way they had come, to his own lodgings.

The front door was open, and she stepped into the hall, which was piled high with trunks and leather suitcases and coats and scarves flung over the top of them. There was a clamour of voices coming from the parlour. Mrs Johnson came through into the hall and greeted Poppy. 'Ah!' she exclaimed. 'I was just coming to close the door. They've brought enough luggage for a twelvemonth.'

'New guests, Mrs Johnson?' Poppy asked. 'Has Mr Harding left?'

'Yes, dear, he's gorn,' she said. 'The Terry Sisters 'ave harrived.' She nodded in a self-satisfied manner. 'They're my regulars. They're no bother, though they will hargue.'

'Could I come in and say hello?' Poppy asked. 'I've met them before, but I don't know if they'll remember me.'

Mrs Johnson ushered her into the parlour where the Terry Sisters were sitting talking to Miss Jenkinson and the kettle on the fire was starting to boil and whistle.

The three women looked up at Poppy as she entered with Mrs Johnson behind her, and Ena Terry, her feet elegantly crossed, her neat ankles showing, said, 'Come on, Johnny, make us a cuppa tea, I'm fair gasping.'

'Give me a chance,' Mrs Johnson said. 'I 'aven't got two pairs of 'ands! This is Miss Mazzini, by the way. She says you've met.'

'Have we?' Veronica Terry screwed up her face. 'I'm Ronny. This is Ena. Where've we met?'

'You were playing at the Mechanics in Hull – Boscoe's is its proper name. You came to my father's coffee house with Mr Damone after one of the shows.' Poppy didn't say she had sung for them; she wanted to know if they remembered.

Ena pursed her lips and shook her head. 'We get about a lot,' she said. 'Though we've been to Hull several times.'

'I remember you!' Ronny exclaimed. 'You were that little girl who sang for us! Dan was most impressed. Don't you remember, Ena?'

'Mm, vaguely.' Ena yawned. 'Gawd, I'm dead beat. Hurry up with that tea, Johnny. I'm ready for my bed.'

'Yes! Dan said you'd make a star,' Ronny continued. 'So what are you doing here? Are you on the boards now?'

'Yes.' Poppy was scarcely able to believe her luck at being here with the Terry Sisters. 'I met Mr Damone again at a competition in Hull.' She refrained from telling them that he had written to her. 'This will be my first professional appearance.' She smiled exultantly. 'I'm appearing at Bradshaw's with you.'

'Are you indeed?' Ena glanced sharply at her, and for a moment Poppy thought she felt hostility, though she remembered her as being friendly. Then Ena added, 'Well, all the best, dearie. Hope you've got stamina. You need it in this game. It fair wears you out.'

'What are you, then?' Ronny asked. 'A singer or a dancer? Or do you do both, like us?'

Poppy hesitated, and then said. 'I'm a singer, but I dance too.'

'Descriptive ballad singer, then?' Ena asked. 'Not like us. We're dancers who sing!'

'I'm playing for Miss Mazzini,' Miss Jenkinson cut in. 'I've been in to see Mr Bradshaw and he's asked me to, seeing as it's her first time. You ladies will require the full ensemble as usual?'

Ronny sighed. 'Yes. We need them to cover up our off-key notes.'

'Speak for yourself,' Ena snapped. 'I don't sing off key!'

'Neither do I,' Ronny retorted. 'But somebody does – that last review said so!'

'Pah! Critics! What do they know?' Ena fished about in her bag and brought out a cheroot and Poppy remembered how astonished she'd been when she had first seen her smoking. Few women in Hull smoked, apart from the poor ones who smoked pipes of tobacco.

'You will excuse me?' Miss Jenkinson rose hurriedly from the table. 'But I have things to do before I retire to bed. I trust you have had a good day, Miss Mazzini?' she said to Poppy.

'I've had a lovely day, thank you,' she replied. 'I've been to the Royal Pavilion. And I've something for you.' She smiled at Miss Jenkinson as she gave her the envelope from Anthony and saw her cheeks flush with pleasure as she opened it. She looked at Miss Jenkinson with different eyes now that Anthony had told her of her background. She saw her capable hands with their polished nails, her neat coiffured hair, her tasteful dress and carefully arranged scarf at her neck, and most of all her polite cultured manner, so at odds with the rather brash Terry Sisters.

'How lovely,' Miss Jenkinson murmured. 'I will look forward to that. Such a dear boy. Well.' She looked up at Poppy, who stood almost a head taller. 'I'll say good night, and see you in the morning at breakfast. We could walk to the theatre together, if you wish, and discuss your music?'

'Thank you, Miss Jenkinson. I'd like that very much.' Then Poppy added, 'I'll be pleased to take any advice you could offer.'

CHAPTER NINETEEN

Joshua had given Albert a key to the back door. He thought that the lad might want to go out to meet friends after the coffee shop was closed, and didn't want to put too many restrictions on him. He insisted, however, that if he was the last to come in, he must bolt the door after him. Tommy had previously had his own key and used to be the last to bed, but he never forgot to bolt the door.

Shortly after Poppy had left for Brighton, Joshua had come downstairs one morning, early as usual, and found Albert's truckle bed still pushed up against the wall, not having been slept in, and the back door locked but not bolted. He opened the front door to the shop, ready for when Nan came in, for she was always on time, and then went back into the kitchen to stoke up the range ready for the morning's baking. He filled the kettle with water and swung it over the fire to boil. There was no sound of Lena moving around upstairs and he guessed that she was still in bed. This, he thought grumpily, will be the second time she's been late.

'Lena!' he shouted up the narrow staircase. 'It's a quarter past five!'

She came down about ten minutes later, her clothes crumpled, her eyes bleary, and her hair brushed roughly into a snood. She blinked at him, then gave a simpering smile. 'What a naughty girl I am,' she said croakily. 'I slept in again.'

'Albert didn't come back last night,' Joshua said brusquely. 'He must say if he's going to stay out and then I can bolt 'door.'

'He must have decided to stay at our place,' Lena said.

'Perhaps he didn't want to disturb us.' She glanced sideways at him, lowering her lashes onto red cheeks. When he didn't respond, she turned and took a flowered teapot and two cups and saucers out of the cupboard and set them on the table.

'I'll see to 'breakfast,' Joshua told her. 'You'd better get started on 'bread or there'll be none ready for 'customers when they come in.'

'There's some left from yesterday.' Her mouth turned down. 'They'll have to have that if they won't wait.'

'What?' Joshua's tone was sharp. 'We have to have fresh bread! My customers expect it. Yesterday's bread is sold off cheap.'

Lena raised her eyebrows, but didn't answer. She went to the store cupboard for the flour, tipped it into an earthenware pancheon, made a hole in the centre and added a knob of yeast. She poured in some warm water from the kettle, and a pinch of sugar to help it froth. Then she casually threw in a lump of lard.

Joshua saw what she was doing. I suppose everybody bakes differently, he thought, but I'm sure that Mary used to dissolve the sugar in the water first and then add the yeast to it. Then he gave a shrug. No-one had complained, at least not to him.

He drank a cup of tea and then went into the shop to start organizing his day. He knew which of his regular customers would come in first and what they required. There was Mrs Forbes who bought a screw of tobacco for her husband. Mrs Brownlow would want one of yesterday's loaves at a reduced price. A child whose name he didn't know always came in for a bag of broken biscuits, which he suspected was the only food he would have that day, and a young boy came in for an ounce of tea for his gran.

Then, as the morning drew on, other customers would come in for the first bread out of the oven, which today, he thought, as he glanced up at the clock, would be late.

'Good morning!' Nan was her usual cheerful self as she came through the door. 'Lovely morning.'

Joshua nodded. 'Not bad,' he said. 'Not bad at all.'

'Everything all right?' Nan asked. She seemed to have an instinct for knowing when something was wrong.

Joshua gave a sigh. 'Yes, I suppose so.' He glanced towards the inner door. 'It's just that Lena's late up and has only just started making 'bread, and Albert hasn't come in yet.'

'Oh!' Nan's eyes flickered uneasily. She knew of the new arrangements, whereby Lena had taken Tommy's room, and Albert was to sleep downstairs, but she hadn't commented on them. She took off her shawl. 'I'd better see if I can help Lena, then, before I start anything else, though I was going to clean 'windows this morning. They're getting very steamy now that 'weather's colder.'

The doorbell jangled and Albert rushed in. 'Sorry I'm late, Josh,' he said. 'I – er, I decided to stay at home last night. I was at the other end of town with some mates so there seemed no sense in coming back here.' He must have seen Joshua's glower, for he added, 'It was late, and I didn't want to disturb you or Ma.'

'Don't call me Josh, Albert,' Joshua said firmly. 'My name's Joshua. We have to have a proper understanding,' he went on. 'The door has been unbolted all night. So you either come back here and lock up properly, or you stay in your own home and give me back my key!'

Albert's face reddened. 'Sorry. I – I think Lena's given notice on our place, so we'll not have it anyway after next week.'

Nan glanced anxiously at Joshua, then hurried through the door into the living quarters.

'Has she?' Joshua was concerned to hear that. The new arrangements were meant to be just a trial, to see how they all got along. He hadn't expected Lena to give up her own house just yet. And, he worried, Tommy and Poppy were right: there was something about Albert that was slightly disagreeable, though he couldn't quite put his finger on it to say what it was. The fellow was good at figures, no doubt about that, and the cash box was always correct at the end of each day, and he did his best to be pleasant, Joshua was sure of that, but he felt that some of the customers were uneasy about Albert and preferred to wait for him to be free to serve them.

He heard a clatter of a pan or something heavy being dropped, and then Lena's raised voice. 'Finish stacking these tins, will you?' he said to Albert. 'Then grind 'coffee beans and open 'door.' He was convinced that the aroma of freshly ground coffee drew people into the shop.

'What's up?' he asked as he went into the kitchen. 'Dropped something?'

'She knocked my arm and the whole lot went down.' Lena was picking up squashed and battered uncooked breadcakes from the floor, dusting them off with floury fingers and putting them back onto a baking tray.

Nan was standing with a pan and brush in her hand. Her eyes were wide and startled and as she glanced at Joshua she gave a slight shake of her head. Joshua put up his hand to stop her from explaining. 'An accident, I expect,' he said. 'Is the bread ruined?'

'It'll have to do.' Lena opened the oven door. 'There's no time to make another batch.' She pushed the tray into the oven and faced Joshua with a red and sweating face.

'You're not . . . you're not going to bake those? They've been on 'floor!'

' 'Floor's clean enough,' Lena said. 'Fortunately I cleaned it thoroughly myself last night before I went to bed. It wasn't very clean up to then,' she added meaningfully, glancing at Nan. 'But there, if you want a job done properly, you're best doing it yourself.'

'I scrubbed 'floor yesterday morning,' Nan broke in. 'As I do every morning.'

'Well, it wasn't clean enough for me.' Lena glared at her. 'You could eat off my floor!'

'Well, it seems that somebody's going to,' Joshua said ironically, but then added doubtfully: 'I suppose 'heat will kill off any germs?'

Lena busied herself at the kitchen table, kneading the remaining dough and roughly shaping it into loaves and rounds. 'What folks don't know about they won't worry about,' she said sharply.

Joshua heaved a sigh as he left the kitchen. The two women didn't get on, that was obvious, but he didn't know what he could do about it. Nan was very reliable and his wife had thought the world of her, but Lena was forever complaining about her.

'That delivery from Donkin's should be coming in this morning,' he said to Albert. 'I thought it would have come yesterday. You did tell them it was urgent, didn't you?'

'Oh, yes,' Albert assured him. 'I spoke to the foreman in the warehouse about it.'

'Foreman? Well, next time give the order to Mr Donkin himself. Then we'll be sure of getting it on time. We're running short of tea and sugar,' he added. 'We must be selling a lot more than usual. It's not a month since 'last order was put in.'

Mrs Forbes came in for the usual screw of tobacco. 'Mister said to ask, is it 'same brand as before?' she whined.

'Same as he allus gets, Mrs Forbes.' Joshua pointed to the tin on the shelf. 'I get it in specially for him.' He kept in a cheap but strong brand of tobacco for those who couldn't afford much.

She nodded and handed over her coppers and went out, as Mrs Brownlow came in for yesterday's bread. 'Last lot was stale,' she said, giving Albert a penny in exchange for a loaf.

'It's yesterday's bread,' he muttered. 'What do you expect?'

Joshua looked up. 'Sorry about that, Mrs Brownlow. It should keep. Here, take this breadcake to make up for it.'

She gave a smile which lit up her sallow face. 'Thanks, Mr Mazzini. We ate it anyway, but it wasn't your usual.'

Donkin's delivery waggon clattered up to the door. 'I'll get it, Joshua.' Albert scurried to the door and Joshua saw him talking to the driver and taking the delivery note from him.

'Breadcakes are ready!' Lena shouted. 'Can somebody fetch 'em?' She had placed the hot breadcakes on the wire trays, and was tapping the bottom of the loaves to determine if they were cooked. 'These are ready as well,' she said triumphantly. 'So we're not behind after all.'

'My, that was quick!' Joshua said and wondered how she had managed it in only half the usual time.

'Nan!' she yelled. 'Come and clear up in here while I have a cup o' tea and some toast.' She sat down on a kitchen chair. 'I'm fair mafted,' she said, wiping her face on a piece of rag. 'I've just one more lot of loaves to put in when the oven comes up again, and that's it.'

'What about 'scones?' Joshua asked, picking up one of the trays. 'You've those to do.'

'We've some left from yesterday,' she said. 'I'm going to sprinkle 'em with water and warm 'em up again.' She laughed. 'Don't look so shocked, Josh,' she said. 'It's what everybody does with leftovers! I bet your wife did the same, only she never told you.'

Nan, coming downstairs, eyed Lena. 'Excuse me, Lena, but she didn't,' she said quietly. 'I worked for Mrs Mazzini for a long time and I never saw her do that!'

'What would you know about it?' Lena snapped. 'You're just a skivvy. What would you know about what goes on in a bakery?' She turned to Joshua, who was standing in the doorway about to go into the shop. 'I'll not have this, Josh. I'll not have my judgement challenged. She's crossed me more than once and I'll not have it!'

Joshua dithered in the doorway with the tray in his hands. He was a man who didn't like discord. Indeed, he had never been used to it. 'Just a minute,' he said. 'Let me just put this down.' He placed the breadcakes in a basket on the counter top and went back into the kitchen.

'Now, ladies,' he said placatingly. 'Don't let's have any argument. I don't know how my wife baked; she just got on with it. It was probably different from how you do things, Lena, but that doesn't mean that either of you is right or wrong. Just different, that's all.'

Nan didn't speak but collected the baking bowls and implements and put them into the deep sink. She ran hot water onto them; it was always red hot, being heated from the range. Lena, however, glared at her, and then rising from the chair she put the remaining loaves into the oven. 'Don't forget to make the tea,' she said spitefully. 'You've done nowt else much this morning.'

Joshua escaped back into the shop. The groceries had been delivered and Albert had opened one of the sacks of tea and was weighing the leaves into four-ounce paper bags, which was how they usually sold it. Few of their customers could afford to buy more than that at one time. Joshua felt despondent. The morning hadn't gone well. If only Tommy had stayed at home, he thought. There would have been none of this disharmony. Tommy was a good baker, too, even better at making bread than his mother had been. Still, it wasn't to be. Youngsters would do what they wanted to do, to make their way in life. We shouldn't stand in their way.

I hope he's all right, he pondered dismally, worrying that he hadn't heard from Tommy since that first letter. Too busy enjoying himself to think of his poor old da. Of course, his ship might not come back into Hull port. He remembered the strikes earlier in the year when the dockers had refused to unload three barges because one of the crew wasn't a union member. The dispute had escalated throughout the docks and shipping federation, and free labour had been brought in. A timber yard had been fired and the police called in to keep law and order had been pelted with stones, but the Wilson company, who owned the ship Tommy had sailed in, wouldn't concede to the strikers and had threatened to take their ships out of Hull.

At ten o'clock, the post arrived. 'Letter from abroad, Mr Mazzini,' the postman said. 'Hope it's good news.'

'So do I,' Joshua murmured. 'I'm due for some.'

It was a letter from Tommy. 'At last!' Joshua breathed, and, opening the envelope, began to read Tommy's account of his seafaring life. 'I'm in the Baltic,' Tommy wrote. 'We're doing the timber run, and it's not very exciting. I don't know how long it will take or when I'll be home. Hope you and Poppy are managing without me. I have to go now, but will write again when I can. Your loving son, Tommy.'

Joshua turned over the page looking for a postscript. Is that it, he thought? I've been waiting all this time and that's all he has to say! At least Poppy told me what she had been doing and that she'd met up with Charlie Chandler in London and that pianist fellow in Brighton. He heaved a sigh. And she said that she missed me.

He heard another crash coming from the kitchen and Lena's raised voice. Albert, up on a ladder stacking shelves with tins, raised his eyebrows. 'Lena's got her dander up,' he said. 'We'd better all watch out.'

Joshua closed his eyes for a second before taking a deep breath. He put the envelope in his overall pocket, then, setting his mouth in a pinched line, he marched through the inner door into the kitchen.

CHAPTER TWENTY

I feel sick! Poppy stood shivering in the wings. The fire curtain, which was decorated with advertisements for local amenities and had willow trees and turreted castles painted upon it, was still down. The stagehands were standing with ropes and pulleys ready to draw it up when they were given the signal. The orchestra was tuning up and she could hear a hum of voices coming from the auditorium. I'm glad that I'm not first on. She had been billed at the bottom of the programme, which should have meant that she was first to appear, but at the rehearsal Jack Bradshaw had decreed that an acrobat should go on first and Poppy second. The acrobat was standing in front of her now, rising up and down on his toes, flexing his calves and swinging his arms.

Poppy hunched into her shawl. I'll be no good, she thought. I'm so frightened. Why am I here? I should have stayed at home with Pa. I don't like being on my own. Her lips trembled and she wanted to cry. She had shared a dressing room with the other female performers, the Terry Sisters and Nancy Martell the comedienne, but they hadn't been good-humoured and barely spoke to each other, let alone her, and she had been too shy and nervous to start a conversation with them.

'How are you feeling, Poppy?' Anthony Marino breathed the words as he came up behind her. 'All set?'

'No,' she whispered back. 'I'm scared. I don't want to go on!'

'You'll be fine,' he assured her. 'I've been out front and there are lots of old ladies in the house, and they'll love you!'

'Perhaps so. But what about tonight? The old ladies won't be there then.' What if the audience heckle me tonight, she thought.

She had been over her routine this morning with Miss Jenkinson, who had been very patient and understanding at interpreting the tempo of Poppy's dancing of the mazurka, and then playing softly as she sang two romantic love songs. 'You'll do very well, my dear,' she had said, when Poppy had finished. 'And I shall speak to Mr Bradshaw about having a violinist play for you also, later in the week. Not just yet,' she had added. 'You and I are fine together until you have got over your nervousness.' She seemed to have guessed that Poppy felt like a sack of trembling jelly.

But now as she waited in the wings, saw the curtain rise and the acrobat somersault onto the stage, Poppy felt that she would never be able to control either her feet or her voice. She watched in a stupor as the performer came to the end of his act, heard the applause of the audience and the tattoo of the drum as he did his final roll across the stage, somersaulted and spun, ran to the wings and then back to centre stage. He gave a low bow, holding his hands to his ankles, then swiftly back-flipped off the stage, over and over, to exit.

It's me! She suddenly woke up, licked her dry lips, held up her head and squared her shoulders as she was announced. 'A young lady – fresh from her astounding success in northern England – come specially for your entertainment . . .'

Anthony nodded encouragingly to her, as Jack Bradshaw, holding out his arm to draw her on, proclaimed, '*Miss – Poppy – Mazzini.*'

She threw off her shawl and ran to centre stage. Bowed. Put her hands on her hips, her head to one side, and Miss Jenkinson began the lively music of the mazurka.

Poppy smiled as she danced the spirited rhythm, for she could hear some members of the audience clapping in time to the music. Then she shut her ears to it and concentrated solely on the piano, as some of the clapping was half a beat behind.

There was spontaneous applause as she finished. She came to the front of the stage and took a bow, and saw that the theatre was only partly full in the stalls, and that, as Anthony had said, most of the audience was made up of elderly people who probably didn't care to venture out in the evenings. She took several breaths as she unfastened the scarf which had bound her head, shook out her hair and announced that she would like to sing two particular favourites of hers, and she hoped that they would like them too.

She sang first of all an appealing, merry tune, one which people were whistling in the streets of Hull. An earnest young swain was urging his ladylove to marry him, and soon. 'Come, pretty May, Come, pretty May, Marry me now 'fore I'm old and grey.' Then she sang the response of his sweetheart, in a voice all sweetness and guile. 'I'll not marry you, Harry, I'm too young and merry.'

She paused for a second's effect, and Miss Jenkinson, taking her lead, held her hands over the keys, before she ended, teasingly, 'But don't go away – for maybe – one day!'

Poppy invited the audience to join in the chorus and found that her nervousness had gone and she was elated at their response.

She took her bow again and began her final song, 'Will You Be Forever True?' She assumed a graceful appealing pose, lifted her arm to let the flimsy scarf float above her head, and began. 'La la, la la, la la-ah, hold me close forever more.'

Though she concentrated on the music and her voice, she couldn't help but think of Charlie. This is my song for him, to show that I love him. If only he would come and hear me, then he would really understand. He wouldn't think that I was only a girl just out of school. She did one more glide round the stage, came to the front and let her voice soar for the final line. 'Gone on the silent breath of night.'

There was polite sporadic applause and she backed away, then she returned, tripping lightly to centre stage and giving a deep bow before exiting.

She breathed hard and stood back as a magician in black tail-coat and tall hat and carrying a tall box with a spangled cover pushed past her. Anthony was still there, but standing back so as not to be in the way.

'They didn't like me!' she said. 'What was wrong?'

He took her arm and they moved away from the wings. 'They did like you,' he said. 'But they don't often get your quality of singing. They liked the merry song best,' he added, looking down at her. 'They want to tap their feet and clap their hands and go home happy.'

'I see,' she said in a small voice. 'Should I give up and go home?'

'Give up!' He was astonished. 'With a voice like yours? Certainly not. But you need to take some advice. I have to go,' he said. 'I need to change.' She was so wrapped up in herself that she had almost forgotten that he was performing too.

'Oh! I shall stay and listen,' she said. 'I so loved your playing when you came to Hull.'

'Ah!' He raised his eyebrows. 'You might find this quite different; but go and put on something warm,' he advised. 'Backstage can be a chilly place.' Though he was wearing black dress trousers, he also had on a thick high-necked jumper over his shirt. 'Don't catch a chill.'

'That's what Miss Jenkinson told me,' she murmured, and he nodded briefly and went off to the men's dressing room.

Poppy shivered as she made her way back to the dressing room. Anthony was right; it was cold and draughty down these narrow passages. She'd dropped her shawl as she'd made her entrance on stage but it wasn't where she'd left it.

'This yours, miss?' One of the stagehands, coming towards her down the corridor, held it up. 'I found it in a corner in the wings.'

'Thank you,' she said, taking it from him and noticing how grubby it had become. Someone must have kicked it to one side.

'Best to hang it up next time, miss,' he said. 'There's some hooks on the wall just inside the wings. Anybody might have tripped over it,' he added.

'Oh! Sorry. I must have dropped it.' She felt foolish. How unprofessional of her. She hadn't been thinking of the other performers but only of herself. As she opened the door to the dressing room she heard the applause for the magician, but then was almost knocked over by the comedienne Nancy Martell.

'Outa my way,' she barked. 'I'm on,' and the large woman, dressed up in a curly red wig and a voluminous apron over a striped bodice and skirt, rushed past her.

The Terry Sisters, who were appearing in the second half, were sitting in front of the mirror finishing off their make-up. Their eyes were heavily outlined in black with bright blue shadow on their lids. Their brows were arched high and long false eyelashes swept their cheeks. As they sat, Poppy would hardly have known one from the other.

They both looked at her through the mirror. Ena didn't speak but reached for a lip brush and paint pot, and began to fill in her mouth with scarlet. Ronny swung round to face her. 'How'd you get on? Your first time, wasn't it?'

Poppy nodded. 'Away from home,' she said. 'So it was different.'

'Course it is,' Ronny said. 'No friends or family to support you and give you a clap. So how was it?' she repeated. 'Did they like you?'

'I'm not sure.' Poppy hesitated. 'They liked the first two numbers anyway. The mazurka and the ditty. I don't know if they liked the romantic song.'

'Probably didn't.' Ena spoke to Poppy's reflection. 'The matinee audiences like something lively. They don't want romantic mush to remind them of what they've lost – or never had,' she added sourly.

Ronny made a moue and raised her eyebrows even higher, causing them to shoot up into her hairline. 'Hark at Miss Crabby,' she said. 'She knows all about it if anybody does!'

Poppy, glancing at Ena, gasped. Ena had mouthed an expletive through the mirror at the back of Ronny's head, and though she had stopped short of saying it aloud, there was no mistaking what she had meant.

'Come here.' Ronny indicated for Poppy to come closer. She peered at her face. 'Have you been on like that?'

'What do you mean? Dressed like this?' Poppy was flummoxed. This was one of her best dresses. The skirt was cut to flounce and the bodice had floating sleeves.

'No! The dress is lovely. Your face! You ain't wearing any make-up.' Ronny stared at her. 'Why not?'

'I am. I am!' Poppy insisted. 'I've rouged my cheeks and I've got lipstick on.'

Ena swung round now. 'Well, they'll not see that from the back of the stalls.' She laughed. 'Your face will have completely disappeared!'

Poppy stared open-mouthed at the sisters. 'Will it?' she said. 'No-one has ever mentioned that before.'

'Well, I dare say that when your family and friends came to see you on your home turf, they were sitting in the front row. Am I right?' Ronny asked.

'Yes.' I've so much to learn, Poppy thought miserably. I'm such a beginner.

Ronny and her sister swung round to face the mirror again and both fastened back their hair and began to pin on their head-dresses. Ronny saw Poppy watching them. 'If you like,' she said, with a mouthful of hairpins, 'I'll show you how to do your face. Maybe tonight at Johnny's, after the show? If I'm not too tired,' she added.

Poppy saw Ena glance at her sister, but she made no offer of help, instead continuing to arrange the feathers and beads around her head. Then they both stood up and seemed to tower above her. They were wearing very high-heeled shoes with the front of the shoe made from transparent material, with sparkling diamante straps around their ankles.

'So how do we look?' Ronny asked.

They were transformed. Poppy could see that. From being rather mousy, unremarkable women who wouldn't merit a second glance out in the street, they were now elegant, glamorous performers.

'Wonderful,' she breathed. 'Just wonderful.'

'Glamour. That's what people come for,' Ronny said, looking down on her. 'That, or to be made happy and merry. And it's our job to satisfy them.'

During the interval, the Terry Sisters drank coffee and rehearsed some of their dance steps. Poppy felt as if she was in the way, so she changed into her outdoor clothes, packed away her stage clothes, and made her way to the back of the stalls where she sat alone in an empty row and waited for the second half to begin. Will I ever be on in the second half, she wondered? Will I ever top the bill as I did in Hull? Will I even have the stamina to continue? I did so want to sing my romantic songs. I wanted to perform with feeling, and not just sing merry ditties!

The lights were dimmed and she sank down into her seat as the curtain rose to show a piano on stage with a potted palm tree in the background. Jack Bradshaw appeared and the audience applauded as he announced, 'Your favourite pianist and mine – returned by special request – the talented – *Mr Anthony – Marino*!'

Anthony strode onto the stage, bowed, flourished a white handkerchief which he then tucked into his trouser pocket, and took his place at the piano. How splendid he looks! Poppy gazed admiringly as Anthony ran his hands across the keys. He wore a black frock coat and crisp white shirt with stand-up collar and a white rose in his buttonhole. His hair curled just below his collar whilst a stray lock hung about his forehead.

He wears his hair like that because it looks appealing, she thought. He seems – she smiled – a romantic figure, I suppose. And just out of reach! The old ladies will love him. How clever! Whereas I need to look older if I'm to sing romantic music. I need to look as if I know what love is. She gave a small sigh. They won't realize that I do know already.

Anthony played merry tunes and marching songs, waltz arrangements by Johann Strauss, and charming lyrical pieces, but not the music that had once made her cry. She sat and listened and watched, not just Anthony but the audience too. She let her gaze wander about the auditorium and saw them nodding their heads in time to the music, tapping their feet to a hornpipe or singing softly to the popular melodies. Poppy realized that Anthony had chosen the music especially for this audience. He has learned to know what they want, and in order to make a living he plays the music they like. And that is what I must do if I'm to succeed. For now, she decided. Only for now.

She joined in the applause at the end of Anthony's performance and then stayed to watch the Terry Sisters, wondering as she did so why they appeared higher up the bill than Anthony when he was so evidently more talented. They looked good though, she thought, from the rear of the stalls, and even if their singing wasn't quite what it might be, they had developed their act to incorporate dance steps which provocatively showed off neat ankles through their split, glittering, befeathered skirts. The lyrics of music hall songs were enhanced by simpering expressions and much fluttering of fans, and Poppy guessed that the singing might be further enlivened at the evening performance.

As the Terry Sisters took their bow, Poppy got up to leave. As she made her way to the exit, an elderly woman blocked her way. 'Excuse me, Miss Mazzini.'

Poppy glanced down at her. She was quite tiny and looked rather frail and was dressed in black. 'Hello,' she said softly, for the next act, a tenor, was about to begin.

'I just wanted to say . . .' The woman whispered so low that Poppy couldn't hear her, and indicated that the woman should follow her through into the foyer.

'I just wanted to say,' the woman repeated as they went through the doors, 'and I hope you'll pardon my intrusion, but I saw you sitting in the stalls.' She nodded. 'The stars often sit at the back, so I look out for them. And I wanted to tell you how much I enjoyed your singing.'

'Thank you,' Poppy said gratefully. 'That is so very kind.'

'And I especially liked that lovely song – "Will You Be Forever True".' The old lady blinked up at her. 'It reminded me of when I once loved somebody and I thought he loved me. Except that he didn't,' she added sadly. 'He left me for another.'

'I'm so sorry.' Poppy was embarrassed. 'So very sorry.'

'Oh, don't be, dear,' she replied. 'It was a very long time ago. But the love I had for him has sustained me all of my life. I never loved again, you see.' She gave a wistful smile that deepened the lines in her face. 'There never was another. But I don't ever want to forget him, and your song reminded me again.' She lifted her head and her blue eyes gazed into Poppy's. She smiled. 'I'm a sentimental old woman, and I do realize that it's only a song and not your own experience. You're far too young to know. But you sounded as if you had really known love.' She patted Poppy's arm. 'I hope that when you learn to love, it will be with someone who will love you in return.'

She turned and hobbled with the help of a walking stick towards the doors of the theatre. 'I shan't stay to hear the tenor,' she called back. 'His voice is too thin, and I don't care for the comic. He's not in the least funny. Goodbye, my dear. I wish you luck in your career. You will go far.' She looked over her shoulder. 'But set your sights higher than Bradshaw's,' she added. 'Much higher.'

Poppy watched her through the windows of the swinging doors. She has paid me such a compliment, she mused. So why do I feel so sad?

CHAPTER TWENTY-ONE

Poppy stepped outside and was about to walk back to her diggings for an hour's rest before the evening show when a voice hailed her from the stage door at the side of the building. It was Anthony.

'Jack Bradshaw's looking for you,' he called, coming towards her. He was dressed again in his warm jumper and an overcoat, with woollen gloves on his hands. 'He wants to see you about tonight's show.'

'Oh!' Immediately she was anxious and it must have shown in her face because Anthony smiled. 'Don't be scared,' he said. 'It won't be anything to worry about.'

'Well, he does scare me,' she said. 'His voice is so loud.'

'That's because he's deaf. He doesn't know he's shouting. I'm just off for a walk by the sea,' he said. 'Want to come?'

'I'd better see what he wants,' she said reluctantly. 'I'll catch you up.'

She walked down the narrow passage from the stage door vestibule towards Jack Bradshaw's small office. She saw him through the open door. He was sitting at his desk smoking a cigar and coughing. She called out, 'Did you want a word, Mr Bradshaw?'

He jumped and looked up. 'Didn't hear you,' he spluttered. 'You girls will creep about!'

'Sorry,' she said. 'Did you want me?' Behind her, towards the stage, she could hear voices and laughter as Bill Baloney concluded his act, and then applause and the orchestra playing the finale as the audience prepared to depart.

'I just wanted to say, will you swap a couple of numbers round for tonight? Put that love song in the middle and finish with something merry. A bit cheeky, maybe?' He narrowed his eyes as he drew on the cigar. 'That's what they like of an evening. Have a word with Miss Jenkinson and arrange it.'

'Yes.' She was relieved it was nothing more than that. 'Was I all right?' she asked.

'What?' He seemed puzzled by the question.

'My act! Was it all right?' I've obviously made a huge impression on him, she thought.

'Oh! Yes. Fine. Fine.' He looked her over. 'But tonight is the telling time. We've two charabanc parties coming in. We'll see how they like you. That's why I say make it a bit saucy!'

And so she didn't try to catch up with Anthony but stayed behind to rehearse another song with Miss Jenkinson, who pursed her lips when she heard what Mr Bradshaw had said. 'Well, I suppose he knows what his audiences want,' she said primly. 'But I would have thought we had sauce enough with the Terry Sisters and Mr Baloney, and that dreadful Nancy Martell, without its coming from the mouth of a sweet young thing like you.'

A sweet young thing. That was how Miss Jenkinson saw her, and probably how the old lady who had spoken to her a little earlier saw her too. And she didn't want to appear brash or bold. She had never sung songs with a double meaning. In fact, she thought ruefully, I've only recently discovered what they mean. She came to a decision.

'You're right, Miss Jenkinson,' she said. 'So I won't do it. I'll sing two love songs, and finish with the mazurka, and I won't do the sauce.' She smiled. 'I'll leave that to the others.'

She was first into the dressing room that evening and sat alone in front of the spotted mirror, looking dispassionately at her face. Her skin was a creamy colour toning with her red hair, and the usual summer freckles on her nose had faded. Ronny's right: my features won't be seen from the back of the theatre. So, foundation cream to give me colour, and then I'll darken my eyebrows, she thought, picking up a pencil. And what colour for my eyes? Green – it's got to be green.

She glanced up as Ronny came in. 'Hello,' she said through the mirror. 'I'm putting on more make-up as you suggested.'

Ronny nodded. She looked glum. 'Good girl.' She sat down and put her feet up on the dressing shelf, her skirt falling around her calves. She gazed at Poppy. 'Did nobody tell you anything about stage life before you came to Brighton?'

Poppy paused in the act of outlining her eyes. 'No. I don't really know anyone from the theatre. I had my dance and singing teachers, but that's what they taught me – to dance and sing, and how to stand and how to breathe, but not about appearing in a production.'

'I can't believe that Dan took you on without any experience and sent you here to Brighton!' Ronny said. 'To sink or swim! It's so unlike him.'

'Perhaps he's just trying me out?' Poppy suggested.

Ronny shook her head. 'No, he wouldn't do that. He has his reputation to think of.' She gave a deep sigh. 'He must have great faith in you. Expectations! Here.' She swung her feet down and stood up. 'Let me show you how to do that.' She opened up her own make-up box and brought out a small container and brush. 'This is what you need for your eyes. Now keep very still so that it doesn't smudge.'

Poppy did as she was told and felt Ronny's light touch around her eyes.

'Try not to blink for a minute,' Ronny said, stepping back to view the effect. 'This is called kohl. Arab women use it to darken their eyes and stage people do too.'

Poppy looked in the mirror. Her eyes looked enormous.

'Now do your lashes if you haven't any false ones.' She peered closer at Poppy's face. 'Mmm. Perhaps you don't need them. Your lashes are long enough anyway.'

Ronny sat down again, opened her bag and drew out a cheroot. Poppy hadn't seen her smoke before. Ronny lit it and drew until the tip glowed. 'Want one?' she asked, seeing Poppy watching her.

'Oh, no, thank you. I don't – at least – I've never—'

'No?' Ronny's eyebrows rose. 'Well, no doubt you will before long. Still.' She knitted her eyebrows into a frown and sighed. 'Stay as sweet as you are for as long as you can.'

Poppy turned back to the mirror. She had half an hour to finish her make-up and get changed. 'Where's Ena?' she said, brushing rouge onto her cheeks. 'Isn't it getting late?'

'Probably.' Ronny drew again on the cheroot, then with it tight between her lips started to peel off her shoes and stockings. 'As for Ena,' she muttered. 'I neither know or care.'

'Oh.' Poppy drew the outline of her mouth with a red pencil, and then filled it in with scarlet. 'Have you had a row? My brother and I were always falling out when we were little, and we had arguments all the time until—'

'She's not my sister.' Ronny unfastened the buttons on her dress and let it slip to the floor. Then she picked it up and threw it over a chair. She put her hands on her hips and, clad only in her silk slip, surveyed her reflection in the mirror. She ran her hands over her flat stomach and turned to look at herself sideways. Then she sighed and turned to the rail where their dresses were hanging with a white sheet over them. 'We're not related.'

'You're not related?' Poppy stared. 'But you said that your parents were stage people!'

Ronny shook out her dress, teasing out the feathers. 'They are. Hers and mine.' She hung the dress at the end of the rail and came to sit in front of the mirror. 'We met when we were youngsters, about ten or eleven, and just starting out. We were in a dance troupe. Our parents knew each other and they put their heads together and suggested we join up as a double act.' She gave a shrug. 'We became the Terry Sisters. The public don't know we're not sisters,' she added. 'Only the stage folk do.'

'And now you've fallen out,' Poppy said anxiously. 'Is it serious?'

'Heavens no,' Ronny said. 'We argue all the time. We live in each other's pocket, that's the trouble. We've nothing in common. We wouldn't even be friends if it weren't for the act.'

'I see.' Poppy stepped into her dress and buttoned it up, then fastened on her red shoes. 'I hope she turns up in time.'

'She will.' Ronny stubbed out the cheroot. 'She has to. Nice shoes,' she commented. 'Very classy.'

'Handmade!' Poppy beamed and was gratified when Ronny gave a whistle. 'A friend made them. He's a shoemaker. He's just come to London to work.'

'I'm impressed!' Ronny said. 'An admirer?'

'Mm – yes!' she answered, but before she could explain the door burst open and Ena rushed in, followed by Nancy Martell who pushed past her, saying, 'I'm on before you. Outa my way.'

Ena dug her elbow into the other woman. 'Don't you push me, you old hag!'

'Who you calling an old hag?' Nancy lifted her hand and for a moment Poppy thought she was going to strike out at Ena.

'That's enough,' Ronny said sharply. 'There's a show starting in fifteen minutes. Fight outside if you want, but not in here, and not before the show.' She glanced at Poppy who had gasped. 'Take no notice, darling. Nance is always late and always blames everybody else for it. It's never her fault.'

Nancy transferred her glare to Ronny but didn't speak and took off her outdoor coat, skirt and blouse and sat in front of the mirror. She had pale fleshy shoulders and a thick neck. She covered her dark hair with a hairnet, rubbed foundation cream on her face, stuck on false ginger eyebrows and rouged her cheeks, then put lipstick on her top lip to make a bright cupid's bow. Then she carefully placed a curly ginger wig on her head before stepping into her costume. Ronny and Ena glanced at each other, raised their eyebrows at a common enemy and continued to prepare themselves for the evening performance.

Poppy stood waiting in the wings once more. She wasn't as nervous as she had been for the matinee; rather she was taut with pent-up excitement. She could hear the buzz from the audience and the occasional guffaws and shrieks of raucous laughter. The charabancs have arrived, she thought. Everybody's come for a good time. The tumbler, who was again going on first, and stretching his toes and limbs as before, gave her a grin. 'House full,' he said, peeping round the edge of the curtain.

Poppy took a breath. She hoped that Mr Bradshaw wouldn't be angry that she wasn't putting in any saucy songs, and mentally rehearsed what she would say to him if he was.

The orchestra began to play, the curtain rose and the show began. Poppy glanced over her shoulder when she heard soft footsteps, thinking it was Anthony, but it was Bill Baloney, the comic and top of the bill. He was a short, plump man, made plumper with padding under his large checked trousers. He stood with his thumbs tucked under his red braces, and with a sombre expression watched the tumbler perform.

'So who are you?' he asked in a low voice. 'A dancer?'

Everybody asks if I'm a dancer, Poppy thought; nobody ever asks if I'm a singer. 'Poppy Mazzini,' she said. 'I'm a singer and dancer.'

'Oh,' he muttered, his manner scornful, and moved back towards the dressing rooms.

Poppy blinked and a stagehand standing near shook his head. 'Take no notice,' he mouthed. 'He thinks he's a star!'

Jack Bradshaw again announced her as a rising star come fresh from northern England especially to entertain them, and Poppy ran onto the stage, her skirts fluttering. She gave a twirl round the stage and then broke into a song about sweethearts pledging their love beneath a silver moon. She followed with a romantic rendition of a popular love song, and finished with the mazurka, during which the audience clapped and stamped their feet and shouted '*Hoy!*'

She bowed and ran off, but was urged on again by Jack Bradshaw to take another bow. 'Good girl,' he said, as she ran back to the wings. 'They really liked that.' He seemed to have forgotten that he had asked her to sing something saucy.

She followed the same routine on Tuesday and Wednesday and on Thursday, shortly before the evening performance, someone tapped sharply on the dressing room door. 'Are you decent, ladies?' a man's voice called. The Terry Sisters both grinned and called in unison, 'When were we ever decent ladies?' whilst Nancy shouted, 'Wait,' and pulled a robe round her bare shoulders.

Poppy rose from her stool. She was dressed and ready for the stage. She opened the door and greeted Dan Damone who was standing with three bouquets of flowers in his hands. 'For my darling girls,' he said extravagantly, giving a bouquet to Poppy and one to each of the Terry Sisters, who both put up their cheeks to be kissed. Poppy blushed and thanked him.

'I've been getting wonderful reports,' he said. 'About all of you. And I shall take you all out to supper after the show, so don't go dashing away to your digs.' He turned to Poppy, and patted her under the chin with his hand, then winked and spoke softly. 'I need to talk to you, Poppy. Don't discuss any future plans with Bradshaw. I've things in mind for you.' He turned to leave, putting his hand on the door. 'I'll see you a little later. Good evening, Miss Martell.' He nodded politely to Nancy who looked at him with distaste and didn't answer.

Poppy felt elated. Dan had heard about her! How? Who had been to see her at the theatre who knew Dan? I know so little about what goes on. I'm as green as grass. But, she thought as a few minutes later she waited in the wings once more, I must do my very best tonight for he'll be out there watching me. He'll want to know whether I've forgotten that I'm a grocer's daughter, and am now a music hall performer.

CHAPTER TWENTY-TWO

Dan had booked a supper table at Orlando's for the four of them. By the smell of the coffee, Poppy was transported back to the time when Dan, Ronny and Ena had come to her father's coffee shop in Hull, though Orlando's was an intimate restaurant and not a grocery. Now wasn't the time to mention it, however, as she realized that this was to be a business meeting. She looked round at the other diners, and hoped that Anthony might be there. But he wasn't and she reflected that it was odd that Dan hadn't wanted to see him as well. After all, he was Anthony's agent too.

Ronny and Ena both looked very smart, though to Poppy's surprise, they still wore their stage make-up, though they had toned down their eyes a little. Ronny was wearing a high-necked classical dress in red and black, with a skirt which just showed her button boots, a black waistcoat and a red toque hat, whilst Ena wore pale blue muslin, cut low and trimmed with pearls, and a pearl necklace wound through her hair. Round her shoulders she wore a chinchilla wrap, which Poppy thought looked out of place in a small Italian restaurant. They shouted 'stage' from their very essence.

Poppy knew she looked young and immature beside them. Before coming out of the theatre, she had washed her face clean of make-up, and brushed her thick hair, using a ribbon to keep it in place. She wore a plain long skirt and peplum jacket in pale grey wool. But she was glad that she had dressed modestly, for some of the other diners looked rather disapprovingly at the unconventional Terry Sisters, especially when Ena lit up a small cigar.

Orlando brought them each a dish of hot tomato pie and another of crisp salad, produced a jug of red wine and murmured, '*Buon appetito.*'

'What I suggest,' Dan said, as he poured the wine for each of them, 'is that the Terry Sisters stay on at Bradshaw's right through the Christmas season until January.'

'Gawd, Dan. We'll freeze to death in Brighton!' Ena complained. 'Can't we go back to London?'

'I can't get you a booking, darling. I've been trying for weeks. Jack Bradshaw wants you, the audiences like you, what more can you ask?'

'It's fine,' Ronny said hurriedly. 'People still come to Brighton in the winter. We've got good diggings. Johnny'll be pleased to have us stay on. Who else will be playing, do you know?'

'I've heard that Bill Baloney's got a contract until the end of January and Jack's booked a magician. Oh, and a ventriloquist.'

Ena raised her eyebrows. 'Oh, well, they'll be good company for each other! And what about Tony Marino? How long is he staying? He always brings people in.'

Dan took a drink of wine. 'He's moving on at the end of this week. He's doing a tour of south coast towns, a week at each until Christmas.'

'We should have his luck,' Ena said sarcastically, her mouth turned down.

'We should have his talent!' was Ronny's rejoinder.

'Oh,' Poppy murmured. 'I didn't know.'

'Mmm?' Dan turned to her. 'Anthony doesn't stay long in one place,' he explained. 'He likes short contracts. Doesn't like to be tied down. He's off to Bournemouth next week.'

Who shall I talk to, Poppy thought? He's been so understanding and helpful. And besides, he's younger than the others. They're all so much older than me.

Dan and the Terry Sisters swapped theatre gossip whilst they were eating and Poppy listened intently to the tales of who had done what, who was popular and who had died on stage. She was aghast at this until she realized that they didn't mean that the performers had actually dropped dead, but that their acts were not well received and they were not asked back.

'So, Poppy!' Dan turned to her. Ena and Ronny had both gone

off to the ladies' powder room to 'freshen up' as they described it. 'How has the week gone? Do you think you can stand this kind of life, or is it too early to say?'

'I was very nervous to start with,' she told him. 'But I think I've got over that, or at least I will. But I'm unsure about what is expected of me. Mr Bradshaw asked me to sing something saucy, only I didn't and I don't think he noticed.' She thought of the old lady who had congratulated her and wished her good luck in her career. 'And, well, I want to be a singer of romantic songs, and I think I have the voice for them, but I've been told that the audiences want something merry.' She looked at him for reassurance. 'So I don't quite know what to do.'

'That's why I'm here,' he said quietly. 'To watch and assess you. And you were good tonight. Very good, and the audience liked you. This is what I propose.' He leaned towards her and lowered his voice still further. 'I'd like you to stay on here until the end of November, which is what? – another five, six weeks? You'll gain stage experience, and then I'm hoping to get you a small role in a Christmas pantomime. That will be theatre work, not music hall.' He gazed at her. 'What do you think?'

'That sounds exciting,' she said. 'Will I be singing in the pantomime?'

He nodded. 'Yes. But in this profession you always need good footwork.' He looked round as Ena and Ronny came across the room. 'But don't discuss it with anyone just yet,' he murmured to her. 'There's a good deal of jealousy about, even with people we think we know, and I have yet to do a deal with a theatre manager.'

Ronny's face was taut, as if she was cross about something and trying not to show it, but Ena was flushed and defiant and as she approached the table she casually ran her fingers across the back of Dan's neck. He started and shrugged them off, glancing up at her, then looking away.

Goodness, Poppy thought, observing the interaction. I do believe Ena is sweet on Dan, but he doesn't return the feeling. She glanced at Ronny, who was glowering at Ena. Perhaps Ronny is jealous, or perhaps Dan prefers Ronny. She looked from one to another, trying to assess the atmosphere between them and feeling only tension.

'Well, ladies. Time you were all tucked up in bed.' Dan called for the bill and rose from the table. 'It's been good to be here and see how successful you are. Look in tomorrow's paper,' he added. 'There'll be a review of the show. *Grazie mille,* Orlando,' he said to the proprietor, who was waiting with their coats. 'A perfect meal as always. Do you think you can get a cab for the ladies?'

'It's not far. We can walk,' Ena said, but Dan, without looking at her, said quickly, 'No, I wouldn't dream of letting you walk at this time of night, and I'm too dead tired to escort you. A cab it is.' He fished in his pocket for coins to pay the driver.

Poppy bit her lip as Dan helped her on with her jacket and she looked up at him. There was more she would have liked to ask. He hadn't answered her question as to whether she should continue with her love songs; the idea of pantomime appealed to her and she wondered which theatre it would be, and which town. She had seen one a few years ago, a comic opera of Dick Whittington. 'Erm,' she said hesitatingly. 'What about – I mean, who will pay me?' She blushed as she asked, but she had to know. Her father's money was getting low.

'Oh! Sorry, Poppy. Yes, of course.' He was flustered. 'You must think me hopeless, and I am; that's why I keep Dora.' He took a slip of notepaper out of his pocket. 'I've negotiated with Bradshaw. He'll pay you every week. Don't let him forget! Dear girls,' he said to the Terry Sisters. 'Keep Jack up to scratch, will you? Make sure he pays on the dot every Saturday.'

'As if we'd let him forget!' Ronny said scathingly. 'Some of these managers think we don't need to eat.'

Orlando came back. He'd been outside to whistle for their transport. 'Thank you for coming, ladies. *Buona notte,*' he said to Poppy. 'Please come again.'

'*Si.*' She smiled. '*Grazie. Arrivederci.*'

The three of them travelled in an awkward silence. Poppy could feel the tension between Ronny and Ena and although she made a few feeble attempts at conversation, there was no response from either of them, so she gave up and stared out of the cab window at the white surf lashing the shore.

Just before they reached Mrs Johnson's house, Ena turned to Poppy. 'So what's Dan got lined up for you? Are you staying until January? Or is he sending you on elsewhere? Bradshaw usually likes to change the bottom of the bill acts every week.'

Poppy felt sure that Ena didn't mean the remark to be derogatory, yet that was how it sounded to her. 'Until the end of November,' she said in a small voice. 'I don't know what else after that.' And if I did, Dan told me not to say, she thought. So I won't.

Ronny seemed to guess that she was hurt. 'You won't always be at the bottom of the bill,' she said kindly as the cab drew up outside Mrs Johnson's gate. 'You're doing just fine. You've a lovely voice and a great stage presence.'

Ena swished up the path towards the house, but Ronny hung back, waiting for Poppy. 'But I'm not sure if you're right for the music hall,' she said thoughtfully.

'What do you mean?' Poppy stood stock-still and looked at her. 'Not right?'

'Well, for the music hall you need to sharpen up a bit; play to the audience, you know – tease the men, as well as pleasing the women.'

'Be a bit cheeky?' Poppy said with a sinking heart.

'Yes, that's it. A bit of a wink, a wiggle of your hips, a glimpse of an ankle, that kind of thing.'

'Yes,' Poppy murmured . . . 'I see. Thank you.'

'On the other hand.' Ronny paused and looked at her before entering the house. There was a sea mist hovering about them, and Ronny's make-up was starting to run. 'On the other hand, if I'm honest, you'll do well just as you are. You look young, fresh and appealing.' She sighed and pushed the door open. A smell of kippers and coffee drifted out. 'Which is, of course, exactly what you are.'

Mrs Johnson was in her parlour, dressed in a wool dressing gown over her nightdress. Her hair was unpinned and hanging down her back, though she wore a pink cotton cap on her head. 'Would you like tea, ladies,' she asked, 'or chocolate? The kettle's hon the boil.'

Ena didn't answer her but immediately started haranguing Ronny about something she had said during supper. 'Don't you tell me,' Ronny snapped back. 'Just watch your own language and what you're doing when we're out. Don't forget that people know us!' She shook a finger at Ena. 'It's easy enough to get a bad reputation.'

'Now, girls,' Mrs Johnson said. 'Save your harguments for the morning. Tea, dear?' she asked Poppy, who was edging out of the room. Poppy shook her head. 'Take a cup up with you, then,' Mrs Johnson suggested. 'I've just made it, so it's nice and 'ot. Shame to waste it.'

Poppy gave a weak smile and came back in as Ronny said, 'You know you're wasting your time with him! Keep up with little tricks like that and we'll lose him as an agent.'

'Little tricks! What little tricks?' Ena shrieked, and Poppy cringed and tried to keep her eyes on Mrs Johnson as she poured the tea, and not look at Ena or Ronny.

'Everybody saw you!' Ronny hollered back. 'Running your fingers round his neck! God, how embarrassing!'

'I did not!' Ena whirled about. 'Did you see me, Poppy? Did I do anything untoward? There, see! Poppy didn't see anything and she was sitting right next to him. All I did was make a friendly gesture and if anybody wants to read something into that . . . !' She bent her head and fumbled in her bag for a cheroot, and when she raised her head Poppy saw that there were tears in her eyes. She lit the small cigar and inhaled. 'God,' she muttered resentfully, 'but you're a bitch sometimes, Veronica.'

Ronny stared at Ena, and Poppy took the teacup and saucer from Mrs Johnson who sighed and shook her head. 'It's for your own good, Ena,' Ronny said at last. 'You know he's not interested. Leave the poor chap alone.'

Ena gazed into the low fire and drew on the cigar. 'I will have coffee, Johnny,' she said, her voice grating. 'Two sugars.'

'I'll say good night, then,' Poppy said quietly. 'See you in the morning.'

'Oh,' Mrs Johnson exclaimed. 'I nearly forgot! Some letters came in the second post.' She went to her sideboard and picked up two envelopes and handed them to Poppy.

'Thank you.' Poppy looked down at the writing. One was from her father; she recognized his bold style. The other she wasn't sure about. She'd open them upstairs, privately. Not down here in this bitter atmosphere. 'Good night.'

Only Mrs Johnson replied. Ronny nodded her head, but Ena continued to gaze into the fire.

'I can't help it,' Poppy heard her murmur. 'I just can't help it.'

How sad, Poppy thought as she climbed the stairs. She loves him, and I suppose he loves someone else. 'I can't stop loving him,' she hummed softly, then, 'I can't stop loving you,' and rubbed the envelopes between her fingers. Then she took a breath. Suppose this is from Charlie! Oh, please! Let it be from Charlie! She took the last few steps two at a time, almost tripping over her skirt.

The fire in the grate was very low, but she riddled it with the poker and put another piece of coal on it. Then she lit the gas mantle on the ceiling lamp and adjusted the thin chain so that it burned brighter. She sat on the floor near the fire and opened not her father's letter but the other one. It was from Charlie.

'Dearest Poppy,' it began and she almost swooned. 'Dearest Poppy,' she breathed. 'I'm coming to Brighton on Saturday afternoon with some other fellows, and shall come to see you at the theatre in the evening. I've told these chaps about you and they can't wait to see you, and neither, of course, can I. Your good friend, Charlie. PS Perhaps we can have supper afterwards?'

'Oh!' She wrapped her arms round herself and squeezed. 'He's coming. He's coming! He can't wait to see me! Oh, bliss. Bliss!'

She got up and danced round the small room, holding his letter. 'He's told his friends about me! And he wants to take me to supper. We could go to Orlando's.' Oh, maybe not. He isn't very keen on Italian food. But somewhere nice. She cast around in her head for somewhere they could go. I'll ask Anthony, she thought. He'll know.

She gave a deep satisfied sigh and then returned to sit by the fire and read the letter from her father. It was short and to the point. He was well, he said, and things were much the same at home. Nan and Lena were having their usual disagreements. At least, he said, Lena was having disagreements with Nan. He'd had to chastise Albert about leaving the door unlocked and there had been a short note from Tommy, who was in the Baltic, but no more news from him than that.

He concluded by saying he hoped she was enjoying her new life and added jokingly that he was expecting her to become a star of fame and fortune so that she could look after her pa when he became old and decrepit.

There seemed to be an air of wistfulness about the letter, yet she couldn't quite put her finger on it. It was cheerful enough, but there was something between the lines, some pathos underlying his breezy words.

'He's missing us,' she murmured. 'Tommy and I have left him alone and there's no-one there to love him.'

She slowly started to undress, then she picked up Charlie's letter and read it through again. 'He's coming on Saturday.' She couldn't contain the joy which unfolded within her. 'He's coming on Saturday and can't wait to see me!'

CHAPTER TWENTY-THREE

After the Friday matinee, Jack Bradshaw called Poppy into his office. 'I'm making some changes for tonight and tomorrow,' he said. 'I want you to open the second half. The juggler will go next, then Tony Marino, and the Terry Sisters will go on before the comic. And don't forget to spice up your act a bit. That's what the Friday and Saturday audiences like: a bit of spice. We've some competition over at the Alhambra; don't forget, they've got some big names over there.'

I'm opening the second half! 'Thank you, Mr Bradshaw,' she said calmly. 'I'll catch Miss Jenkinson and discuss it with her.'

She almost collided with Anthony as she came out of the office. 'I'm opening the second half,' she said excitedly. 'Mr Bradshaw has just asked me!'

He nodded and smiled. 'I know. He told me. Want to come for coffee?'

'Dan Damone told me that you're leaving the show tomorrow,' she said as they walked along the street towards a coffee house. 'I didn't know. I thought – well, I thought you'd be staying longer.' She glanced up at him. 'I'll miss you,' she said shyly. 'You've been so helpful to me.'

He took her elbow and guided her into a small and steamy café and ordered a pot of coffee.

'I'll miss you too,' he said, helping her off with her coat. 'When Dan asked me if I'd watch out for this new young singer and help her along, I thought I was letting myself in for nerves, tears and tantrums, and—'

'Dan asked you to watch out for me?' She was astonished. 'Why did he do that?'

He shrugged. 'He's like that.' He gave a little frown. 'I'm not sure if he'd promised your father he'd find someone to keep an eye on you—'

'So when you asked me to visit the Royal Pavilion, it was because Dan had asked you to keep me entertained and not because you wanted to go? You were doing him a favour!' She felt piqued; she'd thought it was because they were going to be friends.

'No!' he said earnestly. 'That wasn't the reason. Dan wanted me to show you the ropes, to let you know you could come to me if you had any problems.' His face was set as he realized what she was implying. 'I asked you to go to the Pavilion because I've always wanted to visit it, and because I thought you might like it too. Not because I was asked to. It was nothing to do with Dan.'

'Sorry,' she said, lowering her voice and her head. 'You must have thought me a nuisance to begin with, though? Especially when Mr Bradshaw got my name wrong and we went round changing the posters.'

'I never thought you a nuisance,' he insisted. 'We had fun together, didn't we? Poppy!' He reached across the table and clutched her hand. 'I never thought you a nuisance! Honest!' He gave her a reassuring grin. 'I'd have found all kinds of excuses not to be with you if I'd thought that!'

'Well, thank you anyway,' she said, not entirely convinced.

'Tell you what,' he said, releasing her hand. 'Just to prove it, shall we have supper at Orlando's tomorrow night? I'm leaving early on Sunday morning – what?' he asked, on seeing her expression change.

'Oh!' she breathed. 'I can't! A friend . . . a friend of my brother's – the one I told you about – is coming to the show.' She bit her lip in frustration, torn between having supper with Anthony on his last night, and wanting, desperately to see Charlie. 'He's asked me out to supper.'

'Ah!' Disappointment showed on his face for a second, but then he gave her a quick smile. 'Well, never mind. We'll meet up again, I expect.' He sipped his coffee and glanced at her over the rim of the cup. 'Is he, er, special? He's not just a friend of your brother's?'

She was embarrassed and looked down at the tablecloth. It was white with yellow spots. Here and there were tea and coffee stains and she thought that Nan would never have allowed that at Mazzini's. 'I've known him a long time.' She traced round one of the stains with her finger. 'He still thinks I'm a child.'

He kept his gaze on her face. 'And you – how do you think of him?' When she didn't answer, he said softly, 'Ah! You love him?'

She nodded, pressing her lips together. 'Yes,' she said softly. 'I always have. I think of him whenever I sing love songs.'

'I see.' He considered, tapping his lip with his finger. 'When you sing "Forever True", do you sing that for him?'

'Yes,' she whispered.

'But in the song you're asking do you love me as I love you? It's a question,' he said. 'Don't you know the answer?'

'No.' She swallowed hard. 'He still thinks of me as his friend's little sister, although once—'

'Well, you can't blame him for that, Poppy,' he interjected. 'You are young; though I'm not saying that you're too young to know what love is.' He gazed thoughtfully at her. 'But men have to be careful around vulnerable young women.' A slight smile hovered about his mouth. 'Especially the beautiful ones.'

She blushed. 'Now you're embarrassing me,' she said. 'I've not spoken about Charlie to anyone else before,' she admitted. 'But you understand, don't you?'

He nodded and pursed his lips. 'Yes. That's the romantic in me. I'm a songwriter, don't forget.'

She gave a deep sigh. 'Will you write a song for me?'

'For you?' he asked. 'Or for Charlie?'

'It's the same thing,' she murmured.

He drew his fingers through the lock of hair that always seemed to fall over one eye. 'A love song? Unrequited love? Or reciprocated?' His brown eyes were soft and gentle as he gazed at her. 'Music is often more appealing if it speaks of lost love, or of tender feelings that are not mutual or returned.' He gave a wistful smile and looked away. 'That's the trend at the moment, anyway.'

'Well, I don't know then,' she said. 'I can only tell you how I feel. How I've always felt.'

He nodded slowly, and then said lightly, 'Shall I get to meet this paragon? This idol who has stolen your heart?'

'Oh yes,' she said enthusiastically. 'I'll introduce you. Charlie's bringing some of his friends along. After the show?'

'Perhaps,' he agreed. 'Perhaps so. Come on then, Poppy.' He called for the bill. 'I must go and rehearse for an hour.'

'How committed you are,' she said. 'You rehearse so often. That's why your playing is so perfect.'

'Come with me,' he said impulsively. 'You can practise too.'

'Oh!' Poppy put her hand to her mouth. 'I was supposed to speak to Miss Jenkinson about the change of programme tonight!'

'Naughty girl,' he admonished. 'First and foremost you must always be ready for your performance.' He shook his head at her. 'Don't ever leave your rehearsal until the last minute. The musicians can't guess what you want from them. Perfection is what you must strive for.'

'Yes, Anthony.' It was a reproof, if a mild one. 'I won't forget again.'

'You mustn't.' He took her arm as they stepped outside. A wind was blowing off the sea and it buffeted them together. 'You can be a star, Poppy. Top of the tree. But it's a hard climb.' He hung on to his hat and Poppy's skirt flapped around her calves. He looked down at her. 'And don't get waylaid by love.'

The theatre was empty apart from the stage door keeper who let them in, and a cleaning woman in the auditorium. There was just one light burning on the stage, and Anthony pushed the piano towards it and then lit a single candle in a candelabra and placed it on top. 'There,' he said, giving Poppy some song sheets, and sat at the keyboard. 'We'll set the scene. A romantic evening.' He pointed to the candelabra. 'The light of the moon. And a young man or woman in love.' He ran his fingers gently over the keys. 'Choose the one you'd like to sing.'

'I don't know these,' she said, coming towards the piano. 'I haven't heard them before.'

He didn't answer, but played a soft refrain, and she started to hum and then sing the words of the first song. 'Take away this loneliness, take away this aching heart / Wrap your love round me so tight, let your love stay here this night.'

Then another which began, 'Once I thought she loved me.

Once I had such plans. Now she is contented in some other lover's hands.'

She paused and glanced across at him. His head was bent as he fingered the melody. 'These are your songs, aren't they, Anthony?' she said quietly. 'Your words and music?' She noticed that all the lyrics were of lost or unrequited love, but there was something else which struck a chord. She didn't quite know what it was, but it was a nostalgic memory, teasing and tantalizing her.

He nodded and went on playing snippets of popular themes, improvising with his own personal adaptations.

'"Forever True"!' she said suddenly. 'That's yours! Now I recognize your style!'

He looked up at her and nodded. 'Sing it then, Poppy,' he said softly. 'I've never heard anyone else sing it the way you can. You've made it your own.'

And so she did. She took a breath and, sustaining the sweet and appealing harmony, lifted her voice at the last to fill the theatre with a heart-rending emotion and a clear ringing plea. The cleaning woman stopped what she was doing and leaned on her mop. The stage door keeper came and stood with his arms folded, and Jack Bradshaw, coming through the unlocked stage door, chewed on his unlit cigar as he listened.

For Poppy it was the ultimate triumph, singing the song she loved with the man who had composed it; the man who surely had felt love in the same way as she did. Who had perhaps been too young and had lost that love; unlike her, who was determined to keep it.

Her eyes were shining as she finished and her lips trembled. She couldn't speak and neither could Anthony as he gazed at her, before he turned back to the piano and started to play. It was a haunting little melody and he didn't know where it came from; but a refrain ran through his head and he sang in a husky whisper, 'The man's a fool – if he doesn't love you; the man's a fool if he doesn't care / So sweet a face my eyes embrace – la lah, la la lah, hmm, hmm.'

'Will you write a song for me, Anthony?' Poppy came over to the piano, her voice catching with emotion.

He smiled up at her and murmured, 'I rather think I already have.'

CHAPTER TWENTY-FOUR

'Sing like that tonight and I'll be giving you star billing.' Jack Bradshaw came to the front of the stage. 'Forget what I said about spicing it up.' He rolled the cigar around his lips. 'The Terry Sisters can do that. Here.' He pulled a newspaper from under his arm and handed it to her. 'You've got a good review. Page four.'

'You were wonderful, darlin',' the cleaning woman called up to her. 'Both of you. You should team up.'

Jack Bradshaw glared at her. 'What are you then?' he bellowed. 'Some kind of critic?'

'Aye, I am,' she retaliated. 'Course I am! Who do you think comes to your the-ayter of a Friday and Saturday night? Me and my pals, that's who – and we pay,' she added. 'Don't get no free pass even though I work 'ere.'

'Well you've just had a free performance,' he grunted. 'So get on with doing whatever it is I pay you to do.' He turned to Poppy. 'I'm going to telegraph Damone and see if you can stay on over Christmas. I'll give you top billing. Well' – he chomped on his cigar again – 'not top, the comic is top, but you can go on second from top. How does that sound?'

From the corner of her eye she saw Anthony shake his head. 'I'll have to be guided by Mr Damone,' she said. 'I don't know what plans he has.'

'I'll increase your salary!'

'I can't make the decision, Mr Bradshaw,' she said. 'You'll have to ask my agent.'

He grunted but didn't argue. Anthony gathered his music and

he and Poppy walked out of the theatre together. 'Aren't you going to look at the review?' he asked.

'I hardly dare,' she said, but he gave her a nudge and she turned the news pages until she reached page four. 'Here we are,' she murmured, and read: 'Bradshaw's Theatre. In his usual manner, Mr Jack Bradshaw has got together a creditable company of popular artistes to entertain and amuse. Top of the bill is Mr Bill Baloney who aroused great mirth and hilarity with his jokes and *double entendre.* The tenor, Mr Thomas Tearle, though slightly reedy in places, gave a passable performance, whilst the Terry Sisters performed with their usual aplomb. I have to say, and this is purely personal, that in my opinion Miss Nancy Martell should try some new material if she wants to raise a laugh, as we have heard her sketches several times before. Mr Anthony Marino is always welcome in Brighton, and his piano playing was superb as always, and we are honoured to have him during his tour, but the star of the show at last night's performance was undoubtedly the sixteen-year-old Yorkshire girl, Miss Poppy Mazzini. If her singing didn't bring a tear to your eye, then you're either too old or too young for love.'

'Whew!' Anthony exhaled. 'How about that, Poppy? Didn't I say you'd be a star?'

'Goodness,' she murmured. Then, embarrassed, she said feebly, 'They've got my age wrong.'

'But they got your name right!' Anthony said playfully. 'That's what's important. Don't split hairs! I must go,' he added. 'We've got an hour and then we're back on stage. Go and gargle or something, but rest your voice.' He hesitated, and then said, 'Don't mention the review to the others, not unless they do. Performers can be a bit touchy.'

'But you're not,' she said.

'I'm an old hand.' He smiled. 'I don't take too much notice. I know when I'm playing well. I don't need a newspaper critic to tell me.'

Poppy took a walk by the sea and then went for a cup of tea and a sandwich. She felt exultant about the review and kept reading it and smiling to herself. I must buy another copy and send it to Pa, she thought. He'll be so thrilled.

She walked back to the theatre and carefully folded the paper and put it into her bag. She was again first into the dressing room but Ronny and Ena came in soon after. She could hear them arguing as they came along the corridor. 'What does he mean?' Ena said as she opened the door. 'Their usual aplomb! What's that supposed to mean? Ah, here she is!' she said, seeing Poppy. 'The star of the show.'

Poppy looked up, a feigned expression of surprise on her face. 'What?'

'Don't tell me you haven't read the review,' Ena said. 'Of course you have! Rushed out to buy up half a dozen copies, I expect.'

'N-no. Mr Bradshaw gave me a copy,' Poppy said in a low voice. 'I'd forgotten that it was going to be in.'

'And he'll have offered you top billing, I expect?' Ena said sarcastically. 'That's what he always does with new talent. Puts them top of the bill and they just can't cope with it.'

The door crashed open and Nancy Martell rushed in. She had a rolled-up copy of the newspaper in her hand. 'Have you seen this? Who does he think he is? Jumped up little journalist. What does he know about knockabout comedy? I've played this act up and down the coast. If it's good enough for Bournemouth it's good enough for Brighton.'

She didn't notice Ena and Ronny mouthing a parody of the last sentence, but Poppy did. She stifled a laugh, but Nancy heard it. 'Think you're so clever, don't you?' she snarled. 'Well, when you've been on the boards as long as I have, you can be called a star. Until then you're just a flash in the pan! I'll show 'em fresh material,' she said fiercely, throwing off her coat and letting it fall on the floor. 'I'll give them something to titter about.'

'For heaven's sake, Nance,' Ronny cut in. 'It's only a bleeding little tinpot paper! We've all had bad reviews at some time or other. You just have to rise above them.'

'That's what I'm going to do,' Nancy muttered. 'I'll give them something to think about tonight.'

She took off her skirt and bodice, and stepped into the padded stage costume, buttoning it up over her ample figure. Then she sat down and proceeded to put on her usual dark foundation cream, and stuck on the ginger eyebrows on top of her own dark ones, but instead of putting the hairnet over her scraped back dark hair she peeled off the hair, revealing a completely bald pate. She turned to look at the three of them, and said, in a deep masculine voice, 'So what about that, ladies? That'll give them something to write about, won't it?' She turned to Poppy. 'They'll not be talking about you tonight, darlin'. They'll be talking about Mr Norman Martell who's been fooling 'em all these years.'

Ena stood up. She was wearing only her slip and silk stockings. 'Get out!' she shouted, reaching for a wrap. 'Get out! You perverted vulgar hypocrite! How dare you come in here?'

'Hark at her!' Nance bawled. 'You ain't showing nuffink I ain't seen before, and besides, I wouldn't be interested. And if I was,' he spat out, 'I wouldn't look twice at you!'

Ronny got up from her chair and taking one long stride she smacked Nancy Martell across the face. 'I don't care who you are or what you get up to, but you don't belong in here! This is the female dressing room. Go and tell Bradshaw you want your own room if the men don't want you in theirs.'

Martell flushed, but didn't reply or retaliate. He scooped the make-up, the hairbrush, the pins and the ginger wig into the voluminous apron he wore round his waist and stormed out of the room, leaving the door wide open.

'Well!' Ronny sat back in her chair. 'I just can't believe it! Ten years we've known that woman and never an inkling!'

'I've always thought there was something odd about her!' Ena scowled and wrinkled her nose. 'But I don't understand. There are plenty of men dressing up as dames. Nobody doubts who they are. Why would he pass himself off as a woman acting a woman, and an ugly one at that?' She shivered and pulled her wrap round her. 'He's in the wrong box, isn't he? Do you think the men know? My Gawd,' she choked. 'Can't you see the headlines?'

'Yes, I can,' Ronny said quietly. 'And it won't do for it to get out that we've been sharing a dressing room with a man! Heaven knows, our reputations are fragile enough.'

Poppy stared at them. The incident, raw and ugly, had unnerved her. Thank goodness she had always been changed into her stage clothes by the time Nance Martell came into the dressing room. She – he – was always late and now Poppy wondered whether he was giving everyone the chance to be fully dressed before he came in. He didn't look like a man, she thought. In his ordinary clothes with his wig on, he looked like a woman, if a rather broad-shouldered one. His skin was soft and pale. Suddenly she felt sorry for him and she thought of what her father had said about meeting people who were not run of the mill like them. Well, Nancy Martell was certainly not like anyone she had met before.

The evening show went on as usual, except that Nancy Martell didn't appear, being 'indisposed', Jack Bradshaw announced to the audience. Poppy opened the second half and sang an extra song, and the Terry Sisters did another dance routine to make up for the comedian's absence.

Bradshaw told them later that he had persuaded Martell not to disclose his secret, as the last thing they wanted at the theatre was the police descending on them, tracing the scent of a scandal. 'They won't think it amusing that we thought Martell was a woman,' he told the assembled company. 'This has got to be kept quiet.'

'Where's he gone?' Bill Baloney asked. 'Is he coming back?'

'No,' Bradshaw said. 'I've suggested he changes his name and starts again as a character comedian.' He drew on his cigar. 'But he'll not be coming back here.'

They were all subdued. The discovery that Martell was really a man masquerading as a woman could have closed down the theatre and they would all have been looking for other bookings; but Bradshaw was sharp and, immediately after asking Martell to leave, he took on a local youth who could whistle like a bird and was available for the Saturday performances.

'Who'll take your place, Anthony?' Poppy asked him after the Saturday matinee. The posters hadn't yet been changed and wouldn't be until Sunday morning.

'Some fellow with performing dogs,' he said. 'Apparently they can count and sing.' He grinned. 'Though I don't think they can play the piano.'

'I feel as if I've been here for ever,' Poppy said. 'I can't believe it's only been a week. So much has happened. And I feel as if I've known you such a long time. I wish you were staying,' she said wistfully.

They were leaning over the rails, gazing at the sea. Poppy's hair was blowing across her face, and Anthony brushed it back to look at her as he answered. 'You'll be all right. And the time will pass quickly enough to the end of November, and maybe we'll meet up again when you're next in London?'

She nodded thoughtfully. Dan must have told him he'd asked her to stay at Bradshaw's until the end of November, because she hadn't.

'Poppy?' He bent his head to look at her. 'What?'

'Did Dan tell you I was leaving in November?' She pouted. 'Did you know before I did?'

'Ah!' he said. 'So I'm found out!' He rubbed his chin. 'Confession time! I've known Dan a lot of years,' he said, 'and because I don't stay in one place for very long I get to see other performers. Dan uses me as a sort of scout, and I let him know who's doing well.'

He put his finger under her chin so that she would look at him, for she'd turned her head away. 'Don't sulk,' he admonished. 'I'm not a spy! I telegraphed him after your performance on Monday evening and told him how good you were and that Bradshaw would probably ask you to stay on. I also told him,' he added, 'that you deserved somewhere better.'

'Oh,' she said, mollified. 'I'm so green, aren't I? I don't know how things are done.'

'After only a week, I think you've learned a lot.' He smiled. 'Think how much more confident you were for today's matinee than you were on Monday!'

'Yes,' she agreed. 'I am.' Then she gave a great sigh of pleasure. 'And then tonight,' she said, 'Charlie is coming to see the show!'

'Ah!' he said. 'Yes. Charlie!' His expression became serious. 'Don't let him influence you, Poppy. Remember you're now a professional. You're not just singing to impress him. There's the rest of the audience too!'

It was a reproof and for a moment she was annoyed that he thought she might forget everyone else but Charlie. But I might have done, she considered. I might have. She looked up at him. 'I won't forget.'

'Good girl,' he said, and bent to kiss her cheek and smiled at her surprise. 'That's in case I don't have a chance to say goodbye.'

She was nervous again before the evening performance. It was a full house and a rowdy one. She went into the wings to watch part of the first half and could hear the banter of the audience. They whistled along with the young whistler, though he wasn't deterred, and they called out encouragement to the tumbler as he performed his routine. The tenor was heckled and quite put off his music.

At the interval Poppy went back to the dressing room and changed her slippers for the red shoes and pinned a flower in her hair. The Terry Sisters were dressed and sitting smoking, making a thick fug in the room. Both had a glass of wine in their hands. A knock came on the door. 'Flowers for Miss Mazzini,' the door keeper called out.

'Ooh!' Ronny and Ena exclaimed, sitting up. 'An admirer!'

Poppy went to the door and took the bouquet of red and cream roses, sweet peas and carnations. A card was slipped inside. She took a trembling breath. It had to be from Charlie.

'With best wishes for tonight,' she read. 'With love from Anthony.'

'Oh!' Tears sprang to her eyes. Anthony! How sweet and kind. Her mouth trembled. But nothing from Charlie.

She rushed back to the door. 'Wait,' she called to the door keeper. 'Is there anything else? A note or anything?'

He shook his head. 'Nothing else, miss. Sorry.'

'Not what you were expecting, dearie?' Ena drew lazily on her cigar. 'Think yourself lucky to get anything at all.'

'We used to,' Ronny declared. 'When we were first starting out. Who're they from then?' she asked. 'Not the gentleman who makes the shoes?'

'No,' she said softly. 'They're from Anthony Marino. He's leaving the show tonight.'

They both raised their eyebrows. 'Very nice too,' Ronny said. 'He's taken a shine to you, obviously. He usually keeps himself to himself. A bit aloof, you know.'

'That's because he's not really one of us.' Ena looked at herself in the mirror and tapped the corners of her mouth with a fingertip. 'He's concert hall, isn't he? Not music hall like we are.'

Poppy buried her face in the bouquet to hide her disappointment. It smelt sweet and heady. The flowers were beautiful, even if they weren't from Charlie.

'Five minutes, Miss Mazzini!' A rap on the door and the muffled tones of the callboy alerted her.

'Thank you,' she called back.

'This is your first Saturday night, isn't it?' Ronny asked, cupping her chin in her hand. Her fingernails were long and red. 'Well, all the best. They're in a merry old mood out there.'

Poppy walked towards the wings. The stagehands were in position to open the fire curtain. Jack Bradshaw, in a silk top hat, tailcoat and a white cravat, stood waiting. She had told Miss Jenkinson that she wouldn't dance the mazurka, but would save her breath and energy for the songs. She would start with 'Come Pretty May', then the popular sweetheart song, and finally 'Forever True'. Miss Jenkinson had told her that next week she had asked the violinist to accompany her.

She heard the opening bars of the first song and the stage-hands, looking in her direction, began to open the curtain. Jack Bradshaw stepped forward and the audience whooped. He bowed. 'Ladies and gentlemen. We have many fine performers entertaining you this evening, and none finer than the talented – *Miss – Poppy – Mazzini.*'

He held out his hand and as Poppy ran onto the stage he backed away behind the curtains. The audience cheered, the most noise coming from the gallery. 'Poppy – Poppy! Come on, give us a love song!' They were men's voices and she had to raise her own voice to be heard. 'Shh,' some of the audience admonished, but Poppy smiled and smiled and continued with the song.

There was tremendous applause as she finished, and again she could hear voices from the gallery. 'She's a friend of ours, ain't you, Poppy?' someone called and again they were shushed. She sang the second song and they were quieter until she was finished, then applause and cheers broke out again. She took a bow. 'For my final song,' she began, and by the piano in the orchestra pit she detected some movement, 'I would like to sing "Forever True", composed by Anthony Marino.'

She heard the familiar opening notes, but she was now attuned to Miss Jenkinson's playing, and it wasn't hers. She looked down and saw Anthony sitting at the piano. He half rose and gave her a slight bow. She took a breath. He was going to play for her! What a compliment!

He ran his fingers over the keys, playing the opening bars, waiting for her to begin. She closed her eyes. 'La la, la la, la la-ah, hold me close forever more.' She floated round the stage. 'La la, la la, la la-ah. Do you love me as I love you . . .'

There was a hush as she sang and Anthony, glancing up, kept in perfect tempo with her. They came to the end of the song and for a second there was silence. Then a great whoosh of applause rang out, as the audience stamped their feet and stood up and cheered. Poppy bowed and backed away, then came forward and bowed again and this time held up her hands for them to be quiet.

'Ladies and gentlemen.' With a graceful flourish she held out her arm towards Anthony, who rose from the piano. 'Mr Anthony – Marino!'

To tumultuous applause, Anthony bowed to the audience, and the applause grew to wild cheers as he turned to Poppy, bowed, then, smiling, lifted the tips of his fingers to his lips and blew her a kiss.

CHAPTER TWENTY-FIVE

Poppy was flushed and excited as she came off stage. Never, not in her most wishful moments, had she ever expected such an ovation. And it's because of Anthony! What a performer! And blowing that kiss, that was the final flourish. The audience would read so much into that, not realizing that he is the ultimate professional and knows what they want!

She could still hear the house chanting, and the next act, the juggler, was refusing to go on until they had quietened down. Bradshaw was dashing around rearranging the acts. He followed Poppy to the dressing room and asked the Terry Sisters to go on after the juggler, and then he would put Anthony Marino on after them, just before the final act, Bill Baloney.

Ena objected vehemently. 'We're booked for next to the top,' she said. 'Why should we change?'

'It's just for tonight,' Bradshaw wheedled. 'This is Marino's final performance. Next week we'll be back to normal, I promise. If I put him on before you, they'll be shouting out for Poppy and we'll never get you on. We'll overrun.'

'Just for tonight?' Ronny asked. She too was annoyed at the change-round, though she saw the sense of it.

'Just for tonight. You know you'll please them.' He cracked his face into a thin smile. 'Give them a bit of sauce,' he said. 'You know, tease them a bit, a few wiggles. You know what they like. Then you're a complete contrast to Marino.'

Poppy slunk to her chair by the mirror and watched as Ena and Ronny made final adjustments to their headdresses, looked at themselves in the mirror, then walked out of the room. Neither of them spoke to her and she felt disappointed. But then, she thought, they have to concentrate on their own act, not bother about me.

There was a knock on the open door and Anthony stood there. 'Well, Miss Mazzini,' he crowed jubilantly. 'Did we knock them cold?'

She jumped up and running to the door she flung her arms round him. 'Thank you,' she cried. 'Thank you, thank you, thank you!'

'Miss Mazzini.' The stage door keeper interrupted them. 'Here's a gen'leman to see you. Mr Charles Chandler with friends. Did I do right bringing 'em?'

'Oh!' she said, and Anthony backed away as Charlie and behind him two other men came up along the corridor.

'Charlie! Oh, how wonderful to see you.' Her face was wreathed in smiles. 'No, Anthony – please don't go for a moment. I want you to meet Charlie. I've told you about him.'

'Indeed. How do you do?' Anthony said formally, and stretched out his hand to Charlie. 'Very nice to meet you, Chandler. As Miss Mazzini says, she has spoken of you.' He turned to Poppy. 'I'm on next. I must go.' He gave her a smile, which didn't quite reach his eyes. 'Goodbye.'

'Anthony!' she said. 'Will I see you before you leave—?' But he was gone, giving a final wave of his hand as he walked down the corridor.

'My word, Poppy!' At her invitation, Charlie and his friends followed her into the dressing room. He put his arm round her. 'What a star! I had no idea.' He kissed her cheek. 'I told my friends here – this is Bertie Fletcher, and Roger Doyle – I told them we were going to see some talent tonight, and . . .'

'. . . my word, we have.' Roger Doyle took her hand and kissed it. 'Charmed, I'm sure.'

Bertie Fletcher, whom she thought seemed a little worse for drink, also leaned over her hand, but she drew it away before it reached his wet lips. 'Beautiful,' he slurred. 'Ab-sholu-shly beautiful!'

'But who's the fellow on the piano?' Charlie mockingly frowned at her. 'You didn't tell me about him!' He put his finger under her chin and looked into her eyes. 'Don't tell me that you don't love me any more, Poppy? That you've found somebody else?'

'Don't be silly, Charlie.' Embarrassed in front of his friends, she turned her head away. 'That's Anthony Marino. It's his final night at the show so he very kindly played for me. The song is his. He's a songwriter as well as a pianist, and he's a friend.'

'Ooh!' Bertie sighed. 'Sing a song of sixpence!'

'Shut up, Bertie,' Charlie said rudely. 'I'm trying to have a conversation with Poppy.' He smiled down at her and whispered, 'But you do still love me? You haven't had your head turned by all this adoration?'

'Hello! What's this? A party?' Ena, followed by Ronny, came into the room. They were both flushed by their exertions on stage, but Poppy could tell that they were over their ill humour. Obviously they had had a receptive audience.

'Good evening, gentlemen.' Ronny, in her high-heeled shoes, towered over Bertie and Roger. She sat down and unfastened the straps on her shoes and kicked them under the dressing table. 'So which of you is the shoemaker?'

'I am.' Charlie gave her a bow. 'Charles Chandler at your service.'

Ronny eyed him. 'Hmm. Will you make me a pair?' She wiggled a foot in front of him, and then waved a finger across at Ena. 'And a pair for my sister, of course. We always do things together.'

'Well, not always together.' Ena smiled seductively at Roger. 'Some things we do separately!'

'I'm glad to hear it.' Roger pawed over her hand and kissed it. 'Roger Doyle, Miss Terry. Delighted to meet you.'

'We thought we'd go out for supper,' Charlie announced. 'Shall we all go? Are you ladies free?'

'Not free,' Ena and Ronny cried in unison. 'But we ain't expensive!'

Poppy was appalled as they all laughed and joked, and Ronny and Ena told the gentlemen they must go back into the theatre and wait until they were changed. She had been so looking forward to seeing Charlie and spending some time alone with him. Now the evening would be ruined.

She stepped back into the corridor as the men left, and walked towards the stage where Anthony was coming to the end of his performance and playing the final piece of music. It was his own composition and Poppy recognized it from when he had played in Hull. Tears came to her eyes, as they had then, and she wished he had played something merry to finish rather than something that touched her emotions.

He stood up and bowed and the audience, having been told that this was his final performance at Bradshaw's, stood up and applauded heartily, though not noisily as they had previously. He bowed again and turned to come off stage. He saw Poppy watching him and held out his hand.

She shook her head; tears were running down her cheeks. She wouldn't go on. This was his performance. Not hers. She had had her ovation. But he still stood there, and then began to clap his hands. Again he put out his hand for her to join him. The audience, sensing something, began to murmur, 'Poppy . . . Poppy . . .'

She lifted her head and blinked away her tears, then ran lightly to join him. He took her by the hand and kissed her cheek and the audience cheered. 'Give a bow, Poppy,' he murmured, smiling at the audience as he spoke. 'Now brush away your tears with your fingers. That's it. Another bow. Back away. Wave. Throw a kiss.' They left the stage and he squeezed her hand. 'Always leave them wanting more.' He gazed at her. 'I'm going now. Have a wonderful evening with your friend Charlie. And I'll hope to see you again in the not too distant future. Goodbye.'

'Anthony!' she said, but he'd turned away. 'Thank you,' she called. 'For everything.'

'So you're the little lady who loves Charles!' Roger put his face close to hers as they walked away from the theatre. Somehow, Charlie had been ensnared in front between Ena and Ronny, and Poppy was between Roger and Bertie. Both were hanging on to her arms. 'Lucky old Charles.'

Why did Charlie tell them, Poppy thought. And Charles? Is that how he's known now? 'Where are we going?' she called out. 'Charlie!'

He stopped, and Ena and Ronny stopped too. 'Darling girl,' he said. 'The chaps know of a bar round the corner. We can get a bite to eat there.'

'Here!' Ronny said. 'Let's swap. Charles, you walk with Poppy. We'll walk with Roger and Bertie,' and they obligingly swapped over so that Poppy was at the back with Charlie.

'That's better!' Charlie put his arm round her waist and she took in a breath.

'Charlie!' she said. 'Behave!'

'Oh, come on!' he laughed. 'We're not in dear old Hull now. Nobody here knows us and is going to tell your pa.'

She shrugged away from him. 'No-one knows you, Charlie, but there are plenty of people who know me.'

'Oh, hoity-toity!' He stopped walking and looked at her. 'Not getting uppity, are we?'

'No, of course not, but—'

'Not thinking of your piano man, are you?' Charlie's eyes narrowed. 'You said you loved me!'

She put her hand up to her mouth. 'I do love you, Charlie.' Her voice was full of tears. 'You know that I do. But I didn't think that I'd have to share you with all these others.'

He gave a self-satisfied smile. 'Oh, Poppy! Let's have some fun now. We can be alone later, hey? Just you and me?'

'All right,' she said in a low voice. 'I just wanted to talk to you, that's all. Find out what you've been doing since I saw you last.'

'I know,' he said, tucking her arm into his. 'And that's what we'll do. We'll talk.' He kissed her cheek and she could smell ale on his breath. 'And we'll kiss a little too, shall we? And by the way, Poppy,' he murmured. 'It's Charles now, not Charlie. Sounds better, don't you think? I'll tell you everything later, but, briefly, I'm going to set up on my own. Charles Chandler, shoemaker. That's why I wanted to talk to the Terry Sisters. If I can get in with the stage people it will do me a lot of good, don't you see?'

He squeezed her arm. 'So don't be upset if I give them some attention. It's all in the way of business, you understand? I'm sure you can help me in that line,' he added. 'You must know a few people?'

'No,' she said. 'I've only been here a week!'

The others stopped outside a building and waved for them to hurry.

'Where are we going?' Poppy called after them.

'It's a supper bar,' Charlie told her. The others disappeared down the basement steps. 'It's all right,' he added. 'I'm sure it's quite respectable.'

Roger and Bertie had procured a table and ordered champagne and oysters. A pianist at an upright piano was playing popular music accompanied by a violinist, and Poppy relaxed. Perhaps it was going to be all right after all. She had been anxious that the place might be seedy and undesirable, but although the lights were dim and she couldn't see into the corners, it seemed to be respectable enough. But as they walked across to the table and she took her seat, the pianist began to play the introduction to 'Forever True', and then added an animated variation. The lights were turned up, and she saw that the room was full of people and the furnishings were garish.

'Ladies and gentlemen.' The pianist turned to the company. 'We are honoured tonight by the presence of Miss Poppy Mazzini' – he began to play the melody in a forceful manner – 'and the Terry Sisters!'

The fiddle player began a jig and Ena and Ronny, with theatrical smiles, stood up and bowed from the waist, first to one side of the room and then the other. Both were wearing bustled dresses with off-the-shoulder necklines, and a froth of tulle in their hair. 'Stand up, Poppy,' Ena whispered between her teeth. 'Give them a bow.'

Poppy did as she was bid, feeling very embarrassed. She had dressed simply in a pale green wool gown, which had a high-buttoned neckline and a bolero with leg o' mutton sleeves. In her hair she had pinned a cream rose from the bouquet Anthony had given her. She gave a shy smile and bowed her head and the pianist played the melody of 'Forever True' again, but he thumped the rhythm and somehow lost the soul of the music.

'Sing for us, Poppy,' someone shouted, but she shook her head and sat down. Someone else banged on a table. 'Yes, sing for us. Come on, be a sport!' A woman's voice answered back: 'Leave her alone! She's been singing all night. Go and pay to hear her at Bradshaw's!' The pianist began to play other tunes and the waiter came over with the champagne and oysters. Poppy's face had flushed and she bent her head to hide her discomfort. She hadn't expected this. Charlie was still and silent and when she glanced at him he had a stony expression on his face.

'Come along, you young star.' Roger poured her a glass of champagne. 'You're going to have to get used to this kind of thing, isn't she, ladies?' He turned to Ronny and Ena.

'Oh, yes,' Ena said scathingly. 'It happens all the time.'

Poppy sipped the champagne and spluttered as the bubbles went up her nose. It was the first time she had tried it, and she wasn't sure if she liked it. At Roger's urging she took an oyster and swallowed it, grimacing as it slid down her throat.

'Come on, old boy,' Roger said to Charlie. 'Drink up. Are you not having oysters?'

'Don't care for 'em,' he said sullenly, taking a drink from his glass, and Poppy guessed that he hadn't tried them before either. Oysters were not common to the east Yorkshire coast. Mussels and shrimps were in plentiful supply and she had had them often, but she didn't care for the slippery wet texture of the oyster.

The pianist came over to their table and, giving a short bow to the company in general, addressed Poppy. 'I do beg your pardon, Miss Mazzini. I saw you come in and couldn't resist playing your music.'

'It isn't my music,' she said quietly. 'It was composed by Mr Marino.'

'Ah, yes, I realize that.' He was a young man and wore a rather shabby black suit. 'He's a very talented musician and I wish I could play half as well, but you've made that song your own. I heard you sing it tonight at Bradshaw's and couldn't believe it when you came in here.'

'Yes,' Charlie interrupted brusquely. 'But Miss Mazzini is now with a private party, so we'd be obliged if she wasn't disturbed further.'

Poppy took in a breath as the pianist apologized and backed away, but she gave him a quick smile of regret, then turned to Charlie. 'He wasn't disturbing us,' she said. 'He was only—'

'We haven't got long,' he said sharply. 'We've to catch the last train back to London.'

'Oh, we'll stay the night,' Bertie said airily. 'We'll find an hotel. Perhaps where you're staying?' he asked Ronny and Ena.

'No.' They and Poppy answered simultaneously. 'Not allowed, old thing,' Ena said. 'Our landlady is inflexible on that.' She smiled sweetly at him. 'We've asked before – when our brother came to visit.' She shook her head. 'No male visitors.'

'Mmm!' Roger eyed them thoughtfully. 'That's a shame.'

'Yes, isn't it?' Ronny lit a cheroot and drew on it. 'What can we do about it?'

'I need to get back to London,' Charlie said, rising from his chair. 'I've things to do tomorrow. I'll walk you back, Poppy.'

Roger and Bertie objected loudly, though Ronny and Ena said nothing, but Charlie insisted on leaving there and then, so Poppy said good night and was self-conscious, yet gratified, as people at other tables clapped their hands as she passed.

'Is it far?' he asked as they went outside. 'To your lodgings? Should we get a cab?'

'Not far,' she said. 'But perhaps we should. Then you can go on to the train station.' She wished that he would stay overnight as Roger and Bertie were going to do, so they could have spent Sunday together, but his face was set and she didn't like to ask him.

Charlie put his hand up for a horse cab and when the driver stopped he handed her in. 'Look,' he said to her. 'I might as well walk to the station from here. You'll be all right with this fellow, won't you?'

'Oh,' she said, surprised. 'Yes – I suppose so.'

'Fact is, Poppy,' he said, 'I can't afford to stay the night like the other fellows. They're very well heeled. Money no object.' He sounded testy and irritable. 'But they're very well connected, which is why I put up with them.' He leaned into the cab and kissed her cheek. 'If you bump into them tomorrow, be nice to them, won't you?'

'What do you mean?' Her voice trembled. She was unbearably disappointed with the way the evening had gone.

'Well, I want them to help finance me in my new venture. You know!' he said sharply. 'I told you I was setting up on my own. If you see them, reassure them about my ambition, and tell the Terry Sisters too.'

'Are we going or not?' the cab driver called down. 'I haven't got all night!'

'Yes,' Charlie said hastily. 'Goodbye, Poppy. I'll see you again soon.' He flashed her a smile and mouthed a kiss. 'I promise.'

CHAPTER TWENTY-SIX

She went straight up to bed, refusing supper from Mrs Johnson. 'I'm really tired,' she said. 'It's been such a hectic evening.'

'Saturday night,' Mrs Johnson said knowingly. 'My stage folk are always *hexhausted* on a Saturday night. I 'eard' – she nodded her head and pursed her mouth – 'I 'eard from Miss Jenkinson about your reception tonight. She said how good you were and that the haudience didn't want you to leave! My word,' she said. 'The Terry Sisters won't like that.'

'They were all right,' Poppy assured her. 'They didn't say anything.'

'No. They wouldn't,' she said sagely. 'Where are they, anyway? They're generally in by this time.'

'They – they met some friends,' Poppy said. 'So they'll probably be late. I'm going up now, Mrs Johnson. I'll say good night.'

'Good night, my dear. You do look a bit tired. Your first week, ain't it? You'll be glad of a day off tomorrow.'

'Yes,' Poppy said, feeling her chest tighten as she fought back tears. 'I will. Good night.'

She screwed her eyes up tight and felt her way upstairs. When she entered her room she took off her bolero and gloves and dropped them to the floor before unbuttoning her dress and letting it slide over her feet. She sat on the bed in her petticoat, and, putting her hands over her eyes, she wept and wept. In the course of the evening, she had gone from being exalted on the stage to being downhearted over Charlie's attitude at the supper bar, and then his leaving her to come back to her diggings alone. She was full of pent-up emotion.

She talked to herself between sobs. 'What did I do? I don't understand. Did I upset him? Was it something I said?' He had seemed in a strange mood right from the beginning: from the time when he demanded, in front of his friends, to know whether she still loved him, to his odd manner in the supper bar when people had clapped and the pianist had come over to speak to her. Was he resentful that others demanded her attention? Did he begrudge her her popularity?

She blew her nose. No, of course he didn't. He wasn't like that. How could she even think it? He has worries, she thought. Perhaps he had wanted to tell her of his plans and there hadn't been an opportunity. She took the rose from her hair and breathed in its perfume. Dear Anthony. If only he had still been here. I could have discussed it with him. He would have understood.

After rinsing her face and cleaning her teeth she climbed into bed. The refrain of 'Forever True' ran through her head. 'You said we must say adieu. Sweet memories are all I have left of you.' She gave a heavy sigh. Did Anthony write those words thinking of someone? It was such a poignant song. But no, she thought. He's a songwriter, after all. He writes emotional words and music to touch the heartstrings. But still, she thought, I'll ask him when I next see him. But then she realized that she might not see him for a long time, and her tears flowed again.

The next few weeks passed fairly quickly. She wrote and received letters from her father who told her of the hostility between Lena and Nan, and that he didn't know how to resolve it. Poppy also wrote several times to Charlie, and was disappointed not to receive a reply. But she put on a brave face and followed a regular routine at the theatre. A violinist now accompanied Miss Jenkinson on the piano, and complemented her light and sensitive touch. Poppy dropped 'Forever True' from her repertoire and included more popular songs; she learned how to appeal to the audience, dwindling though it was, as the last of the holidaymakers left and the London day-trippers no longer came to Brighton as the weather became colder.

Jack Bradshaw went around with a long face, hunched into the fur collar of his heavy overcoat, chewing on a fat cigar and complaining that the takings were down.

'Don't even think of asking us to take a cut,' Ena warned him one evening when he had been grumbling about the small audience. 'We shall be off to London if you so much as mention it!'

'To where?' he scoffed. 'You'd not get a booking so near to Christmas!'

'We'd go home to Mater and Pater,' Ronny said, 'and rest.'

He'd grunted, but said nothing more and left the theatre. Poppy, Ena and Ronny had started walking back to their lodgings together as the winter nights were dark, and Ena suddenly asked Poppy now, 'So where's your next gaff, Poppy? Has Dan told you yet?'

'No.' Poppy shook her head. She was getting worried. This was her last week. Today was Wednesday; she was finishing on Saturday night and hadn't yet heard from Dan Damone.

'Odd that he hasn't been in touch,' Ronny said. 'Are you sure he's got you a booking?'

'No,' Poppy said again. 'I'm not sure about anything any more.'

'What's up?' Ronny glanced at her. 'Fallen out with your shoemaker?'

'I haven't heard from him for us to fall out,' Poppy said miserably. 'He's not replied to my letters.'

'He's probably too busy getting his business up and running,' Ena commented. 'Roger said he was looking for premises.'

'Roger said?' Poppy turned to Ena. 'You've heard from Roger?'

'Mm,' Ena said casually. 'Had a note a week ago. He and Bertie are coming down next week.'

Poppy fell silent. Ena and Ronny hadn't mentioned the evening when they had all visited the supper bar, but she hadn't heard them come in that night. They hadn't come down for breakfast the next morning either, and Mrs Johnson had been very grouchy, muttering about inconsiderate people.

Poppy wondered if Charlie would come to Brighton with Roger and Bertie. She had written to say she was leaving at the end of November, but that she didn't have a forwarding address as yet.

'Roger told me that he's backing Charles,' Ena explained. 'That's how he knows.'

Ronny tucked her arm into Poppy's. 'Don't break your heart

over him, darlin',' she said. 'Men in business only have time for themselves. And I think your Charles was jealous over your success that evening.' She gave a wry grimace. 'We all were.' She gave Poppy's arm a squeeze. 'But not now. You've got talent. It just needs to be nurtured.'

The next day there was a letter from Dan asking her to come to his office on Monday morning as he had something to discuss with her. Where will I stay on Sunday night? she wondered. Dare I just turn up at the Marinos'? They did ask me to. She decided to ask the advice of Ena and Ronny.

'You've time to write to the Marinos,' Ronny said. 'If you post a letter today they'll get it before Saturday. And if they can't take you, then you can go to my ma. You'll have to pay her. She won't put you up for nothing, but if you tell her I've sent you, she'll find you a room.'

Poppy spent Saturday morning emptying drawers and cupboards and packing her trunk. There was a matinee in the afternoon and a performance in the evening. Jack Bradshaw had put up a poster outside the theatre announcing her final performances for the season, and although the audience was scanty at both houses, she received a good ovation.

'I'll say cheerio now,' Ena said, as they reached Mrs Johnson's after the evening show. 'I shall have a lie-in tomorrow. Thank Gawd it's Sunday.'

Poppy was quite sorry to leave them. They'd been fairly supportive of her as a newcomer; Ronny in particular had offered suggestions and advice, though Ena had held back. 'I hope I'll meet you both again,' she said.

'We only part to meet again, as someone once said,' Ronny quoted. 'We're sure to catch up with you one of these days. But all the best, anyway, gel. Keep on singing!'

The next morning she said goodbye to Miss Jenkinson, who had been so encouraging and helpful. 'Think seriously about your career, my dear,' the elderly pianist said. 'You could do better than Bradshaw's – or at least you could do differently.'

'What exactly?' Poppy asked. 'I like doing what I do, though I like to sing more than dance.'

'Then that is what you must think about,' Miss Jenkinson advised. 'Be a singer, not a dancer.'

She thought about it as the train steamed towards London and considered that if Anthony should, by a stroke of luck, be staying with his parents that weekend, she would ask him. However, he was unlikely to be in London if he was touring the coastal towns. She hired a cab to take her to St Martin's Lane and directed the driver towards the small street off the main thoroughfare where the Marinos' café was situated.

But the blinds were drawn on the window and a notice hanging on the door said they were closed for a week. 'I know of a bed and board place,' the cabman called to her, but she declined, remembering the last time she was recommended to the run-down and dirty lodging house.

'Will you take me to Seven Dials, please?' she asked. That was the area in which Ronny's mother lived.

'Nuffink much there,' he commented. 'Used to be the rookeries till they pulled the 'ouses down. But if that's what you want!'

She gave him the address and he stopped outside a shabby terrace of two-storey houses. 'Will you wait, please?' she asked, and hoped that Ronny's mother would be in and able to accommodate her, for she didn't know where else to go. She knocked on the door and waited, then knocked again. 'All right, I'm comin',' a female voice called. 'Keep yer 'air on.'

A plump middle-aged woman in a dark red velvet dress with an apron over it opened the door. She was wearing a brown curly wig with a white lace cap, and had a tobacco pipe in her hand. 'Yes,' she said. 'What do you want?'

'Mrs Trenton?' Poppy asked.

The woman's eyes narrowed. 'Who wants to know?'

Poppy knew it was Ronny's mother for they looked alike; both had narrow faces and bony noses. 'Ronny said you might be able to let me have a room for the night.'

'Did she?' The woman looked Poppy up and down. 'Did she tell you you'd have to pay rent?'

'She did. Yes, of course. I – I do hope you can,' she said desperately. 'I don't know where else to go.'

Mrs Trenton came closer. 'You're not in trouble, are you?' she whispered, as if the cabbie could hear. 'Cos I'll not take you if you are.'

'Trouble! No! I just need somewhere to stay tonight. I've to see my agent in the morning.'

'Who? Dan, is it? Well, why didn't you say so? You'd better come in. 'ere,' she shouted to the cab driver as a stream of steaming urine flowed from the horse into the road. 'Don't you let that 'oss mess up my clean front!'

'What d'you expect me to do about it, lady?' he said, jumping down from his cab to carry Poppy's trunk into the house and up the rickety stairs. 'Ask if she can use your privy?'

Poppy paid him, and as she came into the house she saw that Mrs Trenton's home had a scrubbed doorstep and clean lace curtains at the window.

'There's some criminals about,' Mrs Trenton muttered in front of her. 'You can't be too careful about who you invite indoors.' She took Poppy into her front parlour, which though furnished with cheap furniture had a brightly polished brass fender and fire irons in front of the grate, and on the mantelpiece hung a red embroidered valance, with an ebony clock in the middle of it. The windowsill was adorned with green plants; the chairs were covered with cushions, antimacassars and shawls, and pinned to the walls were theatre posters and bills advertising various shows, reviews and comedies. Teddy Trenton was a recurring name as was Dolly London, music hall artiste. There were several photographs of the Terry Sisters and others of young girls and boys in Pierrot and stage costume.

She asked Poppy to sit down and she sat down opposite her. 'You on the boards, then?' she queried. 'You don't look the type.'

'I'm a singer,' Poppy said. 'I've been appearing at Brighton with the Terry Sisters.'

'Is that where they are? Up to no good I'll be bound, specially that Ena.' She scratched at her head, knocking the wig and cap sideways over one ear. 'What do you sing? All the Marie Lloyd songs, I'll bet? Everybody does. Nobody does their own material any more, not like in my day.' She eased herself out of the chair and humming a tune took a photograph from the wall. There was a brighter patch on the faded wallpaper where it had been. 'That's me,' she said. 'Or was. Don't look much like that now, do I?'

The photograph showed a round-faced buxom young woman

with a cheeky grin, wearing a milkmaid costume and carrying a pail in each hand. 'Fifteen I was, when that was took.' She bent her head and scrutinized Poppy. 'About your age, I reckon?'

Poppy nodded. 'Were you a singer?'

'Me? No! I was an entertainer. A bit of comedy, bit of knock-about, spoofing, and then I learned to clog dance. I can still do it,' she said, and lifting her skirts did a few shuffling movements with her slippered feet. 'Though I get breathless after a few minutes, and it gets your back in the end, you know, cos you've to keep it so straight – it's all legwork, you see. Then me and Teddy, that's me 'usband, 'im up there in the picture, 'e's gorn now, God bless 'im, we did a double act. He was a comic and I was his side-kick and we did a song and dance routine.'

She sighed and sat down in silence for a minute. Then she said, 'I miss them days. Best days of my life they was, even though it was 'ard, specially when the youngsters came along. Do you want somefink to eat?' she asked suddenly. 'It's extra, o' course. I 'ave to charge to keep body and soul together.'

'Yes please,' Poppy said. 'That would be very nice.'

'Good.' Mrs Trenton rose to her feet again. 'I'm just cooking an eel pie. A pal o' mine comes round on a Sunday and we have a bite to eat together. But there's plenty. I always do enough for three, just in case.'

Poppy unpacked what she would need for the rest of that day and the following morning. She lifted the faded coverlet off the bed to check the sheets, but they were clean and smelled as if they had been freshly laundered so she didn't need to use her own. The marble washstand had a crack in it, but the bowl and jug were clean. The fire in the grate was laid with newspaper curls, sticks and coal and she guessed that Mrs Trenton kept the room constantly ready for any visitors.

She was called down for supper at six o'clock. Mrs Trenton's friend, Nelly Gorman, was already seated at the table in the small kitchen with a knife and fork at the ready in her hands. In the middle of the table was a huge crusty pie with dishes of carrots and floury potatoes.

'This is Nelly. She used to play in penny gaffs,' Mrs Trenton said. 'She's a bit deaf so you'll have to shout up if you want to talk to 'er.'

Poppy tried to converse, but to no avail as Nelly couldn't hear her, and eventually she asked Mrs Trenton to explain to her friend that she couldn't shout in case she damaged her voice. Mrs Trenton passed on the message in a piercing shout and Nelly looked at Poppy, then shouted back at Mrs Trenton. 'She'll be no good at the gaffs, then, will she?'

Mrs Trenton shouted back. 'She's a singer. She ain't going to the penny gaffs; she's been doing music 'all, like our Ronny.'

After supper, the two women cleared all the crockery into a deep earthenware sink. Mrs Trenton poured boiling water from the kettle onto it and then the three of them moved into the parlour where a fire had been lit in the grate. 'We 'ave a little singsong on a Sunday,' Mrs Trenton shouted at Poppy, then she gave an apologetic grin. 'I gets used to shouting at Nelly,' she said. Poppy really wanted to go out for a walk, but felt it would be rude if she didn't join them for a while, so she sat down and prepared to be entertained.

The women pushed back the furniture and lined themselves in front of Poppy. 'Nice to 'ave an audience, ain't it?' Mrs Trenton said, and began a lively song with Nelly joining in, slightly behind the beat and raising her eyebrows, wiggling her hips and lifting her skirts.

> 'I was going for a walk in the park,
> When this feller calls to me, let's have a lark,
> Come on pretty miss, let's 'ave a little kiss
> For you know how much I care for you.
> Says I, if I do, will you marry me and be true?
> He gave a saucy wink and said I'll have to have a think
> Of what my darlin' wife might say,
> That I'd never be good enough for you.'

Poppy sat with a fixed smile on her face. How can I get out without offending them? She sat through another three slightly suggestive songs, and then stood up. 'I must take a walk before bed,' she announced. 'Otherwise I'll never sleep.'

'It's raining cats and dogs!' Mrs Trenton told her. 'You'll be soaked. And besides, it's not safe for a young girl out there on her own.'

'I'll be all right,' Poppy assured her. 'I've got an umbrella and I don't mind the rain. I won't be long, just a turn round the block.'

She backed out of the parlour and ran upstairs for her rain cape and black umbrella, and then down again and out of the door before they could persuade her not to.

The rain was torrential, sharp and needle-like, and she huddled beneath the brolly and hurried down the narrow road, keeping her eyes on her feet for the road was cracked and broken in parts. But she hadn't gone far when she lifted up the umbrella and stopped, realizing she could no longer see where she was going. There had been gaslight outside the row of houses where Mrs Trenton lived, but ahead of her there was none. She seemed to have run into a wall of darkness concealing dilapidated buildings with shadowy low arches and murky passages dividing them, whilst beneath her feet ran a thick stream of putrid water. She took in a quick startled breath and was about to turn back when she heard the rasp of a match. There was a sudden flare of yellow light on a level with her eyes and behind it she saw the features of a man.

' 'ello, little lady,' he said softly, but his voice had a hoarse edge to it, and she was instantly reminded of the comic song which Nelly and Mrs Trenton had been singing. Only now it wasn't in the least comical, for she saw something sinister in his expression. 'Where are you off to on this dismal night?' She flung her umbrella at him and turning swiftly on her heels took flight, picking up her skirts about her knees and sprinting back the way she had come.

CHAPTER TWENTY-SEVEN

She hammered on Mrs Trenton's door, terrified that the man would come after her. 'Mrs Trenton. Mrs Trenton. Let me in! Please let me in!'

She saw a light in the lobby as an inside door was opened and she hammered again. 'Mrs Trenton!'

'Who is it?'

'It's Poppy. Let me in. Quick. There's a man—'

She heard the key turn and the door opened a crack. She saw one eye and Mrs Trenton's long nose peering through. 'You're soon back,' she said. The chain on the door rattled as she unfastened it. 'I've only just locked it after you. Come in. Come in. What's up? Somebody chase you?'

'I don't know,' she said breathlessly, stepping inside. 'I walked and then ran out of light and then there was a man! He spoke.' She suddenly felt foolish for having gone out alone in the dark.

'I told you,' Mrs Trenton said. 'But you young women, you don't listen. It's not like in the old days when we knew everybody hereabouts. Now all the old streets are changed and there's all sorts of vagabonds moved in.'

Nelly Gorman appeared, dressed ready to leave. She had a moth-eaten fur stole round the neck of her black coat and a bent feather in her large hat.

'Don't go out, Mrs Gorman,' Poppy pleaded. 'Tell her, Mrs Trenton,' for Nelly had obviously not heard her. 'There's a man out there!'

'There's lots o' men, darlin',' Mrs Trenton laughed, 'but they'll not bother Nelly. You ain't 'eard 'er shout, 'ave you? She could fetch a mountain down with her voice. Besides, look at her. She's wearing black. Nobody'll see her on a night like this. And another fing – she only lives three doors down. You might think it ain't worth the effort, but she likes to dress up, just as we used to in the old days when we trod the boards.'

Nelly stood watching them and nodding her head as if she was making sense of what they were saying. As they stood there, a knock came on the door and Poppy jumped.

'Who is it?' Mrs Trenton cried out, and then muttered, 'It's like the Old Kent Road tonight.'

'Harry!' a hoarse voice called back. 'I've got somebody's gamp 'ere.'

Mrs Trenton turned the key and opened the door and Poppy and Nelly shouldered each other to see who it was. An elderly man stood outside, holding Poppy's umbrella over his head. 'Somebody threw it to me,' he said. 'Must 'ave thought I was getting wetter than she was. I followed 'er to your door.'

'There you are then.' Mrs Trenton turned to Poppy. 'It was only old 'Arry after all. 'e'd not 'arm you. Not that you'd know that. 'e always goes out for a smoke at night, raining or not. 'is wife won't let him smoke indoors in case he sets the 'ouse on fire.'

'She give me a fright, I can tell you.' Harry handed over the umbrella. 'Don't expect to see anybody down there. I was just sheltering from the rain.' He touched his cap, and water dripped off it onto his nose. 'I'll wish you good night.'

'I'll walk with you,' Nelly shouted after him and hurried out. 'See you same time next Sunday, Dolly. Good night, miss.'

'I'm so sorry to have bothered you,' Poppy said after they had gone. 'But I was so frightened.'

'Well, he could have been anybody,' Mrs Trenton said. 'But there we are, it was only old 'Arry. Now then, a nice cup o' cocoa and then I'm off to bed.'

Poppy lay sleepless for some time. The mattress, though soft and warm, tickled her as feathers poked through the cover, but she kept thinking of old Harry out in the street and what she would have done if he really had been a criminal on the lookout for a victim.

She awoke to the sound of Mrs Trenton singing. She had a

tuneful voice though rather raucous. Then she heard her step on the stairs and her call to say it was seven o'clock and she had brought up hot water.

'There you are, darlin'.' In her hand she had a copper jug filled with steaming water, with a cloth wrapped round the handle. 'Piping 'ot. I've just drawn it off so don't scald yourself. Breakfast in quarter 'n hour. Sausage and bacon all right, is it?'

The morning was dull and when Poppy looked out of the bedroom window she saw yellow fog swirling round the lamp posts. She washed, then pulled on her grey wool skirt, which had a matching caped jacket, buttoned up her white and green striped shirt, and donned her elastic-sided boots. Then she dipped her comb into the bowl of water and ran it through her hair to tame it. Though large hats were fashionable, she often wore a smaller boater type and she laid on the bed a yellow felt one, which she wore perched on the back of her head and fastened with a ribbon beneath her chin.

'You look nice,' Mrs Trenton remarked when she went downstairs. 'Very classy, ain't you?' She put her hand on her hip and surveyed her. 'Mm, you don't look the type for music 'all. Not showy enough, if you don't mind me saying so.' She looked her up and down. 'I'd say you're more theatre or concert hall; though I dare say when you're dolled up in your frippery and gewgaws and with slap on your face, you'll look quite different.'

She placed a plate piled high with bacon, sausage and beans on the table and bade Poppy sit down and eat, then she brought another plate with a hunk of bread and a saucer of butter. 'Fing is, darlin',' she said, sitting opposite her and pouring two cups of tea from a huge brown teapot, 'and you mustn't mind me giving you a piece of advice, cos I was in this business for a long time; the fing is, you need a bit o' swank, a bit o' swagger, you know. And you need somefink – some little dodge to catch the attention of the public.

'You've seen that picture o' me with the milk pails? Well, I ain't never been near a cow in my life, but one time I used to bring a little lamb on the stage. Bless it, it would keep bleating for its ma whenever I was going through my patter, so I used the milkmaid routine instead, and that lasted for quite a few seasons.'

She put her elbows on the table and gazed at Poppy as she

sipped her tea and Poppy self-consciously continued her breakfast. 'But surely,' Poppy murmured, 'I shouldn't need to use a novelty if my voice is good enough?'

'No, you shouldn't,' Dolly Trenton agreed. 'And is it?' Without waiting for an answer, she went on, 'The Terry Sisters can't sing for toffee, but they can dance and they tart themselves up so's you'd never know it was them if you saw them out in the street like what they really are; and folks love 'em. They like a bit of vulgarity, you see, so that's what they get. Have you seen Marie Lloyd?' she asked. 'No?' as Poppy shook her head. 'Well, she's saucy, gives them a wink and a bit of how's your father.' She wiggled her eyebrows and flashed her eyes. 'I've seen her and I can tell you, she has 'em eating out of 'er 'and and she's only young! Now take Vesta Tilley . . .'

Poppy finished her breakfast. She could tell that Mrs Trenton was in a reminiscent mood and she wondered how she could excuse herself.

'Now she's a star and a really nice lady,' Mrs Trenton went on. 'And Dan Leno, why, you couldn't wish for a finer feller, and they all have a special somefink.'

'Mrs Trenton,' Poppy said desperately, 'I have to go. Mr Damone is expecting me.'

'Lovely feller.' Mrs Trenton rose from the table. 'Seems a waste, don't it, 'andsome chap like him? That Ena sets her cap at him.' She shook her head. 'But she don't stand a chance. Nobody does.'

It was only a ten-minute walk to St Martin's Lane from Mrs Trenton's house and Poppy's hat bobbed bright and yellow in the grey morning as she set off. She had put her rain cape over her jacket and wore a warm scarf round her neck. In her gloved hand she lightly swung her walking umbrella.

Miss Battle was in the front office when she arrived at Dan Damone's, but this time she went into his room to tell him that Miss Mazzini had arrived.

'Lovely to see you, Poppy.' Dan kissed her cheek. 'How are you? You've had a successful season! I had a request from Bradshaw asking if you could stay on, but I told him that I had other plans for you. Come and sit down.'

'Mr Damone,' she began.

'Dan!' He smiled. 'You're not a schoolgirl any more, you know, and in this business, privately at any rate, we can be informal.'

'Dan,' she began again. 'Am I suited to the music hall?'

He tipped back in his chair and gazed at her and she thought that Mrs Trenton was quite right. He was handsome, with his smiling blue eyes and mutton chop whiskers. 'Why do you ask that,' he said, 'when you were moved up the bill at Brighton? Bradshaw would have put you in the penultimate spot if you'd stayed on.'

'Well, a few people have said to me that a singer in the music hall needs to be a bit saucy and use *double entendre* and that kind of thing.' She took a breath. 'And I can't. Don't want to.'

'Of course you can't, and you don't need to,' he reassured her. 'And not all do. There are lots of straight singers, balladeers and vocalists who don't use sauce and don't use novelties to entertain. Some are good at it, but it wouldn't be right for you. You're not the type.'

'That's what Mrs Trenton said,' she murmured.

'Dolly Trenton!' He brought his chair back with a crash and laughed. 'Dolly London as was! Have you been staying with her?' At Poppy's answer, he laughed again. 'What an old girl she is! Did she sing for you?'

'Yes.' Poppy smiled. 'With her friend Nelly Gorman.'

Dan roared. 'Wonderful! They were great in their time. They'd dash from one penny gaff to another, halls or clubs, on foot or catch a hansom; they'd go anywhere to earn a crust! They were true music hall.' Then he leaned towards her. 'But that's not for you, Poppy. Let me tell you what I think you should do. You might not want to and if you don't . . .' He lifted his hands in an apologetic gesture. 'Well, it's up to you. I can always get you a booking in a hall like Bradshaw's anywhere in the country.'

'Yes?' she said. 'But?' She felt nervous. What was it he had in mind for her? 'You mentioned pantomime.'

He nodded. 'I did. That's still on.' He hesitated for a second. 'I can recognize quality when I see or hear it, and so can others who are more, shall we say, musically attuned than I am.' He leaned back again and folded his arms in front of him. 'I'm not doing myself any favours in suggesting this, because I could make money out of you by letting you sing just as you do. But it has been suggested to me that your voice could be improved if you took further singing lessons with a coach.'

'Oh!' She swallowed. 'I see. Who suggested it? Anthony!' she gasped. 'It was him. Wasn't it?'

'Yes,' he admitted. 'It was, though he did ask me not to tell you. He thought you might feel he was interfering. I put great faith in his judgement,' Dan continued. 'He's young and talented and has a great deal of experience behind him. And he's a friend,' he said. 'I've known him since he was a boy and I first became his agent, and I know he wouldn't make the suggestion if he didn't believe it would work.'

'I don't know of a coach,' Poppy said, her mind working furiously. 'Would it cost a lot of money? Would I be able to sing to pay for the lessons? I don't want my father to have to pay.'

'It would cost, but you could still work. I can get you bookings in London; not the best places in town, but they would pay your rent and the cost of a tutor.'

'Do you know of someone?'

He nodded. 'I do. She's good, used to be a concert hall singer herself until she married and raised a family. She's my sister,' he admitted, and abstractedly flipped his bottom lip with his finger. 'She has a daughter who used to sing too, but she also married and gave it up.'

'I wouldn't do that.'

Dan smiled. 'You might if your husband was rich and influential and didn't want his wife on public display.'

'Ah!' Poppy thought for a moment. 'So why does she teach if she's rich?'

He shook his head. 'I was speaking of my niece. She's the one with a rich husband. My sister married for love and needs the money.' He gazed at her for a moment, then said, 'Have a think about it. You don't have to tell me now. Talk to your father. He's a sensible man; ask him his opinion. You're young, Poppy. You've a long career in front of you. Make sure you take the right path.'

'All right.' She gathered up her cape, gloves and umbrella. 'So what about the pantomime? What is it and when do I start?' She smiled at him. He wasn't very organized. No wonder he needed Miss Battle to help him. He hadn't given her any details of the part she would play, where it was or the date.

He scrabbled on his desk amongst a pile of papers, and then opened the desk drawer and looked in there. Then he shouted, 'Dora!'

Miss Battle came in holding a sheaf of papers. 'Is this what you're looking for, Mr Damone? The contract for Miss Mazzini?'

He gave her a rueful grin. 'What would I do without you, Dora?'

She turned without a word and went out again and Dan raised his eyebrows. 'She's a treasure,' he murmured.

Poppy laughed. 'So what is the pantomime and what part do I play?'

'Ah,' he said. 'Aladdin . . . and you're to be . . .' He looked over the papers. 'Ah! Yes, here we are. Fairy Fancy, the Good Spirit of Pantomime. Not a big part but important, for you need to empathize with the audience.' He glanced up at her. 'And being local they'll no doubt give you topical allusions. And there'll be some good songs. Starts on December twenty-second, so you've ample time for rehearsal.' He shuffled the papers round again and took a page out. 'So, if you'll sign just here.'

Poppy picked up the pen and hesitated. 'Local? But where, Dan? You haven't said where I'm to go or which theatre!'

'Didn't I say?' He seemed astonished at his oversight. 'Why, it's the Grand Theatre. In Hull!'

CHAPTER TWENTY-EIGHT

'I can't be doing with you two women arguing!' Joshua had had enough; the problem had to be resolved. To be fair to Nan, she didn't argue; it was Lena who constantly complained about Nan. But it was getting him down today. He didn't feel well. He'd had a pain in his gut all night and had risen this morning feeling hot, sweaty and sick.

'I'm giving in my notice, Mr Mazzini,' Nan said quietly. 'I'm never going to please Mrs Rogers, no matter what I do.'

Joshua stared at her. 'Don't leave, Nan. Whatever will we do? You've been here so long. Why, Mary—'

'It was different when Mrs Mazzini was alive. I'd never have left her.' Nan turned to look straight at Lena. 'But Mrs Rogers has been trying to get me to leave ever since she came—'

'I have *not*,' Lena asserted vehemently. 'If you'd done your work properly – anyway, leave if you want. I can soon get somebody to replace you.'

Joshua suddenly felt he was going to be sick and covered his mouth with his hand. 'Just a minute,' he gasped and dashed from the kitchen.

Lena gave a triumphant sneer. 'Best collect your wages and go now,' she said. 'No sense in your hanging about.'

'I'll wait for Mr Mazzini, thank you,' Nan said bluntly. 'And I don't need you to tell me what to do. I'll finish the work I'm paid to do.'

Joshua came back a few minutes later looking grey and washed out. He sat down at the table. 'Something's upset me,' he groaned. 'That pork you cooked last night, Lena. Did it look all right? Wasn't green, was it?'

She bridled. 'Well, I'm all right. It hasn't affected me.'

'No, but you ate 'crackling and 'top slice of meat and that was very crisp. Look, Nan,' he began. 'Sorry.' He put his hand to his forehead. 'I feel rotten. I don't want you to leave.' He got up from the table again. 'I'm going to be sick.'

Nan picked up a polishing cloth and went towards the shop door. Lena called after her. 'Make sure them windows are clean before you go. Don't leave any streaks.'

When Joshua came back, Lena said in a confidential whisper, 'I'd let her go if I was you, Joshua. She's set on leaving; she's just said so. I wouldn't put it past her to have got another job lined up already.'

Joshua wiped his mouth. 'Do you think so?' he said weakly. 'I never thought that Nan—' He took a deep breath. 'I'd better not go in 'shop this morning. I feel terrible. Are you sure that meat was all right? Did you get it from Brown's 'same as usual? He's always had good meat.'

'Well, as I say, I feel all right.' Lena evaded the question. 'Perhaps you'd better go and sit down. Me and Albert will manage. We're not that busy.'

That was true, Joshua thought as he sat by the range in his easy chair. They were not very busy. Trade seemed to have dropped off. Some of the regular customers were not coming in and although he knew that people could be fickle in their shopping habits, even people like Mrs Forbes no longer came in for her husband's screw of tobacco, nor Mrs Brownlow for yesterday's penny loaf, and when he thought of it he hadn't seen the two youngsters lately, the one for the broken biscuits or the other for an ounce of tea. I could worry over those two, he mused. I hope they're all right. Scraps, they were, just skin and bone.

Nan finished her work an hour later and came through into the kitchen. Joshua was still sitting in his chair. 'Can I get you anything before I go?' She wore an anxious frown. 'You don't look so good. A drop of brandy and hot water? It's 'finest thing for an upset stomach.'

He shook his head. 'No, I can't face anything.' He looked up at her. 'Don't go, Nan,' he said weakly. 'I'll have nobody left from 'old days.'

She blinked. 'Old days are gone, Mr Mazzini. We've onny got 'present and 'future. If ever Mrs Rogers leaves, I'll come back.' She pressed her lips together. 'But I can't work with her any longer. She wants me out.'

'You've never called me Joshua, have you?' he murmured bleakly. 'Always done things right.'

'You're my employer,' she said flatly. 'I've never forgotten that. It doesn't do to become too familiar.'

It was almost a reprimand, he thought. Lena had called him Joshua – even Josh, until he told her not to – right from the start. 'I need Lena here,' he pleaded. 'I need somebody who can bake. I thought I was doing 'right thing in taking her, and she knew Mary.'

Nan put her chin up. 'So she said.' Her voice was without accusation, yet Joshua felt it was there, some hint that Nan didn't believe Lena. Yet why should Lena lie?

'I onny want wages up to today,' she said. 'I would have stayed until 'end of 'week, but I think it's best if I go now and we can all have a fresh start.'

'What will you do, Nan?' He rose from his chair. His legs felt weak and he doubled over as a stabbing pain hit his bowels. He groaned. 'Ask Albert to give you 'cash box and bring it here, will you? I'll have to go out to 'back again.'

He stumbled to the back door and Nan went into the shop. 'Mr Mazzini needs 'cash box. He said for me to take it in to him.'

Albert looked at her and then at Lena. 'Give it to her.' Lena indicated Nan with a toss of her head. 'If that's what he said.'

Nan took the box without a word and went back to the kitchen. She put the box on the table and sat down and waited for Joshua to return. When he did, a few minutes later, he looked greyer than ever, his mouth was pinched and his eyes were watery. 'Something's upset me,' he said, going to the sink to wash his hands. 'Something I ate.'

He opened the cash box at the table. He counted out some coins and then scanned the remaining contents. 'Mm, not been very busy this morning. There's not much more than the float here.'

Nan opened her mouth to say something but then seemed to think better of it, and remained silent. She took the coins that

Joshua gave to her and then said, 'You've given me a week's wages! I only want up to today's,' she repeated. 'You paid me on Saturday.'

'I know,' he said. 'But I feel bad about you going, Nan. I want you to have that, just to cover you until you find other work. Are you still working nights?'

'Yes.' She nodded. 'And washhouse. I have to. That pays 'rent, this pays – paid – for everything else.'

'What about Mattie? Is she still at 'flour mill?'

She blinked and swallowed and for a second he thought she was about to cry. 'At 'moment she is, though they're cutting down on 'workforce.' She caught her breath and glanced around the kitchen. 'Everything's done,' she told him. 'Upstairs and down. I've cleaned Poppy's room, but not Mrs Rogers's. She says she likes to do it herself.'

'I'm really sorry, Nan,' Joshua murmured. 'Will you drop in and see us?'

She gave a wistful smile. 'I don't think so. I'll not be welcomed by some folk.'

'You'll always be welcomed by me, Nan, you know that. If you can't manage or you need help, you know where to come.' But he knew she wouldn't. She was far too proud.

After she had gone, he put his head back and closed his eyes. Women, he thought. I don't know how to handle 'em! Who would have thought there could be so much discord? There was never a cross word when Mary was alive. He sighed. If he hadn't felt so ill he would have probably tried to resolve the situation between Lena and Nan, help them come to some working arrangement, but he felt so weak, he had no fight in him.

He heard the shop bell ring and shortly afterwards Lena came in for the cash box. 'We're a bit down wi' cash this morning,' he said. 'You haven't been giving credit, have you?'

'Why, no!' Her voice was sharp and startled. 'We had a bit of a rush on earlier.' She opened the box and looked in. She pursed her lips, and then commented, 'Course, you'll have paid Nan out of the takings?'

'Not that much,' he said. 'I've had to dip into 'float to pay her.'

She drew herself up. 'Well, there was plenty of cash in when she brought it in to you.' She glanced narrowly at him. 'I'm not suggesting anything,' she said. 'I know how you've always trusted her.' She raised a finger and shook it. 'I'm only saying there were takings in there when Albert gave it to her. Ask him,' she said defiantly. 'He'll tell you the same.'

He lifted his hand in resignation. 'Leave it,' he said. 'Forget I ever said anything.' Nevertheless it worried him. Whom could he trust? If only Tommy was here, or Poppy. He needed somebody.

'Why didn't you wait until 'end of 'week before handing in your notice, Ma?' Mattie's usually cheerful face was creased with worry. 'We could have done with 'extra money.'

'Mr Mazzini's paid me till 'end of 'week, bless him.' Nan sat down to take off her boots. 'But I couldn't stand a minute longer with that woman. She was determined to have me out and I wouldn't put it past her to tell Mr Mazzini lies about me. This morning I'd had enough and I could tell that Mr Mazzini had as well. He's not well, poor fellow. She's fed him some rotten meat, I shouldn't wonder.' She bit on her lip. 'I might find out about that. I know 'butcher at Brown's.'

'Oh, leave it, Ma. It's finished now,' Mattie said. 'We'll have to manage 'best we can. Did you tell Mr Mazzini I'd been put on short time?'

'No,' her mother said. 'As you just said, it's finished. Nothing to do with anybody else how we manage. And manage we will.' Her voice broke. 'One way or another.'

In the course of her search for daytime work as a cleaner, she called in at the butcher's shop to ask if any extra staff were needed, though she quite hoped he would say no. She didn't relish the thought of cleaning up bloodstained counters or floorboards, though she would have done if all else failed.

'Don't need anybody just now,' Brown's manager said. 'The lads wash down when we're finished. Mr Brown's very particular about cleanliness.'

'Does Mr Mazzini still get an order from you?' she asked casually.

'No!' he proclaimed with feeling. 'Not since that woman he lives with took over. Huh! Can't think why a nice chap like him would take up with a bitch like her. Is she a friend o' yourn?' he asked, seeing Nan's shocked expression.

'No, she isn't. But she doesn't live with Mr Mazzini! She has a room there and does 'baking. They're not, you know . . . Her son stays there too,' she added feebly.

'Sounds 'same to me!' He started to slice up a side of bacon. 'Still, it's nowt to do wi' me what he gets up to, but I miss his regular order. He used to buy a goodly amount o' meat from me; but then she wanted a bit o' this and a bit o' that. On 'quiet, you know. So I told her no and she's not been in since. She'll have found somebody to let her have cheap meat, I reckon. There's plenty who will if you're not too particular.' He gazed keenly at her. 'Don't you work for him?'

She shook her head. 'Not any more,' she said quietly. 'That's why I'm looking for another job.'

He put on a knowing expression. 'Got rid of you, did she?'

She nodded ruefully. 'Seems like it!'

When she arrived home at the end of that fruitless day, Mattie was already there. 'I've been stood off, Ma,' she said mournfully. 'When I arrived this morning, 'foreman said there was no work till after Christmas and to apply then.' She shrugged her shoulders. 'He didn't say how we were expected to manage in 'meantime.'

'Where've you applied since?' Nan asked, knowing that Mattie wouldn't have come straight home but would have looked for work.

'All over. I've been down to 'fish dock but there's some trouble there and they're not taking anybody on till after Christmas.' She shrugged again. 'They're asking 'workforce to join a union – and hey, Ma.' She laughed. 'What do you think? I heard there's going to be electric trams running through 'town next year, so I applied to train as a driver!'

Nan gasped, her mouth open in astonishment. 'What did they say?'

'Oh, well, what do you expect! They're onny taking men on. 'Chap I saw said how could women expect to do summat as technical as driving a tram! And,' she went on, 'do you know, I applied for cleaning jobs, scullery maid or laundry, in those houses in Albion Street – up where Poppy used to go to school – and some of those houses have electric light! Yes, really. They just press a switch and 'light comes on. They don't need to light a match or have a mantle or anything!'

'And will they take you?' Nan asked eagerly.

'No.' Mattie shook her head, her expression grave. 'What're we going to do, Ma? We can't manage on what we earn at 'King's Head.'

'We'll manage,' Nan said. 'Same as we allus do.'

'It's less than a month to Christmas Day,' Mattie said gloomily. 'I don't suppose we'll get an invite to Mazzini's this year?'

Her mother gave a grim smile. 'Even if we do, love, we won't be going.'

CHAPTER TWENTY-NINE

Poppy decided that she would travel back to Hull the next day rather than rush to catch a train that afternoon and arrive late at her father's. After leaving Dan's office she walked towards the theatre area and gazed at the posters announcing the artistes. Some of the theatres served melodrama, some farce, and some burlesque, which the present-day audience seemed to prefer, though serious theatre work was more acceptable than it once was, and theatres such as the Lyceum where Henry Irving had directed and acted in Shakespearean plays attracted a more genteel audience.

She gazed through the doors of the Royal Italian Opera House in Covent Garden and wished that she could hear a performance. But she couldn't go alone, and there was no-one she knew who could take her. Opera wouldn't be to Charlie's taste, she was sure of that, and the only other, Anthony, who she felt would appreciate opera, was no longer around.

Covent Garden swarmed and bustled with people, buying and selling, for this was London's fruit and flower market. Early each morning the porters heaved huge crates and sacks around as if they were a mere nothing; they shouted and whistled and by eight o'clock their job was done and the customers were gathering. The air was filled with the combined heady odours of fruit and flowers and the ground scattered with straw, horse dung, vegetable pods and parings.

The expansion of the railway into London forty years before had brought thousands of people to the capital looking for work. They came without money or jobs to go to and many of them shared a bed with strangers, living in cellars or on the streets, or beneath the arches which had been built to carry the railway lines which had brought them here in the first place. Most never went home to wherever it was they had come from. They stayed and increased the population until London overflowed with humanity. Some grew rich, and founded shops and industries; others stayed poor and lived in the workhouses, or if they were fortunate enough were given accommodation in newly built mansion flats, a scheme envisaged by philanthropists to ease the housing problem.

Some of the music halls were tucked away from the main thoroughfares but Poppy sought them out and took notice of the performers who were appearing there, and then she found the Savoy Theatre where the D'Oyly Carte Opera Company put on the Gilbert and Sullivan operettas which, it was said, the Queen enjoyed so much.

She stopped for coffee and cake, and wrote a postcard to Charlie telling him she was going home for Christmas. She posted it and then walked alongside the Thames, watching the mass of river traffic. Water taxis rowed by, tugs chugged past throwing out thick black smoke, sailboats with canvas sails creaking took advantage of the sharp wind, and ragged boys waded at the water's edge, searching for treasure within the detritus of old boots, bits of rags, empty bottles and sewage. She leaned against the embankment wall for a time and then, as her feet were aching and she was beginning to feel a chill, she hailed a hansom cab to take her back to Mrs Trenton's house.

Dolly Trenton made her a cup of tea, and when Poppy told her where she had been she regaled her with tales of the places where she and Nelly had played.

'Held the audience in the palm of our 'ands, we did. They loved us. We could do no wrong; whatever we sang, they joined in.' She sighed and grew wistful. 'Them was the days, all right,' she murmured. 'They'll never come back.'

The next morning Poppy went out into the street to look for a cab to take her and her trunk to King's Cross railway station. She saw old Harry standing outside his house smoking a pipe, and gave him a wave. The street didn't seem threatening in the daylight hours and she could laugh at her previous fears.

She bought a magazine at W. H. Smith's bookstall and settled down in her seat on the train. She hadn't asked for a ladies-only carriage this time as her father had done when she had travelled to London, and she reflected that although she hadn't been away from home so very long, it seemed as if a lifetime had passed.

I wonder if Charlie will go home for Christmas, she thought as the engine gathered steam. The guard shouted and waved his flag and the train jerked into action. I do hope that he does. I so want to see him. And Tommy, she thought, will there be a letter from him? Her father had written to her that he had heard nothing more from her brother since that first note.

When she arrived at the Paragon station it was early evening and she guessed that her father would be busy in the coffee shop. Office workers often popped in after they had finished work and before they walked home, as did some of the factory managers and clerks from the nearby dock office. He'll be so surprised to see me, she thought gleefully, and it's so nice to be home.

A porter took her and her baggage through to the front concourse and hailed a cab. 'To Mazzini's, please,' she said to the driver. 'Savile Street.'

'Aye, I know where it is,' the cabbie said, lifting up her trunk. 'And this is a deal heavier than when I took you to catch 'train to London! How've you bin? Had enough of bright lights o' London, eh? My missus has been watching 'newspaper for news of you.'

'Oh!' She was surprised that he remembered her. 'No, I've come home for Christmas and I'm appearing at the Grand Theatre, in pantomime.'

'My,' he said, handing her into the cab. 'We'll have to have a penn'orth o' that. I've not been yet. They say it's one of 'best theatres in 'country.'

She shook the creases out of her skirt and adjusted her fur hat, which was trimmed with velvet. She was wearing a navy wool jacket which had belonged to her mother and carried a fur muff.

The cab drew up at the shop and eagerly she peered inside to see if her father was there. But disappointingly, Albert was the only person she could see, and there were no customers inside. The driver handed down her trunk but she didn't wait for him to help her. She lifted her skirt and stepped down onto the footpath. She thanked him and paid him, and he tipped his cap before driving on as she turned to the door.

'Hello, Albert,' she called cheerfully, determined that neither he nor Lena would spoil her homecoming. 'Where's Pa?'

Albert stared open-mouthed. Then he licked his lips. 'He's in bed,' he said thickly. 'He's not been well.'

'Oh no!' She was immediately worried. 'What's the matter with him?'

He shrugged. 'He's been sick. Something he ate, the doctor said.' He looked at her. 'Is he expecting you?'

She gave a short laugh. 'No! But this is my home.' Then she asked, 'Would you mind helping me in with my trunk? I can't lift it by myself.'

He came round the counter and she noticed that the door to the medication cupboard was slightly ajar. He pulled the trunk into the shop and straightened up. 'Looks as if you're staying for a bit?' he said.

'Yes,' she said. 'I am. I'm appearing in the pantomime at the Grand. You say that my father's in bed? I'd better go up. Where's Lena?'

'She had to go out. She's had to do the ordering and the banking and things while your pa's been laid up.' Albert shuffled his feet whilst he was talking and occasionally glanced up at the cupboard. 'We've had to manage as best we could.'

'You're not very busy, though,' she commented. 'The coffee shop is usually full at this time.' She looked round. The tables had cloths on them but were not set with cutlery or flowers as they always used to be.

'No,' he agreed. 'Folks don't seem to be coming in.'

'I'll go up then,' she said. 'Will the trunk be in the way?'

He said that he would bring it through into the kitchen and she thanked him politely and went into the private quarters. The fire in the kitchen range was low and the room seemed gloomy. She reached for a match from the mantelpiece to light the gas lamp. One of the mantles had a hole in it and it pop-popped, so she turned to the oil lamp which was always kept on the dresser and lit that instead, turning it up so that there was a warm glow in the room. Then she turned to the stairs door and went quietly upstairs.

'Pa,' she whispered. 'Are you asleep?' Her heart gave a sudden lurch when she saw his hunched form beneath the covers and she was reminded forcibly of when her mother was ill in this same bed. Hot tears sprang to her eyes. What would she do if her father should die? How would she ever bear it?

'Papa!' she said, more urgently, and she heard a sigh and saw a slight movement. She came nearer the bed. 'It's me! Poppy.'

He turned over and put one arm above the coverlet. 'Poppy! Am I dreaming?'

There was no lamp lit and only a grey light coming in from the window, but she saw his pale face and reddened eyes. 'You're ill,' she said. 'Why didn't you send for me?'

He struggled to sit up. Beads of sweat were on his forehead, his chin was bristly and his hair stood on end. 'I've onny been sick for a few days, and besides, I wouldn't have bothered you.' She reached to hold his hand but he pulled it away. 'Don't,' he said. 'In case it's something catching. Lena said it might be. What're you doing here?' He licked his dry lips and she glanced at the empty water glass on the bedside table. 'Oh,' he sighed. 'I'm so glad to see you, Poppy. I can't tell you how glad.'

She opened a window, for the room smelt stale, and then went downstairs to fetch a bowl of warm water for him to wash with, and a jug of cold for him to drink. She poured him a glass and sat on the side of the bed whilst he drank thirstily.

'I've been gasping for a drink since dinnertime,' he said hoarsely. 'I hadn't 'strength to get up. I called for Lena but she didn't hear me. She must be busy in 'shop.'

'She's out,' Poppy said. 'Albert said she's had to see to the ordering and banking whilst you've been ill.'

He turned a puzzled frown towards her. 'I've not been ill that long. There can't have been overmuch to do.' He gave a weak grin. 'I feel better already now that you're home. Have you come for Christmas?'

'Yes.' She smiled. 'I have, and listen to this! I'm going to be in the pantomime at the new Grand Theatre and Opera House!'

'At 'Grand! Why, that's grand!' He gave another grin. 'Champion!'

'Have you had anything to eat?' she asked. 'Could you manage something light?'

He hesitated. 'I'm not sure. Doctor came and he said I'd eaten something that was off, though Lena swears that I've caught an infection from somebody.' He shook his head. 'I reckon it was that joint o' pork. I don't think she'd cooked it enough.'

'Let me make you some gruel,' she said. 'That's what Ma used to give Tommy or me if we were sick.'

'She did, didn't she?' he said pensively. 'I still miss her, you know, Poppy. Three years, and I still reach out for her in bed every morning.' She saw tears flood his eyes and she reached for his hand and this time he didn't pull away.

'I know,' she said huskily. 'I do know.'

She put the bowl of water by his bed and left him to wash and shave, and went downstairs. She had taken off her jacket and washed her hands, but still had her hat on as she stirred the gruel, when Lena came in.

'Well,' Lena acknowledged her. 'Never expected to see you so soon! Had enough of treading the boards, have you? I suppose it's not the same away from home where nobody knows you? You won't have had the same acclaim?'

Poppy glanced at her. She looks slovenly, she thought. Whatever made Pa take her on? Surely there must have been other bakers. Or did she catch him at his most vulnerable after her mother had died?

'I've had a very successful season, thank you,' she answered calmly. 'And I have another engagement here in Hull.' She wondered why Albert hadn't told his mother, but perhaps he hadn't thought it mattered. 'What do you think made my father ill?' she asked. 'He doesn't seem at all well. He's lost weight.'

'Don't know,' Lena answered casually. 'It's not something he ate as he seems to think, cos I ate the same. I reckon he's picked up a contagion from somebody. There's all sorts of things going about.'

'Are there? I didn't know. Perhaps we should ask Nan to give everything a good scrub with carbolic!'

'Nan isn't working here any more.' There was a hint of defiance in her voice, a warning against Poppy's challenging her authority. 'She left.'

'No!' Poppy was incredulous. 'Why?'

'She wanted to leave.' Lena's mouth turned down. 'She told

your father she was leaving and went the same day. Didn't even work a week's notice, which in view of the length of time she's worked here, I thought was very paltry. Just left us in the lurch.' She folded her arms in front of her. 'I've not found anybody to take her place as yet, but I'm asking around. At the moment I'm doing everything. Baking, cleaning, and Albert's looking after the shop.'

'What about the coffee house?' Poppy frowned. There was too much to do for two people, though she hoped her father would soon be up and about.

'We don't seem to be doing much there. I've stopped baking cakes, doesn't seem worthwhile, so I'm just offering coffee and biscuits.'

'Oh.' Poppy paused with the spoon in her hand. 'But Mazzini's was known for its cakes!'

'Can't be helped.' Lena was dismissive. 'I've only got one pair of hands.'

'Pa! Why did Nan leave? I can't believe that she just walked out as Lena said.' Poppy placed the tray with the dish of gruel on his lap, and then plumped up his pillows.

'She and Lena didn't get on,' her father said wearily. 'And it just came to the crunch. I said I'd had enough of them arguing and Nan said she was leaving, and it was best if she went straight away. I was feeling ill on the day she left or I might have found some solution.'

'Like sacking Lena,' Poppy said bitterly.

'And then Albert would have gone too and I would have had to shut up 'shop. I was too ill to manage on my own.'

'Lena said she isn't baking cakes any more. Could we get another baker to supply us?' Poppy's forehead creased. 'We can't have a coffee shop without cakes!'

'Don't you worry about it, Poppy. I'll sort things out when I'm up and about.' He spooned the gruel into his mouth. 'But that's enough about 'shop. Tell me about 'pantomime. When do you start?'

'I'm to go in tomorrow to meet John Hart, or Fred Vine if he's arrived. They're producing it. It's Aladdin, by the way.' She smiled. 'And I'm going to be the Good Spirit of the Pantomime. At least, I hope so. Dan Damone was a little vague about it.'

'Is he a good agent?' Her father finished off the bowl of gruel and sat back on the pillows, satisfied.

'Yes. I trust him. And he's come up with a suggestion for me. He doesn't think, and I agree with him, that I'm a suitable type for the music hall.'

As she told her father what Dan had said, she reasoned that if his business wasn't doing well, she definitely couldn't ask him to pay for singing lessons. I'll take the engagements in London, she mused. There are lots of small theatres that would probably have me as a fill-in act. I shall pay for the coach myself.

'A singing coach?' Joshua repeated. 'And where will that lead you? Where will you sing then?'

'Theatres,' she said. 'Or pantomimes like the one at the Grand. I think Dan has offered me this engagement to see how I like it.'

'But pantomimes are onny a short season! What will you do for 'rest of 'year?'

'I'm not sure,' she confessed. 'Perhaps I'll work as a single performer, or in operettas – not grand opera,' she added hastily. 'I haven't got the voice for that.'

'So you'll be guided by this coach, will you?' he asked. 'Do you know who he is?'

'He's a she, Pa.' She smiled. 'So you don't need to worry – and it's Dan Damone's sister.'

'Ah!' His face cleared, then he said, 'I do still worry about you, Poppy. I think of you all by yourself in these unfamiliar places, mixing with I don't know who!'

She patted his hand. 'I have to grow up sometime, Pa. I'm having another birthday in a couple of weeks.'

'Grown up!' He nodded thoughtfully. 'And I suppose you'll be meeting up with young men and falling in love before we can wink an eye!'

She smiled. What would her father think if she told him she already loved Charlie? 'Yes,' she said. 'I suppose I will.'

CHAPTER THIRTY

When she arrived at the Grand Theatre the next morning she found John Hart in his office. He seemed surprised to see her so soon. 'We're still in production with *Pepita*,' he said. 'It's going very well. Have you seen it?'

She confessed that she hadn't, and told him that she had just returned from a season at Brighton. He immediately gave her two complimentary tickets for the comic opera. 'Another week before Fred Vine and the company arrive, and then we'll start rehearsals. You'll be glad of a week off, I expect,' he added. 'You'll have had a busy time in Brighton. Have you enjoyed the experience? I came to see you at the Mechanics. You've a lot of talent and it's good to know that you're trying out other shows and not just music hall.'

'That's what my agent says,' she replied, thanking him for his compliments. 'He wants me to take further singing lessons.'

She told him that she would see him the following week and decided that she would put the days to good use. On the way back from the theatre, she went to see Miss Eloise to tell her what she was doing. She was sure she would be interested to know. Miss Eloise was thrilled to hear that she was to be in pantomime.

'It will give you a chance to stretch your voice,' she said. 'Aladdin is not quite operetta as Rossini's *Cinderella* is, but nevertheless is a good vehicle for a pure voice.' Poppy explained that she would have only a small part, but Miss Eloise said she would book tickets immediately they came on sale and would buy one for Miss Davina, who was away at present.

Poppy called back at home and found that her father had risen from his sick bed and come downstairs. He was sitting in his chair by the range and Lena was scurrying round him, clearing up from the morning's baking, her face set and her mouth pinched.

'I have to go out again,' Poppy told Lena. 'Is there anything I can get for you? Do we need meat for supper? Chops or anything?'

'No,' Lena said sharply. 'I'll get it. I've ordered some mince. The butcher knows what I like. You can help Albert in the shop when you come back,' she sniffed, and glancing at Joshua she added, 'That's if you're not too proud.'

'I'll never be that,' Poppy said quietly. 'I know who I am and where I belong.'

Lena flushed and turned away. 'I need some help,' she muttered. 'I've a woman in mind to come in and do the rough. I'll slip out and see her a bit later.'

'Fetch her here, why don't you?' Joshua said in a low voice. 'I'd like to see who she is before we tek her on.'

Lena put her hand on her hip. 'Well, if you don't trust my judgement!'

'It's not that,' he began, but Lena had turned and gone to the sink, and Poppy could see how her father was worn down by the pettiness and so was giving in to Lena. She too felt powerless, for if she argued with her she might leave, taking Albert with her as her father had said, and then there would be no-one to help him.

She made coffee for her father and Lena, and then prepared to go out again. 'I won't be long,' she told him. 'I just need a few things.' But she didn't tell him that she was going to see Nan.

As she went through into the shop she heard raised voices. 'Look at this!' a woman's voice complained. 'Why, I wouldn't chuck it out for 'pigeons, let alone eat it myself. I don't know what's come over this place.'

Albert was staring sullenly at the customer and fingering a soggy bread loaf. 'Looks all right to me,' he muttered. 'We've not had any other complaints.'

'Not yet you haven't,' the woman stated. 'You wait till dinner-time when folk come to eat it.' She looked up as Poppy came through the door. 'Poppy!' she said. 'About time you came home! What's going on here? Can't get a decent loaf o' bread. Can't get a cup o' coffee.'

'Hello, Mrs Thomas.' She was a long-standing customer of both the grocery and the coffee shop. 'What's the trouble?'

Mrs Thomas took the bread from Albert and handed it to Poppy. The outside of it was crisp, but the inside where it had been pulled apart was soft and doughy and uncooked. 'That's the trouble. Can't expect Mr Thomas to eat that! It'll make him right badly. It's not 'first time it's happened,' she said. 'I'll start making my own again and tek it to 'baker to be cooked!'

'I'm so sorry, Mrs Thomas,' Poppy said. 'I don't think the oven can have been hot enough. Albert, give Mrs Thomas her money back and another loaf if you have one.'

'What's this? What's this?' Lena had heard the raised voices and come marching through from the kitchen. She snatched the bread from Poppy and examined it. 'Why, you've cut it with a knife while it was still hot, haven't you?' she said. 'Anybody'll tell you that you should break bread with your fingers when it's just out of the oven. Give her her money back, Albert,' she said aggressively. 'But we've no bread left. Sold out!'

'Sold out! Already? At this time of a morning? Then you're not making enough,' Mrs Thomas accused. 'Or mebbe you can't sell it.' Mrs Thomas snatched the money from Albert's hand and headed for the door. Then she turned back. 'All these years I've been coming here, but this'll be 'last time!'

'Mrs Thomas!' Poppy called futilely, but she had gone, her long coat swirling on her short body and her hat bobbing furiously.

'Oh, let her go,' Lena said callously. 'We can do without folks like her!'

'But she's been coming here for as long as I can remember!' Poppy was dumbfounded. 'When I was little she used to bring me bon-bons and sugar mice.'

'Did she?' Lena sniffed. 'Well, them days are gone.'

Poppy walked briskly towards the High Street, trying to rid herself of anger. Lena has the wrong attitude towards customers, she thought. She should be trying to please them, give them what they want, not what she wants them to have. And what did Mrs Thomas mean when she said that you couldn't get a cup of coffee? There was always coffee at Mazzini's.

She knocked on Nan's door and thought how shabby and

rundown the area was. Some of the houses in the court were left empty when tenants moved out to the newer streets out of town. Only the very poor who couldn't afford a higher rent stayed in the old town courts.

She only half expected Nan to be at home and was surprised when the door opened and both Nan and Mattie stood inside. Both were wearing old coats with shawls over the top, and when they invited Poppy in she realized why. There was no fire lit in the grate and the room was freezing.

'Poppy!' They both greeted her with pleasure. 'How grand to see you.' Nan gave her a kiss on her cheek and Poppy felt the coldness of her face. 'Have you come home for Christmas?' Mattie asked. 'Come on, come and sit down and tell us all that you've been doing.'

'Sorry there's no fire,' Nan murmured. 'We – we were just going out. Not that there's any hurry,' she added hastily. 'We've plenty of time to talk to you.'

Poppy gazed at her. 'Tell me where you were really going, Nan! Are you looking for work?'

Nan nodded. 'Aye. Well, we've been out this morning already. We've both just come back.'

'Are you not working either, Mattie?'

'Onny at night,' Mattie said. ' 'Flour mill's stood off some of 'workers till after Christmas. They'll take us back then,' she said brightly. 'At least – that's what they said.'

Poppy pondered. Last night she had offered to help Lena with the morning's baking, but she had refused her, saying that she and Albert had a routine, so whilst she was having an extra sleep in bed this morning Nan and Mattie were trawling round looking for work. Unsuccessfully, it seemed.

'I'm sorry you felt you had to leave, Nan,' she told her. 'It's not the same without you. And Pa misses you too.'

Nan shook her head. 'I couldn't stand it any longer,' she said. 'It wasn't an instant decision. I knew one of us, me or Lena, would have to go; and it's just bad luck that Mattie came off work on 'same day.'

'Anyway,' Mattie chipped in, 'that's enough about us. What about you? Tell us about London, and Brighton. Was it really exciting? Oh, how I wished I could have gone with you that day you got on 'train.'

'Charlie met me at King's Cross,' Poppy told her. 'He hired a cab and took me to my agent.' She went on to tell them about Miss Battle and the awful lodging house and having supper at the Marinos'. And then she told them about going to Brighton and being on the same bill as the Terry Sisters and Anthony Marino, who had written 'Forever True' and played for her at her last performance.

'So – this pianist, is he 'son of 'people with the café?' Mattie had worked it out. 'And is he nice? 'Pianist, I mean?'

'Yes,' Poppy said enthusiastically. 'He is. He's lovely! I was so nervous and he was so good and helpful towards me.'

'You were nervous?' Nan said. 'I can't believe that!'

'It was different being away from home,' Poppy explained. 'Nobody knew me, so I had to prove myself.'

'And did you?'

Poppy nodded, pressing her lips together in embarrassment. 'Yes,' she said. 'I think so.'

'Any news of Tommy?' Mattie asked. 'Has he written?'

'No.' Poppy shook her head. 'Pa's not well, but when he's up and about again he says he'll go and enquire at the shipping company. He's getting really worried now.'

'Your pa's not well?' Nan frowned. 'Not with 'same thing as 'day I left?'

'I think so,' Poppy said. 'The doctor said he'd probably eaten tainted meat, but Lena pooh-poohed that and said he'd picked up a contagion from somebody. But Pa thinks it might have been a bad piece of pork.'

Nan tutted and looked angry and frustrated. 'I wasn't going to say anything, but I'd better tell you. Lena's not using 'same butcher any more. I went into Brown's,' she explained. 'I was looking for work but I asked if he still supplied Mazzini's. Apparently Lena hasn't shopped there for some time.'

'She's buying cheap meat!' Poppy gasped. 'The pork might have been rancid. And if it wasn't cooked enough—'

Nan nodded and bit her lip. 'You can die of that,' she muttered. 'That woman's a menace.'

After leaving Nan and Mattie, Poppy went to Scale Lane, intending to call on Mr and Mrs Chandler. Perhaps, she thought hopefully, they'll have news of Charlie. Mr Chandler was in his chair by the window of his workshop, his arms outstretched as he pulled thread through a welt to attach to the sole of a shoe, and Poppy mused that he was sitting in the selfsame position as when she saw him the last time. Does he only rise from his chair when he goes to bed? she wondered. Does he never take a walk outside to find out what is happening in the world?

He looked up as she knocked on the door and signalled for her to come in. 'You're back then?' was his comment.

'For a while, Mr Chandler. I'm playing at the Grand Theatre and then I'll be going back to London.'

'Hmph. Seen anything of my son? Or is he too busy to keep in touch with you as well?'

'I saw him in Brighton,' she said. 'But that was when I first went down there. I wrote to him to say I was coming home for Christmas.'

'I've written to him several times.' Mrs Chandler stood in the doorway to the house. 'But he hasn't replied. I expect he'll write when he's run out of money.'

They can't know about his new venture, Poppy thought. And it's not up to me to tell them.

'Are you still wearing them shoes he made for you?' Mr Chandler asked.

'Oh, yes,' Poppy said eagerly. 'I always wear them when I'm on stage. They're lovely. As a matter of fact,' her tongue ran away with her, 'the Terry Sisters who were on the same bill as me asked if he'd make some for them.'

Mr Chandler grunted, and Mrs Chandler, without commenting, sat down at the sewing machine. Poppy thought it was no wonder that Charlie wanted to leave home when his parents were so dour and taciturn. At least her father had always encouraged her in her singing, even though he was reluctant to let her go.

'Aye, well. He wanted to make shoes for 'rich and famous,' Mr Chandler muttered, knotting the ends of the thread. 'Mebbe those stage folk would be a start, though I doubt they'll be rich even if they're famous.'

'I'm sure they are not, Mr Chandler. I haven't met anyone yet who is.'

Poppy walked back along Whitefriargate looking casually in the shops. She'd stopped to look at a grey and red wool costume in the window of one establishment and then turned to walk on when a small elderly woman almost bumped into her. 'I beg your pardon,' Poppy said. 'So sorry.'

It was Mrs Thomas. 'Well, Poppy,' she said, looking up at her, and Poppy thought that either she had grown or Mrs Thomas had shrunk. 'Have you come home to look after your da before that woman ruins him? I'll not shop there again until she's gone and there's others feel 'same!'

'I don't know what to do, Mrs Thomas,' Poppy said miserably. 'Pa took her on because she's a baker and because she knew my mother.'

'Pah!' Mrs Thomas bristled. 'She's no baker! Where did she learn to bake, that's what I'd like to know? Not round here, she didn't. And as for knowing your ma, I don't believe that either. I don't remember her being about, and I'd known your ma for a long time.' She shook a finger. 'I reckon she heard as your poor ma was dying and kept her eyes and ears open. Then when opportunity came, when your da was at a low ebb, she turned up.'

She nodded solemnly at Poppy, who was astounded at this discourse. 'And as for that son of hers. You take a look at him.' She tapped her nose. 'If I'm not very much mistaken, he's having a dip into your da's medicine cupboard.' She patted Poppy on the arm and said, 'I'm sorry, but there's onny one thing you can do, young woman. You'll have to stop at home or your da will be ruined.'

CHAPTER THIRTY-ONE

Poppy's conscience smarted. Mrs Thomas's words had hit home. She was telling her that she was being selfish by concentrating on her own wishes, when she ought to be staying at home as a good daughter should, running the grocery shop with her father. It was totally unheard of among the people they knew for a young woman to go off to live her own life away from her family.

My father is so generous and caring, she mused. He only wants us to be happy and fulfilled. Although she had a suspicion that when he told Tommy he could go to sea, he was presuming that he would come home after having had a taste of it. But he's wrong there, she sighed. Tommy seems to have settled into seafaring life so well that he doesn't even have time to write.

The following day she walked down to the Queen's Dock, which was situated behind Savile Street, and looked at the ships just as Tommy used to do. From their bedrooms above the shop they were used to hearing the clang of iron and steel, the hoot of steamers and the shouts of porters and seamen as they went about their daily business. This ten-acre dock was once the biggest in the country and had served the whaling trade, which gave Hull its first major industry.

She turned and cut back towards Monument Bridge, then waited as the bridge was raised to allow a tall-masted barge to come through the Whitefriargate lock. The lifting and lowering of locks and bridges to let the shipping traffic through frequently delayed pedestrians and road traffic.

Poppy was going again to see Nan and Mattie, to offer them the tickets that Mr Hart had given her for *Pepita.* Tomorrow was

Friday and she had asked her father if he would like to see the comic opera, but he was still feeling low, he said, and didn't want to.

'You go,' he'd suggested. 'Ask Mattie if she'll go with you, and find out if Nan has found work,' he added anxiously. 'I'd like to help her, but she's so proud I know she wouldn't accept any money.'

Poppy knew this to be true, so had decided to give the tickets to them both as a treat, and she would buy one for herself. As she waited for the bridge to be lowered, she saw someone waving to her from the other side. It was Mattie, barely recognizable, muffled up as she was in several shawls. It was an extremely cold morning and Poppy was wearing a warm coat with her fur hat and muff.

'Poppy! Where are you off to?' Mattie asked.

'I was coming to see you.' Poppy smiled. 'To ask if you and Nan would like to come with me to see *Pepita* at the Grand.' She saw the doubt appear on Mattie's face and swiftly added, 'I've been given complimentary tickets. Pa isn't well enough to come and I don't want to go on my own.'

'Oh! When?' Mattie asked eagerly. 'We can't come at night as we're working at 'King's Head and if we give up even one night they might sack us!'

'A matinee then? Tomorrow or Saturday?' I should have realized that Mattie and Nan couldn't afford to give up an evening for something as frivolous as entertainment, she thought. 'I start rehearsals next week.'

'Saturday then! Lovely.' Mattie's face lit up with enthusiasm. 'Ma is out this morning anyway. She's found temporary work at 'washhouse and won't be back till later.' Then she frowned. 'Is your pa no better, then?'

'I think he's over his sickness,' Poppy said. 'But he's very low-spirited. Come and have coffee with me, Mattie,' she said impulsively. 'Here.' She looked back along the street towards where St John's Church and a group of shops and a coffee shop stood. 'This place is all right, isn't it?'

'Not as good as Mazzini's,' Mattie grinned, linking arms. 'But it'll do.'

They went into the coffee shop and Poppy ordered coffee,

cakes and scones, for she wondered if Mattie had had any breakfast. And she might not have had, judging from the way her eyes glistened when the waitress brought the food.

'The thing is, Mattie,' Poppy said thoughtfully, 'I wanted to talk to you or Nan. I wasn't just coming to ask about the theatre tickets.'

Mattie licked her buttery fingers. 'Mm? Aren't you going to have a cake?' Her eyes were enormous, Poppy thought, and she saw what she hadn't noticed last time, that beneath her shawls Mattie had lost weight.

'I don't think I want anything,' Poppy said, even though she knew she could have eaten something. 'You finish them. I'm worried, Mattie, and I don't know what to do.' She took a deep breath. 'I shouldn't bother you,' she said guiltily. 'You've got more worries than I have.'

'What are friends for?' Mattie asked. She rubbed her fingers together to dispose of crumbs and then pressed Poppy's hand. 'We've known each other a long time.' She drew her eyebrows together anxiously and narrowed her eyes. 'You're not in any kind of trouble, are you?'

'What do you mean?' Poppy asked innocently. 'Trouble? No.' She shook her head. 'Oh! No!' She flushed. 'Nothing like I think you mean.' She recalled Mattie's giving her advice on women's matters when she didn't know who else to ask.

'That's all right then.' Mattie gazed at her. 'But young girls can get in trouble, especially when they're on their own away from home.'

Poppy swallowed. 'I suppose so,' she said. 'And especially in the sort of business I'm in,' she admitted, thinking of the Terry Sisters who had stayed out all night. Then she laughed. 'But no-one has propositioned me yet.'

'No?' Mattie raised her expressive eyebrows. 'What about that pianist feller you told us about? Didn't he want to take you out for supper or anything? That's how it would start.'

'He's a perfect gentleman. No, really!' she insisted, when Mattie hooted derisively. 'We did go out to supper and he also took me to see the Royal Pavilion at Brighton, but I didn't know until later that my agent had asked him to keep an eye on me.' She sighed pensively. 'I don't know when I'll see him again. He's touring the south coast now.'

'And – erm, Charlie?' Mattie threw in the question casually. 'Have you seen him again? Apart from when he met you in London, I mean?'

'Just once,' Poppy murmured. 'I thought he might have come to see me again, but he didn't,' she said miserably. 'Though I can excuse him, I suppose. He's about to start in his own business and is bound to be busy.'

'You're fond of him, aren't you?' Mattie asked, and when Poppy nodded, she said, 'Well, be careful you don't get hurt. He's – well, he's older and more experienced than you,' she finished lamely.

'Everybody's older than me, Mattie.'

'So what is it that you're worried about?' Mattie scraped up the crumbs from the plate with her fingers and popped them into her mouth. 'If it's not some feller.' She winked.

Poppy sighed. Mattie was so cheerful and positive in spite of her hard life. She was just like her mother. 'I'm worried because—' she began. Then she corrected herself. 'That's not right. I'm not worried. Worry is when you've no job and no money coming in, and you don't know where the next meal is coming from, isn't it?' Mattie nodded in agreement and Poppy went on. 'I'm confused and I'm anxious and I don't know what to do for the best.'

She told her about Lena and the row she had had with Mrs Thomas over the bread, and then about meeting Mrs Thomas and being advised that she should stay at home and help her father.

'Perhaps I should stay at home,' she said. 'I hate to think of Pa being in that woman's clutches; and if customers are staying away, then it won't be long before the business is finished!'

'Your pa won't let that happen,' Mattie assured her. 'He's been in business too long to let some harridan like that spoil it for him.'

'You don't understand!' Poppy said fretfully and felt tears fill her eyes. 'Pa's got so low. He's not really over the loss of my mother, and then Tommy and I have let him down by going away and leaving him!'

'I'm really sorry,' Mattie said huskily. 'I like your father – he's just 'sort of da I'd have liked. But if you stay at home he'll feel guilty for stopping you from doing what you want to do. And would it help?' she asked. 'Wouldn't you still want somebody who can bake and serve in 'shop?'

'Yes,' Poppy agreed. 'But I could choose who came, and she wouldn't have to live in.'

'Is that what you're bothered about?' Mattie came swiftly to the point. 'You don't like Lena living in 'same house as your da?'

'No, I don't,' Poppy said petulantly. 'I don't like it at all. It's as if she's trying to take over.'

'Well . . .' Mattie hesitated. 'If it was me – if I was in your shoes—'

'Yes?' Poppy knew what Mattie would do in her situation. She would give up her singing and help her mother or her father if she had one. Mattie was totally unselfish. Unlike me, she thought mournfully. I want to sing and if I can't, then I'll be miserable for ever.

'I think you should talk to your father. Tell him how bothered you are about him and tell him that you'll give up 'stage if needs be. He's got a couple of weeks to think about it until you've finished at 'Grand, hasn't he? It might be just 'boost he needs to consider a way of getting rid of Lena and Albert and taking somebody else on instead.'

'Yes,' Poppy said. 'You're right. It's no use my mulling it over on my own. I've got to bring it out in the open. Take the bull by the horns, as they say.'

Mattie grunted. 'Cows don't have horns,' she said. 'But you could get hold of Lena by the nose!'

Poppy laughed unhappily. It wouldn't be easy getting Lena out. Her father was such a kind man. He wouldn't want to hurt her feelings. But there surely must be a way?

Poppy paid and they prepared to leave. 'Which Mrs Thomas was it, by the way?' Mattie asked. 'The one who had 'row with Lena?'

'She and Mr Thomas used to come in for coffee on a Saturday night after they'd been to the Mechanics,' Poppy said. 'You know, he used to be a barber in Posterngate until he got rheumatism in his hands.'

Mattie nodded. 'I know,' she said. 'I know who you mean.' She flashed a smile at Poppy as they stood outside. A sharp wind was blowing in off the estuary, gusting up the dock and churning up the water, rattling rigging and dragging on anchors, and swirling rubbish round their feet. She huddled into her shawls. 'Don't you worry, Poppy. Talk to your pa. We'll think on some way of getting rid of Lena.'

Nan was thrilled to have been asked to the theatre, and on the Saturday afternoon she brushed down her shabby coat and unearthed the hat that she had worn when Joshua had made up a party at his expense to hear Poppy sing at the Mechanics. 'How that girl has come on since then,' she said to Mattie. 'She's done so well! I'm really pleased for her.'

'So am I.' Mattie brushed her unruly hair and looked at herself in the tin plate on the wall that served as a mirror. My freckles have gone, she thought. Wish I was better-looking. She sucked in her cheeks. If onny I had good bone structure like Poppy, instead of a round face. She's a real looker. She sighed. Not that it would make a deal of difference to my life. 'I'm ready, Ma,' she said. 'Can't do any better with what I've got.'

'You're lovely.' Her mother smiled. 'Anybody would be glad to be like you.'

'Come on!' Mattie picked up her coat. It was one that had been her mother's and before that had belonged to Mrs Mazzini, who had given it to Nan years ago. 'Compliments would buy you a glass of ale if I had any brass.'

Nan locked the door behind them and put the key in her pocket. 'We've not got much,' she murmured. 'But mebbe more than some, and I'd like to think it's still here when we get back.'

'Nobody would break into our place, Ma,' Mattie said. 'They'd have to be desperate.' She took hold of Nan's arm and they walked off through driving rain to meet Poppy outside the Grand Theatre and Opera House. They cut across Bridge Street, skirted round the eastern end of Queen's Dock, dodging the bustle of seamen which told them of the arrival of another ship, and walked down Charlotte Street towards George Street where the Grand was situated.

'Ma!' Mattie said as they hurried along, heads bent against the rain. 'Do you know Mrs Thomas? The woman whose husband used to be a barber?'

'Yes,' Nan said. 'Course I do. Known her for years. Why?'
'Do you know where she lives?'
'They still live above 'shop. He sub-let the barber's when he couldn't handle a blade any more. Why do you want to know?'
'There's Poppy waiting for us,' Mattie interrupted. 'Yoo-hoo, Poppy!'
'Hush!' Nan said, conscious of the better-dressed people waiting to go in. 'This isn't music hall, Mattie. This is opera!'
Mattie turned to her mother. 'You mean I can't sing along?' she said in mock amazement.
'Certainly not,' Nan reprimanded her. 'So please. A little decorum!'
'Decorum isn't me, you know that, Ma!' Then she grinned. 'Only fooling! I'll be as good as gold.'
But she could have sung along, she decided, as she sat glued to her seat, if only she had known the words. Lecoque's *Pepita* was bright and amusing, the costumes and sets were charming, and the singing was delightful, or so it seemed to her. Mattie turned to Poppy in the interval and saw that her eyes were sparkling.
'Do you know what, Poppy?'
'No. What?' Poppy seemed to have lost her anxiety and found her high spirits again.
'I think you could do this. Sing in light opera. You can certainly sing as well as . . .' She consulted the programme. 'Pepita – Miss Anne Rees. Couldn't she, Ma? Can't you see it? Miss Poppy Mazzini taking the lead!'
'Well, we'll see.' Poppy looked suddenly downcast. She took a deep breath. 'After Aladdin is over. Then I'll make a decision.'
As they walked home after the performance, Mattie said to Nan. 'We've got to do something, Ma, to keep Poppy on 'stage. It's such a waste of talent otherwise.'
Nan nodded, but said, 'It's out of our hands, Mattie. We're not involved any more. What can we do?'
They both shrunk down into their coats. The sky was as black as if it was night. Rain was still pelting down, sharp as sleet, and they didn't have umbrellas. 'Got to do something,' Mattie gasped. 'I'm going to find out about that Lena woman. Discover where she's come from.'
'It won't help,' Nan replied. 'Joshua will be in a worse state

than before if she leaves. Poppy will have to stay at home then.'

'No, she won't,' Mattie argued. 'We'll go and work for him. For nowt, if necessary.' They turned into their dark court. It was awash with water. 'Damn and blast this place,' Mattie said, splashing towards their door, and her mother hushed her, telling her to be thankful they had a place to go to and a roof over their heads.

'Give us 'key, Ma,' Mattie said. 'I'm frozen! Though there's no point in making a fire when we've to go out again in a couple of hours. Mother of God!' She sprang back, away from the huddled shape on the doorstep. 'Who on earth—'

'We've got nothing!' Nan's voice broke as she saw the figure rise up above them. 'We're as poor as you are.'

'Nan! Mattie!' A man's voice, young and trembling. 'Don't be scared. It's me. Tommy!'

CHAPTER THIRTY-TWO

Poppy turned up for rehearsals on the Monday morning as arranged, but few of the cast were assembled. Some were still travelling from their last engagement. 'You're local, I hear?' Fred Vine asked. He was the producer and stage manager for the company.

'Yes, I was born in Hull,' she said. 'Just across from here, in Savile Street.'

'But you're a professional singer?' He frowned. 'I'm sorry, but I don't know of you. I'm only going by what Dan Damone said about you.'

'You won't have heard of me – yet,' she added, and was gratified to see him smile. 'I've been working in Brighton – at Bradshaw's.'

'Music hall! This is different.' Again he frowned. 'What did Damone tell you?'

'I know it's different from music hall,' she said. 'I've been going to the theatre and music hall and pantomime all my life. I know that I need to sing well and to dance and I can do both.' She looked earnestly at him and wondered why Fred Vine had agreed to take her on. Was it because the show was opening in Hull? Surely Dan had told him she was new to the business? 'Dan wants me to try all aspects of the theatre before making a final choice of career.'

'What part did he tell you I might give you?'

'The Good Spirit of Pantomime.' She was feeling nervous under his scrutiny.

'A red-haired Spirit!' he murmured, almost to himself. 'Well, why not? A flame to keep the Spirit alive.' He looked closely at her. 'Mm. Sparkling glitter in your hair as if it's on fire. Could work. Just one snag.' He worried through his beard with his fingers. 'Miss Gosse usually plays that part. You'll know her, probably? Miss Ellen Gosse? Her agent wrote weeks ago to say she couldn't play, which is why I cast round for someone else. But now I've had a letter from him to say that she's available after all.'

'But – I've signed the contract.' Poppy was dismayed. 'Surely she won't expect to come now?'

He had the decency to look embarrassed. 'It's not her fault,' he said. 'She's very reliable and she knows the part backwards. It's her agent who's at fault and so am I, if I'm honest. I suppose I panicked when I heard she couldn't come. Tell you what – and I'm really sorry about this, Miss Mazzini – would you learn the script and the songs? I'll know by the middle of the week what's happening and if she does turn up I'll create another role specially for you.' He nodded. 'You'll be a good draw if people in the town know there's someone local playing a part.' He peered anxiously at her. 'What do you think?'

I'm too inexperienced to know what I should do, she thought. And if I write to Dan to ask him, by the time I receive a reply it will be too late. 'I've given up another engagement to come here,' she hedged. 'I could have stayed on at Brighton. All right. I'll do it on condition that if I don't play the Spirit, then I'll play some other character, as you say, and you don't put me in the chorus.' There, she thought. I've asserted myself. Let's see what he says to that.

He heaved a sigh. 'Wonderful!' He smiled. 'You are most obliging, Miss Mazzini. So very accommodating! You wouldn't believe the trouble I have sometimes with a temperamental cast.'

She smiled sweetly and said, 'You caught me in a good frame of mind, Mr Vine.' She didn't want him to think he could manipulate her. 'A contract is binding, after all. And I'll write to my agent and tell him to make sure it doesn't happen again.'

He nodded. 'Quite right,' he said. 'I do apologize. It's just that Miss Gosse has played the part so often and I might want her to play it again, whilst you . . .' He looked at her and there was a twinkle in his eyes. 'You will no doubt be spreading your wings elsewhere?'

'Perhaps I will,' she said. 'But you haven't heard me sing yet, Mr Vine, so how do you know?' She was being bold, she knew, but felt she had to appear self-assured.

He gave her a little bow and stretched out his hand towards the stage. 'Then let's begin.'

She ran through a repertoire of popular songs from the music hall and then lyrical pieces, waltzes, sweet melodies and songs of love. She could sing without accompaniment, but there was a pianist down in the orchestra pit who played quietly in the background, picking up the harmony as she sang.

'Well done,' Fred Vine said as she finished. 'Lovely!' He gazed at her for a moment and then said, 'You are young for this kind of role, Miss Mazzini.' He nodded thoughtfully. 'But you have a voice beyond your years. Nurture it, and it will serve you well.' He smiled. 'You'll go far.'

'Thank you,' she said, and gave a deep breath of contentment.

'I could quite hope that Miss Gosse won't turn up,' he murmured. 'But even if she does I will create a role for you. We can't let that voice go to waste.'

When she wasn't at rehearsal or studying the role of the Good Spirit, she spent as much time as she could helping out in the shop. But trade was slack. She saw few of her father's regular customers, and this bothered her. She harboured the suspicion that Lena and Albert's attitude had driven them away, for they both had an indifferent disposition towards the people who came in. They sullenly served coffee and biscuits to those who wanted refreshments, and stood around as if waiting for them to leave so that they could clear away.

Poppy's father came back into the shop mid-week and found that Albert had rearranged the grocery shelves, which were in any case much emptier than usual. 'Where are 'tinned peas and haricot beans?' Joshua asked one morning whilst Poppy was out. 'And 'jars of barley sugar? And where've you put 'Pontefract Cakes and liquorice sticks? Everything's been moved!'

'I shifted 'confectionery so that the bairns didn't put their sticky fingers in it. Too much temptation,' Albert said glumly. 'That's what Lena said, anyway.'

'Candy and confectionery needs to be at 'front so that they can see it,' Joshua said. 'We want them to be tempted, otherwise they don't buy. And them tinned peas should be on 'bottom shelf so we can get at them easier. They're a regular seller in winter, same as dried peas.' He looked round. 'Are we out? Do we need another sack?'

Lena appeared at the door. 'I've to take another order to 'supplier. I've been busy whilst you've been sick,' she said accusingly. 'I've not had time and Albert couldn't go, seeing as he's been minding the shop.'

'But why hasn't Turner been to take our order? He comes regular every week.'

Lena's eyes shifted. 'He didn't have what we wanted when he came last time, so I told him not to bother coming back again. I've found another supplier.'

Joshua put a hand to his forehead. Things seemed to going terribly wrong. 'Who?' he asked. 'Which one?'

'Cassell,' she muttered reluctantly.

'But he's bankrupt!' Joshua exploded. 'And he was accused of selling stolen goods.'

'Wasn't proved!' She glared at Joshua and then Albert as if they shared a common conspiracy. 'Anyway, he's started up again in his wife's name, not his own. I've had some good deals from him. Better than you'll get from Turner any day.'

'No!' Joshua made a stand. 'I won't deal with him.'

'I've put in an order,' she stated flatly.

'You just said that you hadn't had time to go!' What was going on? Joshua felt ill again when he'd thought he was better. He hadn't been eating much; he couldn't face the greasy mince and heavy puddings that Lena was serving up and so had refused the meals, saying he wasn't hungry. He knew his strength was being sapped, not just by lack of food, but also by her aggressive behaviour. She's going to ruin me, he thought, just as Tommy and Poppy had said she would.

'Not for extras, I haven't,' she explained in a wheedling manner. 'I've given him a regular order for cheese and butter and flour and all 'things we need every day. He's given us a discount,' she added. 'A good one!'

For rancid butter and mouldy cheese, I'll be bound, Joshua thought, but he merely said. 'I'll go round and see him. No! I'll go,' he persisted, as Lena started to protest that she would attend to it. 'If we stop with him I have to find out his terms.' I'll cancel the order, he thought, and call and ask Turner what it was he was out of, that made Lena tell him not to come any more. It's time I took charge again.

The doorbell jangled and Poppy came in. Her step was lively and her eyes sparkled and Joshua could tell that something had happened. She looks lovely, he thought proudly, his gloom dissipating. She's the light of my life.

'I need to talk to you, Pa,' she said, and he knew she meant alone, away from Lena or Albert.

'Well, I'm going out, so you can come with me,' he said. 'I'll just get my coat and hat.'

As they walked towards the old town he told her what had happened that morning. 'Lena's trying to take over,' he said. 'I can't think how I've allowed it to happen! And I don't know why, but I've got the feeling I can't trust her any more.'

'I never did,' Poppy said grimly. 'A woman's sixth sense, I suppose. Pa!' she said impulsively. 'I've made a decision! But first let me tell you what happened at the theatre this morning.'

'Something good?' Her father smiled. 'I could tell by 'look on your face.'

'It's a mirror, isn't it.' She laughed. 'I could never keep my feelings inside me.' She hunched up her shoulders. 'Mr Vine has created a special part for me in Aladdin! I'm to be the Lambent Flame! You know,' she explained as her father frowned in puzzlement. 'It's a flame or light which doesn't burn. And it's meant to keep Fairy Fancy, the Good Spirit of the pantomime, alive, do you see?'

'Mm, yes, I think so. I was never very good at fairy stories and suchlike. I allus left that to your ma. But I'm right glad for you, Poppy.' He gave her arm a squeeze. 'You looked so happy that I knew we'd made 'right choice for you.'

'Well, that's what I want to talk to you about. My decision! After the pantomime I'm going to give up the stage.' She took a breath. 'I can see how things are at home and in the shop and I'm not going to let you down. We'll ask – no, *tell* Lena and Albert we don't need them any more because I'm coming back, and then we'll get someone else in as a baker. Perhaps it could be a man?' she said. 'But whoever we find couldn't do worse than Lena.'

'We'll see,' her father said quietly. 'I've been thinking of some changes, but they didn't involve you giving up your singing!' He sighed. 'I might close down,' he said. 'Have a bit of a rest. It's been hard, Poppy, these last three years without your ma.'

'Close down!' She was horrified. 'But what would you do? Savile Street wouldn't be the same without Mazzini's!'

'Nothing stays 'same for ever,' he said. 'Maybe it's time for a change. For me, anyway. Look,' he said, pointing down the street. 'There's Mrs Thomas. She was allus a regular customer of mine. Now she doesn't come any more.'

'She was given her marching orders by Lena when she complained about the bread,' Poppy said quietly, stunned by her father's announcement. She narrowed her eyes. 'That's Mattie with her, isn't it? They're having a good old gossip.' She waved to them and Mattie looked up. She said something to Mrs Thomas, and then, giving a quick wave back to Poppy and her father, she turned on her heel and sped off down Whitefriargate.

As Joshua and Poppy caught up with Mrs Thomas, she nodded at them and said hurriedly, 'Can't stop. I've done enough gabbing for today.'

'Mrs Thomas!' Joshua began, wanting to apologize, but she shook open her umbrella, for it was starting to spit with rain, and dashed away.

They both stared after her, then Joshua said, 'She didn't want to talk to me, and who can blame her?'

'Odd, though,' Poppy murmured, watching Mrs Thomas's determined figure until it was lost to view. 'I'd have thought she would have wanted to give you a piece of her mind. She did with me! I'll go home, if you don't mind, Pa,' she went on. 'I've this new part to learn, and some new songs. We open on Saturday night so I haven't got long.'

'Only two days! Can you do it in time?'

'It's only a small speaking part, but there are some lovely songs. New ones that I haven't heard before.'

'Off you go, then,' her father said. 'And we'll talk again after the pantomime.' He squeezed her arm. 'Don't do anything hasty, will you, Poppy? Don't go cancelling your contract with Damone. Not without talking to me first.'

She promised that she wouldn't and made her way back

towards Savile Street. Now that she was alone she could drop the pretence that all was well. Miss Gosse had arrived in Hull to play the part of the Good Spirit, unaware that her agent had almost ruined the engagement for her, and was very pleasant towards Poppy, sympathizing with her when she heard what had happened, and thoroughly approving of the new role of the Lambent Flame which Fred Vine had created for Poppy to play. Poppy herself was thrilled with the part, but underlying her excitement was the knowledge that this might be her last engagement. She knew she couldn't leave her father to the mercies of Lena or anyone else like her. The other niggling anxiety which was upsetting her was that she wouldn't be near Charlie, who would surely never come back to Hull again. I'll lose him, she thought, if I'm not near him. Lose him before he's even mine.

CHAPTER THIRTY-THREE

Nan and Mattie were not usually frightened of the dark or the neighbourhood round the river Hull where they lived and worked. They were used to finding their way in the ill-lit alleyways and streets and knew which unsavoury quarters to avoid and which were safe. But when the tall, dark figure loomed up in front of them, the night they returned from the theatre, they had been scared witless until he spoke.

Mattie had found her voice first. 'For heaven's sake, Tommy! What you doing here?'

'I went home—' His voice cracked. He sounded fatigued.

'Come in. Come in!' Nan said. 'Open 'door, Mattie, quick. 'Lad must be frozen through.'

Mattie fumbled with the key and once inside fiddled with the lamp. When she had a light she turned to look at Tommy. 'Crikey,' she said softly. 'What happened to you?'

'Let's get 'fire lit,' Nan was all practicality. 'He's wet through. Good job I laid it ready.' She struck a match to the paper in the hearth and it caught, sending a blue-green flame up the chimney and igniting the twigs. She stood up to gaze at Tommy. He was thin and anxious-looking beneath his weathered skin, and very, very wet. 'Did you say you'd been home?'

'I didn't go in,' he croaked. 'There was no-one there – at least, Pa and Poppy weren't there. Lena and Albert were both in 'shop, but the blind was down on the door and it looked as if it was shut, and I couldn't think why. Where would they be, do you think? I tried 'side door but it was locked and I didn't want to knock in case Lena or Albert came to answer it.' He shivered and came nearer to the fire. 'I had all sorts of horrible thoughts running through my head.'

'Poppy was out with us at 'theatre,' Mattie said, 'and your pa might have gone to have a lie-down. He's not been well.'

'Oh? What's 'matter with him?' Tommy said, concerned.

'Stomach upset,' Nan said. 'But he's getting better. A lot better, in fact, since Poppy came home.' She bent to put a small pan of water over the fire to boil. 'This won't take long,' she murmured. 'Then you can have a hot drink.'

Tommy crouched down beside her. 'Poppy? Why, where's she been?'

Nan and Mattie glanced at each other. 'There's been a few things happening since you went away, Tommy. We'll tell you all about everything,' Nan said. 'But first get your wet things off.'

Mattie gazed at him. 'There's a towel hanging on 'door there, so rub yourself down. We've no change of clothes for you. Unless you want my other skirt!' She grinned, seeing his bewilderment. 'Here, take this and wrap it round you.' She took a thin blanket from the back of a chair and handed it to him. 'Then we'll hear what you've been up to and why you turned up here.'

He sat by the fire with the blanket round him, his bare legs sticking out from beneath it and his hands clutching a cup of cocoa. 'I almost daren't go home,' he said. 'I feel such a failure and I've let Pa down. I've been hanging around not daring to go back. And then, when I did, Pa wasn't there. I don't know why, but I had a horrible feeling that Lena had taken over and that Pa and Poppy had gone.'

'Mm,' Mattie said. 'It was looking that way. You're home just in time. But then . . .' She hesitated. 'When are you sailing again?'

'I'm not!' he said harshly. 'I've hated every minute of it. I stuck it out for the first few weeks; didn't want to come crawling back so everybody could say told you so. I wrote to Pa,' he said in mitigation. 'But I didn't tell him about how sick I'd been. How ill I felt, or homesick,' he added. 'Then I got stuck out in 'Baltic when the ship needed repairs. I tried to get another to bring me home, but there wasn't one that would take me on.'

Mattie and Nan both beamed at him. 'So you'll be staying?' Mattie asked, and when he nodded, she said, 'Good! Listen,

Tommy. We've a lot to tell you and I've got a plan, but Ma and me have to go to work now. Will you stay here till we get back? There's enough wood to keep 'fire going.'

'A plan? What sort of plan?' He almost grinned but he was so weary.

'To get rid of Lena and Albert. I think they've been fiddling your da!'

'You've no proof,' Nan protested.

'I will have,' Mattie said in a determined voice. 'I'm halfway to finding them out, but I need some help.'

This time he did grin. 'I'll be glad to give it.' Then he frowned. 'Nan, do you think Pa will want me back? I know he said I could always come back, but will he be mad at me?'

'I don't work at Mazzini's now,' she explained. 'Lena made sure of that. But your pa will be glad to see you home.' She heaved a breath and smiled. 'And so will Poppy.'

As they were about to go out, Nan bit her lips together anxiously and said, 'There's 'remains of a loaf if you're hungry, Tommy. I'm sorry I can't offer you more, but—'

'You've no money? Pass my jacket, Mattie.' Tommy half stood, clinging to his blanket. 'I've plenty of cash. Haven't spent anything for weeks.'

'We can't take your money!' Nan was aghast.

'I wasn't suggesting you should.' Tommy dug into his coat pocket. 'But you can buy a pie and peas from 'King's Head and bring it back with you when you come home. Enough for three,' he said, handing several coins to Mattie, who took them without a word. 'Then we can talk as we eat.'

Mattie exhaled a breath. 'Tommy, I could kiss you!'

'Well, you can if you like.' His voice was husky. 'I can't tell you how I've missed everybody.'

Nan gave him a hug. 'We've missed you too, Tommy. Welcome home.'

Mattie stood in front of him. 'I'm not sure if I should kiss a man with no clothes on,' she joked, but she put her face up to receive his kiss. Then she awkwardly patted his bare arm. 'I'm glad you're back,' she murmured and looked away.

As they went out of the door, she glanced back at him. He looked more relaxed now and had leaned his head against the back of the chair. 'What did you do, Tommy? On board ship, I mean? Did you have to scrub decks or what?'

He turned towards her, a sheepish grin on his face. 'Promise you won't tell anybody?' At her nod, he admitted, 'I was 'ship's cook. Can you believe that? My life's ambition to go to sea, and the onny job they'd give me was as a cook!'

When they came home later that evening with a large meat pie and a dish of peas, he was fast asleep across the bed, and no matter how they tried to wake him he didn't stir.

'We'll have our supper, Mattie, and then try again,' Nan said. Mattie agreed. She'd carried the pie home and the smell of it reminded her that she was famished; they hadn't had a proper meal since her mother had finished at Mazzini's. The wages they earned at the inn went towards their rent, first and foremost. They ate half of the pie and most of the peas and then tried again to waken Tommy. But he was dead to the world and finally they pulled him to one end of the bed and got into the other.

Mattie had a fit of the giggles, which she transmitted to her mother who laughed as she hadn't laughed in a long time. 'I'll tell him in 'morning that he's got to marry me, Ma,' Mattie stuttered. 'That my ma was witness to him being in 'same bed as me!'

Nan quivered with laughter. 'Well, he'll have to marry both of us,' she gurgled. 'For I was a respectable widow woman and now he's undone me by sharing *my* bed as well!'

They laughed so much that the bed shook and Tommy murmured something and turned over, but the next morning they were both up before him. He lay with one hand tucked beneath his cheek as he slept. Mattie looked down at him for a moment. She'd felt his feet next to hers during the night and she had hardly slept afterwards as she'd tried to keep her own tucked under her. She gently touched his bare shoulder. 'Tommy!' she said softly. 'Cup of tea whilst it's hot?'

There weren't enough tea leaves left to make another pot and she had to have a drink before going on the hunt for work. Her mother had already gone out to the washhouse.

Tommy sat up and stared at her. He ran his tongue over his dry lips. 'Mattie?' He glanced round the small dark room. 'Am I at your house? Yes, of course I am!' He ran his fingers through his hair. 'I couldn't think where I was for a minute.'

Mattie handed him the cup of weak tea. 'We couldn't wake you last night,' she said. 'You were so hard asleep.'

'I've not slept properly in weeks,' he said, gulping the hot tea. 'Couldn't sleep on board ship, and then when I got back to Hull . . .'

'So where did you stay?' She sat on the edge of the bed. 'Before you came to us, I mean?'

'I slipped back on board, day before yesterday. I'd been back home and looked through 'shop window a couple of times. Nobody noticed me – I had my hat over my eyes – but each time I onny saw Lena and Albert. Then yesterday I was found on board so I was turfed off. I hung round 'dock for a bit, but then it started to rain so I came here. I thought Nan would know what was happening at home. But there was no-one here either. I was beginning to get desperate, wondering where everybody was!'

'Poppy had some theatre tickets given her,' Mattie told him. 'And your pa couldn't go on account of him being poorly. That's what she said, anyway. But I think she was giving ma and me a treat.'

'What did you mean last night when you said about Poppy coming back? Where's she been?'

'It's a long story.' She turned her eyes away from his bare chest. 'How long have you got?'

'As long as it takes to tell.' He seemed suddenly aware that he was in somebody else's bed. 'Mattie? Where did you and Nan sleep last night?' he asked awkwardly. 'Am I in your bed?'

She raised her eyebrows. She couldn't joke about his having to marry her as she'd told her mother she was going to do. Not now, not when he was half naked in the same room as she was. 'Ma and me don't take up much room,' she murmured. 'We slept fine. I want to ask you something,' she added quickly to cover her confusion. 'Are you willing to stay a bit longer? It's just that – well, I'll tell you about Poppy first.' She put aside her plans to go out hunting for work. This was more important. 'Then I'll tell you about Lena. Albert told your father that she was giving up 'house where she and Albert used to live. Well, I bet she hasn't and I've got my spies out to find out her address.'

He put down the empty cup and folded his arms across his chest. 'What good will that do? What if she does still have 'house? There's no law against it!'

She blinked, and then licked her lips. The sight of him made her uneasy. She had kept her feelings for Tommy to herself for such a long time, and now she was in danger of revealing them.

'Look,' she croaked. 'I'm just going to step outside so you can get dressed. Then I'll tell you.' She gave a false laugh. 'I wouldn't want anybody to call and catch you without your clothes on!'

'You're right.' He too laughed nervously. 'Wouldn't do anything for your reputation!'

'Haven't got one,' she quipped as she went to the door.

'But what about Lena's house?' he asked, his hand on the blanket ready to throw it aside.

She turned away. 'I think it's a thieves' kitchen.'

Mattie told Tommy all that had happened whilst he had been away, from Poppy's entering the competition in Hull to her signing a contract with an agent and going to London and Brighton. 'She's home now and starting in pantomime on Saturday at 'Grand Theatre.'

'Gosh. So – you mean – that Pa's been on his own with them two? Lena and Albert?' He was astonished.

She nodded. 'Now Lena's got rid of my ma. She's been trying to for weeks and finally Ma cracked up. Said she couldn't stop any longer. And poor Poppy has been thinking that she'll have to give up her career to help your pa.' She looked at him anxiously, her brows knitting together. 'I hope she doesn't have to, because she's just wonderful, Tommy. You should see her; she's such a star! Will be, at least, if she gets 'chance.'

She told him then what she had heard about Lena from Mrs Thomas, who was convinced that Albert had been stealing from the medication cupboard and that Lena was fiddling the cash box. 'Mrs Thomas said that whenever she paid her for groceries, Lena would give her 'change from out of her apron pocket, and that she didn't always open 'cash box drawer unless your father was there. But 'final straw was when 'bread wasn't properly baked and she took it back and Lena said it was her own fault for cutting it when it was still hot.

'Lena's been buying cheap meat as well,' she added. 'That's what Ma says, anyway. And I bet she's been pocketing 'difference.'

'Well, I'm back now,' Tommy asserted. 'I'll sort them out.'

'But we need to find out what they've been up to!' Mattie said urgently. 'They're not going to get off scot free. Not after 'way she's treated my ma!'

'My, what claws!' Tommy said admiringly. 'Where's that flippant lass I once knew?'

Mattie gazed steadily at him for a moment. 'You never knew her, Tommy. Nobody does. Now.' She swiftly changed the subject, but still his eyes watched her. 'Listen to this. I'm waiting for Mrs Thomas to find out where Lena was living before she went to Mazzini's. If she's still paying rent on it, it means she's using it for something else,' she explained.

'Not necessarily,' he said, surprising himself by arguing Lena's side. 'Perhaps she's hanging on to it in case Pa asks her to leave.'

'No, not her,' Mattie said vehemently. 'Albert told your pa they were giving it up. She's up to something, I know she is. Will you stay, Tommy, until I find out? I mean, I don't want to upset Poppy when she's rehearsing, and I don't want to trouble your pa when he's not been well, so 'timing has to be right.'

'How long?' Tommy was keen to get home, but then he thought that as Lena was using his room it would be better to have some ammunition to get her out. 'Where's Albert staying?' he asked. 'Is he at our house?'

'Seemingly he's sleeping in 'kitchen cos Poppy insisted he couldn't have her room. Ma says it was kept locked.'

Tommy nodded thoughtfully. What a fiasco, and all because he wanted to go to sea. Now he couldn't wait to go home. 'Then what?' he asked. 'What if you do find out her address?'

She looked at him in surprise. 'Why, what do you think? We go in and have a look round!'

CHAPTER THIRTY-FOUR

Tommy wasn't very keen on the idea of breaking into someone else's house, but Mattie did her best to persuade him. 'It isn't as if we were stealing anything,' she wheedled. 'We're only looking. We might not even have to go in. We can mebbe just look through 'window. But,' she added cautiously, 'don't mention it to Ma, will you? She'll be dead set against it!'

But Mrs Thomas couldn't at first find out the address and it was Tuesday morning before she came knocking on their door. Nan was out at the washhouse and Mattie had gone job-hunting. Tommy peeked out of the window and on seeing Mrs Thomas he opened the door a crack.

'Tommy! Whatever are you doing here?' she exclaimed. 'Why aren't you at home?' She gazed narrowly at him. 'You're not on 'run from 'authorities, are you?'

He opened the door to let her in. 'No!' he said. 'I should be at home, but Pa doesn't know I'm back yet. Mattie's got some crackpot idea about Lena Rogers and Albert.'

'They're ruining your father,' Mrs Thomas said. 'I've never seen a man so run down. But Mattie's right. We should find out what they're up to!' Mrs Thomas's eyes gleamed and Tommy reckoned she was enjoying the scheming. 'If you go home now, they'll be cautious. They think they can get away with owt while your pa's on his own and under 'weather!'

'But Poppy's there,' he argued. 'They'll not get up to anything when she's around.'

'I don't think she's in much. I've seen her trotting off to 'theatre most days. She's rehearsing for panto, I think. Anyway, tell Mattie I know where they live.'

The house in question was in Dagger Lane, the area near the Holy Trinity Church in the centre of the old town, and as soon as Nan and Mattie had gone off to work that evening Tommy pulled his hat over his forehead, hiding his sandy hair, pulled up his coat collar and went off to look for the address. It was a dark and gloomy area but he found the place, an unlit downstairs room, and he leaned despondently against a wall across from it. A light drizzle was falling and he thought that he was doomed for ever to get wet. He waited a few minutes and was about to walk towards the house when he heard the sound of footsteps coming down the narrow lane.

He pulled back into a corner, and saw Albert walking towards the door of the house with a large bag in his hand. Tommy waited a moment longer for Albert to go inside, and then slipped across the lane. There was torn newspaper hanging down inside the window and he repressed the urge to wipe the grimy glass in order to get a better look. Then a candle flame flickered and Tommy took in a sharp breath as he saw Albert take out the contents of the bag.

He arrived back at the house in Stewart's Yard before Nan and Mattie came home from work and sat brooding by the fire. He had given Mattie some money and she'd bought a bag of coal. Nan had refused it but he'd insisted, telling them he was cold, and finally Mattie had agreed to take it to buy coal and food.

'You ought go home,' Nan had told him, but Mattie had said no, another few days wouldn't matter and they must get the business of Lena and Albert settled. Now, as he sat gazing into the flames, he conceded that Mattie was right. If he confronted Lena and Albert and accused them of stealing the goods which he had seen stacked in boxes and cartons against the walls of the room in Dagger Lane, they would just pack up and disappear out of town.

When the two women arrived home he was still sitting gazing into the flames. He looked up and raised his eyebrows. 'You were right, Mattie. It's a thieves' kitchen. The place is like a warehouse, stacked with goods. I recognized 'manufacturers' names on the cartons as 'same ones that Pa buys.'

'What?' Nan had a puzzled frown on her tired face, so they

explained that Mrs Thomas had discovered the address and Tommy had gone round to have a look. 'Then we have to inform 'police,' she said. 'We can't go taking 'law into our own hands or we'll get into trouble.'

Mattie looked disappointed. 'I wanted 'pleasure of confronting them,' she said. 'Especially after 'way they've treated you, Ma.'

'We'll ask 'police if they'll keep watch,' Tommy said. 'Albert went in bold as brass with a bag stuffed full of tea tonight. He's obviously getting careless.' He frowned. 'But what are they doing with it? They must be selling it, but how, if Lena is in 'shop most of the time?'

Mattie shook her head. That she didn't know.

'This is Mrs Spivey. She's come to give me a hand with the cleaning.' Lena confronted Joshua with a hard false smile on her face. 'You remember I said I had somebody in mind?'

Joshua opened his mouth to protest. He had said he'd like to take a look at her first when Lena had mentioned it, but she'd taken the woman on anyway. Well, he thought, I'll keep an eye on her, see how she shapes up. Then he grunted to himself and pondered that Lena had been rather sharp, bringing the woman in when Poppy was at the theatre. She thinks she can get round me, he thought, and she's probably right. I'm no match for a scheming woman.

'Where've you worked before, Mrs Spivey?' he asked. She didn't look as if she was strong enough to do any cleaning. She was very small and thin, but wick, he thought, as if she could move quickly when she wanted to. He wasn't entirely happy about her; she didn't look very clean, for one thing. Not like Nan. He gave a sigh. Nan was as neat as a pin in spite of her shabby clothes. I really must assert myself, he thought wearily. I must decide what to do.

'Ooh, all over town!' Mrs Spivey whined and Joshua clenched his teeth. She had a sharp voice which grated. 'Anybody'll tell you about me.'

He nodded, a fixed look on his face. 'All right. Start in 'morning. We'll give you a fortnight's trial. Mrs Rogers will tell you what needs doing.' But he was troubled. He didn't like the idea of her cleaning upstairs. He fancied that she might be the type who would have a nosy look into things that didn't concern her. I'll ask Poppy what she thinks when she comes in, he thought.

But when Poppy came home she was full of the excitement of the rehearsal and told him that she had three tickets for the opening night on Saturday. 'I know that Nan and Mattie work at night but I'll still ask if they'll come. The opening night will be special. I'll slip round and ask them in the morning.'

It was raining hard the next morning so she decided to wait until it cleared, which it seemed it would; the sky was lightening and an occasional glimpse of blue sky could be seen above the cloud. She went through into the shop and asked Albert if there was anything she could do to help. 'I'll make the coffee, shall I?' she asked. 'Pa always says that people will come in out of the rain if they smell coffee.'

He shrugged. 'If you like. I wasn't going to bother this morning.' His eyes shifted to a little woman whom Poppy hadn't noticed, as she was bending down behind a table. She had a duster in her hand.

'Oh!' Poppy said. 'Hello! Who are you?'

'Mrs Spivey,' the woman whined. 'Lena's just set me on.'

'As a cleaner?' Poppy was surprised that her father hadn't mentioned it, though perhaps he had forgotten as he was spending the morning looking over his accounts. Lena hadn't mentioned it either. She was still rattling around in the kitchen. 'I didn't know.'

'She's only just started this morning,' Albert interrupted. 'Not ten minutes since.'

Rather late for a cleaner to start, Poppy thought; it's gone nine o'clock. She said nothing, but felt uneasy. I wonder where Lena found her? She made the coffee and then opened the door. The windows were steamed up and Mrs Spivey was reaching up to clean them. She was far too short to get very high.

'You need a pair of steps, Mrs Spivey. You'll not be able to reach the top. Albert,' Poppy turned to him, 'would you get Mrs Spivey the steps from the back, please? I doubt if she can lift them herself.'

Why has Lena employed her, she wondered as Albert went to fetch the steps. She's not big enough to move the tables or reach into the corners without help.

'Good morning!' A cheerful voice greeted her.

'Mattie! Hello. How nice to see you. Come and have a cup of coffee. I've just made it. Compliments of the management,' she added.

Mattie's attention seemed to have been caught by the sight of Mrs Spivey. 'Erm, no thank you,' she said vaguely, her eyes on the woman. 'I'm on my way somewhere, but I thought I'd drop in and ask how your pa is and how 'pantomime rehearsal is going. Morning, Mrs Spivey,' she said. 'Haven't seen you around for a bit.' Mattie's eyes seemed to brighten and she chewed on her mouth and gave a brisk nod of her head as if she'd just realized something. 'Not for ages!' She turned to Poppy. 'Everything all right, is it?' She had a smug grin on her face, which she was trying to conceal. 'As I say, I can't stop, but I thought I'd drop in.'

'I was coming round to see you anyway,' Poppy told her. 'I was just waiting for the rain to stop. I've got some tickets for the theatre on Saturday night. I hoped that you and Nan could go with Pa?'

Mattie drew in a breath then exhaled. 'Saturday? Mm, that would be nice. Can I let you know?'

'I've got the tickets anyway.' Poppy was puzzled by Mattie's attitude. She thought she'd have to persuade her to take time off work, but here she was practically agreeing without even consulting Nan.

'Yes!' Mattie beamed at her. 'I think that would work out just right. Thank you very much, Poppy!'

Work out right? What does she mean? Poppy stared after Mattie as she left the shop. Still, it will be lovely if they'll go to the pantomime with Pa. He won't want to go on his own.

Albert came back in. 'You're not rehearsing today, then?' he asked, as he opened up the steps for Mrs Spivey.

'This afternoon,' she answered, thinking that this was the first time he had shown any interest. 'The children are in this morning.'

'Ah!' He nodded. 'And, erm, when does the show start?'

'Saturday evening.' She removed a dirty tablecloth from one of the tables and took a clean one from a drawer.

'I expect your pa will want to go and see you, won't he?' She looked at him in surprise as he added, 'Lena and me will be able to manage all right if he does.'

'I'll come in and give you an 'and,' Mrs Spivey piped up from the top of the steps, and rubbed the back of her hand across her nose. 'I'm not doin' owt on Sat'day.'

'Oh, that's kind of you, Mrs Spivey, but I'm sure it won't be necessary.' Poppy was aghast. Maybe Mrs Spivey was good at cleaning, but her presence in the coffee shop would not be an advantage; rather the reverse. I must speak to Pa. There have to be some changes. A great despondency swept over her. It's no good, she thought miserably. I can't let Pa cope with this on his own. Aladdin will be my last show.

CHAPTER THIRTY-FIVE

The pantomime opened with a great clash of gongs and cymbals as the orchestra began the overture, and the curtain rose showing Emperor Souchong's palace. Around the elaborate oriental set, designed to represent Chinese life by bridges, doves, flowers, strange animals and ancient symbols, the emperor's coolie servants, musicians and acrobats scurried with much bowing, scraping and tumbling, preparing for the emperor and his beautiful daughter Princess Badroulbadour to put in an appearance.

Poppy watched from the wings. She didn't appear until the end of the first act so she was able to absorb the atmosphere and thrill of the performance. She listened as the deceitful Congue, the Grand Vizier, made crafty plans for his son, Hyson, to ensnare the princess into marriage, and to his artful son's endeavours to marry her serving maid.

The chorus maids sang, their hands tucked into the sleeves of colourful kimonos, and the children of the ballet, in their black-fringed wigs, danced and sang appealingly. Then the scene changed to the poor hovel where Aladdin and his mother Widow Twankey lived. The audience laughed and hooted at the widow's red petticoats and voluminous under-drawers, and at Aladdin's futile attempts to shoo away the two bailiffs, Snipper and Snapper, who had come to collect their rent and were booed and hissed at by the audience.

Poppy's costume had been specially made for her as the Lambent Flame was a new part in the pantomime, and the seamstress had excelled herself. She had been told of the role and had fashioned a tunic of gold satin with slits at each side for free movement which fitted Poppy like a second skin. Over it she had sewn an overskirt of gold and silver muslin panels, which shimmered and floated like tongues of flame as she moved. These were replicated in the long flowing sleeves, which reached to her fingertips. On her head she wore a circlet of gold and silver which flashed and scintillated as she turned her head.

In the last scene of the first act, Fairy Fancy, the Good Spirit of the Pantomime, dressed in shimmering white, appeared by a deep cave, to assure the audience that the pantomime would live for ever, but she was disturbed by the magician Abanazer, wearing a pointed hat and a black cloak decorated with stars, who, in his search for the magic lamp, threatened to overwhelm and diminish her power. The light which shone on her began to dim and fade; her figure drooped, the hand holding the silver wand began to sink, her head with its circlet of white diamonds slumped to her chest and she fell to the floor.

The lights on the stage dimmed, and as the children in the audience began to wail and call out and the grown-ups started to boo the magician, there came from a dark corner a shimmering, flickering gleam of yellow light which increased to a glow, and Poppy as the Lambent Flame appeared with the spotlight playing on her, the panels on her costume fluttering like a golden flame and singing:

'I am the radiant Lambent Flame
Let no-one ever forget my name
Come, children of this pantomime
Will you clap and sing a happy rhyme?
And bring good cheer to Fairy Fancy
Let not the wicked Abanazer take our
Spirit – but by flame and pyromancy
Bring back her magic power.'

Poppy lifted her arms and began to spin round and round the Good Spirit, the panels of her costume swirling and her gold tunic glittering beneath as if on fire. As she danced she exhorted the children to clap and sing and the theatre resounded with the sound of their voices calling 'Fairy Fancy! Fairy Fancy!' and their hands clapping so loudly that everyone's ears began to buzz.

As Poppy swirled round and round, the Good Spirit began to raise her head and then her shoulders and finally she lifted high her arms and hands, holding her wand, and rose to her feet. The children began to applaud, standing up from and onto their seats, cheering and shouting.

The Good Spirit and the Lambent Flame began a chant together in which they exhorted the good spirits of the world to crush the bad, and Abanazer, to hisses and whistles from the audience, cowered, bent his head and slunk away off the stage.

'Spirits of the world unite
And by your powers stand firm this night
Condemn this evil, let it fail, and bring forth a steadfast male
A man who by his honesty – will one day be – *His Majesty*!'

There was a crash of cymbals, a reverberating roll of drums, and a brilliant flash of light, and Aladdin, covering his eyes from the brightness, appeared apparently out of nowhere, in front of the cave.

'Wonderful,' Fred Vine whispered as Poppy and Miss Gosse came off the stage. 'Just wonderful!'

Poppy laughed. She had enjoyed herself enormously, and she still had several entries to make and songs to sing. Each time the Good Spirit's powers diminished, the children would shout for the Lambent Flame and she would appear as a flickering yellow light to save her. Near the end of the pantomime, Aladdin captured the princess's heart and hand and sang to her, 'A whole new world'.

'I can show you the world
Shining shimmering splendour
Tell me, princess, when did you last let your heart decide?
I can open your eyes, take you wonder by wonder
Over, sideways and under, on a magic carpet ride.'

All is happily concluded and the final wedding scene is set. Poppy had a solo spot in which she sang that she was destined to be always alone as a single flame.

'Alone am I, and meant to be – with no-one in the world to love just me
My flame is gold, my heart is true – who will love me? No, not you.
My kiss is warm – my passion tender but without true love –
Light fades and lessens.
It ebbs and wanes – and so – expiry –
No more to glimpse its radiant glory.'

Her light dimmed and she drifted flickering and fluttering like a spent candle flame until the Good Spirit arrived just in time and begged the children in the audience to save the Lambent Flame as she had been saved by her. 'Tell her you love her,' she begged. 'Keep her light shining or we are all lost.'

The children shouted and screamed. 'We love you, Lambent Flame! Come back! Come back!'

The stage lights were dimmed and the flame grew brighter as the spotlight, powered by the newest gas arrangements, flickered from yellow to white. Then came a flash and the Lambent Flame appeared in all her shining glory to the cheers of the audience.

Down in the stalls, just out of the sight of the stage performers, Poppy's father sat wiping his eyes and blowing his nose. He sniffed and took a breath. 'Marvellous, isn't she, Nan? Best of 'em all, even them seasoned players.' He turned to her. 'I wish – I just wish—'

Nan patted his arm. 'I know,' she said softly. 'You wish that Mary was here to see her. She would have been very proud.'

Joshua swallowed and with the rest of the audience rose to his feet to applaud the company as they took their final bow. 'I was going to say Tommy. I wish he was here. He knows nothing of any of this. He'd gone before Poppy started on her career.'

Nan gave a vague smile and nodded, but before she could comment, Joshua went on, 'Shame that Mattie couldn't have come with us. Pity she couldn't get 'time off. She'd have enjoyed it.' He took his timepiece out of his waistcoat pocket and looked at it. 'It's onny just gone nine. She'd have been back at work by half past.'

They eased their way out of the auditorium and Nan said, 'Let's wait for Poppy. We can walk back with her.'

'She'll be ages,' Joshua said. 'There's sure to be folks waiting to talk to her.'

'You should go backstage,' Nan said urgently. 'She'll be expecting you. She'll be disappointed if you don't.'

'I ought to get back to 'shop,' he said worriedly. 'I've a doubt in my mind about Lena and Albert. There's summat not quite right.'

'Don't worry,' Nan assured him. 'Seeing Poppy is what is important right now. And,' she added, 'mebbe some of 'cast will come back for coffee.'

'Mm,' he said doubtfully. 'If Lena hasn't turned off 'coffee and shut up for 'night.'

Nan's mouth curved into a smile, but she put her hand up to hide it. 'Never mind just this once,' she urged, and edged him towards the stage door. 'You can make up for it.'

'I don't think so,' he said dismally. 'It might be too late. I've lost a lot of customers. I'm going to have to rethink, Nan. I'm in a quandary. I called to see my supplier Turner who told me that Lena wanted to do some shifty deal, and he refused. She told him not to bother coming again, and went to Cassell, who I know is a rogue. But I can't let Poppy give up. Not with talent like she's got.'

The stage door keeper knew Joshua and let them through, though there was a crowd of admirers waiting by the door to see the performers. They could hear laughter as they walked down the corridors, and the excited chatter of the children who had performed. Joshua knocked on the dressing room door and waited. Poppy opened it. She had already changed out of costume and was in her dressing robe. She still wore the golden face paint of the Lambent Flame but down it were long streaks where she had shed tears.

'Oh, Pa!' Her mouth trembled on seeing him. 'What am I to do? How can I give up?'

He put his arms about her. 'You can't,' he said. 'Don't you worry your head now. We'll think on some way round it.'

They waited in the corridor while she changed into her outdoor clothes, her warm coat and hat and buttoned boots. When she rejoined them, she carried a bag containing her red dancing shoes. She always took them with her wherever she went, worried that they might disappear if she left them in a dressing room.

It was bitterly cold. There was a hard frost and a tingling in the nostrils, which made them think that snow was on the way. Nan shivered; her coat was a summer one, not meant for winter weather.

'Come home with us, Nan,' Joshua said as they left the theatre. 'Have a cup of chocolate to warm you up and then I'll walk you back home. Or were you intending going to 'King's Head?'

'N-no, I don't think so. I'll give it a miss tonight.' Nan seemed tense over something, anxious almost.

'Did you enjoy the pantomime, Nan?' Poppy wondered if Nan was worried about losing wages, or even her job, for missing an evening at the King's Head.

'It was grand, Poppy. I loved it. Your costume was – well, it looked just like a guttering candle flame with 'spotlight on it.' Nan shook her head in wonder. 'I just can't work out how they do that with them new gas appliances.'

'Nor can I,' Poppy said. 'And they say that when they bring in electricity it will be even more amazing.' But I shan't be part of that, she thought. Not if this is to be my last show. My final curtain.

'What's going on?' As they turned out of George Street Joshua craned to see along Savile Street. 'Summat's up! Bobbies are out. They're at my shop!' He started to run. 'Hey!' He waved his arms. 'Hey! What's up?'

Ahead of them they could see a crowd of people, a number of policemen and their bicycles, and a police vehicle, the Black Maria, all clustered round Mazzini's shop.

Poppy ran to keep up with her father. 'What is it?' she said breathlessly. 'What's happened?'

Nan followed more slowly. She knew that Tommy and Mattie had informed the police about the goods in the Dagger Lane house, and that they had been keeping a watch on it to see what was being brought in and taken out. Tonight was to have been the night when they would swoop on the perpetrators, Lena, Albert and Mrs Spivey.

'It's all right, sir.' A police sergeant, three chevrons on his sleeve, stopped Joshua in his headlong rush. 'We've got 'em. Caught 'em red-handed. You'd have had an empty shop if we hadn't come when we did.'

'What? Who?' Joshua looked on bewildered as Lena, Albert and the little woman who had only just started this week as a cleaner were handcuffed together and put into the Black Maria by two burly police constables.

'We'll get all 'other merchandise brought back to you as soon as we've ascertained that it belongs to you and not some other tradesman.' The sergeant lifted his helmet and scratched his forehead. 'Beats me why it wasn't missed. There are enough provisions in that house to stock another shop.'

'Provisions? What provisions? What house? I don't understand!'

Nan came up to stand beside him. 'Lena and Albert have been robbing you, Mr Mazzini. I'd suspected it for some time but I'd no proof. But after I left because of Lena, Mattie was so mad that she decided to find out about them. She went to see Mrs Thomas.'

'Mrs Thomas! What's she to do with anything?' Joshua stared after the disappearing carriage.

'Right, Mr Mazzini, sir, we'll be off.' The police sergeant and a constable stood in front of him. 'We'll be round in 'morning to take statements from you and your son.'

'Son!' Joshua's face grew red. He jabbed his finger towards where the police carriage carrying Lena and Albert was turning the corner. 'He's no son of mine, so don't even think it!'

'I wasn't talking about Albert Parker, sir,' the officer said. 'That's his proper name, by the way, not Rogers. I was talking about your son, Thomas Mazzini, who told us of the offence.'

Joshua was stupefied; he looked at Poppy, who was as bewildered as he was, and then at Nan.

'Let's go in,' Nan said quietly. 'Then it'll all be explained.'

The crowd dispersed though, one or two lingered, talking excitedly together about the prisoners and who knew of them.

There was an aroma of freshly ground coffee as they entered the shop and Joshua wrinkled his nose appreciatively. Mattie stood behind the counter putting out cups and saucers. She gave a saucy grin and raised her eyebrows at her mother. 'Hello, Mr Mazzini,' she said. 'Guess what I've just found.' She looked down and with her knee nudged something below the counter.

'Hello, Pa! Hello, Poppy!' Tommy stood up. He had a striped

apron tied round his waist and a very bashful countenance. His face was flushed. 'I hope I've done right, Pa. I've come home!'

Joshua closed his eyes for a second whilst Poppy squealed in delight. Then he strode towards Tommy and put his arms out. 'I'm so glad to see you, son!'

Tommy came round the counter, a huge relieved smile on his face as his father hugged him. 'I've missed you, Pa.' His voice was muffled as he was lost in his father's embrace. 'I've really missed you.' He looked up as he saw Poppy in tears. 'And I've missed you too, Pops,' he choked. 'I really have.'

CHAPTER THIRTY-SIX

Tommy told his tale, of rough seas, of harsh weather, of seasickness and of the difficulties of preparing food for the seamen when the ship was rolling and dipping in gigantic troughs.

'I thought I was going to die time and again,' Tommy said. 'But 'other seamen just laughed at me. They said it was onny a capful of wind. They stood on deck singing, the gale blowing in their faces, and there I was, on my knees, puking up green bile.' He shuddered. 'I thought if I came out of it alive I'd never go near a ship again.'

Then Mattie and Nan told jointly of their suspicions of Lena and Albert and of the confirmation when Mattie saw Mrs Spivey working in Mazzini's. 'I couldn't work out how they were selling 'goods until I saw her. Then 'penny dropped.' Mattie grinned. 'She's known all over the old town,' she said. 'She's only just nicely out of jail for thieving. Now she'll be back in and with some company. Lena and Albert are wanted in York, Huddersfield, Bradford and Bingley. Lena pretends that she's a widow and searches out for somebody on their own in businesses like yours, Mr Mazzini. That's what 'constable told me, anyway. And not just men,' she added. 'Apparently she's pilfered from women too. She takes a house and fills it with stolen goods, and then moves on before anybody realizes what's going on. Albert isn't even her son,' she said. 'He just works for her. He's her lookout, an accomplice. And by the way,' she murmured. 'The police found some bottles of laudanum.'

Poppy nodded. 'Mrs Thomas told me that she thought he was taking it. She said she could tell from the way he was behaving.'

Joshua was bewildered. 'I still don't see what Mrs Thomas had to do with anything. Did she know Lena?'

'No, that was just it! She didn't know her. And Mrs Thomas knows just about everybody,' Mattie said. Her eyes were sparkling and Poppy thought that maybe Mattie hadn't had such excitement in her life before. She glanced at Tommy who was leaning on the counter with his chin in his hands, watching and listening to the animated Mattie.

'But 'only reason Mrs Thomas got involved was because she was that mad about her bread!' Mattie continued. 'She said she'd been coming to Mazzini's for years, so she was really peeved when Lena as good as told her she could go elsewhere. She was only too pleased to find out where Lena's house was and what she was up to!'

'Mattie told me what was going on.' Tommy picked up the tale. 'So we decided that before I came home I would keep watch. I saw Albert taking goods into their house and so I informed 'police. They put police officers in civilian clothing on watch, and with their own eyes they saw Lena and Albert taking bags of provisions out of our shop and transferring them to their house. They guessed that they would be moving on soon when they saw Albert talking to a York carrier and money changing hands!'

'And *we* guessed, Ma and me,' Mattie said, 'that it would be tonight, cos Lena knew that Mr Mazzini was going to see Poppy in 'pantomime.'

The doorbell jangled and they all turned. 'Is this a private party or can we come in? We smelt the coffee.' A crowd of performers came through the door. Aladdin, Abanazer, Widow Twankey and Miss Gosse were there, and it was Fred Vine who asked the question.

'Come in. Come in!' Joshua welcomed them with open arms. 'Welcome to Mazzini's. We're having a celebration.'

'In honour of your daughter?' Miss Gosse asked. 'Her performance was wonderful.'

'And of my son,' Joshua beamed. 'I'm going to change the sign above the shop to Mazzini and Son! We shall redecorate and restock—'

'New tablecloths?' Poppy added.

'Curtains?' Nan suggested. 'These ones are faded.'

'What about a theatre theme?' Miss Alice Maiden who played Aladdin asked, getting into the spirit of the conversation.

'Yes!' Fred Vine agreed. 'Paint this wall like a stage, with drapes and say a palm tree.'

'A clown!' Poppy laughed. 'And a juggler!'

'Whoa!' Joshua said, glancing at Tommy who was making more coffee, whilst Mattie was searching in tins for biscuits, but finding only a few. 'Tonight, coffee is on the house.'

The theatre performers cheered. It wasn't often they were given something for nothing, one of them remarked.

'But I want you to tell everybody in 'theatre world that Mazzini's make 'best coffee and cakes you've ever tasted.'

'But we've not had any cake,' said Abanazer, who was only a young man and very handsome. 'How can we say it until we've tasted it?'

'You will,' Tommy said. 'Come on Monday night and I can promise you cake!'

'We can't come on Monday night,' said Miss Gosse. 'We'll all be going home for Christmas. But we'll come again as soon as we can.'

After everyone had gone and the shop was closed, they cleared the tables, washed the coffee cups and made everything ready for the next morning.

'Did you mean it, Pa? About redecorating and everything?' Poppy asked.

'Aye, I did,' her father said. 'We'll have a clean sweep. Get rid of any trace of that woman and her so-called son.'

'We'll need some more help then.' Tommy winked at Poppy before adding, 'Unless our Poppy's stopping at home.'

Poppy held her breath until her father said, 'No, Poppy can't stop: she's got a career to make. She's going to take singing lessons, did you know?'

Tommy shook his head. 'So if Poppy isn't staying, I vote that Mattie comes to work here – if you will, that is.' He glanced at Mattie, who was sweeping up crumbs from the floor.

She straightened up, her eyes bright. 'If you'll have me, Mr Mazzini. I'd like to.'

Joshua hesitated. 'I can't pay as much as you'll get at 'mill,' he said. 'But you could have extras like bread, and your dinner here.'

She beamed at him. 'I've been stood off at 'mill,' she told him. 'There's no guarantee that they'll take me back after Christmas.'

'So how've you been managing?' Joshua turned to Nan. 'What have you done for money?'

She gave a little shrug. 'I've allus been a good manager,' she said. 'Ever since I was widowed. I had to be. I'd a child to bring up and no man to support me.'

'Will you come back?' he asked humbly. 'It's not been 'same since you left.'

Poppy felt a sudden joy. She could go away without any worry if Nan and Mattie were here. They wouldn't cheat or steal; they'd only work for the good of Mazzini's. Then she felt a little prickle of merriment. She'd noticed covert glances between Mattie and Tommy, each looking at the other when they thought they weren't aware of it. Oh, what if, she thought. Just suppose! Yes, of course. Mattie is sweet on Tommy. She wouldn't admit it, of course. She's always had that jocular manner to show that she was carefree and indifferent. What was she hiding? Poppy smiled to herself. A warm and loving heart, that was for sure.

Tommy walked Nan and Mattie home. His father had said that he would but Tommy insisted. When they had gone, Poppy and her father locked up the shop. Tommy had his own key again, but Joshua was going to have the locks changed, just in case Lena ever came back. 'Shelves do look bare,' he said. 'I kept going over my books time and again, wondering why we weren't making a profit. I never guessed that them two were robbing me hand over fist.'

'Pa!' Poppy said thoughtfully. 'It's nearly Christmas.'

'Aye,' he sighed, 'I know, and there's nowt ready. No pudding made, no goose ordered.'

'Well, I was wondering,' she said. 'What about us having an Italian Christmas instead? We don't have to have Christmas pudding. We're part Italian, after all!' She told him of eating at the Marinos' restaurant. 'And we can invite Nan and Mattie, can't we?'

'Well, yes, of course. It's to be expected. They've allus had their Christmas dinner with us.' He rubbed his chin thoughtfully. 'I wonder what Lena had in mind? Do you think she'd have stayed over Christmas if she hadn't been rumbled?'

Poppy shook her head. She couldn't imagine what Lena had in mind. Something devious, no doubt. 'And another thing, Pa. Could we invite Miss Maiden? She plays Aladdin. And Abanazer, as well. They neither of them can get home in time for Christmas and then back for Boxing Day.'

'Why not?' Joshua said. 'We'll eat in here.' He looked round the shop. 'Plenty of room – put 'tables together. And,' he added, 'I'll invite Mr and Mrs Chandler. They'll be on their own with Charlie away.'

'Yes,' Poppy said softly. How wonderful it would be if Charlie came home for Christmas. It would make everything just perfect.

Tommy agreed, and was all for having a different Christmas dinner. 'Let's have wild boar instead of goose,' he said, when Poppy put it to him the following morning. 'That's if Brown's can get it for us in time. Wild boar with apple,' he said. 'Mmm. Wild boar with apples and rosemary, and onion soup flavoured with cinnamon to start. Yes, I'll enjoy doing that. I'll have to think about a pudding, though.'

'Can you do that, Tommy? Really?' Poppy was amazed at her brother. He had been so reluctant to cook before he'd gone to sea, yet now he was brimming with ideas.

'Well, you see, I enjoyed doing the cooking. I was given the ingredients and had to make what I could of them. What I didn't like was being seasick and not being able to eat any of the food I'd cooked. But the men all seemed to like what I gave them.' He pondered thoughtfully. 'There were days when I felt so ill that I mixed up all kinds of things that I wouldn't normally have done. But no-one complained.' He laughed.

Tommy made a batch of bread on Monday morning, and whilst Poppy was appearing in the matinee on Monday afternoon he trawled round the town buying ingredients for the Christmas dinner. Mattie and Nan came to help in the shop.

'I'm giving in my notice at 'King's Head,' Mattie announced to Joshua. 'I'd rather work here at Mazzini's of an evening. But Ma will stay on for 'time being, and give up her mornings at 'washhouse.'

Joshua was troubled over Nan working at the King's Head and walking home alone, especially at this time of year when drunks might be roaming around. 'I've allus done it,' she said, when he mentioned it. 'It's what I did before Mattie started working with me.' She smiled at him, gratified by his concern. 'Besides, Mattie has to walk home from here. She can't expect to be escorted by Tommy like we were the other night. Don't worry,' she said. 'It's what we're used to.'

'I wish I could come and see you in 'pantomime,' Tommy said to Poppy when she slipped home for an hour after the matinee.

'Oh, so do I,' Mattie said. 'Ma said how lovely you looked and what a grand show it was.'

'Well, why don't you both go?' Joshua said. 'It's quiet in here on a Monday night. I can manage.'

Tommy and Mattie looked at each other. 'I don't know,' Tommy said doubtfully. 'You might get busy.'

'Folks will wait. What would I have done if you hadn't come home?' Joshua argued. 'And anyway, I'm going to shut up 'shop for a week in 'New Year while we get decorated.'

'A week!' Tommy exclaimed. 'We won't need as long as that. I can paint; I can do 'walls and windows.'

'And I'll help,' Mattie said, suddenly anxious that she might not get any wages if the shop was closed.

'No!' Joshua was adamant. 'We'll have it done right and you two can order new stock and think on what we're going to do in 'coffee shop. So,' he continued, 'you can take tonight off because once we get busy there's no knowing when you'll be able to take time off again.'

'Good.' Poppy smiled. 'So I'll see you both later. Will you wait for me after the show?'

'I can't go, Tommy,' Mattie whispered to him later when they were alone. 'I only said that I'd *like* to go. But I've no money, and besides, I'm too shabby. I don't have a coat fit to be seen in. Not for going to watch Poppy at 'Grand.' Not for going out with you, she thought.

'You're fine as you are, Mattie,' he told her. He hadn't noticed her clothes before, but now he saw that her skirt was faded and worn. 'Tell you what, then,' he said. 'We'll go up in 'gods. Nobody up there has much money so they'll not notice us.'

'I wouldn't want you to be ashamed of being with me, Tommy,' she raised her chin defiantly. 'Your sister's a star. You should be at 'front where everybody can see you!'

A slow flush suffused his face. He was eighteen and his feelings for Mattie were changing. She'd always been a pal, someone to have a joke with, but she was so spirited, so bold and confident, she could have any man she wanted. And did, according to Charlie, but Tommy wasn't sure he believed him. Charlie tended to exaggerate at times.

'I'd never be ashamed of being with you, Mattie,' he said. 'It's more likely to be 'other way round. Why would anybody want to see me? I'm nobody! Who'd notice me?'

'Plenty of lasses, I'll tell you that for nowt,' she said softly. 'A good catch, that's what you are. Mazzini's son!' Her lips curled into a mild taunt. 'Still, if you're with me it might make some of 'em jealous,' she quipped. 'Then you'd have your pick!'

He sighed. There was no getting the better of her. 'Do you want to come or not?' he asked.

'All right.' She shrugged. 'If you like. But I'll pay for myself.'

Poppy was booked to play for only a week after Christmas, but the pantomime would continue without her. When she arrived at the Grand she saw that her name had been put up on a board as a special attraction. *Local girl stars as Lambent Flame. One week only. Miss Poppy Mazzini!* She felt a frisson of excitement when she saw it. Was this what stardom was about? Seeing your name at the front of the theatre!

The audience wasn't as large as it had been on Saturday as most people were preparing for Christmas. Boxing Day would be busy as children were taken to the pantomime as a treat. But it was a good evening for trying out extra humour, some of it immodest, especially on the part of Widow Twankey who had difficulties holding up her under-drawers. There were numerous allusions to the town of Hull and its citizens, particularly the councillors and notables of the town, which the crowd loved, jeering and cheering by turns.

'That's it, then! Happy Christmas.' Some of the performers dashed away to catch a train home and would return on Boxing Day; others, including Aladdin and Abanazer, would stay in the town for Christmas Day and make what merriment they could.

'See you tomorrow,' Poppy called to Miss Maiden, and Mr Vaughan who played Abanazer. 'Come early.'

They thanked her and said that they would, and she made her

way to the front of the theatre where Tommy had said he and Mattie would wait. The lights had been dimmed but she could see two figures waiting by the door. 'I'm coming,' she called, and saw Tommy swing open the door into the foyer.

'Poppy!' Mattie said softly. 'There's—'

'Did you enjoy it?' Poppy smiled. She hadn't yet come down from the euphoria. Everyone had been elated and good-humoured, probably because it was almost Christmas.

'Look who's here!' Tommy grinned. 'What a surprise. Who would have guessed?'

Poppy stood still, her lips parted. Hadn't she wanted this above anything else? Christmas would be perfect after all.

'Hello, Poppy,' Charlie said, his eyes searching her face to discover her response. 'You were magnificent!'

CHAPTER THIRTY-SEVEN

Christmas Day had been wonderful. Poppy lay dreaming in her bed at the end of the evening. Charlie was so attentive, so obviously pleased to see her. His mother kept casting suspicious glances in their direction as if she was assessing whether there was anything between them.

Tommy had cooked a superb meal as he had promised. He'd prepared *crostini di fegatini*, chopped chicken liver and anchovy, flavoured with a touch of brandy, which he served on crisp toast as an appetizer whilst he was putting the finishing touches to the meal to follow: onion soup flavoured with cinnamon and crushed almonds to begin, and then, as they were wiping out their bowls with fresh bread, he brought in the wild boar, which had been sliced and cooked with apples, onions and rosemary.

'Of course,' Tommy had sighed, 'it should have been left longer in the marinade, but there wasn't time.' He lifted his shoulders. 'I hope it's all right.'

'It's delicious,' Mattie said. She licked her lips, her eyes wide. 'Where ever did you learn to cook like this, Tommy?'

'Ma and me used to discuss food,' he said, 'but there was never time to do anything out of 'ordinary. We were always too busy baking bread and cakes. But I did like cooking.' He glanced cheekily at his father. 'Even though I sometimes made a fuss about doing it.'

Mrs Chandler commented that it was a very tasty piece of pork and that Tommy had done well.

'You can't beat English cooking, though, can you?' Charlie had said. 'You know, roast beef and Yorkshire pudding! Tripe and onions!'

Poppy remembered that Charlie hadn't liked the food they had been served at Mario's and she hoped that Tommy hadn't taken offence, but she reckoned he knew Charlie well enough not to. Charlie had eaten most of the meal anyway, though he'd refused the pastry tart filled with custard made from eggs, cream, almonds and pine nuts.

Mr Vaughan, Abanazer, had risen from the table to give his thanks on behalf of the guests, and Miss Maiden, who had had too many glasses of wine, had turned rather pink and said, 'Tommy! Will you marry me?'

Everyone laughed uproariously, though Poppy had noticed that Mattie had merely turned up her mouth, and had then got up from the table to clear away.

And Charlie says he wants to see more of me when I go back to London, she mused contentedly. She turned over in bed, knowing that sleep was a long way away. He's got his workshop ready, and some commissions. I think Miss Maiden is going to order some shoes from him. She had her foot in his lap at any rate, for him to measure it.

The following week flew past. She hardly noticed her birthday; her role as the Lambent Flame was considered a great success and given reviews in the local paper. Then it was time for her to pack again and return to London. She had written to the Marinos to ask if she might stay with them and had received a reply saying they would be glad to accommodate her for as long as she wished.

'That's such a relief, Pa,' she said. 'You'd like them. They're such nice people.'

'They're Italian,' he replied. He had paint in his hair even though he wasn't doing any painting. 'That's why. Fellow countrymen.'

'You're as Yorkshire as they come,' she teased. 'Hardly a drop of Italian in you.'

The shop was closed for decoration with a notice on the door stating, 'The new Mazzini and Son, grocer and coffee shop, will be opening shortly at your service.'

Her father saw her off at the railway station. The weather was freezing cold though the expected snow hadn't materialized, just sleet and rain. Poppy had wrapped up warmly for the journey. She'd raided her mother's wardrobe again and discovered a dolman coat, with a quilted lining, wide enough to cover a bustle, and this she had given to Mattie to wear in the cold weather. Mattie was broader in the shoulder than she was and fuller in the bosom. Poppy had sighed, for though she had an hourglass waist and didn't have to wear a corset, she was slender, unlike Mattie who had a very fashionable figure and needed no extra padding. Poppy travelled in a warm cloak over her costume, and elastic-sided pointed-toed boots.

'Poppy! How well you look!' Dan Damone greeted her exuberantly the next day. 'My word, but you look splendid. You know, I've heard such reports about you that I'm beginning to have doubts about you breaking off your career to take singing lessons.'

They were seated in his office and without bidding Miss Battle had brought them coffee and biscuits.

'I still think I'd like to,' she said. 'But I need to earn money as well. I don't want my father to have to pay. He's had a difficult time lately. Someone he trusted was swindling him, and he's only just getting back on his feet.'

He's to find wages for Nan and Mattie as well as himself and Tommy, she'd calculated on the train journey. If I can fund myself, so much the better.

'I can get you engagements in the evenings,' he said. 'There are plenty of theatres in London who'll take you. You might have to travel about a bit between theatres, so find a hansom driver you can trust and make an arrangement over the cost.'

He took her to meet his sister, who lived in Bloomsbury. 'You'll like her, I think, though she's a stickler over practising. She used to get on to me about piano practice when I was a youngster.'

Marian Bennett was a tall, handsome woman, a few years older than her brother. She appraised Poppy as they took tea in her airy sitting room. 'May I ask how old you are, Miss Mazzini?' she queried.

'I've just had my fourteenth birthday,' Poppy smiled. 'On New Year's Day.'

'So young!' she said. 'Well, that's good.' She turned to her brother. 'Jeanette was about the same age, wasn't she? A little older. My daughter,' she explained. 'But she gave up her career in favour of marriage,' she told Poppy. 'Such a pity, I always thought. She had a very good voice. She would have done well if she had continued.'

'Not to be, Marian,' Dan said. 'Don't keep regretting it.'

Marian Bennett shook her head sadly. 'If only she had stayed with – still, what's done is done.' She smiled at Poppy. 'That's the thing with some young women; they see an opportunity to live in luxury and security and give up a promising opportunity. At least that is what Jeanette did. Gave up love and gave up singing.'

'Oh!' Poppy said earnestly. 'And I could give up neither!'

'Well, I'm off then.' Dan finished his tea and stood up. 'I'll leave you ladies to discuss your arrangements. Can you find your way back from here, Poppy? I've an appointment to see a theatre manager. Call into the office tomorrow and we'll see what bookings I can get for you.'

Mrs Bennett told her the cost of her lessons. 'But first of all I must hear you sing,' she said. 'I must ascertain how much training you will need, and I will tell you now, Miss Mazzini, that I don't allow any slacking, otherwise it wastes your time and mine.'

She led Poppy into another room, slightly smaller than the sitting room, which housed a baby grand piano. She sat down on the piano stool and said, 'I'd like you to sing a simple air, a ballad or folk song perhaps, or a favourite melody. *Not* a popular music hall song,' she emphasized. 'We are not here for those. Do you have a favourite piece?'

'Yes,' Poppy said. 'I have. It's called "Forever True".'

'Ah, yes.' Marian Bennett gave a wistful smile, and ran her hands lightly over the keys in the introduction. 'I know it well.'

Poppy felt so happy. She was doing what she loved best, and she was going to meet Charlie tomorrow. He would, she knew, always be true. He had been so attentive, kissed her lips on Christmas Day and promised that he would see her in London. She sang with fervour, her voice ringing out.

'Well done, Miss Mazzini,' Mrs Bennett said.

'Please call me Poppy,' she implored. 'Miss Mazzini sounds so stuffy.'

'Very well,' she said reluctantly. 'Though it wouldn't do for us to become too familiar at first. Now what I want to say is this. You obviously know the song and convey the love of a young girl very well. But where is the pathos when you discover that he is bidding you adieu? That he is leaving you for another? Which he undoubtedly is. The songwriter makes that quite obvious.'

'Oh, yes, of course. Perhaps I can't express sorrow because I feel so happy within myself, Mrs Bennett.'

'You are in love?'

'Yes,' Poppy admitted shyly and breathlessly.

'And does he love you?' Mrs Bennett kept her eyes on Poppy's face.

'I don't know for sure,' she said, a little crestfallen.

'Then let's start again, only think this time how you would feel if he had left you for another!' She smiled at her. 'I'm sure he won't, but let's pretend. You must act as well as sing.'

Poppy closed her eyes and tried to imagine how she would feel. She would be devastated! Never more would she love. She took a breath and began again.

'Better!' Mrs Bennett proclaimed. 'That time I could tell how lovesick you were! Good,' she said. 'So, we can start next week, if that suits? Six months' tuition three times a week, then we can cut it down to twice a week for the following six months, and after that, well we'll see. How does that sound? You perhaps think that you won't need so much teaching, but singers can become so familiar with their own voices that they don't notice if they become a little sloppy or out of control. You will learn breathing, concentration, relaxation, and how to focus on the music and the words. Then you will sing,' she said.

Dan booked engagements in theatres and music halls in and around the Covent Garden and St Martin's Lane area, and Poppy soon built up a reputation for reliability, often being able to fit in with managers at short notice, when they sent a runner round to the Marinos' with a message asking her if she could appear.

Charlie took her to see the premises for his new workshop. He had ordered a specially adapted Singer treadle sewing machine, for although he intended to be known as a bespoke shoemaker he realized that for some bread and butter work he would need mechanization. He showed her his order book, which contained several familiar stage names. 'I've ordered the leather and the fabric,' he said, 'and the thread and buttons, and I shall give in my notice to my employers just as soon as I receive my supplies.'

'Have these people paid you anything in advance, Charlie?' Poppy asked. 'Because, well, if they go out of town, they just might forget they've ordered from you.'

'No!' he scoffed. 'These are regular people, don't you know? They're not likely to forget! Your friends the Terry Sisters have each ordered two pairs of kid shoes and a pair of patent leather boots.'

Poppy was bothered about that. The Terry Sisters had never had any money when she was with them, and were always scratching about for coppers for a cup of coffee. She pondered. Perhaps they spent their money on things like clothes and shoes? Then the thought came into her mind that maybe Roger, who was putting up finance for Charlie, was buying the shoes for Ena. But it's most improper of me to even consider it, she thought, and dismissed the idea. Anyway, Charlie won't discuss business with me. I just hope he isn't too trusting, that's all.

'And by the way, Poppy,' Charlie reminded her, 'you keep forgetting. It's Charles now. Not Charlie! Charlie's all right for home, but not here. Do try to remember.'

'I'll try,' she said. 'But you've always been Charlie. I never think of you as anything else.'

He put his arms round her and pulled her towards him. They were quite alone in his workshop. 'We're different people here, Poppy.' He kissed her forehead. 'I'm going to be a successful shoemaker. I shall be well known. I don't want people calling me Charlie Chandler. Charles Chandler has a much better ring to it.'

He bent his head and kissed her neck, then ran his hands through her hair and kissed her mouth. 'You grow lovelier, Poppy. When I think of the child you were; you remember, when you said you loved me?' He gave a slight smile. 'That day in Hull down by 'dockside?' Just for a second, he slipped back into the Hull accent.

She nodded and licked her lips, disturbed by his wandering hands, yet glad that he'd remembered. But then she recalled that he'd betrayed their secret and told Roger Doyle and Bertie Fletcher that she loved him. 'How could I forget?' she said softly. 'Yet you never said that you loved me.'

He held her back and looked at her. 'Of course I did,' he said jocularly. 'How could I not love you? But I said that you were too young for love, which you are – for serious commitment, I mean,' he added quickly. 'But there's nothing to stop us . . .' He kissed her again and ran his hands over her breasts.

She pulled back. 'No,' she breathed, agitated by the wanting of him and the confusion she felt. Did he love her or not? 'No. We mustn't, I mean – I love you, Charlie – Charles – but . . .' She swallowed. 'I'm afraid!'

'Of what?' he teased. 'Not of me?'

'No,' she whispered. 'Of myself.'

'You're still a child, aren't you?' He looked down at her and she thought she saw impatience in his eyes.

'No,' she answered, gazing back at him. 'I'm not. I'm growing up.'

'Well!' He shrugged and said abruptly, 'I suppose I'll have to wait.'

The first six months of lessons had flown past and they were now into September. Poppy could tell that her voice was improving. Her breathing was more controlled, her musical instincts more acute in relation to the lyrics and the composers' intentions. Mrs Bennett gave her different types of musical scores, some of which she found very challenging yet exhilarating.

She arrived back at the Marinos' one evening after a theatre performance and was greeted by huge smiles from Mario. 'Come. Come!' he said. 'We are having a celebration. Anthony is here! He has been away for so long.'

'Oh, how lovely to see you!' She was very pleased to see him again.

'And you, too, Poppy.' He rose to greet her. He took her hand and his dark hair flopped over his forehead as he bent to kiss it. He appraised her with his brown eyes. 'How well you look, Poppy. Are you enjoying life? Was it the right decision to take coaching?' He looked a little sheepish. 'I wasn't interfering when I suggested it to Dan?'

She kept hold of his hand and gently squeezed it. 'No! I'm so grateful to you, Anthony. It's been the very best thing for me.' She let go of his hand as Mario handed her a glass of wine, insisting that she had just one, for usually she refused.

'She doesn't drink enough wine,' Mario said. 'But tonight is special. Tell her, Anthony!'

'Oh, in a moment, Father,' Anthony said. 'I want to know about Poppy first and how she's progressing with Mrs Bennett.'

'Do you know her?' she asked eagerly. 'She's such a perfectionist. I can't leave my lessons until she's satisfied!'

'I know her very well.' He nodded. 'She's Dan's sister; of course you'll know that?' He drew his eyebrows together in a slightly anxious way and Poppy thought there was a flickering questioning glance at his parents.

Mario had prepared supper, and although it was late, Poppy agreed to stay up and join them.

'How is your friend Charlie?' Anthony asked. He was sitting next to her at the table. 'Is he still in London?'

'Oh, yes,' she said enthusiastically. 'He's set up in business as a shoemaker. I have to try to remember to call him Charles! He's very busy, but sometimes he comes to see me at the theatre if he has the time.'

He smiled and raised his eyebrows quizzically. 'You must have a string of admirers by now, Poppy, who would happily find the time?'

She blushed. It was true there were many men who came to the stage door, both young and middle-aged. But the door keepers at the variety theatres and music halls knew by now that she wouldn't see anyone but Mr Chandler. 'There are one or two who are persistent,' she admitted. 'They send flowers and chocolates, but I refuse their invitations.'

'So if I came to hear your next performance, would I be turned away if I offered you supper afterwards?' he asked teasingly.

'Of course you wouldn't.' Her cheeks dimpled. 'I'll always be pleased to see you.'

The next evening she was to appear at a small music hall off the Strand and Anthony said he would come to hear her and book a supper.

'Book a supper!' His father overheard their conversation. 'You can eat here! I do something special for you and this beautiful young lady!' He stretched out his hands and looked from one to the other. 'You want to be alone, yes? It can be arranged. I put a table in the corner, with flowers and candles.'

'Don't be ridiculous, Father!' Anthony's manner was slightly crotchety. 'Poppy and I just want to talk theatre, that's all.'

'Tch! Too much talk, that is the trouble with young people today.' He blew an exaggerated kiss with both hands towards Poppy. 'You must know love, and then you sing and play better.' He clutched his chest. 'It come from 'ere.'

'Poppy knows that,' Anthony said tetchily. 'We all do!'

'Ah! You not think about the Englishman?' Mario asked Poppy. 'Ze one who doesn't like my food? Ah, he doesn't know about love. Pah! He is cold, that one. Not for the beautiful Poppy. And Anthony – he needs to know about love again.'

'Sorry, Poppy. My father has had too much wine,' Anthony said. 'I told him my news and he started celebrating early.'

'What news?' She had been so busy answering questions about herself that she hadn't asked Anthony what he was doing or where he was playing. She knew he hadn't been home since his tour of the south coast.

'I've been invited to tour Europe,' he told her, a reflective look in his eyes. 'I leave next week.'

CHAPTER THIRTY-EIGHT

'I can't believe the difference,' Anthony told her as they ate supper in a small restaurant near the theatre. 'Your voice is much improved. It was good before, but so much better now! Mrs Bennett is an excellent coach. You'll soon be ready for the concert hall.'

'That's what Mrs Bennett said,' Poppy replied. 'But never mind about me, tell me about you! I didn't quite take it in last night. How long will you be away?'

'About a year in total, though I'll come back for a week in six months, just to check up on the old folks, you know,' he said with a grin. 'They're so pleased for me, mainly because I shall be going to Italy during the tour: to Florence and Pisa, and Siena which is where their families are from.'

'How wonderful.' Poppy clutched her hands beneath her chin. She was thrilled for him. 'I can't think of anything more exciting.'

He leaned across the table and took hold of her hands. 'Are you happy, Poppy?' he asked earnestly. 'Is everything as you hoped it would be?'

His fingers entwined with hers. 'More than,' she whispered. 'Life in the theatre is so exciting. I love the atmosphere, the applause, the response from the audience.'

He nodded. 'It's food and drink, isn't it?' He gazed at her intently. 'And Charlie? Is he attentive? He must be very proud of you.'

A small furrow came to her brow and she absent-mindedly toyed with his fingers. In truth, Charlie wasn't proud of her. She thought, in fact, that he was just a little jealous and irritated by her success. 'I suppose he is,' she said softly. 'But as I said, he's so busy getting his business under way that he doesn't often come to the theatre. But that's all right,' she said excusingly. 'I quite understand, and it means I can concentrate much more if he isn't there.'

He nodded silently and released her hands. 'Sometimes love gets in the way, doesn't it?'

He looked wistful, she thought, and slightly melancholy. 'What did Mario mean when he said that you needed to know about love again? Were you crossed in love, Anthony?' she asked softly. 'Or shouldn't I be so forward as to ask?'

'I was,' he admitted. 'That's when I wrote "Forever True". It was an epilogue, I suppose – an ending!'

'I knew it,' she breathed. 'When I first heard the song, I knew that whoever had written it had felt love, and then lost it.' She searched his face. 'Did you – did you get over her? Did you find love again?'

He gave a slow smile, and his brown eyes gleamed. 'I think I've recovered. At last! It's taken a long time, but I was very young, and so was Jeanette.' Then his smile disappeared and he said in a slightly bitter tone, 'But she wasn't too young to know that she could do better for herself than loving an impoverished pianist. She chose money, position and status rather than love.'

'Jeanette?' she whispered. 'Mrs Bennett's daughter?'

'The same.' He lifted wistful eyes to hers. 'Have you met her?'

'No.' Poppy shook her head. 'But Dan told me that his sister had married for love and his niece had married for money.'

'Dan was very supportive of me,' he said. 'He saw how hard I'd been hit. He kept me so busy with engagements that I hardly had time to think about her.'

'But you still wrote a song for her?' Poppy said.

'About her,' he quickly corrected. 'Not for her. I wrote it for me.' Then he again gave a sudden smile. 'But someone has stolen it from me!'

She thought afterwards that he hadn't said whether he had loved anyone since Jeanette. Perhaps he's too bruised, too vulnerable, to fall in love again. She'd said goodbye to him a few days later before he set off on the start of his journey to Europe.

'Write some more music, Anthony,' she urged. 'And let me be the first to sing it!'

He'd bent and kissed her hand, and the next day when she arrived at the theatre there were flowers waiting for her. There was a card attached. *For the beautiful Poppy, bright flower of the field. From your greatest admirer. Anthony.* Under his signature he had added a quotation from Shakespeare's *Love's Labour's Lost*: *When Love speaks, the voice of all the Gods make Heaven drowsy with the harmony.*

'Oh! How true,' she'd murmured, pressing her nose to the bouquet to inhale the sweet perfume of the roses. She found a container and placed them on her dressing table. She kept looking at them and smiling as she prepared her make-up and changed into her stage clothes. They gave her such pleasure. Dearest Anthony, she mused. How kind. How considerate and talented he is. I do hope he succeeds abroad. My goodness, how famous he will be!

That evening after the show, Charlie knocked on the dressing room door. One of the dancers opened it. 'It's for you, dearie,' she said to Poppy. 'Your young gentleman. My,' she commented as she invited Charlie in, for they were all fully dressed, 'you must be proper smitten to send such gorgeous flowers.'

Charlie uttered a sardonic quip when he saw the bouquet. He'd seen other flowers that Poppy had received from her admirers and always made a joke of them. This time he idly read the card. 'The piano player! What's he mean?' He tossed the card onto the table. 'The man's a fop! Full of jargon and folderol!'

'No,' she said in dismay. 'He's not! It's a quotation. He was telling me about . . .' I can't speak of it, she thought. Not to Charlie. Anthony wouldn't want me to discuss his lost love. He told me in confidence. 'We were – we were discussing music and – and song, and how love always plays a part.' She looked anxiously at him. 'He was only home for a short time,' she said. 'He's going to tour Europe.'

'What sort of tour?' he asked grumpily. 'Has he got time and money enough to travel?'

'A concert tour!' she explained, and wondered why Charlie always misconstrued everything, and why she should feel so apprehensive as she clarified the matter, not wanting to upset him.

'Oh!' He bent towards her and whispered, 'Good riddance! He won't be sneaking behind my back, then, and running off with you!'

'Of course he won't.' She laughed, relief surging through her at his change of manner. Perhaps after all it did Charlie some good to be a mite jealous.

They went out for supper and he pressed her hand. 'You know, Poppy, it will be years before I can marry or make a proper commitment. But there's no reason ' – he turned her hand over and kissed her palm – 'why we can't . . . well, we're away from our folks; nobody would know . . .'

'What?' she asked softly. 'Wouldn't know what?'

He gave an exasperated sigh. 'Poppy! You're no longer a child. The sort of life you're leading, you know what goes on between couples,' he whispered. 'We don't have to wait!'

She swallowed. She knew perfectly well what he meant. It would be easy to give in to his urgent demands, she loved him so much. But what if – what if he changed his mind about her? Suppose she became pregnant? What would she do then about a singing career? And whatever would her pa think? He'd trusted her to come away on her own, when his instincts had urged him to keep her under his protection.

'Do you mean that we would live together as man and wife, but not actually get married?' she parried. 'Until later?'

'Well, no!' He looked taken aback. 'My landlady wouldn't allow us to live together in my lodgings.'

'Well then – what?'

'Oh!' Again he seemed exasperated. 'There are ways and means! A weekend away now and again,' he said, and added sarcastically, 'if your career allows it, of course!'

'I want to sing, Charlie,' she said quietly, though her heart hammered at the thought that he didn't really respect her if he could suggest such a thing.

'Charles!' he corrected. Then he said pedantically, 'If we should ever marry, Poppy, you'd have to give up your singing, you realize that? I couldn't have my wife careering all over the country. Not once I'm successful, at any rate.'

Her spirits plummeted. She couldn't believe what he was saying. 'You know it's what I've always wanted,' she said. 'Just as you wanted to start your own business as a shoemaker!'

'But I'm a man!' He stared at her in astonishment. 'I have to earn a living. You're only playing a game, dressing up and singing to entertain people, just as you did when you were little! You've a lovely voice, I admit, but it's not proper work like a man has to do! Not in the theatre. Not in some grubby little tinpot variety show! I mean, this pianist fellow. You can't say that he's doing proper work!'

Her lips trembled. There were only a few people in the café, but they must have heard his words, which he hadn't bothered to speak quietly. She felt tears trickle down her cheeks. How could he be so cruel?

'Poppy!' he said beguilingly, seeing her tears. He pulled his chair nearer to hers. 'Don't be upset. You know that I'm right.'

A few days later she arrived at Mrs Bennett's for her lesson as usual. She felt very downhearted, and as she had walked from the Marinos' she had yet again gone over her conversation with Charlie. He would never have made such improper suggestions had they still been living in Hull. And if he really wanted to marry me, he would have spoken to my father. But then to say that I'd have to give up my singing! An image of Mrs Chandler sitting over the sewing machine in her husband's workshop came to her mind. Is that what would await me? She sighed, feeling troubled and anxious, as she mounted the steps to Mrs Bennett's front door. I'm so confused.

Mrs Bennett's maid answered the door. 'Good afternoon, Miss Mazzini,' she said, taking Poppy's coat. 'Mrs Bennett said would I take you into the sitting room. Her daughter is with her,' she added, on seeing Poppy's questioning glance, for she generally showed her straight into the music room.

Poppy took in a sharp breath. Jeanette! Whom Anthony had loved and lost. I wonder if she is content?

'Poppy, come and meet my daughter, Mrs Herbert Marsden,' Mrs Bennett said. 'Jeanette, this is Miss Poppy Mazzini. I've told you about her.'

'Indeed!' Mrs Marsden gazed curiously at Poppy. 'How do you do? A most unusual name, if I might be permitted to say so. Is it your own or one you have appropriated for the stage?'

'It's my own,' Poppy answered. 'My father's family were Italian.'

'Ah!' Mrs Marsden sank back into a chair. She was plump and pretty with a pert upturned nose and dimpled cheeks. Her fair hair, dressed in a pompadour style, was swept under her velvet hat, with a loose fringe of curls on her forehead which emphasized her large blue eyes. Poppy could see why Anthony had been so enchanted by her.

Jeanette Marsden was dressed to go out; she wore a tiered shoulder cape over a pleated day gown and dangled a silk muff in her hand. 'I was about to go out visiting,' she said. 'But Mama said I should stay and meet you and listen to you sing. I used to sing, you know. I think Mama wants me to know what I could have achieved if I had continued, and hadn't married Herbert.' Mrs Bennett protested but Jeanette simply shrugged. 'I have everything I want,' she said airily. 'I have a house in the country and my own cabriolet; I travel abroad, and our children want for nothing.'

'Then it was right for you,' Poppy said quietly. 'Music wasn't your world.'

Jeanette lowered her long lashes. 'No,' she said. 'It wasn't! There were other things I wanted more, so I gave it up. But I sing to entertain my husband's friends. I still have a pleasant voice. And,' she added, 'I had a song written for me. Not everyone can say that!' She rose gracefully from her chair. 'But, if you don't think me rude, Miss Mazzini, I really must go out now. Perhaps I could hear you in concert sometime? I spend so little time in London that I have masses of things to do when I'm here. You do understand?' She looked pleadingly and sweetly from Poppy to Mrs Bennett.

'Of course.' Poppy was relieved to see her depart. She didn't want Mrs Marsden to hear her sing. She was convinced that if that patronizing lady discovered that she was performing in variety halls she would turn up her pretty little nose in disdain.

Poppy and Mrs Bennett watched from the curtained window of the music room as Mrs Marsden was assisted into her smart conveyance, and as if she knew they were there she waved a gloved hand from the window.

'Does she miss him, do you think?' Poppy asked softly, thinking of Anthony's heartache when Jeanette had told him she was marrying someone else.

'Anthony?' Mrs Bennett answered vaguely, still gazing out of the window at the disappearing carriage. 'I don't know. She would never admit it, if she does.' Then she and Poppy looked at each other guiltily. 'Oh!' Mrs Bennett drew in a breath. 'Do you know him? Anthony Marino? Yes, of course you must!'

'I spoke out of turn,' Poppy said hurriedly. 'I shouldn't have asked. I'm so sorry.'

'No, that's all right.' Mrs Bennett was flustered. 'It is all over. A long time ago. But I still do feel for the dear boy.' She put her hand to her chest. 'I did so want them to marry. He writes such beautiful music and I think he still writes for her.'

Should I tell her that Anthony told me he wrote that song for himself? No, she decided. Mrs Bennett is a romantic, just as I am. Dan Damone said that his sister had married for love and not for money. It would shatter her idealistic dreams if she thought that someone could recover from a broken love affair. She turned towards the piano. And how could anyone recover, if they had truly loved? Does Anthony have a secret longing for Jeanette even though she is married to another man? She sighed and murmured, 'Love is a sickness full of woes, all remedies refusing . . .'

'A plant with most cutting grows, most barren with best using,' Mrs Bennett continued. 'Samuel Daniel. I remember that from my schooling!' She smiled. 'Come along, no more talk of love. Let's make music.'

They were only halfway into the lesson when the front door bell rang. Mrs Bennett tutted crossly. 'I will tell the girl to say I am not at home.'

But the maid opened the door and Dan came rushing in, his cape flying and his hair awry. 'I'm so sorry to interrupt,' he told his sister. 'But this just couldn't wait. I need an answer! I've come at full speed and I hoped that I'd find you here,' he said, turning to Poppy. 'Tremendous news, if you are ready for it.'

'News! What news? Has something happened?' Poppy asked.

He sat down and then got up again. 'We'll take your advice, of course, Marian. You must say if Poppy is ready.'

'Ready? For what?' Mrs Bennett asked.

'To sing in concert. In Paris!'

CHAPTER THIRTY-NINE

'To sing – in Paris? But—'

'A French agent has been in London, on holiday with his wife, and seemingly they went out to the theatre one evening and heard you.' Dan put up his hands as Poppy opened her mouth to ask questions. 'I don't know where or what you were singing, but he was sufficiently impressed to go back to France and inform the managers of several concert halls and theatres. He mentions Lyon, Reims and Rouen too as possibilities.'

He fished around in his pocket and brought out a sheet of paper. 'I've enquired into his credentials, and he's bona fide.' He waved the paper at her. 'They sent a telegram. If you agree, they'd like you to go over next month!'

'But I can't speak French, and what would I sing!' Panic filled her. It was one thing singing in England, quite another singing in France.

'Nothing too grand,' he said soothingly. 'Small halls or theatres and possibly salons for private performances. But it would be good for you, Poppy, don't you think, Marian?' he said to Mrs Bennett. 'Better to start in concert halls and legitimate theatre over there, than here where you are known in music hall.'

'You mean that if I'm not successful then no-one in England will hear of it?' Poppy lifted her chin defiantly. 'Is that what you mean?'

He patted the seat of the sofa. 'Come and sit here. No, of course I don't mean that! Not at all. But the theatres and variety halls in London are asking for you as a popular singer. In France you can stretch your repertoire.' He looked at his sister for confirmation. 'Could she become another Jenny Lind?'

'Jenny Lind! I've heard of her. She sang "*La Sonnambula*".' Poppy almost whispered the name as she remembered singing for her mother.

'She did,' Marian Bennett said. 'She was known for it. *Ah, non giunge.* Do not mingle. It was one of her set pieces when she sang in concert.' She shook her head. 'Poppy is a different kind of singer entirely.'

'I know it,' Poppy told her softly. 'I can sing it.'

Dan gave a huge smile. 'Well, there you are then! What else? What else can she sing, Marian?'

Marian Bennett put her fingers to her head. 'You've caught me off guard. Erm, Strauss waltzes. Ballads – "Greensleeves"! Folk songs. Rossini. But she can't go abroad alone! It's different here in music hall – everyone starts young and they're not always chaperoned – but France! She *must* have a travelling companion; she would be considered immoral otherwise. It would be disastrous. There would be rumour and innuendo – especially as she doesn't know the language, or the customs!'

He pursed his lips and teased his whiskers as he surveyed the women. 'But does it appeal?' he asked Poppy. 'Is she ready?' he questioned his sister.

Poppy nibbled her bottom lip. Already she was getting excited just at the idea of it.

'Y-yes. She has to start sometime – but . . .' Mrs Bennett looked doubtful and Poppy guessed that she would have had similar misgivings if the same had been asked of her own daughter.

Dan sat back and crossed his legs. 'Then you go with her,' he suggested. 'John can manage without you for a few weeks.'

Poppy and Marian Bennett looked at each other. Poppy had never been introduced to Mr Bennett, though she had sometimes seen him walking down the steps from the house, his head in his newspaper and a pipe in his mouth. What he did for a living she had no idea.

'Leave John? How ever would he manage without me?'

'You've got a maid and a cook. Anyway, he's so absent-minded he probably wouldn't notice that you weren't here.'

'I couldn't afford to go,' she exclaimed. 'What about my pupils?'

'Who would I sing with?' Poppy asked. 'Will I have a pianist or an ensemble – what?'

Dan shrugged. 'I'll find out about all that before we agree on a contract. There will no doubt be other singers too.'

'So . . .' Poppy gazed at Mrs Bennett. 'If I were to take a companion who is also a pianist . . . ?' She let the question hang in the air, but her eyes brightened.

'I . . .' Mrs Bennett clasped her hands to her chest. 'I've never played the piano in a concert hall!'

'You play the piano every day!' Dan jumped up. 'Of course! Well thought, Poppy. We can say that you will accept, and will bring your own accompanist and chaperon. What say you, Marian? Is it agreed?'

'I must ask John.' Marian Bennett had gone quite pink. 'He won't refuse, I'm sure, but – oh dear!'

It was then that Poppy thought of Charlie. What would he say? What would he think? He couldn't object, of course, unlike Mr Bennett who could refuse to let his wife go; but, she thought, Charlie would most likely disapprove. And I do so want his approval.

She went straight round to his workshop on leaving Mrs Bennett's. He was sitting in his window and she was struck by his likeness to his father, who was always in his chair.

'One day I shall take on an apprentice and have women to do the machining for me,' he said, by way of greeting, as she entered the door. 'I shan't be bent over a piece of leather all day like my father!'

'But surely customers will want *you* to make their shoes?' She came and put a hand on his shoulder. 'You're such a fine shoemaker.'

'Well, yes,' he said, mollified. 'But just take a look at my order book! Another six pairs of shoes to make, and all for the theatre or for Roger's friends. I'm going to be working day and night to finish them.' He looked up at her. 'Could you slip out and get me a meat pie for my dinner?'

'Yes, of course I can,' she agreed. 'And when I come back I've something exciting to tell you.'

'What?' He picked up his awl and began pressing holes in the welt of a shoe to make it ready for stitching.

'I'll tell you when I get back.' He might be in a better mood after he's eaten. He seems very grumpy now, and who wouldn't be, she thought, glancing round the small dark workshop. The only place he could afford, he'd told her, when first showing it to her.

On the way back with the meat pie, she slipped into a nearby hostelry and bought him a small jug of ale. I'm sugaring the pill, she thought. Wheedling him so that he'll be pleased for me. Surely I shouldn't have to do this?

'So will you go?' he asked, when she had told him the news. He looked downcast and took a gulp of ale. 'Is that what singers do? Travel abroad before they've made a name for themselves at home?' He gave a slight shrug. 'Nothing to do with me, of course. I can't influence you.'

'But it is to do with you, Charlie – Charles. I – I want to go, but . . .' I want him to say well done, or what a wonderful opportunity. 'I'd like your opinion,' she tailed off quietly.

'Well, seeing as you ask, my opinion is that you should stay here. Plenty of places to sing at in London, if it's really what you want to do.' He took another sup of ale, but pushed the half-eaten pie away. 'You've spread your wings already by moving away from Hull. London's the place to be; it's the hub for theatres, for business, for anything you can think of. I shall make my name here.' He drew nearer to his bench and began working beeswax into the threads of hemp which he would use for sewing. 'Although when I'm established I might try Europe.'

She left him, saying that she was still thinking about the offer; that she hadn't yet made up her mind. As she walked down the street a young woman was alighting from a brougham, and looking around her as if she was in unfamiliar territory.

'Pardon me,' she said to Poppy. 'I'm looking for Charles Chandler, the shoemaker. Do you happen to know where his premises are?'

She was expensively dressed in rich brown velvet: a full-skirted tailored jacket with large sleeves and a wide panelled skirt. On her head she wore a neat velvet boater with a short veil.

I'm glad I cleared away Charlie's dinner plate, was Poppy's first thought. He would be cross to have someone like this catch him unawares. 'I'll take you.' She smiled. 'I've just this minute left him.'

'Is he any good, do you know?' the young lady asked. 'I've heard excellent reports, but I don't know of anyone *personally* who has had a pair of shoes made.' Her voice was haughty; it held no warmth at all, Poppy mused. But still, what does that matter if she's a potential customer?

'I have a pair,' Poppy told her. 'He made me a pair of dancing shoes. I wear them constantly.'

'Really? Oh, that's splendid! That's just what I want for a special occasion. A supper dance.'

'Here we are!' Poppy pushed open Charlie's door. 'He's inundated with work, but I'm sure he'll see you. Charles!' she called. 'A visitor for you.'

The Marinos had received a letter from Anthony and he had enclosed one for Poppy. She opened it as she was having supper with them. It was brief, telling her of his travel plans. 'I am leaving France in a few days to go to Switzerland; to Basel and then Zürich. After that I shall travel to Milan, Florence, Bologna and Siena. I am giving you this information, Poppy, in case you should ever need to get in touch with me – for whatever reason. I trust that you are happy – you seemed to be when I saw you last. Yours in affection, Anthony.'

'France, Switzerland, Italy!' she murmured and Mario beamed.

'It is good, yes, all this travel? You should do it too. Travel broadens the 'orizons.'

His wife nodded. 'It is true what he says. But *we* only go to Italy in a blue moon, *we* never go anywhere else, not to France or Germany, only we travel through these places!'

Mario lifted up both hands and looked round the small restaurant. 'Why should we go? We have everything we want 'ere. It is the young who should travel, as we did.'

His wife waved a hand in dismissal. 'Yes,' she said to Poppy. 'You must travel while you can or else you meet an 'usband who wants always to stay at 'ome.'

Poppy sat listening to them chuntering good-heartedly at each other. Should she tell them of her offer? She decided that she would. 'As a matter of fact,' she said, 'I've been offered engagements in France. I have to make up my mind by tomorrow, so that Dan can write a proposal and send a telegram. What should I do?' she asked. 'I can't ask my father, there isn't time.'

'Alone?' Rosina asked, and Mario, who had just said that she should travel, shook his head. 'Not alone,' he said. 'It is too dangerous for a young lady.'

'Mrs Bennett, my singing coach, might be able to travel with me. If her husband approves, that is.'

'Mrs Bennett? Ah, yes.' They both nodded their heads in complicity and looked at each other.

'I do know about Anthony and Mrs Bennett's daughter,' said Poppy. 'Anthony told me.'

'Yes?' Mario came and sat next to her, putting his chin in his hand and gazing at her. 'He discussed her with you? That is good.' He gave a big smile. 'Rosina – that is good, yes?' he said to his wife. 'He talks about her at last!'

Rosina heaved a sigh. 'I knew it. I knew that one day he would be over her.'

A few days later, Poppy told Charlie that she had decided to travel to France. Mr Bennett had decreed that his wife should accompany Poppy and indeed said that he was delighted that the opportunity had presented itself. He had been introduced to Poppy and she found him to be of courtly and old-fashioned charm, yet worldly enough to agree that his wife should travel without him.

'You see, I can't miss the chance,' Poppy explained to Charlie. 'It might open so many doors for me.'

He nodded, biting his lip and pondering. Then he said, 'Will you see that pianist fellow whilst you're over there?'

'Anthony!' She laughed. 'Why no!' Goodness, she thought. Is he jealous? Warmth spread over her at the idea. 'He's gone to Switzerland – I think,' she added cautiously.

He came towards her and put out his arms and drew her towards him. 'I shall miss you,' he said, and bent to kiss her. 'How long will you be away?'

'Dan has suggested I take other engagements whilst I'm over there, so perhaps several weeks, maybe a month or more. Will you really miss me, Charlie?' she asked. 'Truly?'

'Of course, you little goose! Of course I will. I shall be slaving away here whilst you're enjoying yourself, taking bouquets and being flattered by compliments.' He looked down at her and smiled and she felt overwhelmed with love for him. Perhaps after all he did really love her, though he could never love her as much as she loved him.

'I love you, Charlie,' she whispered. 'And I'll think of you every day I'm away.'

He kissed her again, his lips tender against hers. 'One day you'll prove it,' he said softly. 'One day you'll show me how much you love me.'

'I've loved you since I was ten,' she murmured. 'Isn't that proof?'

'How sweet you are, Poppy! My adorable girl.'

'How old do I have to be, Charlie, before you believe I love you and you say that you love me?' She gazed up at him, her emotions in confusion.

He shook his head and said tetchily. 'I've told you that I love you, Poppy. Of course I do.'

She blinked as tears filmed her eyes. Why did she always have to ask him? Why was her happiness always tinged with doubt and uncertainty? Her heart told her to believe the words he uttered. Her head told her that she must have a care, or her heart would break.

CHAPTER FORTY

A month later they crossed to France. Poppy had written to her father to tell him her news, and regretting that there was no time to come home to Hull before she went away. There were rehearsals of her chosen pieces of music, three new songs to learn and a duet with a tenor she had been asked to consider. There was also a wardrobe to prepare, and Mrs Bennett was helping her with this.

The first thing she had suggested was a corset to accentuate Poppy's tiny waist and uplift her breasts, for the two gowns they had chosen for her performances were cut low on the bodice. One was in apple green with diaphanous sleeves of chiffon, the other in creamy white satin with frilled lace sleeves over net and edged with satin ribbon. Both emphasized charm and youthful sensuality.

Charlie had come to say goodbye at Mrs Bennett's where she was staying for the last few days before their journey, and had imparted the news that he was taking on an apprentice.

'So soon?' she exclaimed. 'Have you business enough to do that?'

'Yes,' he'd said enthusiastically. 'I've promises of lots of work. You remember the young lady who came the day you were there, Miss Amanda Burchfield? Roger recommended her. She's ordered several pairs of shoes, and I went to visit her father who asked me to make him a pair of boots. He's a self-made man,' he added. 'Has his own carriage and a house full of servants.'

She was pleased for him, of course, but he seemed uninterested in her own plans, although as she showed him out he took her hand and said bon voyage, and that he would miss her.

'I hope you do, Charlie,' she'd whispered. 'I shall think of you whilst I'm away, and I hope you think of me, even though you will be so busy.'

He'd kissed her cheek and said that he would never be so busy that he didn't have time to think of her, and she had to be satisfied with that.

The concert hall was packed at her first appearance. The wildly enthusiastic audience had come to hear an Italian tenor who, although Poppy hadn't heard of him, was extremely popular in France. Poppy too was greeted by great applause at the end of her performance. She took her bow and gave an encore.

She and Mrs Bennett had been invited to stay with the French agent, Michel Auber, and his wife whilst in Paris and Mrs Bennett had gratefully accepted on their behalf. They lived in a roomy first floor apartment overlooking the Seine and one of its many bridges. Mrs Bennett told Poppy that they couldn't be too careful in protecting her reputation. When Poppy looked puzzled, she explained that even well-run hotels could be regarded as places for assignations and intrigue, fatal for an innocent female artiste.

Dan had arranged with Michel Auber that he should plan Poppy's schedule over the next few weeks, but told him that he should always discuss the venues with Mrs Bennett first for her approval. After the first performance, reviews were impressive and led to a flood of invitations to sing at private gatherings and salons. These were carefully considered and she accepted three engagements a week for a month. Whilst they were in Paris, they were taken to view the Eiffel Tower, newly built in 1889 for the Grand Exhibition, and the twelfth-century cathedral of Notre Dame, and climbed the steps in Montmartre to reach the heady heights of the church of Sacré Coeur. Then they moved on to the ancient Roman city and university town of Reims.

Two of the other female singers who had shared the billing at Poppy's first appearance, Madame Solari and Mademoiselle Lablanche, were also going to engagements in Reims and Michel Auber suggested that they should travel together, while he made bookings for the three of them to sing at the same venue. Poppy was pleased with the arrangement. They were older and more experienced than she was, one French, the other Italian, and they cushioned any nervousness that she felt at being in a strange country, by having visited the place before and therefore being able to advise her. Marian Bennett too was satisfied with the plan; always aware of social protocol, she felt it was safer and more respectable for them to travel with a party.

A letter was forwarded from Poppy's father, who told her that the shop was once again busy and the coffee shop with its new decorations in a theatre theme was doing well. 'There's some attraction between Tommy and Mattie,' he wrote. 'They've said nothing but there's something going on there for sure. Nan has noticed it as well. We'd both be pleased if it came to a proper relationship. She'd be good for him and she's such a help in the shop, full of ideas. I've got very fond of her, and of Nan too. I admit I was foolish, not to have had them both here in the first place. But I was at my wits' end after your mother died and not thinking straight.'

There was also a letter from Anthony, sent on to her by Dan. He had just arrived in Italy where he said he intended to stay for the next three months, in spite of the bitterly cold weather and the snow which had started to fall. He wrote, 'I'm so proud of you, Poppy. Dan has written of how well you are being received and I'm only sorry that our paths haven't crossed. I seem always to be moving on in front of you. I hope that perhaps one day you will catch up with me. I have written several songs whilst I have been in Europe and the music publisher Schott has shown an interest. I am enclosing one of them. It might not be suitable for you to sing in private salons, but maybe in the theatre.' He signed his letter, 'Your good friend, Anthony.'

Poppy showed the song to Marian Bennett, who having hummed it through said, 'He's quite right; it won't do for the salons. The audiences there seem to prefer the old-established songs from operetta, though the themes are similar, of lost or unrequited love.' She gave a little smile. 'Anthony is such a romantic. He writes songs from the heart.' Then she said wistfully, 'Such a dear boy. I wish him happiness . . .' She gave herself a shake. 'But there.' She turned to Poppy and gave her back the song sheet. 'You could sing it in the theatres. It would appeal to those in an audience who like to shed a few tears, and then have a happy ending.'

When Poppy was alone, she hummed the song softly. It was a yearning lyrical melody suitable for voice, piano or orchestra arrangement.

My love she sits a-weeping beneath the greenwood tree
My love she sits a-weeping – but not for me.
Her tears flow for another, to me she was not true
For though I love those pale pink cheeks and starry
 eyes so blue
The tender lips I fain would kiss their nectar sweet to
 claim
Love only him who cares not and whisper on his name.

My love she sits a-weeping beneath the greenwood tree
My love she sits a-weeping – but not for me.

I wait for her as the year doth pass when winter turns
 to spring
When fresh green grows on the greenwood tree, my
 dearest love will turn to me, to bring her comfort still.
And when I look upon her face the light of love to see
And with my arms I do embrace her wounded gentle
 heart
I'll claim it for my very own and tell her soft, my dearest one,
I'll never part from thee.

My love she sits a-smiling beneath the greenwood tree
My love she sits a-smiling – she smiles for me.

It's beautiful. I'll sing it tomorrow evening, she mused. And announce it as a new composition by Anthony Marino. She was to sing at a small theatre where Madame Solari and an English tenor, Mr Andrew Richardson, would also perform. Marian Bennett was to accompany her on the piano.

The theatre had a full house and Poppy was the first performer. She wore her green gown and had dressed her hair in a loose chignon with ringlets at the side of her face. She didn't like to wear false curls, as the nearest match to her own was always coarse and gingery and not red and shiny like her own hair. She looked young and fresh as she sang 'Greensleeves' in her clear crystalline voice and received rapturous applause.

Marian Bennett was beaming as she too took applause from the audience. It was the best reception they had had on the tour. The tenor then portrayed the character Hoffman from *The Tales of Hoffman* – followed by Madame Solari who sang arias from *La Traviata.* A short interval, and Mrs Bennett once more took her place at the piano, a full-size concert grand. Poppy came to stand by it; she folded her hands in front of her and announced that she would like to sing a new composition by the pianist and composer Anthony Marino. She smiled shyly and sweetly at the audience and told them that this was the very first time the song had been heard.

There were appreciative murmurings from the auditorium and as Mrs Bennett began the introduction, emphasizing the phrasing of the melody, Poppy took a breath, clasped her hands against her breast and began.

The audience was hushed as Poppy's voice, soft and low, expressing all the tenderness of unrecognized love, wistfully caressed the poignant passages of the first verse. She charmed them with the evocative chorus, and in the second verse sang lyrically and joyfully of the fulfilment of romantic rapture.

As she finished and bowed her head there was a sudden silence in which Poppy could hear the beating of her own heart. Then, as one, the audience rose to its feet and began to applaud. 'Bravo! Encore! Encore!'

She stood startled for a moment and then a smile lifted the corners of her lips. What was it Anthony had said? That to perform and hear the applause of the audience was food and drink to an artiste. He is quite right! She came to the front of the stage and gave a deep curtsy. I feel as if I have dined on heady sweet wine. She bowed again and held out her hand to invite Mrs Bennett to take an acknowledgement, and backed away. She remembered something else that Anthony had said, the time he had invited her to join him on the stage at Brighton. Always leave them wanting more. There was no time for an encore in any case. The other singers were waiting. She touched her hands to her lips, threw the audience a kiss and left the stage.

Reviews were ecstatic and hailed her enchanting performance. Flowers and champagne, the speciality of the region, were sent to her at every appearance and offers flooded in. Michel Auber travelled to Reims himself to discuss them and they then journeyed on to spend a week in the industrial city of Dijon, followed by the long journey on to Lyon.

In Lyon Poppy saw for the first time, and was invited to ride in, a petrol-driven motor car. It was, she thought, one of the strangest contraptions she had ever seen. 'It travels as fast as two horses,' she said excitedly to Mrs Bennett. 'It bangs and spits and sets off with such a jerk that I had to hold on to my hat.' She remembered being with her father at the theatre in Hull when they saw the trick cyclists on stage with their motorized bicycle.

'I miss my pa,' she said suddenly. 'It's such a long time since I saw him.' She didn't know why she felt so homesick. She was having a wonderful time, but she was getting tired. They had been travelling abroad for six weeks and she had been singing several times a week at theatres or salons during that time.

'I miss my husband too,' Mrs Bennett confessed. 'We have never been apart for so long during the whole of our married life. But your voice needs a rest, Poppy. I thought you sounded a little husky at your last performance.'

Poppy nodded. It was true, her voice felt strained and reaching the higher notes was no longer as easy as it had been at the beginning of the tour. 'Should we make Lyon our last stop?' she said. 'And then go home? We could be home for Christmas.'

She was longing too to see Charlie. She had sent him several letters and topographical postcards of Paris, including some picturing the Arc de Triomphe and the Eiffel Tower, but hadn't received a reply, even though she had included a forwarding address. In Reims she had posed in her green gown, with her red hair flowing to her shoulders, for hand-coloured photographs for *cartes de visite*, which she distributed to admirers, and one of these she had placed in an envelope and posted to Charlie, being careful to address it to Charles Chandler. But still no reply.

Perhaps he has moved to new premises and hasn't received them, she pondered, prepared to forgive his laxity. And I expect he will be so busy he won't have had time to enquire of Dan Damone or my father as to my whereabouts. Nevertheless, she felt rather hurt that she hadn't heard from him.

'Yes, I think we should return,' Marian Bennett said in reply to her question. 'There are no forward bookings after Lyon, but you must honour those that are already made.' She smiled. 'It will be good to go home, though I have really enjoyed being here. It's been such a pleasure to play. Going back to teaching my pupils will seem very dull in comparison.'

Poppy gazed at her. 'Does that mean that you won't be able to come with me again, if I should return to Europe?' Mrs Bennett had been the perfect companion as well as coach and accompanist.

'Oh, my dear,' Mrs Bennett said wistfully. 'I don't know if I can leave my husband again for so long.' She seemed almost shy as she added, 'We have a good marriage. I wouldn't want to do anything to upset that.'

'Yes, of course,' Poppy said quietly. 'I do understand. Mr Bennett will want you with him.'

She sighed inwardly. How wonderful to inspire such devotion. Then she pondered. So if I want to continue travelling abroad, I must find another companion. Not necessarily one who played the piano, for wherever they had been there was always a pianist, violinist or ensemble able to play, and indeed the other singers hadn't had their own accompanists.

But I realize now that I must travel with an older married female or with a theatre party. She had seen for herself when gentlemen had arrived at the theatres and halls, bringing flowers and chocolates and invitations to supper, how easy it would be for a young single woman to give the wrong impression. Whom would I ask? Whom do I know? There was no-one she could think of. I won't worry about it now, she decided. There will surely be someone.

She sent a *carte de visite* to Anthony to tell him that they would be returning to England after she had completed the engagements in Lyon, and he had written back to say how pleased he was to receive it. 'I see that you are no longer a child,' he'd put, 'but a charming and beautiful young woman.' He also expressed regret that their paths wouldn't cross in Europe, and hoped that they would meet up again when he returned to London in the New Year.

He says I'm a beautiful young woman, she mused, smiling as she read his letter. Many of the reviewers in the newspapers had declared their astonishment at such a pure clear voice in one so young, and at her command of range and tone. Her age, according to the critics, ranged from thirteen to eighteen.

The last two weeks were very tiring, for Michel Auber, having been told that she was returning to England, had pleaded to be allowed to book several more engagements, and she was forced to sing less taxing roles in order to save her voice. Nevertheless she was applauded wherever she went, though she always refused to sing an encore on the advice of Mrs Bennett.

'Your voice is still immature,' she warned her. 'Don't overstrain it.'

She took her final bow at a theatre in Lyon after singing Anthony's song, 'Beneath the Greenwood Tree', and once more was given rapturous applause. Flowers were thrown onto the stage, and she took one rose from a bouquet and threw it into the audience. A young man in the second row reached high above everyone else's head and caught it.

He was waiting at the door of the theatre as she left with Mrs Bennett and the other members of their party. 'Mademoiselle!' He bowed and spoke to her in fractured English. 'Please, you will come back to France one day?'

She said that she hoped so, and he pressed the rose to his lips and declared he would keep the flower for ever.

'You've made several conquests during your time here,' Mrs Bennett drily remarked as they were driven away in the brougham. 'But you are a sensible young woman and I can't see such adoration going to your head!'

'It's very flattering,' Poppy said softly. 'But my heart is already spoken for.'

CHAPTER FORTY-ONE

Poppy was tense with nervous exhilaration when she arrived back in England. She chattered animatedly to Mrs Bennett about what to do first as they boarded the train to London. 'Do I go first to see Dan? Should I stay with the Marinos? I must go home for Christmas. And I want to get in touch with Charlie! How will I find him if he's moved premises?' Mrs Bennett had met Charlie when he had visited Poppy at her house before their departure for France. Reading between the lines she had realized there was an attraction, on Poppy's part at any rate.

But Poppy was also extremely tired. Her voice was croaky and although she had dashed to buy some refreshments and magazines for the journey, when she sat down in the ladies' compartment she put back her head and closed her eyes and tears trickled down her cheeks.

'What is it, Poppy?' Mrs Bennett leaned across from her seat and touched her arm. 'Why are you crying? You've had a great success. You can go back, you know. When you've rested, that is.' She looked anxiously at her as Poppy opened her eyes and she saw the glistening tears.

'I don't know why I'm crying,' Poppy choked. 'I just—' she swallowed. 'I just feel that I want to. I'm not unhappy or anything. It's all been just wonderful!'

'I think you're overtired,' Marian Bennett said. 'You've had a great deal of excitement, and then all the travelling too. I must admit that I feel quite exhausted, and I haven't been on show as you have.'

Poppy nodded. Right now she longed for her own little bed

above the shop. She wanted her father to give her a hug the way he used to when she was a child, but more than anything else she wanted Charlie to be waiting for her at the barrier when they arrived in London. She had sent one last letter to his old address, telling him of her arrival, and had written on the envelope a request that the Post Office forward the letter if necessary.

But he wasn't there, and Mrs Bennett, seeing her obvious disappointment, insisted that she went home with her to rest that evening and then think about what to do the following day. 'Dan will want to see you, of course. I will send a first class letter to him in the morning, asking him to call.'

He came the next evening, bearing flowers, chocolates and champagne. He also brought newspapers with reviews and articles saying that Poppy Mazzini had returned to England from a triumphal tour of Europe. Charlie will surely see these, she thought, as she scanned the reports, even if he hasn't received my letter. Surely someone will tell him? The uncertainty was making her feel quite dizzy.

Dan saw how tired she was. 'I'm putting you on the first train home tomorrow,' he told her. 'You need peace and quiet. I've had letters from your father. He's most anxious to see you after so long.' He looked steadily at her. 'You are a very lucky young woman to have such a supportive father, concerned for your well-being.' Then he added, 'Will a week be enough? I can get bookings for you whenever you're ready.'

'Two weeks at the minimum,' Mrs Bennett insisted, 'and then only one performance, just to let people know that she's back in England. Then she needs to give her voice and herself a complete rest.'

'Well, that's fine,' Dan agreed. 'You've made sufficient money to be able to take time off if you want to, Poppy.'

Part of her wanted to say she'd keep on singing. But another part of her knew that she would have to rest or her voice would fail her. 'I'll see,' she said. 'When I get back from visiting my father.'

She dozed on and off during the whole journey to Hull, only waking when she heard the shout of the guard to change trains. She gathered her personal belongings together as the train reached Hull, and realized that she hadn't even opened the magazine that she had bought to read. The porter carried her luggage; she had brought only hand baggage, having left her trunk at Mrs Bennett's, and as she followed him to the gate she saw a crowd of people carrying a banner and heard the sound of a brass band playing.

Welcome home, Poppy Mazzini, the banner proclaimed, and as she neared the gate there came a loud 'Hurrah'.

Her father stood there, his arms open wide to greet her and his eyes glistening. 'Here she is!' he shouted, as if no-one else could see her. Nan stood beside him, clapping her hands and beaming. 'Welcome home, Poppy. Welcome home!'

The crowd gathered round her, calling to her and thrusting theatre programmes towards her that she might sign her name. Her father gathered up her luggage and propelled her towards the exit. There was a hired cab waiting to take them home and as she stepped out at the shop in Savile Street she saw another banner over the shop window. *Welcome home, Poppy. International Singing Star.*

She laughed. 'I'm not quite international, Pa! I've been to France!'

'It's all 'same to me,' he said. 'France is onny 'stepping stone. It'll be America next, you mark my words.'

The door to the shop was open and Tommy and Mattie were waiting to greet her. Mattie was all smiles, her eyes sparkling. She looked very well and had put on weight since Poppy had seen her last, as had Nan. They were both wearing neat plain gowns and not the shabby garments they used to wear. Tommy had a huge grin on his face as he gave her a hug. 'Been waiting for you to come,' he said. 'We're going to shut up early, and have a celebratory supper.'

But that was easier said than done, as customers old and new kept coming in to greet Poppy and say how they had kept up with her progress. Finally, her father shooed everyone out and said to come back in the morning, when Poppy would talk to them.

'I'm not supposed to talk too much,' she said huskily. 'I've got to save my voice.'

'Well, we'll do 'talking,' Tommy said. 'But first we'll pull 'blinds down, and then we'll set a table and eat.'

Poppy admired the new décor. The grocery side had been

painted cream with brown doors and window frames, and there was a new glass counter. The coffee shop side had been decorated in green, with simulated stage drapes round the walls and windows, a dark green palm tree painted on one wall, and high up in the corners white clown masks depicting smiles and despair. Theatre posters, day bills and photographs of Poppy adorned the walls.

'Can we eat in the kitchen?' she asked. 'The way we always used to do.'

'Aye, if you like.' Tommy was buoyant and merry, whilst Mattie, although smiling as she glanced at Poppy, wasn't quite as chatty as usual, which was unlike her.

She went up to her old room. Nan had obviously cleaned it, for it looked fresh and cosy. There was a posy of winter jasmine on the windowsill and a fire burning in the grate. She sat on the bed and gave a sigh. How good it was to come home. She had missed everybody so much.

After washing and changing out of her travelling clothes, she went downstairs. A bright fire burned in the range, the table was set and there was a smell of cooking beef. Her father was already seated at the table.

'Come and sit next to me, Poppy. You don't have to talk; I just want you by me. How long can you stay?' he asked.

She was grateful to him for realizing that she would be going back, that she would be continuing with her career. She smiled. 'I can stay for Christmas, maybe one week, maybe longer,' she said softly. 'I have to rest my voice, but I will sing at just one performance in London. Then I shall take some time off.'

'Then why sing at one performance?' He frowned. 'Why not wait?'

'It's so that the theatre managers know I'll be available later. They need to see and hear that I'm back in England.'

'Supper's ready.' Tommy put the joint of beef on a platter, and Nan and Mattie placed the dishes of vegetables and a jug of gravy on the table.

'I'm not very hungry.'

'I can see that you've not been eating,' Tommy declared. 'Just look at you – nowt on you.'

'She was always slender,' Mattie said. 'She's not meant to be fat.'

'Not like you, eh?' Tommy grinned. 'Don't you think our Mattie looks bonny, Poppy? That's what good food does for you!'

Poppy nodded, noting the *our* Mattie. 'You do look well, Mattie, and so does Nan.' She smiled at Nan who had taken the seat at the other side of Joshua. 'You all do,' she added. 'You too, Pa.'

'Aye, well I'm a lot easier in my mind now that I've got folks I can trust about me.'

Tommy stood poised with the carving knife and glanced down at Mattie, who smiled up at him. 'Ah!' he said. 'Well, on that subject I've summat to say.' He chewed on his lip and looked at his father. 'I have to ask your permission, Pa, as I've not yet reached my majority, but – well, Mattie and me are going to get wed.' He put down the knife and rested his hand on Mattie's shoulder. 'She's been 'best thing that's ever happened to me, and I know we're both young, but we're prepared to wait if we have to. There's no rush, nobody need think there is, but it's what we both want.'

Poppy and her father both stood up, Poppy to kiss Mattie and give Tommy a hug, Joshua to shake his son's hand and offer congratulations and give Mattie a kiss. Nan sat smiling, and Poppy realized that she already knew when she saw her and Mattie exchanging glances.

'Well, Nan.' Joshua bent down and patted her shoulder. 'So what about that, eh? I suppose you knew all along, did you?'

Nan blushed. She admitted that Mattie had confided in her, and that they had decided to wait until Poppy came home before breaking the news.

Poppy squeezed Mattie's hand during supper. 'I'm so pleased, Mattie,' she said. 'You're just right for Tommy.'

Mattie pressed her lips together. 'Are you? Really?' she said. 'I've been so worried. I was afraid that you might have come back so – grand . . .' She blinked her eyes. 'I should have known better. I should've known that you'd be just 'same. It's just that we're nobody, Ma and me, but we're so fond of you and your pa, and I've always loved Tommy.'

'Mattie! How can you say that you're nobody? You and Nan have always been special people. You've always been like family.' She squeezed her hand again. 'And now I've got a sister.'

She glanced across at Nan who was in a quiet conversation with her father and at the same time helping him to a slice of beef and vegetables. She turned to Mattie and raised her eyebrows. Mattie gave a grin and Poppy turned again to look at Joshua and Nan. She took a deep breath. How lovely that would be, if Nan and Pa— And then, she thought wistfully, there'd just be me.

Poppy visited Mr and Mrs Chandler in the vain hope that they would know whether Charlie had moved premises, but they told her in their usual disgruntled manner that they hadn't had a letter from him for months. 'We heard you were back in Hull,' Mrs Chandler said. 'We'd hoped that you'd know where he was.'

Poppy said she was sorry that she didn't but once she discovered his whereabouts she would let them know.

Nan and Mattie were still living at the house in Stewart's Yard, and Mattie told her that the rent had been paid in advance. 'Your pa's been so generous,' she said. 'He's paid 'rent up front for us so that we'd feel secure and has promised that he'll increase our wages as soon as he can, though when Tommy and me get wed he won't have to pay me and I'll be living above 'shop.'

'But what about Nan?' Poppy asked. 'She won't want to live there alone. I wouldn't mind her having my room.'

'She won't move in, not like Lena did. She said it wouldn't be proper. She won't let me either, not until Tommy and me are wed.'

The five of them spent a quiet Christmas, and on the day following her birthday she received a telegram from Dan. The message read that he could secure a performance for one night only at the Savoy Theatre in three weeks' time. 'Shall I say yes or no?' he queried.

The Savoy Theatre, she pondered, where D'Oyly Carte staged the Gilbert and Sullivan operettas. She wasn't an opera singer by any means, but she knew that she could sing light operetta. The idea excited her, but she would need to make sure that she didn't strain her voice. For the last week she had spoken only in whispers, but now she felt stronger and more rested and ready to go back. She telegraphed 'Yes'.

Dan met her at King's Cross station. 'The Savoy have put up posters outside the theatre and an advertisement in the *Illustrated*

London News. "Special performance",' he quoted, ' "for one night only, the celebrated Poppy Mazzini!" '

'Really?' She was astounded. Everything was happening so fast.

'Yes, really! Though Marian says you should have been given more time.'

'I'm fine,' she insisted. 'I feel really well and although I haven't sung properly I've been going over some of my songs on the piano at home.'

She moved back in with the Marinos who were pleased to see her again and gave her news of Anthony, who was still in Italy, and she travelled each day to see Mrs Bennett.

Her tutor asked her to concentrate on the breathing exercises she had given her, and to learn the words and music of the songs she had chosen to sing. 'Concentrate on the essence of what you are singing about,' she reminded her. 'Think of the emotion of the words and what it might mean to the listener: let them smell the roses in the arbour, hear the rustle of the trees when the breeze blows through them; let them hear the ripple of the stream, and feel the heartbreak or joy of love. Listen also to what the music is telling *you.*'

For two weeks they practised and then Mrs Bennett sat down at the piano and asked her to sing. When she had finished she clapped her hands. 'Tremendous, Poppy,' she said. 'Your voice is much improved. It will get even better,' she declared. 'After this performance, you must take time off again for a few weeks, and then come to me for some more coaching. Your voice will become more mature. You are using variations of tone and expression already, but you have a young voice, and we must be careful not to overdo it. Now,' she smiled, 'I'll meet you at the Savoy tomorrow as arranged for a rehearsal with the musicians. Try not to talk too much and then in three days we'll be ready.'

Poppy was desperate to find Charlie, yet something held her back. After the concert I'll look for him, she decided. She knew how important it was that she concentrated only on her debut at the Savoy. Marian Bennett was to be her pianoforte accompanist, with a harpist and a violinist, and they spent the next three days arranging the order of the music.

On the day of the performance she arrived early at the theatre to change and put on her make-up. She dressed herself in her green gown. She was to sing 'Greensleeves' as part of the programme. One day, she thought, as she pinned back her hair and pulled some curls down around her face, I might be famous enough to have my own wardrobe mistress and a dresser to attend my hair, for it is always so unruly.

Someone knocked on the door. 'Flowers for Miss Mazzini!' a voice called.

She jumped up. From Pa? From Dan? Not from Anthony, for he wouldn't know where she was or what she was doing. She opened the door to receive them. The bouquet was immense: chrysanthemums, lilies, roses, wisps of fern. 'Goodness,' she murmured. 'Whoever has sent these?'

She opened the card and her lips parted as she read the message. 'From Charles.'

CHAPTER FORTY-TWO

'Charlie!' she whispered. Tears gathered in her eyes and she fought to control them. She mustn't become too emotional. She must save that for her singing. But she felt joy rushing through her, making her heart beat faster. 'He came,' she murmured breathlessly. 'He cares after all. He'll be out there in the audience listening to me!'

The musicians were grouped on the stage as Poppy made her entrance. She felt exhilarated and it showed as she swept towards the front of the stage and sank into a deep curtsy. There was a murmuring from the well-dressed audience in the stalls, the gentlemen in formal suits and the ladies in glittering gowns. Most of them were hearing Poppy for the first time. From the gallery came the sound of loud clapping and cheering and she guessed that this was from people who had heard and seen her at lesser theatres before she went abroad.

She turned towards the piano and stood beside it. The harpist began to play with evocative gentle notes. Marian Bennett caressed the keys as she developed the melodic phrasing, the violinist put his bow to the wood and Poppy began to sing.

She barely knew where she was. She only felt sheer joy coursing through her as she sang. Her voice, sweet and touching, ardent with passion, captivating and dulcet, ranged over all the emotions in its intensity. She took sips of water during the interval but spoke to no-one and came back on the stage to tremendous acclaim. At last she sang her final song and the audience rose to its feet in acknowledgement.

Mrs Bennett clapped softly, her eyes on Poppy. The harpist

smiled and nodded, the violinist tapped his bow, whilst the audience went wild. Poppy seemed to wake up. She bowed low, her hand on her breast, then came to the front of the stage and gave another deep curtsy. She backed away, caught Marian Bennett's eye and in answer to her raised eyebrows and unasked question gave a slight shake of her head. She did not have the energy or the voice to sing an encore as the audience were requesting.

'Thank you,' she mouthed. 'Thank you.'

Someone threw a white rose, and smiling she bent to collect it and threaded it into her hair. She smiled again, mouthed 'thank you' once more, and left the stage with the chants of the audience ringing in her ears.

Someone opened the door into the dressing room for her and she swept in and sank into her chair, absolutely spent, yet full of excitement as if she could soar like a bird above the treetops. She took several more sips of water and then Marian Bennett tapped on the open door and asked if she could come in.

'That was wonderful, Poppy,' she said. She too was exultant. 'Truly wonderful! I have never heard you sing so well. Dan is in the audience; he's going to want to make more bookings for you.' She held up a warning finger. 'But you can be choosy. Don't let him rush you into anything. He is my brother, but I have your best interests at heart and we must look after your voice.' She caught sight of the flowers. 'My goodness! What a huge bouquet! That must be from a very special admirer?'

'From Charlie.' Poppy gave a delighted smile. 'He must be out there in the audience.'

There was another tap on the door. This time it was Dan, and behind him the harpist and the violinist, waiting to add their congratulations.

Where was Charlie, she wondered. I want to see him so much.

'There's a queue of admirers waiting outside the stage door, Poppy,' Dan told her. 'Will you see them? Or shall I tell them no?'

'I shall be a little while,' Poppy hedged. 'I must change, and – well, I don't want to rush.'

'I'll tell them you'll be at least an hour; that'll put off all but the most determined.' He gave her a grin as he turned to go. 'You were just perfect tonight,' he said. 'You've been drinking champagne, I can tell! You just sparkled.'

She laughed and denied it, but it was true; she had felt vitalized and elated, and it had shown in her voice.

The stage door keeper tapped. 'Gentleman for you, Miss Mazzini.' He handed her a card. 'He said as you would see him.'

She took the card, which was of good quality with embossed lettering, and read, 'Charles Chandler. Prestigious Shoemaker.' The address was in an arcade off Piccadilly.

She raised her eyes to Marian Bennett. 'It's Charlie,' she whispered.

'Then I'll leave you,' she said. 'But we'll wait, Dan and I, and see you home.'

'No,' she replied urgently. 'I shall be all right.' She smiled happily, joyfully. 'We might go out for supper!'

'Ah!' Mrs Bennett murmured. 'Yes, of course, but – you're well known, Poppy. You must take care. Think of France.'

Poppy laughed. 'But this isn't France, this is London!'

Marian Bennett left, leaving the door open. Poppy quickly looked in the mirror and touched her cheek and hair. The white flower she left in place. She rose from her chair as someone tapped on the door. 'Come in,' she called. 'Charlie! Do come in.'

She would hardly have recognized him as he entered, so debonair had he become. His sideburns were long, down to his jawbone, and his hair cut to just below the ear, but it was his dress that astounded her. He wore a formal black overcoat with a silk collar. The buttons were unfastened and beneath she saw a black evening suit, and white collar and tie. He carried a silk top hat, white gloves and a silver-topped cane.

'Charlie,' she breathed and held out both hands. 'I'm so glad to see you. My word! What a swell you are!'

He put down his hat, gloves and cane on a chair and bending very formally he took one hand and kissed it. 'Indeed!' He gave a suave smile and murmured, 'We must move on, Poppy. We must show the world that we are successful. You know that.'

She kept hold of his hand and drew closer. 'And are you, Charlie? Is business so good? I've tried to get in touch with you,' she added quickly, in case he thought that she had been too bound up with her own affairs to think of him. 'My letters were never answered.'

'I'm sorry. I've been very busy,' he said. 'I've moved premises. Lots of orders.'

'I'm so glad you came tonight,' she said softly. 'I've been longing to see you. I was going to search you out if you hadn't come. I was anxious about you.'

His manner was reserved, yet touched with tension as he answered. 'Well, of course I would come, Poppy. I've read so much about you – how successful your French tour was – how could I not come to see you?'

She gazed at him. There was something amiss, some hesitation, and a slight awkwardness that unnerved her. Was he pleased to see her or not? 'Are you free, Charlie?' she asked. 'I was wondering about supper. My agent and companion . . .'

'Ah!' he murmured and they both turned as they heard a rustling against the door. 'A little difficult.'

A young woman stood there. She was very lovely, was Poppy's first impression. She was also beautifully and expensively dressed in a sealskin coat and a large hat trimmed with plumes and feathers. As Poppy gazed at her, she realized that she had seen her before.

'P-Poppy,' Charlie stammered. 'May I introduce . . .' He indicated the young woman, who, smiling gracefully, came into the room, holding out her gloved hand. 'My fiancée, Miss Amanda Burchfield. Amanda, this is my very good friend, Miss Poppy Mazzini.'

Poppy felt that she staggered as he spoke. Yet she didn't. She was rooted to the spot as Miss Burchfield inclined her head at the introduction. Poppy was in a dream, or a nightmare. Her head buzzed as if a thousand bees had invaded her, and her mind drained of thought. She was as shocked as if she had taken a physical blow. From far off she heard Miss Burchfield say how much they had enjoyed the concert, and that they had met previously when she had visited Charles's workshop for the first time.

'Who would have thought,' Miss Burchfield trilled, 'that that meeting would prove so fateful?'

'Charlie!' Poppy whispered, turning to him. 'Is it true?' Tell me it is not, she silently pleaded. Tell me it is not!

Charlie looked at neither of them, but kept his gaze lowered. 'Miss Burchfield and I announced our engagement two months ago.'

Two months. Poppy counted. November. Whilst I was away!

'We haven't known each other so very long,' Miss Burchfield interjected. 'My parents wish us to wait a little before announcing our wedding plans.' She lowered her eyelashes. 'We would rather not wait, isn't that so, Charles? Charles is impatient to be married straight away, but I must submit to my parents' desires.' She smiled indulgently. 'So whilst Charles is building up his empire, I can plan where we shall live and what kind of house we shall have.' She came and tucked her arm into Charlie's and gazed up at him. 'We can wait,' she said softly.

Charlie said nothing, but he turned a pale face towards Poppy.

Poppy felt sick and faint. Her whole body was trembling. 'Ch-Charles – isn't any good – at waiting.' Her words, mumbled and inarticulate, were muffled, low and tremulous. 'Isn't that so, Charles?' She realized she was repeating Miss Burchfield's earlier question.

'Poppy – I . . .' He turned to his fiancée. 'Dearest! Would you wait outside for me for a moment? I'd like to speak to Miss Mazzini about a private matter.'

Miss Burchfield raised her eyebrows, but gave Poppy a graceful adieu, and left the room.

Poppy sank down into her chair and closed her eyes for a second. When I open them I shall know that I'm dreaming, she thought. This isn't really happening. But when she opened them, Charlie was still standing there with a concerned look upon his face.

'Poppy! I couldn't think of any other way to tell you. It's all happened so suddenly – Amanda and I – even my parents don't know yet!'

'You were going to wait for *me*!' she whispered. 'You said – that you loved *me*. You wanted me to prove that I loved you,' she breathed, her words melting in the air. 'Did I mean – nothing – after all, for you to change your mind so quickly?'

'No. No!' He grasped her hand. 'I've always cared for you, Poppy. Since you were just a child. But . . .' he hesitated. 'You were a child – still are so young.'

'I'm not!' she said, on a faint husky breath. 'I am not a child and I have always loved you!'

'I'm sorry, Poppy,' he said, straightening up and fingering his collar. 'So very sorry.'

There came a soft tap on the door. Mrs Bennett stood there. 'Miss Mazzini has to change now, Mr Chandler,' she said coldly. 'If you will excuse us?'

'Of course. Of course.' Charles backed away, and picking up his possessions he gave a brief bow. 'I hope I shall see you again, Poppy. We – I really enjoyed tonight – you were wonderful. I wish you' – he swallowed, barely looking at her – 'further success.' He glanced at Mrs Bennett's stony expression and turned for the door. 'Goodnight!'

Poppy stared after him. She felt empty, from the top of her head to her toes. I can't believe this is happening! How could he? How could he come tonight of all nights and bring her with him? Did he think I would be pleased for him? Did he think that my love for him was only a childish infatuation?

Mrs Bennett busied herself by the dressing table and then handed her a small silver container. 'I always keep a phial of brandy and water in my purse,' she said softly. 'For any occasion when I might feel unwell.'

Poppy sipped the liquid. Her mouth was dry and the spirit, though weakened with water, burned her throat.

'I don't know what has happened, Poppy, and I don't need to know,' Mrs Bennett murmured. 'But when I saw the young lady waiting outside as Mr Chandler came in to see you, I – I felt I should come back, that perhaps – things were not as you had hoped.'

Poppy licked her lips; she was trembling as she croaked, 'His fiancée! They – they're going to be married.' Tears appeared in her eyes and ran unchecked down her face, down her nose and onto her lips. She could taste the salt blending with the brandy. 'He said – he told me . . .' Did he ever say those words, she anguished, or did I only think that he did? 'He told me that he would wait for me!' Her grief was threatening to overwhelm her. He did say those words! But he wasn't true. He has found someone else that he loves more.

'But he *hasn't*. He *didn't*.' She lifted her eyes, appealing, and the tears began to flow again. She wiped them away with a towel, and took a deep breath. 'What am I going to do?' she pleaded. 'What am I going to do?'

CHAPTER FORTY-THREE

Marian Bennett and Dan took her back to the Marinos' house. Mrs Bennett wanted her to go home with her, but Poppy said no, she'd rather stay with Mario and Rosina, using the excuse that her belongings were there. She knew that Mrs Bennett would be kind and solicitous, but the small room above the Trattoria Mario reminded her of her own room at home and she felt comfortable and safe there.

'Take tomorrow off,' Mrs Bennett said, as they left her. 'Don't come for your lesson. Come the day after. You must continue with your life, my dear,' she said anxiously. 'You have taken a blow and you think that you will never recover, but she will, won't she, Dan?'

He looked very wistful as he nodded. 'Yes, you are young enough to love again. But just now you'll feel that there will never be anyone else deserving of your love.'

Words, words, she thought as she stumbled up the stairs. What do they know? Marian Bennett has a lasting marriage and hasn't felt the loss of love. Dan? He's a single middle-aged man. He's probably never felt such a love as I have just lost.

She lay fully dressed on her bed and wept. How could he? How could he not write to tell me? How could he just arrive like that? And sending flowers! Did he think that such an ostentatious, *extravagant* bouquet would soften his treachery? She gave a sob. Why, this one white rose means more to me than his *poisonous* lilies! He can keep them and put them on his grave, for I wish him *dead* and myself as well!

As she'd come out of the theatre, supported on either side by

Mrs Bennett and Dan, a solitary figure had been waiting to greet her. It was the young man who had thrown a rose to her tonight. The one she had retrieved from the stage.

'Miss Mazzini,' he'd said passionately. 'You was wonderful tonight.'

'Thank you,' she began in a whisper, but Dan interrupted, saying, 'Miss Mazzini is extremely tired. I'm so sorry. Thank you for waiting, but we must get her home.'

The man clasped his hands together. 'You're not ill, Miss Mazzini? Say that you ain't? I'd be devastated if you couldn't sing!'

She'd shaken her head. 'Just very tired,' she croaked. 'Please excuse me.' She'd managed a weak smile. 'Thank you for the rose. It was you, wasn't it?'

He'd smiled gratefully at her awareness, and bowing reverently and in worship stood back to let them pass. She'd looked over her shoulder as she stepped into the hackney cab and had seen him standing under the stage door lamp, gazing adoringly at her.

She fell asleep, worn out by crying, and when Rosina awakened her the next morning with a piping hot cup of coffee, she knew that her whole world had collapsed.

'Pah!' Rosina said, for Mrs Bennett had told her what had happened. 'He is not worthy of you, that young man! He 'as no passion, no fire.'

'But I love him, Rosina. I've always loved him.' Tears began to flow again and she wiped them away with the bed sheet. She took a deep breath and picked up the crumpled rose which had fallen out of her hair. She put it to her nose, the perfume still sweet, and began to cry. 'I'll never *ever* love anyone again. It's too painful to contemplate.'

She looked in the mirror after Rosina had left her and saw her bedraggled hair, her swollen eyes and lips, and her crumpled gown, which she had slept in. She undressed, slid down her garters and stockings, washed her hands and face and clad only in her under-drawers and cambric bodice climbed back into bed. I shan't go out, she thought. I shall stay here in my room and wait to die. Then he'll be sorry! I shall be on his conscience for ever.

Throughout the day, first Rosina and then Mario tapped on her door, trying to tempt her with food, but to no avail. She refused to come down and spent the day crying, and finally dropped asleep through sheer exhaustion. When night came she was wide awake and walking the floor, unable to comprehend that Charlie loved someone else and not her.

'He can't love her,' she muttered, and then came the thought that perhaps Charlie wanted to marry Miss Burchfield for her money. 'He said that her father was a self-made man.' She wondered how Charlie had been able to move premises so quickly, when the last time she had seen him he was only speaking of taking on an apprentice. She climbed back onto the bed. 'Mr Burchfield is helping to finance him! That's why Charlie wants to marry her. He doesn't love her.' She clung desperately to the idea. 'He loves me but must marry her!'

The thought made her weep again. So his love for me isn't strong enough. He's weak and self-centred! Yet I love him still. What can I do? Whom can I ask for advice? Who would understand? No-one, she cried again. There is no-one at all.

She felt even worse the next day. Without food or drink apart from water, her spirits and energy dropped even lower. Rosina knocked on her door and said that Dan Damone was here. Would she see him, or could Rosina give him a message? Through the closed door, Poppy said no, she didn't want to see anyone. She spent the whole of that day in bed just gazing into space, going over the past and knowing that she had no future.

She fell asleep, and woke with a start when she heard the sound of Mario's voice bidding someone '*Grazie mille. Buona notte*' as they left the restaurant. She glanced at the clock on her table. Eleven o'clock. She had the whole of the night to get through. She felt weary, hot and tired. I'd go for a walk, but Mario would want to come with me. I'll wait, she thought. I'll wait until they've gone to bed and then go out. I need some air.

As she sat propped up on her pillows waiting for the clattering of crockery to subside and listening for the sound of Rosina's and Mario's footsteps on the stairs, the fog in her head started to clear. Anthony! she thought. He'll understand how I feel. He was crossed in love by Mrs Bennett's daughter. He'll understand the torment I'm going through.

She climbed out of bed and took her writing paper and pen from the drawer and started to write. She poured out her heartache and told him how she would never love again, and wondered if she would ever sing again, for, she said, 'how can I sing of love when I have lost it? I need to get away,' she wrote. 'I know that Dan is very well intentioned and that he and Mrs Bennett will want me to perform again soon, but I know that I can't. Something inside me has died and I want to go away to where no-one knows me, to hide in some small corner like a sick animal and lick my wounds. I'm writing to you, Anthony, because I know that you'll understand how I am suffering. I don't know what to do to take away this ache and sorrow. I am unbelievably sad and have been given a mortal blow.

'Forgive me if I should remind you of your loss, but I could think of no-one else who would understand. Yours in friendship, Poppy.'

She scrabbled to find an envelope and stamp and directed it to the last address she had for him. She slipped it into her purse and put that on the bed, then she dressed in a wool skirt and a high-necked blouse and took her outdoor coat from the mahogany wardrobe and laid it on the bed beside the purse.

As she sat waiting, an idea came to her. Perhaps I will go away for a few days. Right away where I don't have to answer questions on how I am feeling, or sing when I'm not yet ready. But where? Not home to Hull, for Pa would be angry and would want to write to Charlie and give him a tongue-lashing over his treatment of me; and then Mr and Mrs Chandler would hear about it, and Tommy would say I told you so.

Brighton then? But no. Ronny and Ena might still be there, or I might run into Mrs Johnson or Miss Jenkinson or Mr Bradshaw from the theatre. My hair stands out like a beacon, she thought. The colour of her hair had always pleased her, but now she knew it meant that she would be easily recognized.

It was almost midnight when she heard Rosina and Mario come upstairs to bed. She waited another half-hour and then put on her coat, wrapped a scarf round her neck and picked up her purse. She opened the door cautiously and listened. No sound. They must be asleep. She crept downstairs and unlocked the side door with her own key and slid back the bolt. It worried her that she would have to leave it unbolted, so she moved a wooden chair as near to the door as possible, so that if by chance anyone should try to break in, then the door would clatter against the chair. She stepped outside and carefully locked the door again.

It was bitterly cold and she huddled into her scarf, pulling it up about her ears, then set off at a brisk pace down the street towards St Martin's Lane where it was better lit. She knew there was a posting box there into which she could drop Anthony's letter.

She came to Dan's office, which was in darkness, but she could see the posters, bills and photographs in the window. One of them was of her, taken in France. It had been tinted to show her red hair and green dress. She stared at it. It was like looking at someone totally unrelated. How happy I was then, just a few weeks ago. Her mouth trembled. I shall never be happy again.

Her feet took her onwards to Drury Lane and then to Piccadilly. Her intention hadn't been to go to Charlie's new premises, but curiosity led her on. The address on his business card had indicated an arcade off Piccadilly, but she had no idea whereabouts it would be. Some of the streets off were in darkness and she hesitated about going down them. There were some well-dressed people about, leaving hotels or clubs, but there were others who leered at her or turned to watch her progress.

Finally she saw the name of the arcade on a wall. It was a small courtyard of shops and businesses. A light gleamed from halfway down and, taking courage, she hurried towards it. The window was bow-fronted and freshly painted, and through the glass she saw the back of a fair-haired man. He turned, and she retreated into the shadows when she saw that it was Charlie.

He had an unfinished red shoe in one hand and in the other a flat brush and a length of hemp. He sat down at his bench in the window and she saw from the pucker of his lips that he was whistling.

She gazed, her mouth parted. Whistling! How can he whistle when I am here, distraught at his betrayal? Charlie! A sob shook her. He doesn't care. He has no thought for me! She took a breath. Shall I confront him? Tell him how he has ruined my life? She was about to step out of the darkness and tap on the window when he raised his head and his mouth moved. He pointed with his finger as if telling someone something and she saw a glimpse of another figure, a young boy, behind him.

'The apprentice,' she breathed. 'He said he was taking one on.' She heard a clock strike two o'clock and she wondered at his working so late. Lots of orders, he'd said, so he has to work into the night to complete them. I wonder if his ladylove objects to that, she thought bitterly and turned away, out of the arcade and into Piccadilly.

She walked she knew not where, her mind dulled and her feet moving mechanically. Men spoke to her but she walked on, ignoring their jeers and shouts. A hansom cab drew up beside her, but she lowered her head and didn't respond to the occupant and it went away. Another clock struck three. She looked round her and had no idea where she was, though she thought that she wasn't so far from Bloomsbury where Mrs Bennett lived. She had passed grand hotels, elegant houses, a large area of green which looked like a park and the emporium of Fortnum and Mason whose windows displayed cut glass, clocks, and food of all kinds packaged in tin, glass and china containers. She had walked by bookshops, umbrella shops, tobacco shops and shops selling perfume which she could smell as she went by the closed doors.

Charlie is doing well if he can afford to have a workshop in this area, she considered. All the richest and most affluent people must shop here. Was it Miss Burchfield's idea and her father's money? He advised me to stay in London and not go abroad, she remembered. Would he still have been influenced by Miss Burchfield if I had stayed? She gave a sob. I shall never know.

She felt suddenly faint and giddy and made for the nearest shop doorway and sat down abruptly as her legs gave way under her. What am I to do? She put her head in her hands. Where shall I go? Should I go home? What will Pa say?

A hansom cab went swiftly past and she looked at it through her fingers. Should I go back to Mario and Rosina's? I feel such a fool. So young and stupid. What will they think of me, sneaking out in the middle of the night?

She heard the slow clop of a single-horse carriage coming along the road and on a sudden impulse stood up, holding on to the doorframe of the shop. She staggered towards the road and put out her hand to stop the approaching vehicle. It was a staid four-wheeler, a growler, with the driver hunched up on his box seat. 'Cabby,' she called in a strained shout, waving at him.

He slowed the horse, took a pipe out of his mouth and called to her, 'I'm going home, lady. Not taking any more fares.'

'Oh!' Poppy gasped. Just when she had made a decision, and it was starting to rain. 'Which way are you going?'

He drew up beside her and looked down. 'Are you in trouble, gel? Somebody after you?'

'I'm in trouble, yes.' She began to weep. 'I have to get home.'

'Where's that then?' He was an older man from the sound of his voice, though she couldn't see him properly in the darkness.

'Yorkshire.' She pulled a handkerchief out of her pocket to wipe her eyes.

'Yorkshire!' He pushed his top hat to the back of his head. 'I can't take you all that way, lady. I'll take you to King's Cross if you like, since I'm passing that way, but there'll be no trains running at this time o' night.'

She stifled a sob; she was beginning to have second thoughts. If he was off duty, would it be safe to go with him? Some drivers were notoriously regarded as being preyers on young women. She glanced at the carriage to see if he was licensed and saw that he was. He also had his cab number on his coat.

'Are you coming or not, lady?' he asked impatiently. 'I'm tired, Dobbin is tired and we both need a bit o' hay and to get to our beds.'

'Sorry! Yes please.' She climbed in and they moved off.

The driver opened the window in the roof and called down to her. 'I'll drop you in the station yard,' he said. 'The railway company don't like us private hire men to hang about. They've got their own fleet of cabs. Is that all right?'

'Yes, thank you.' She looked up but couldn't see him. There was just one lantern and that was swinging outside. I'll wait at the station until morning, she decided, and then catch a train home.

She scurried across the station concourse. The gas lamps placed high on the walls cast gloomy shadows and she looked anxiously round at the few people who were about. All of them, she thought, seemed furtive and suspicious. Two police constables glanced curiously at her and then at each other. The ticket office was locked and she wondered where she could sit until the morning.

The constables strolled across to her as she hesitated. 'Now then, miss,' said one. 'What're you doing 'ere at this time of a morning? Ain't you got an 'ome to go to?' He was a big burly fellow with a thick beard and two chevrons on his sleeve.

The other one, younger and without any stripes, grinned. 'Hoping for one more customer?' he asked. 'You'll not find any here; we've cleared 'em all out.'

Poppy was confused. What did they mean? 'I – I want to catch a train,' she whispered hoarsely. 'I'll have to wait until morning, I know, but—'

'Well, you can't wait here,' the first constable said. 'Not allowed.'

'But – it's not long. It will soon be morning,' she stammered.

He shook his head. 'Off you go 'ome, there's a good gel. Plenty of pickings elsewhere but not on our patch. We're after a quiet night.'

With horror she realized what he was implying. They thought she was a prostitute! A street woman! How could they make such a mistake? Then she thought of how she must look. Her eyes were swollen with crying. Her hair, without a hat, would be bedraggled. A young woman on her own. She backed away from them.

'No,' she cried. 'It's not what you think.'

She saw them both grin and move closer to her. They're going to lock me up! They're going to put me in handcuffs! 'No,' she screamed. 'Don't touch me,' and turning from them she ran out of the station, out of the yard and into the darkness of the night.

CHAPTER FORTY-FOUR

'So where is she?' Dan, called in by Mario, stood and looked at him and then Rosina. 'She surely can't have gone far, not without telling you and especially if she's left all her clothes?'

'She was 'eartbroken, Dan,' Rosina said. 'So very upset.'

'Yes, I know she was,' Dan muttered. 'But still, to go off without saying! When did you say you last saw her?'

'Yesterday, in the morning, you know – you came and she wouldn't see anyone, and this morning I take her some coffee, she wasn't there,' Rosina said. 'And now, it is seven o'clock and still she not come back.' She shrugged her shoulders. 'That is why I say to Mario, 'e must send and ask you where she is, is she with Mrs Bennett? And you say no she is not!'

Dan pursed his lips. 'Marian hasn't seen her since we brought her home from the theatre. We thought she was resting. Two days,' he mused. 'Should I wire her father?'

'No!' Mario said. 'He will be alarmed. Wait a little longer. She will come back soon. She is wounded. The wounded always come back 'ome.'

'Except this isn't home,' Dan murmured. 'I wonder if that's where she's gone? I think I'll take a cab down to King's Cross. She might have been seen there. With that hair someone would remember her.'

A station porter directed him to the police hut and he asked the two constables there if they'd seen anything of a young woman with red hair. 'She's missing,' he said. 'We can't find her.' They looked at each other and one of them said, 'Sorry. Don't think so,' but then the other, an older man, said cautiously,

'There was a young woman in the station last night; well, it was early morning, more like. She had red hair. Said she wanted to catch a train, but we thought – well, we thought she was one of the gels come in for shelter. It was raining, you see.'

'One of the girls?' Dan boomed. 'One of the street women, do you mean? Good God, man! Can't you tell the difference between a woman in distress and a whore! Where did she go?'

The constable shook his head. 'We told her she couldn't wait in the station and she just ran. Scarpered. Took off and ran like a bat out of hell. We were only going to ask her some questions,' he added. 'We didn't mean to frighten her.'

Dan swore, leaving them in no doubt of his opinion of their intelligence, and went to some of the privileged cab drivers who had a contract to wait in the station yard and questioned them. But most of them had gone home at that time in the morning and so hadn't seen Poppy, if indeed it had been her. The following morning, when Poppy still hadn't turned up, Dan went to the post office and sent a telegram to Joshua Mazzini.

'What does he mean? Is Poppy with us?' Joshua scratched his head as he read the telegram. 'Nan! What does he mean? Can you understand it?' He handed the telegram to her.

Nan carefully read the message. 'He says that Poppy went off without telling anyone where she was going!' She glanced up at Joshua. 'That's not like Poppy,' she murmured. 'Why would she do that?' She called to Mattie who was in the shop. 'Have you heard from Poppy? Recently, I mean?'

Mattie shook her head. 'No. Not since her last visit. Why? What's up?'

Nan explained about the telegram whilst Joshua stood with his hand over his mouth. 'She'd come here if she was in trouble, wouldn't she?' he said to them both.

'Who's in trouble?' Tommy came out of the shop into the kitchen to see where everyone was.

'No-one, we hope, Tommy,' Mattie said. 'But Poppy seems to have gone missing.'

Joshua put on his raincoat and went to the post office to send a telegram back to Dan Damone, asking if he should come to London to help look for her.

'Tommy!' Mattie said when they were alone. 'I don't suppose you've heard from Charlie?'

'No, not a word since he went to London. Fine friend he turned out to be. Why?'

'I just wondered,' she answered. 'You know that Poppy had been seeing him now and again?'

'What about it?' He looked puzzled. 'Do you think he might know where she is?'

She gave a little shrug. 'She was keen on him, you know!'

He laughed. 'Since she was a bairn.' Then he frowned. 'Come on, Mattie, what are you saying? That they're together?' He grabbed her arm and lowered his voice. 'You don't mean that she might be in trouble? Not with Charlie?'

'Well, he's not 'marrying kind, is he? We both know that.' Mattie's face flushed.

'I know that! How do you know?' His eyes searched her face. 'Has he ever tried anything on with you?'

'Course he has,' Mattie said. 'Me and all 'other lasses in Hull.' She smiled at his shocked expression and patted his cheek. 'You don't have to worry, Tom Mazzini,' she whispered. 'I didn't succumb to his charms. I was onny ever interested in you.'

He put his arms round her and nuzzled her neck. 'And yet you won't let me near you,' he said softly.

She laughed and pulled away. 'No,' she said. 'I won't. Not until we're wed.' Then she kissed him on the mouth. 'I want you to know for sure that I've kept myself only for you. But Poppy might be vulnerable,' she added. 'Especially in a place like London where there's no family to warn her. If she's seeing Charlie . . .'

'And Charlie isn't 'marrying kind – I'll kill him if he's got her into trouble,' Tommy said fiercely.

'We don't know that,' Mattie said. 'But it's a possibility. On the other hand,' she said slowly, and her eyes opened wide as something else occurred to her, 'she's just got back from France. You don't know what those foreign gents get up to with their fancy ways. Oh, Tommy, it doesn't bear thinking about!'

Dan Damone read Joshua's telegram. Having Poppy's anxious father here was the last thing he needed. Why, he would probably want to put up posters or print something in the newspapers about her disappearance and that wouldn't do at all. No, this must be kept quiet at all costs. He sank his chin into his hand as he pondered. I'll tell anyone who might enquire that she's resting for a few days. She'll be back before long, I expect. I know how she feels. It's terrible to lose someone you love. But she's a mere child. What can she know of love? Infatuation, that's what it is. It's not the same as losing someone when you're a grown man or woman.

He opened a drawer in his desk and took out a photograph in a silver frame. He looked down at the serene face in front of him. 'That's love, my darling,' he whispered. 'That's real love.'

Marian Bennett looked up as her daughter came into the room. 'How lovely to see you, dear,' she said. 'I was in need of some company.'

'Why? Where's Papa?'

'Busy, as always.' She smiled. 'But I wanted to talk to you. I need your advice!'

'My advice?' Jeanette raised her fine eyebrows. 'Surely not!'

'Yes. You remember Poppy Mazzini? She's disappeared. But I don't want you to tell anyone,' she added hastily. 'We don't want it to get out. The poor girl is in love with someone and he's become engaged to someone else. She's distraught. Gone to pieces and run away.'

'Well, how can I help with that?' Her daughter was offhand. 'I hardly know her.'

'No, but she's young, and . . .' Marian Bennett hesitated. Her daughter was so self-assured; perhaps she was the wrong person to ask. 'Well, you were young when you and Anthony broke up—'

Jeanette gave a short laugh. 'Yes, but, Mama, I wasn't the one with the broken heart! I was the one who chose to end our relationship. I knew who would serve me best and it wasn't Anthony. Can you see me as the wife of a piano player? No, of course not!'

She played her fingers around her lips. 'I'm not saying that I don't miss his devotion and I was sorry that he was hurt so badly. But we were young and I'm sure he's got over it; or if he hasn't, then he will.' She gave a little shrug and looked at her hands. She wore diamond rings on her fingers and gold bracelets on her wrists. 'I'm happy enough with what I've got, even though my husband probably isn't always faithful to me.'

Her mother looked shocked but Jeanette merely smiled. 'He always comes home,' she declared. 'He knows where he is best off. I'm a perfect hostess, the mother of his children. What more could he want?'

'But you don't love him?' her mother said slowly. 'And he doesn't love you?'

'I love what he's able to give me.' Again came the nonchalant shrug. 'It's enough. I'm not like you and Papa. I've seen you struggle, never having quite enough money. I wanted a life of ease. So, if you want advice on what to do about poor lovesick Miss Mazzini, I'm the wrong person to ask. You'd do better asking Anthony.'

Rosina dropped the letter to Anthony into the post box. Mario had insisted they write and tell him about Poppy's disappearance. 'He is her friend,' he said. 'He might guess where she has gone and tell us where to look.'

Rosina had nodded. She had intended to write and tell Anthony anyway. She needed no second bidding from Mario. But her reasons for writing were different from her husband's. Mario was concerned for Poppy's safety, and she was too, of course, but she had plans of her own. Poppy was just the kind of young woman she wanted her son to marry. Warm, loving, beautiful and talented, and she was part Italian. They would be perfect for each other. Not like the cold, hard-hearted Jeanette Bennett with her grandiose ideas. How delighted Rosina had been when she had chosen to marry someone else. Delighted, even though her son had been so devastated.

'*Ciao, Antonio,*' she murmured, patting the pillar box as she slipped the letter inside. '*Scrivi presto!*' He was over Miss Bennett. He was writing his music again. Now he must come home and look for Poppy.

CHAPTER FORTY-FIVE

Poppy lay on the cold hard bed in the rooming house. She had stumbled out of the railway station and run. Her skirt had flapped round her ankles and she had scrunched it up to her calves to assist her escape. She knew what the policemen had thought of her. They thought she was a street woman. How could they? Surely they could tell? But then, she thought, why would a respectable young woman be wandering the streets of London alone in the middle of the night?

She shuddered. Suppose they had locked her up? How shameful that would have been. She would never have been able to hold up her head again, and suppose someone had recognized her! Poppy Mazzini, well-known singer, recently returned from a triumphal tour of France, locked up on a charge of immorality! Her head was filled with possible lurid headlines. After Mrs Bennett's careful protection of her reputation, she had almost ruined it by her stupidity.

The streets around King's Cross were unfamiliar to her and it wasn't long before she had realized that she was quite lost. She had stood for a while in a shop doorway contemplating what to do and where to go next. It was raining quite hard and there was no-one about. The buildings were shrouded in darkness and there were few gas lamps in the vicinity. Her feet ached and she was desperately tired. She walked on a little further and came to a low brick wall with iron railings set into it. In some relief she perched on the edge of it. There was an iron gate in the middle of the wall and half turning she had looked behind her and seen the leaning slabs of gravestones.

Is this what I've come to, she had thought, sharing the night with the dead? And so she had moved off again. Soon it became light, a weak sun filtering through the grey dawn, and she had come to a row of houses, some of which had notices in their windows of rooms to let. All were shabby and rundown but she chose one where a woman was washing her doorstep at that early hour and asked if she had a spare room.

The woman, who was skinny with a grey complexion, had looked her up and down, then hoisted herself up from her kneeling position and asked bluntly if she was on the game.

'The game?' Poppy had asked without thinking. 'Which game do you mean?'

The woman had laughed and told her to come in. The house smelt of boiled cabbage, old carpets and damp walls, but all Poppy wanted was somewhere to lay down her head and think about what to do. But she didn't think, not immediately. She was so exhausted by the trauma of the night that she had fallen asleep and slept all through the following day, not waking until seven in the evening. The lodging house keeper had told her there was a pie shop further down the street and she had gone to buy a pie and brought it back to her room in a paper bag. The pastry was dry and the meat tough but she had eaten it because she was hungry. Then she had dozed through the night, her sleep broken by lurid dreams of being chased by men in uniform and trains steaming towards her.

Now she lay thinking what she should do. If I go back, Dan is sure to say I should start singing again so that I'll forget Charlie. But I can't. I can't! Tears streamed down her cheeks and she searched for a handkerchief to blow her nose. And if I go home, Pa will want to know what has happened, and I don't want to talk about it. He might even go to see Charlie! And anyway, I can't face any of them. I feel so foolish. They will all think me so childish and immature. None of them will understand how I feel.

Someone knocked on the door and Poppy slipped shoeless and stockingless to answer it.

'I just wanted to know 'ow long you'll be stoppin',' the landlady said. 'This'll be your second day and you've only paid me for one. I want another bob for today. If yer gonna stay fer the rest of the week I'll knock you a tanner orf on Saturday. If you ain't stoppin' then you'll 'ave to leave now.'

Poppy's mouth dropped open. Now? But I haven't decided, she thought. I still don't know what to do. 'I'll stay today,' she said impulsively though she thought the rent excessive, and reached for her purse. 'And I'll let you know tomorrow if I'm staying any longer.'

'Righty-ho.' The woman took the shilling that was offered. She gazed at Poppy. 'Got into trouble, 'ave you?' she asked. 'Got in the pudding club?'

Poppy blushed scarlet. 'No,' she gasped. 'No, I haven't. I'm – I'm seeking work, that's all. I've just come from Yorkshire,' she lied. 'And I got lost coming from the railway station. Someone was supposed to meet me and didn't turn up.'

The woman's face told her she didn't believe a word, and no wonder when Poppy had arrived without luggage, but she turned away. 'Not much work round 'ere,' she said. 'You'll 'ave to go up west if you want anyfink decent. What do you do? I thought your face looked familiar. On the stage, are you?'

'N-no,' Poppy stammered. 'I – I'm a seamstress. Thought I'd try my luck in London.'

The woman nodded and went downstairs, leaving Poppy wondering if she really had recognized her or if she was only fishing for information.

When she had given the shilling for the extra rent, Poppy had realized that she hadn't much money left, only enough to last until the end of the week if she should stay. She pondered. Do I go back with my tail between my legs? Everyone will be worrying about me. She stifled a sob, and her mouth trembled. But go back to what? I always had the hope that Charlie would love me and I suppose that kept my spirits high. But now I know that he does not, and I feel so low, so depressed, how can I sing when I have no happiness left in me?

She poured the tepid water that stood in the earthenware jug into the bowl and rinsed her hands and face. There was no soap, and she looked into the cracked and spotted mirror that hung above the marble washstand. Her eyelids were swollen, her eyes like slits, her cheeks were puffy and her nose was red. 'What a mess I look,' she snivelled. 'How can I go back looking like this? What will everyone think?'

I'll go out for a walk, she decided. I can think better when I'm outside. The small room was beginning to feel oppressive and she felt as if she was in prison. She wrapped her scarf round her head to hide her hair, picked up her purse and went out.

She walked aimlessly, glancing now and again to look in shop windows, which were mostly selling old clothes or second-hand furniture. She crossed the street on seeing a confectioner's and bought a slab of chocolate, for she hadn't eaten, apart from the stale meat pie. She ate the chocolate and huddled into her coat, wondering what she should do. I have no option, she thought. I must go back, yet I'm reluctant. I'm so ashamed at having come away without telling anyone.

She passed a shop with a revolving rack containing postcards outside the door, and she stopped to look. Most were coloured views of London; others were comic cards of hen-pecked husbands, or cats and dogs dressed up in hats and scarves. There were also some of theatre personalities: Marie Lloyd, Vesta Tilley and George Robey.

The shop doorbell tinkled as she went inside holding four postcards, all of them showing a view of London that would tell her father, Mario and Rosina, Dan, and Mrs Bennett that she was still in the capital. She bought stamps from the shopkeeper, determining that she would go back to the room and write them, explaining that she needed some time to herself but that she was perfectly well.

She stood for a moment outside the shop. It stood on the corner of a crossroads. But which way had she come to it? She looked up and down the four streets. They all looked the same, dark redbrick buildings containing offices, houses and shops. Poppy bit on her lip and frowned. She had walked aimlessly, crossing and recrossing roads, turning corners into narrow streets, and now once again she was lost. What's more, she couldn't recall the name of the road where the rooming house stood.

She took the road on her left but she couldn't remember having walked along it, so she turned back, crossed over and walked the other way. She didn't remember anything on that road either, but she continued, hoping for recognition of some landmark. There were horse-buses going past, hackneys and growlers, and she wondered whether to hold out her hand for one and ask to be taken to King's Cross station where she could start again.

But I don't remember the name of the street and I don't think I could find it again, she thought miserably. What am I to do? She put her hands to her face and wept. I'm so stupid! Stupid and wretched. I want to go home and I haven't enough money for a ticket!

'Now then, dearie, what's all this?' A smiling, florid-cheeked man stood near her. 'Lost your way, 'ave you?' he said unctuously. 'Tell me where you want to be and I'll take you.'

She stared at him. He wore a shabby greatcoat, and a bowler hat which had turned green with age. His beard was dark and stubbly and he had a twisted grin on his face. 'Go away!' she shouted and started to run. 'Leave me alone!'

Now she was totally lost. She found herself in a road of model houses built for the working classes, with inns and taverns tucked away in small courts. She looked up as she heard the clatter of hooves and saw a horse-bus trundling towards her. There were three men sitting on top; she couldn't see if there was anyone inside but she ran towards it, putting out her hand for the driver to stop.

A conductor in a buttoned jacket, striped trousers and top hat stood on the step at the rear and he jumped down to let her on. 'Where to, miss?' he asked, and she glanced at the side of the bus. Sloane Street, Piccadilly and Strand was written on the side.

'Strand, please,' she said breathlessly and in some relief. At least I shall be in familiar territory, she thought as she took a seat inside. Then I can make up my mind what to do. If I decide to go back I can walk to St Martin's Lane from there.

The route was busy with traffic: horse-buses, cable-drawn trams, private carriages, hackneys and wooden drays. People spilled out of the Underground exits adding to the masses: working men, men of the law, gentlewomen with their escorts and beggar women with children at their feet. As the bus clattered into the Strand and continued on towards Chancery Lane, Poppy remembered her triumph and then the blow she had received at the Savoy Theatre just a few days before.

The thought of it made her weep again and hurriedly she rose from the seat and made to get off. I can't go back, she wept. I can't face anyone! She ran down a street off the main thoroughfare, turned down narrow lanes in an attempt to get away from the crowds, then leaned against a wall and wept. She wiped her cheeks and blew her nose, and then put her hand to her throbbing head. I don't know where to go!

She heard the sound of shouting, a man's voice and a woman's. The man was berating the woman, telling her to get out and not come back. Poppy turned to where the commotion was coming from, and saw a woman emerging from a passageway close to where she was standing. She was stout and poorly clad, with ruddy cheeks and straw-coloured hair. She picked up a stone and threw it at whoever was rebuking her. 'Keep your bleedin' job,' she shouted. 'I can find work anywhere in London town.'

She passed Poppy and muttered, 'Finks I need to work in that fleapit! I'm not that 'ard up.' She glanced at Poppy. ''e'll miss me, I can tell you. 'e'll not get anybody else working for 'im in an 'urry. They all know 'im too well. Black by name, black by nature, that's what 'e is.'

Poppy stared after her, still wiping her reddened eyes, and then peered down the alley. It opened up into a courtyard and at the bottom was a tavern with beer barrels standing outside. An irate, middle-aged barn door of a man in a landlord's leather apron was gesticulating to two elderly men with tankards in their fists, who were silently nodding their heads.

'I'll soon find somebody else,' she heard him shout. 'Bitch! Needn't think she can come back 'ere.'

Poppy nibbled on her fingernails. I wonder what the woman did? A saloon maid? Charwoman? Then she shrugged and looked round to find her way out. Nothing to do with me, she thought; I have troubles of my own. Nevertheless, something niggled at her mind. I need some money if I'm not going back straight away, and I'm not ready to, not just yet. I will, of course, she told herself. When I'm ready. She sniffed and gave a heaving sigh. I just need to gather myself together. Put my thoughts into perspective and try to think of living a life without love or music.

She was in the middle of theatreland where hundreds of theatres catered for those who loved melodrama, opera or serious plays. The music halls had developed from the singing rooms of inns and taverns for those whose tastes were less subtle and who liked to join in a singsong whilst enjoying a glass of ale. Some of these singing halls still remained.

On her way back to the Strand Poppy paused outside a shop selling second-hand theatrical clothing. It had in its window elaborate satin gowns, red military uniforms that had never seen service, false moustaches and beards, daggers and rifles, shiny tin medals and a selection of tawdry looking wigs. 'Used only twice,' a notice above a scarlet flounced gown pronounced in misspelled letters, 'by the Selebrated Madam Brissini.'

Shall I go in? Only to look, not to buy. She pulled her scarf round her head and pushed open the door, for an idea was emerging. The shopkeeper was attending to a customer and merely glanced at Poppy as she pinned a waistcoat round the waist of a stout man who was wearing a full periwig and knee breeches. Poppy headed toward the counter where there were piles of sheet music, and wig stands where a curly red wig and a black wig were displayed. She looked round. A cubicle with a curtain was in the corner of the shop.

'Can I try these?' she asked, picking up both wigs.

'Yes, darlin',' the woman said, her mouth full of pins. 'There's a mirror in the cubicle. Be wiv you in a minute.'

Poppy closed the cubicle curtain and took off her scarf, then screwed her hair into a tight bun on the top of her head and put on the black wig. She gasped. Transformation! She teased her fingers through the ringlets. It was thin hair, not like her own, but it was shiny and from a distance . . . from a distance, she breathed. No-one would know me.

She kept it on and handed the shopkeeper one shilling and sixpence for it, which was the price on the ticket. 'I'll take this one,' she said. 'The red one doesn't suit me.'

'Righty-ho.' The woman put the money in her pocket. 'The red one's a better quality,' she added. 'But if you're 'appy with that? It suits you,' she said. 'Fair, are you?'

Poppy nodded and made her escape, back the way she had come. She took a breath on coming to the alleyway and impulsively went down it towards the tavern. I need to earn some money, she thought, but more than anything I need a chance to think about my future: to make up my mind about what to do. Here is an opportunity right in front of me. The landlord was still outside, this time with a yard brush in his hand, sweeping the doorstep.

'Yes?' he said abruptly as Poppy approached him. Then he glanced at her again, and added, 'What can I do fer you, miss?'

Poppy cleared her throat. 'I, erm, I'm looking for work. Just to tide me over, you know,' she said. 'I wondered if you had anything? I've worked as an assistant in a grocery shop and in a café,' she went on. 'Or I can clean.'

He sniffed. 'Yer don't look like a cleaner to me. Where're you from?'

'I'm – I'm from the north. I came looking for work as a seamstress, but there doesn't seem to be any. I've spent all my money.' She continued with her white lie. 'I can't go home until I've made enough for the train fare.'

'Huh,' he said. 'So you'd not be stoppin' long?'

'Depends,' she said. 'I might.'

'Well it just so happens that I do need somebody.' He leaned on the brush and stared at her. 'You'd 'ave to live in. I want somebody to clean the place every morning and serve in the tavern every night.'

'I'm used to getting up early,' she told him, 'and working at night,' and she considered that serving ale couldn't be much different from serving coffee.

'All right.' He leaned the brush against the wall. 'I'll try you. But if you're no good then you're out! Understood?'

'Yes, thank you, Mr Black.'

' 'Ow do you know me name?' he barked.

'Oh! Everybody round here knows you,' she said nervously.

He gave a grim laugh. 'And they didn't put you off?'

She shook her head. 'I really need the work.'

'What's your name?' he grunted.

'P-Paula,' she stammered. 'Paula Ma— Mason.'

CHAPTER FORTY-SIX

Black was dictatorial, brusque and domineering. He shouted at everyone, from his customers at the Pit Stop and his neurotic wife, to the lad who worked in the cellars and attended the hydraulic beer engines which brought up the beer into the saloon. He'd led Poppy into the tavern, which was dark and low-ceilinged and reeked of tobacco smoke. There was only one room and that had a bar counter, long wooden tables and rough deal benches, so that the customers sat side by side to drink their ale or gin and play dominoes. On one side of the room was a hearth with a fire burning and opposite was an upright piano with sheet music on the stand.

'Who plays the piano?' Poppy had asked tentatively.

'Anybody who can bash out a few notes,' he'd said curtly. 'Can you play?'

'A bit,' she'd answered and followed him up to the room which was to be hers. It was at the top of the building, small, cold and damp, without a fireplace to warm it. There was a narrow iron bedstead and a wooden chest of drawers with a jug and washbowl. A towel rail stood empty.

'Ask my wife if you need anyfink,' he'd said, and then, glancing at her, remarked, 'I expect you're used to somefink better, ain't yer? Come down in the world?'

She'd only nodded, and then asked him what her duties were. Now she was into her third week and her hands were sore with washing glasses and tables. She swept and washed the saloon floor, scrubbed the doorstep and cleaned the windows, for Black was quite particular about the cleanliness of the place. But she didn't mind; the fact that she was kept so busy meant that she didn't think too often about Charlie and his betrayal. When she did think of him she was sunk into misery.

What she had objected to were the impertinent comments she had endured on her first night serving the customers. Because everyone sat at the long tables, it was her duty to go up and down with jugs of beer, and the difficulty wasn't in leaning over the customers and pouring without splashing, but in avoiding the wandering hands of many of the men, who fumbled with her skirt and bodice and made various suggestions. She had complained to the landlord and told him she wouldn't put up with it, and he had immediately warned everybody that if they did anything untoward, they would be banned from the hostelry. 'This isn't Dora,' he'd bellowed. 'She didn't mind, but this wench does.' And sheepishly they had listened and complied.

The postcards were sent off to her father, Dan, Mrs Bennett and the Marinos telling them not to worry about her, she would come back when she was ready. On the day she posted them, she had passed the costumiers where she had purchased the wig, and on seeing the shop was empty she had gone in to look at the sheet music.

'Take what you want, darlin',' the woman had said. 'I'm sellin' off the old stuff at a ha'penny a sheet, but there's some new music there as well that's just come in.'

Poppy had bought several song sheets which looked interesting – not to sing, she told herself, but just to familiarize herself with the words and the music; she sat down now on her bed with the printed sheet music for 'Greensleeves', which had been published by Schott and Company. She was looking for the arranger's name, for although it was a very old song, various adaptations had been made of it. Hah, she breathed. *Marino.* You've followed me here, Anthony. She folded it up and put it in her apron pocket and went downstairs.

There was just one old man in the saloon and he was asleep at one of the tables, his head cradled in his arms and a tankard of ale in front of him. The landlord was nowhere to be seen, and Poppy sidled over to the piano. She had heard it being played, very badly, by several of the customers, mostly in burlesque style. The tone was quite mellow, though the instrument was in need of tuning. She wasn't a pianist, but she could play a few chords and pick out a harmony, and had a good ear. She took the sheet for 'Greensleeves' from her pocket and saw that she had inadvertently picked up another song sheet with it. She read through it and her pulse quickened.

'Anthony again,' she whispered, seeing his name at the bottom of the sheet. She noticed how he had written '*affettuoso*' and '*amoroso*' above some of the notes. 'With feeling,' she murmured, remembering her piano lessons. 'Lovingly!'

Poppy glanced round again. The old man was snoring. She sat down on the stool, lifted the piano lid, placed the music on the stand and with the lightest of touches and the softest of voices began to play and sing.

'In the town where I was born there flowed a river
Its rolling tide was swift and deep and strong.
In the town where I was born there lived my lover – he stole my heart
He stole my love when I was young.

'He kissed my hand and I was blithe and bonny
He kissed my lips, his words so soft and sweet as honey
My heart, my life, is thine for ever and never will there be another.
In the town where I was born there flowed a river
Its rolling tide swift and deep as a maiden's dreams.

'In the town where I was born once lived my lover
On these deserted moon-lit banks I stand and grieve
He stole my love, my heart, my tears and did deceive, drowning them by his treachery.'

Poppy bent her head as her tears fell. Anthony's words and music always touched her emotions. She groped in her pocket for a handkerchief to blow her nose and was suddenly aware of other people. The old man was sitting up and both the landlord and his wife were standing in the doorway to the living quarters. He had his arms folded in front of him, and she was fiddling with a corner of the apron she always wore.

'I'm sorry,' Poppy began, but Black interrupted her as the old man began to clap.

'That was good,' the landlord said. 'Do you know any more?'

'Erm . . .' Embarrassed that they should see her cry, she swallowed away her tears. 'I've got an arrangement of "Greensleeves" here.'

Black nodded. 'Let's 'ear it then.'

She began again. This at least was very familiar to her, for she had sung it often before. But she sang it low and huskily and not in her usual style. Not because she thought they would recognize her voice – she didn't think they were the type to frequent concert halls or theatre – but because she was so choked with emotion.

'Alas my love you do me wrong
To cast me off discourtesly
For I have loved you oh so long
Delighting in your company

'Greensleeves was all my joy
Greensleeves was my delight
Greensleeves was my heart of gold
And who but my lady Greensleeves'

'Loverly,' Mrs Black said. 'Really loverly, dearie.'

Mr Black nodded. 'Yers, very good, but don't yer know somefink jolly? Everybody'll be going 'ome in tears if you only sing them sorts o' songs.'

Poppy rose to her feet. 'I didn't intend them to be heard by anyone,' she said hastily. 'I was – well, just trying them out.'

'Ooh, but you've got a loverly voice,' Mrs Black proclaimed. 'Hasn't she, 'Enery? Got a loverly voice! You oughta be on the stage, dearie. Shouldn't she, 'Enery? Shouldn't she be on the stage?'

'All right, you silly old bat,' Henry Black bellowed. 'Gerroff back to the kitchen. I'll talk to 'er. 'Now listen,' he said to Poppy, and the old man came closer to hear what he was going to say. 'You've got a good voice, and if you sing 'ere, I'll up your money another bob a week. 'ow does that sound?'

'I'm not sure that I want to sing,' she said, looking wistfully at the piano.

'I'll get it tuned. Pianner, I mean.' His brow creased and he pressed his lips together. 'Go on then, one and six, but that's my final offer.'

'Make it two bob,' the old man piped up. 'She'd be worth it,' he added as Black glared at him. 'You don't often 'ear a voice like 'ers. Not round 'ere, anyway.' He leaned towards Poppy. 'I don't suppose you know any of our Marie's songs, do you?'

She confessed that she did, and hid a smile at the landlord's offer, as only a short while ago she had been earning so much more. Perhaps I might sing, she thought. There would only be the regulars at the Pit Stop to hear her; no-one from the theatre world would ever come to this hostelry. They were all working people who drank here, those earning a pittance and struggling to keep out of poverty. Why shouldn't they hear a different kind of music?

'All right,' she said. 'I'll sing some of the music hall songs as long as I can sing some of my own choosing as well.'

'Done!' Black said. 'Start tonight. But now get on with cleaning them winders. They're covered with cobwebs.'

If she'd thought she would have a respite from cleaning, she was mistaken. He still expected her to do the same work as before, except that halfway through the evening he would signal to her to stop serving the customers and go to the piano. She sang the music hall songs and the customers joined in with great gusto and then she sang her own choice. She sang 'Pretty May', which everyone loved and hummed along with, then followed it with 'Forever True'.

Two weeks on, the hostelry was packed every night as word got round that there was a new singer performing at the Pit Stop.

Poppy took care not to stretch her voice; she sang the love songs low and huskily, her tone sad and full of longing, and the women listening would wistfully stroke their cheeks with rough fingers and cast downward glances at each other, whilst the men would shuffle uncomfortably and then reach for their glasses or tankards and take a hasty swallow.

Poppy had got into the habit of calling in at the costumier's, for there were new song sheets arriving regularly. The woman there, whose name was Betsy, would wave her in if she was passing by.

'You're that singer at the Pit Stop, ain't you?' she said one day. 'You oughta go on the halls. You're as good as I've ever heard. Here,' she said. 'Some young fella just brought these in. He's trying to make a living with his songwriting. He's taking these all over town. I bought them thinking of you.'

Poppy held her breath for a second. Not Anthony come back to England? Automatically she looked for the name of the songwriter, but the name wasn't his. T. Martin. Not anyone she had heard of, and the music was handwritten, not published. But the songs were the kind she liked to sing, so she bought them at sixpence a sheet.

> Sweet eyes that smiled but not for me
> They smiled for him who was untrue
> Dear heart I love you and will be
> Forever faithful just to you.
>
> Sweet lips that kissed a mouth that lied
> Sweet lips so soft and red
> Her gold-red hair like silken thread
> That when untied will capture me
> And bind me by her side.

Poppy paused as she read and hummed the refrain. There was a familiarity about the words, but perhaps that was because they had the old theme of love, lost and found. The melodies were simple, wistful and yearning, and she wished she could play better than she did to do the music justice.

> Dear heart forget him
> Let his memory dim
> Come live with me
> And forever faithful I will be.

Again, she thought. Again it is about lost love and someone patiently waiting.

If I could only love again I'd choose to love just you
Listen and hear my silent voice, my words a muted tune
Of some romantic melody
Question not the but or why
I love you now and for evermore until the day I die.

She turned to another sheet. What's this? This is a mistake, it shouldn't be here. Yet it's fastened to the others. It's – yes, it's Robert Burns!

My love is like a red, red rose
That's newly sprung in June
My love is like a melody
That's sweetly played in tune.

Poppy could hear Henry Black calling upstairs for her to come down, that there were customers waiting to be served. Why would the songwriter, T. Martin, slip in the popular air by the Scottish poet when everyone would know that it wasn't his? And written in English and not Scots dialect. She went downstairs with the sheets folded and slipped into her pocket. And then she realized that the words were linked with music – 'My love is like a melody that's sweetly played in tune.' She reflected wistfully as the poem ran through her head. 'And I will love thee still, my dear, till a' the seas gang dry.'

How romantic! How wonderful to be the recipient of such love. To know that that love would always be true.

CHAPTER FORTY-SEVEN

'Look at this, Nan! Another postcard, saying she's all right.' Joshua handed the coloured card to Nan. 'What am I to do?' He nibbled on his thumb. 'Should I go to London, do you think? Never mind what that Damone fellow says!' His face creased. 'I'm that bothered about her. I know she says she's all right, but what if she's not?'

Nan was worried too, and she was concerned about Joshua as well. Since Poppy's disappearance he had lost weight and his thick dark hair had developed several silver streaks. 'How would you find her?' she asked sensibly. 'Where would you search? You don't know London, and it seems that that's where she might be. And you know, don't you,' she added, 'that Poppy would come home if she was in real trouble? She knows who cares for her.'

Joshua put his hand to his eyes. 'Yes, but I can't sleep for thinking and wondering where she is. It's worse, somehow, than when Mary was ill.' He took a handkerchief from his pocket and blew his nose. 'I feel so – so alone, Nan. I know that I've got Tommy and he's as worried as can be, but I lie awake in bed and—'

Almost without thinking, she went up to him and hugged him to her. 'Try not to worry,' she whispered. 'She'll be all right, I know she will.'

He put his arms round her and rested his chin on the top of her head. Then he absently kissed her forehead. 'Thank you, Nan,' he sighed. 'I don't know what I'd do without you.' He pulled back slightly and looked at her with a dazed, bewildered expression. Then he bent his head and kissed her cheek. It was soft and smooth. He gazed at her as if seeing her for the first time and kissed her again and she didn't say anything, but only closed her eyes. 'Nan?' he said softly, and stroked her face.

Nan opened her eyes and looked up at him. 'Yes,' she said gently and waited, and he kissed her once more, this time on the lips.

She saw him swallow and then he said in an undertone, 'Forgive me, Nan. I'm just a man and so lonely. I can't cope with difficulties without knowing that there's someone near to love and care for me.'

Nan stretched up to kiss his cheek. 'I know about loneliness,' she said softly. 'Show me a widow who doesn't.'

'Could we – could we care for each other, do you think?' He seemed almost boyish in his shyness.

She smiled and her face lit up. 'I've cared for you for a long time, Joshua,' she said. 'Longer than I'd ever admit to.'

His brows creased together. 'Have you? I didn't know!'

'Of course you didn't know,' she said softly. 'You were a happily married man and my employer. Besides, I was very fond of Mrs Mazzini. I would never have done anything to hurt her.'

'But Mary's been gone all these years,' he began, and he still had his arms round her.

Nan laughed. 'Why would I think that you'd ever look at me after being married to such a beautiful woman? She was a perfect wife and mother. I couldn't possibly match her.'

'You don't need to,' he smiled. 'I wouldn't want you to change. What Mary and I had together was very special, and I expect it was 'same for you and your husband?' He saw her give a slight nod. 'But perhaps we could have something special together?'

'It's too soon,' she said wistfully. 'You've been caught at a weak moment. One or two kisses don't make a marriage, and I wouldn't agree to anything less.' She patted his cheek. 'You're a good man, Joshua. I wouldn't want you to regret anything done in a hurry.'

He threw his head back and laughed. 'In a hurry! How long have we known each other? Donkey's years!'

'Seventeen!' she told him. 'I came not long after I was widowed. Mattie was onny a bairn.'

Joshua nodded. He remembered the sad-eyed young woman with an infant in her arms who had come knocking at their door looking for work. 'Anything,' she'd said. 'I'll do anything: scrub 'floors, serve in 'shop, washing, ironing, baking.' And Mary, with a spirited Tommy hanging on to her skirt, had taken to her immediately and asked her in.

He grinned, his eyes twinkling. He felt happier than he'd felt in a long time. 'So, shall we start courting? Are we too old for that?'

Nan's face brightened. 'I'm not,' she said breathlessly. 'It's more than I've ever dared dream of. But only if you're sure,' she added.

He drew her towards him again. 'I am sure, Nan,' he said softly and kissed her tenderly. 'I've never been more sure of anything.'

They said nothing to Tommy and Mattie, though Mattie wondered at her mother's unusual exuberance, and Tommy puzzled over his father's sudden habit of whistling, when he had previously been so worried and down in the dumps about Poppy's disappearance.

'What's going on with Pa and Nan?' Tommy grumbled one morning when first his father and then Nan had separately had to slip out on an urgent errand. 'They know we're allus busy on a Friday morning. That's 'second time this week they've both cleared off and left us to it.'

'Perhaps your pa's trying us out,' Mattie said. 'Mebbe he wants to see if we can run 'business without him.'

'Well, we need him here – and Nan,' Tommy complained. 'I don't know what he's thinking of!'

'He said he wouldn't be long,' Mattie reasoned. 'He wouldn't have gone if it hadn't been important.' Her forehead creased. 'Though I can't think why Ma's gone to 'butcher's now, when she passed his shop on 'way here this morning. He was open, cos we gave him a wave.'

They continued serving customers as they came in and stacking shelves and writing lists of what stock they needed. An hour went by and then a windswept Joshua blew in. 'By,' he said heartily. 'It's a bit wild out there.' Then, rubbing his hands briskly together, he went through into the kitchen. Five minutes later Nan swept in.

'It's *very* cold,' she said, beaming. 'Very cold indeed,' and she too hurried through to the kitchen. 'I'll make a pot of tea,' she called over her shoulder. 'Is your pa back, Tommy?'

'Ye-es,' Tommy said to her disappearing back. 'He's just come in.'

He and Mattie looked at each other, then Mattie began to grin. She rushed to Tommy's side. 'They've been meeting up somewhere!' she said in a hoarse whisper. 'They could have gone out and come in 'shop door at 'same time if they'd wanted and we'd have thought nothing of it.'

Tommy's mouth dropped open. 'What's going on?'

'Don't you see?' Mattie could hardly contain herself. 'They've both been acting oddly all 'week.' She gave a beaming grin. 'I think they're courtin'!'

'Never!' Tommy said. 'Pa and Nan? Why, they've known each other for years.' He stared at Mattie and his eyes sparkled. 'Do you really think so? Why would they court at their age? Why don't they just—' He shrugged as he saw Mattie frown at him. 'Well, I mean, there's nowt to stop 'em, is there?'

Mattie shook her head at him. 'Perhaps that's what they want to do, Tommy. They've both been widowed. Your pa's had a good marriage and my ma . . . well, I don't remember my father, but—'

'Do you think they'll get married?' Tommy said hoarsely, and when Mattie smiled and raised her eyebrows questioningly, he picked her up and whirled her round. 'Wouldn't that be just great?' he said, and put her down as his father came through into the shop.

'What's going on, you two?' he said in mock admonishment. 'Such frivolity in 'place of work.'

'We might ask you and Nan 'same question,' Tommy replied boldly. 'Both taking time off together. Just what's going on?'

Nan appeared in the doorway. She had taken off her hat and coat and put on her apron. 'What?' she asked, catching the tail end of Tommy's question.

Joshua cast his eyes from Nan to Tommy and Mattie, who were both grinning. 'We're not very good at subterfuge, Nan,' he said solemnly. 'I think we've just been found out.'

'I will find her,' Anthony told Dan. 'Be quite sure that I will. She won't be able to stop singing any more than I could stop playing when Jeanette and I parted company.'

'It's really good of you to come back, Anthony,' Dan said. 'You didn't have to. But I do appreciate it,' he added. 'How did you know Poppy had gone missing, anyway? Who told you?'

Anthony laughed. 'Just about everybody, except you. Your sister Marian and my parents wrote to me.' He looked down at his hands and stretched his fingers. 'But by the time I received their letters I was packed and ready to leave. Poppy had already written to me to tell me what had happened. How that wretch had become engaged to someone else and how heartbroken she was.'

'Had she? Really? I didn't realize you knew each other so well.'

Anthony nodded, choosing not to answer Dan's remark, and went on, 'I had two more engagements that I couldn't break, but fortunately one came immediately after the other and as soon as they were over I came back to London. She's here somewhere, I know she is, even though I've looked and looked already. I've even been to Brighton. I thought she might have gone there, but then I realized that she couldn't hide there as people would recognize her.'

'Yes,' Dan murmured. 'With that hair she'll stand out.'

Anthony gazed at him. 'Yes,' he said thoughtfully. 'Everywhere I've been, I've been asking for a red-headed young woman but—'

'What?' Dan asked. 'What are you saying?'

'If she doesn't want to be found – she'd disguise herself, perhaps wear a wig, wouldn't she?'

Dan shrugged. 'Possibly. But we don't know if she's still in London, do we? She could be anywhere.'

'Where did you go, Dan?' Anthony asked quietly. 'When Maria died? You were away for weeks. Everyone was very concerned about you.'

A shadow fell across Dan's face. 'Do you remember? It's a long time ago.' He sighed.

'I was only a boy,' Anthony said. 'But I remember my parents whispering about her and saying how sad they were for you.'

'I stayed in London,' Dan said quietly. 'I wanted to lose myself in the crowds. I thought that if I was hidden amongst the masses, then no-one would ask who I was or where I'd come from. I didn't want anyone asking me how I felt or saying how sorry they were, or telling me I would find someone else one day. I thought', he said reflectively, 'that it would help me forget. I was wrong. Nothing did, nor ever will.'

He gave a small shrug. 'And then, some years later, when Jeanette gave you up for that elderly Don Juan, I knew for sure there was no true love left in the world. Except for my sister and her husband.' He smiled pensively. 'They are the only exception I know of. Real life isn't a love song with a happy ending.'

Anthony smiled back, a light in his eyes. 'No,' he said. 'You're wrong on that score too, Dan. It can be. I know I'm young and foolish—'

'And I am old and wise,' Dan broke in.

Anthony nodded. 'But some songs are meant to be about enduring love, like yours for your wife,' he said seriously. 'And others are about loving for a second time.'

Dan laughed, though his voice cracked, and he rose to his feet. 'Then go away and find her, you romantic young swain, and bring her back here! There's a whole world waiting for her.'

CHAPTER FORTY-EIGHT

Dan had told Anthony that Poppy hadn't been paid for her time in France, that her fees and expenses were sitting in the bank waiting for her. His parents had told him that she had gone out at night and taken nothing with her as far as they could tell, for they didn't want to look through her belongings. So, he had deliberated, she might only have her purse with her, and he pushed to the back of his mind how near breaking point she might have been, as he remembered how he had once stood distraught by the river Thames, when Jeanette had coldly told him she was marrying another. And if she hasn't any money she'll have to earn some in order to eat and sleep.

He had already enquired at music halls and theatres, though not giving her name; had pored over programmes and examined posters. He had scoured the obvious places around Leicester Square, Oxford Street, Drury Lane, the Haymarket and Covent Garden, and enquired at music shops, selling his song sheets at a pittance as he asked if anyone had seen or heard of a red-haired singer looking for work.

Now he was about to try the meaner streets where clubs, hostelries, smoking halls and beer taverns often had singing rooms to entertain their customers. But where to start? London teemed with such places. He opened a map that he'd bought, looked at it, and then folded it and put it back in his pocket, pondering that Poppy, who didn't know London all that well, might have stayed within a sphere that she was familiar with. She's somewhere within the theatre area, he thought. I just know that she is. He walked down St Martin's Lane towards the Strand, and as he stood undecided, a tram trundled towards him. He put out his hand and, grabbing the rail, hopped on.

'Only going as far as Fleet Street,' the conductor told him. 'We're taking the tram out of commission.'

'That's fine.' Anthony handed him a copper. 'That's as far as I want to go.' Off the main thoroughfare were narrow entries and small squares and here Dr Johnson had made his home in the previous century, dining well at the Cheshire Cheese with his literary fellows. Here, by the Law Courts and Chancery Lane, was the discreet abode of legal London, the Inns of Court, and a warren of courtyards, dark passageways and chambers which housed the frock-coated lawyers and their legal students.

Anthony jumped off the tram as they reached Fleet Street and headed towards Fetter Lane. Fleet Street was one of the most famous and ancient streets of London, famous for its mighty printing presses, including those which serviced *The Times* and other newspapers; infamous for the dank and stinking sewer, the Fleet channel, which ran beneath it to Bridewell, once the dreaded place of correction.

Hidden away off the noisy street which teemed with dashing crowds, rattling trams, and horse-drawn vehicles, and away from the inky fingers of journalists and newspaper men, were coffee houses, inns and taverns, and this is where Anthony's feet took him. He had been here before when he had called at music shops and costumiers, for these streets also held small theatres, concert halls and singing rooms.

He stood for a moment, wondering which direction to take. There was a fine drizzle falling and it was very cold; no sign yet of an early spring. He hunched into his coat collar and sighed. Where are you, Poppy? Where are you hiding? He headed towards a music shop which he had visited before. It sold song sheets and second hand violins, and advertised 'Tuning of Pianoforte and other Instruments'.

Anthony pushed open the door and stepped inside, glad to be out of the rain. 'Good afternoon,' he said to the old man who was sitting on a wooden chair restringing a violin. 'I called previously and brought in some song sheets.'

The old man looked at him over his round wire spectacles.

'Indeed you did,' he said, adding, 'I don't need any more at the moment.'

Anthony inclined his head. 'No? Erm – I was wondering, have they been selling? Is it the right kind of music? It's not music hall, I realize, but I am interested to know what is popular just now!'

'Well,' the shopkeeper deliberated. 'Had you asked a few months ago, I would have told you that my customers only wanted music hall songs. You know, "The Ratcatcher's Daughter" or "Polly Perkins", "Burlington Bertie", that kind of thing, but tastes seem to be changing, thank goodness, and I have sold some of yours. They are yours, presumably?'

Anthony admitted that they were.

'You're very good,' the shopkeeper commented. 'You are a musician, are you not, as well as a lyricist?' and when Anthony nodded he said, 'Yes, I thought so. Well, I can tell you, young man, that you will go far.'

'But I need a singer,' Anthony butted in. 'Someone who can interpret my songs.'

'Exactly!' The old man shook a finger. 'Just what I was going to say. You need someone to popularize them. Now let me tell you, Mr – Martin, isn't it?'

'Erm, yes. Tony Martin.'

'I'm led to believe that there's a young woman round here with a very fine voice. I haven't heard her as I don't frequent the type of venue where she performs, but apparently she's singing your songs and there isn't a dry eye in the place.'

'Oh!' Anthony's spirits shot up. 'Where?' he said. 'Do you know where, sir? Do you know the name of the concert hall?'

A frown creased the old man's forehead. 'Not a concert hall,' he corrected, 'otherwise I might have gone along to hear her myself. No, this whereabouts, so I hear, is not for a decent body to visit. There's drinking and rowdyism and a very rough landlord.'

'So, an inn then, or a tavern?' Anthony said, muttering more to himself than the shopkeeper. 'There are so many.'

'Just a moment!' The old man got up from his chair and with bent spine slowly wended his way to the back of the shop. 'Mr Fisher,' he called through a passageway. 'Can you come here a moment, if you please?'

A tall, angular young man came through the door into the shop. 'Yes, Mr Cord?'

'The name of the hostelry where that young woman sings? You've frequented the place, I believe? You said that you'd heard her.'

'I have, sir.' Mr Fisher cast a suspicious eye over Anthony. 'I, er, I'm sorry I don't know the name of it, or its vicinity. Some friends took me along. It was dark; I didn't know where I was.' He looked down at his feet.

'What did she look like?' Anthony asked. 'Was she young? I'm looking for a singer for my songs,' he added, feeling the man's antagonism towards him and wondering why.

'Black hair!' Mr Fisher blurted out. 'No, not young! Sorry, I can't help you further. Excuse me, please,' and he retreated away back into his cubbyhole.

'Mm!' Mr Cord murmured. 'How very odd! I could have sworn he'd been more than once. He came back very agitated after the first time.' He ran his fingers over his grey beard. 'I was sure he'd been again. Quite het up, he was.'

'Thank you for your help, sir,' Anthony said. 'I'll ask about and try to find her.'

'Be careful,' Mr Cord warned. 'Young women who work in such low places are not of the best kind. Not the kind you would take home to Mother.' Again he looked at Anthony over his spectacles. Then he sighed. 'Of course, I'm very old-fashioned. It's not all that long ago that ladies wouldn't have been seen in theatres, but our dear queen has changed all that. I understand that she is very fond of Gilbert and Sullivan.' He shook his head sagely. 'But I'm quite sure she wouldn't approve of young women singing in taverns.'

Anthony walked on. He was sure that Mr Fisher knew where the tavern was, but for some reason didn't want to tell him. Now why? He stopped outside a costumier's. The light was fading fast and the woman inside was lighting a lamp. She looked up and smiled at him through the window. He went in and she greeted him by name.

'Mr Martin!' she said. 'Your songs are going very well. There's a new singer come to work round here and she's bought quite a few.'

'Where is she singing?' he asked. 'I've heard good reports of her already. I'd like to hear her.'

'She's at the Pit Stop,' she said. 'It's not far from here, but difficult to find, it's so tucked away.' She looked at him, her head on one side. 'It's not a very salubrious area,' she advised. 'But the landlord doesn't stand any trouble.'

Two points of view, he thought. Mr Cord said it was rowdy, but then he hasn't been.

'Have you heard her?' he asked. 'Is she any good?'

'I've not heard her sing, but she's been in a few times to buy song sheets.'

'What does she look like?' he asked. 'Fair, dark, young . . .?'

'Oh, very young, and pretty,' she said. 'And dark.' She frowned a little. 'I think she's dark, but I can't be sure – she's like someone else who came . . .' She shrugged. 'I've got people coming and going all the time.'

She gave him directions for the Pit Stop, but in just a few minutes he had lost his way. The area was full of passageways, courts and dead ends; not all were lit and it was now quite dark. He thought that he would be better going back to the costumier's to start again, and stood for a moment to reassess his bearings. Had there been anyone about, he would have asked directions, but there was a lull in the passage of people. Either they were safely in their houses or they had not yet left their offices.

As he was about to turn back, a man came out of the darkness towards him. I'll ask, he decided, but realizing there was something familiar about the tall thin figure he melted back against the wall instead. Mr Fisher! He watched as the man took a right turn out of the street into a narrower lane. He followed him and considered that at the sure pace he was walking, Mr Fisher certainly knew where he was going. There were some gas lamps lit along here so he was able to keep him in view without getting too close, but suddenly he disappeared.

Anthony would have walked past the entrance to the courtyard if he hadn't been looking carefully to see where Mr Fisher had gone, and if he hadn't also seen other people coming towards him and slipping down the same opening. He stopped and looked down it and saw the hostelry with its lighted lamp outside the door and another in the window. He stepped back as other people, men and women, came past him, hurrying as if they had an urgent appointment or a train to catch.

'Come on, Jim,' he heard one woman say to her lagging husband. 'Don't dawdle. I want to sit near to pianner, then I can hear 'er.'

This is the place, he thought with mounting excitement, though he couldn't see a name above the inn door. This must be it! He waited a while longer as more and more people streamed in. He didn't want to look conspicuous, and he guessed that the sale of ale or gin would be the first priority for the innkeeper, before the entertainment began. He heard the sound of laughter and loud voices and went to the window to peer in. The glass was steamed up inside, but he could see the flicker of firelight and customers, mainly women, sitting at long tables, whilst men stood at the bar counter at the far end of the room. The landlord, a big man, was standing behind it, a woman was helping him, and a girl carrying a jug was serving at the tables.

I hope this is it. His confidence was diminishing. I'd better go in and take a look.

Inside the hostelry were far more people than had passed him so he guessed that this was a very popular drinking venue. They stood against the walls and fireplace and round the piano, which was on the opposite wall, to the left as he had come in. The tables were full and the area at the counter was packed with customers. The landlord was drawing ale from a pump into jugs and tankards and pouring gin into glasses.

I'll wait awhile, Anthony thought and stood back in the crowd nearest the door. He looked round for Mr Fisher and saw him across the room in a corner where he would have a full view of the piano. I wonder why he didn't want to tell me, he thought. Why did he want to keep Poppy, if it is she, secret?

He would have bought a glass of ale, for the room was hot, but the serving maid had gone and the landlord and the woman with him were busy. The people at the tables had full glasses and several jugs of ale in front of them. If I go to the counter, he mused, I risk drawing attention to myself, for even in my everyday coat I'm better dressed than this down-at-heel crowd.

The landlord banged on the counter with a gavel and raised his voice to a bellow. 'Has everybody got their ale? Get it now if you want a fill-up, for there'll be no ale served during the entertainment.'

How very odd, Anthony thought. Why is that, I wonder? Does he sell more after the entertainment? But then he saw the rush towards the counter and how the jugs of ale on the tables were poured into extra glasses and handed back empty over the tops of heads to be refilled.

After about ten minutes, the landlord wiped his hands on a towel and bellowed again. 'Quiet please! A round of applause for Miss *Paula Mason*!'

It was almost a command, but everyone enthusiastically cheered and clapped and Anthony cast his eyes round the room for the entertainer. Paula Mason? The same initials. Poppy was upset when Bradshaw had spelt her name wrong in Brighton. But she wouldn't want to use her own name here. Is it her or not? He saw that Mr Fisher had his eyes glued to the door nearest the piano.

The door opened and another cheer went up as a young woman came through. Poppy? Was it her? She was dark-haired with a pale face and none of the exuberance which always lit up Poppy's expression when she was about to perform. But she gave a smile and an acknowledgement as she sat down at the piano and ran her fingers over the keys. She's not a pianist, that much is certain, Anthony mused and wished that he had placed himself nearer, for he could now only see the back of her head, unlike Mr Fisher who was gazing adoringly at her face.

'Welcome to my world of song,' she announced, and when she began to sing, in a soft, husky and wistful tone, Anthony knew for certain it was Poppy. Her voice was expressive and emotional, yet the singer was keeping it strictly under control, saving it perhaps for something more.

She began with 'Greensleeves', which appeared to be popular with both men and women for he could see heads swinging gently from side to side and lips moving as if their owners were singing, and then she began the song he had written for her.

CHAPTER FORTY-NINE

Poppy had felt all eyes on her as she sat down at the piano. She wasn't self-conscious as a rule, but the last few nights she had been uneasy. She was sure there was a shadowy figure watching her. She had felt a presence looking only at her, whereas usually the crowd who had come to hear her sing would take their eyes away to glance at or whisper to their companions, or take a drink. These watching eyes upon her were for her alone and they made her uncomfortable, yet when she glanced up at the end of her performance she only saw the smiling, clapping crowd, some of whom were recognizable to her now as regulars at the Pit Stop.

I'm imagining it, she told herself the following day as she went about her business of cleaning the tables, sweeping and washing the floor, and throwing out tobacco ash, and yet a prickle ran down the back of her neck. There had been someone. She paused with the broom in her hand and concentrated. There was a man, tall and thin, who always stood in the same place across from her, yet when she had finished singing he had gone. A memory eluded her. Who did he remind her of? Someone!

She continued with her tasks, humming a little. Last evening's audience had been very appreciative; they were a lively crowd, not afraid to show that they had enjoyed her performance. They were not polite in their applause, but robust and enthusiastic. I enjoy singing for them, she mused, wielding the broom, and— She stopped as she remembered who the man in the shadows was. He threw the rose at the Savoy, she recalled. He waited for me to come out of the theatre, and— She caught her breath; it was the night Charlie told me he had become engaged to Miss

Burchfield. He asked if I was unwell, and I had the rose in my hair.

He knows who I am! Her eyes grew wide at the discovery. She leaned against the piano as she absorbed the implications. Will he betray me? Will he announce to the audience who I am? Am I ready to be revealed? She was unnerved and distressed.

I'll have to leave, she decided. I'll move on. But where to? Am I ready to go back? I don't hurt as much as I did when I think of Charlie. It's more that I feel empty and humiliated and wonder if I was just a foolish child with an infatuation. Yet he seemed to be fond of me, she thought wistfully. He shouldn't have encouraged me if he really didn't care. I wanted him to love me, but I also wanted to sing and it seemed that with Charlie I couldn't have both. He wanted me to love him and pander to his desires. To look after his needs, his wants and comforts. I would be expected to be happy just because he was pleased with me. He didn't want a wife who had dreams of her own.

I'm missing my pa, she reflected. His love has no conditions. And I'm missing Nan too; she would give me a hug like my mother used to do if ever I felt sad, and that's what I want, someone to hold me close and say that everything will be all right. And yet . . . She took a deep, sighing breath. I can't seem to find the courage to go back. I've let so many people down: Mrs Bennett, Dan . . . and whatever will Anthony think of me, sending out that hasty, impulsive, *imprudent* letter, telling him of my heartbreak? Will he have really understood?

'Come on, gel.' Henry Black's strident voice broke into her brooding. 'I don't pay you to hang about daydreaming. There's jobs to be done before folks start coming in.' He peered at her. 'Dreaming of fame and fortune, ain't yer? Well, I'll tell yer, gel, them things only comes to a few, and not to folks like us, though I'll admit you've got a good warble; but it ain't going to fetch you riches. Only hard work can do that.'

'Yes, Mr Black,' she said quietly, and thought to herself, I'll sing tonight, collect my wages and leave in the morning. Then she added, 'There's a man who always comes to hear me sing; he's tall and stands over by the wall opposite the piano. Do you know the one I mean?'

'Thin, is he? As a beanpole?' He nodded as she agreed he was.

'He only ever has one drink and then he leaves.' He pursed his mouth to a downward sneer. 'He doesn't come for the ale. He only comes to hear you. Not one of my regulars! Works round here somewhere. Why? Does he bother you?'

'N-no,' she lied. 'I just wondered who he was.'

'Mm,' Black murmured, frowning at her. 'Well, if he's a nuisance, tell me and I'll throw him out. Don't want hangers-on causing trouble. I'll not 'ave that!'

I won't tell him I'm leaving until the morning, Poppy decided. Then he can look for someone else, though I'm sorry to disappoint the customers. Some had become very friendly towards her and would greet her with a cheery wave if they saw her out in the streets.

That evening as she served the ale she looked round for the tall thin man, but he wasn't there. He comes late, I think. She couldn't remember ever having served him. As Mr Black says, he doesn't come for the ale, he only comes to hear me. The knowledge didn't bring her pleasure. Rather it made her feel anxious and wary, as if she was being observed or spied upon. She went upstairs to her room to wash her hands and make sure her wig was secure, and brushed a little carmine onto her cheeks. The black wig doesn't suit my complexion, she thought. It drains my face of colour.

She went downstairs again, signalled to Henry Black that she was ready, and waited for him to announce her. She felt nervous tonight and glanced towards the corner where the man usually stood. I'm being stupid, she thought. He's an admirer, he doesn't mean me any harm, and besides, what could he do with all of these people around?

The landlord's voice rang out and she entered the saloon. She bowed her head at the applause and gave a smile and made her way to the piano. She turned again to the audience and said, 'Thank you so much. Welcome to my world of song.' She smoothed down the back of her skirt as she was about to sit down, and then hesitated. On top of the upright piano lay a single red rose. Oh! she thought, her senses reeling. Is it from him? What does he want from me?

Anthony spent the day at the piano in his parents' rooms behind the restaurant. His mother spent the day trying to persuade him to eat. '*Niente. Non ancora,*' he told her. 'Only espresso. I work better when I'm hungry, you know that.'

Grumbling slightly, she brought the coffee as he had asked but brought him a plate of biscuits too. 'Why you sit 'ere?' she chided. 'Why you not out looking for Poppy?'

'I've found her,' he answered absent-mindedly. 'But I need to leave her a message. I don't want to frighten her away.'

His mother raised her eyes heavenwards. 'Thank God!' she exclaimed. '*Molte grazie.*' She clasped her hands together. 'Where? You must bring her back 'ere.'

'*Madre!*' he said impatiently. He held a note pad on his knee and had a pencil behind his ear. 'Will you please go away and leave me alone! Go. *Arrivederci.* Vamoose!'

What am I to say? How am I to say it? She's been hurt and will probably think that she'll never love again. He ran his fingers over the keys, picking out a poignant refrain. I could write a song without words, but would she understand it? Or I could say . . . he hummed softly.

> Think no more of the lonely tears
> Mourn no more the wasted years
> Dear heart forget him, let his memory dim
> And come to me
> For forever faithful I will be.

I've used some of the words before, he thought, as he scribbled them down on his pad, with a notation of symbols to remind him of the melody and rhythm. Then he sighed and tore it out and pushed it into his pocket. He glanced at his pocket watch and jumped up. He was going to be late. He grabbed his coat and dashed out, calling to his mother not to keep supper for him.

'Will you come back with Poppy?' she called back.

'Don't know!'

He ran towards St Martin's Lane and hailed a horse cab. The first one was occupied but the second one stopped. 'Fetter Lane, please, and could you hurry?'

He was dropped off on a corner, for he felt that he would find his way better on foot. He hoped that he could remember the turnings to get him to the Pit Stop. He stopped at a flower shop to ascertain if he was going in the right direction and bought a red rose. The woman gave it to him wrapped in a thin piece of paper. He felt in his pocket and drew out the notepaper he had been scribbling on and as he walked he folded it into a cone and wrapped it round the stem.

'Mr Martin!' A voice startled him and Anthony turned abruptly to see Mr Fisher bearing down on him.

He stopped. 'Yes?'

'You're going to hear Miss Mason, ain't you?'

'I am.' Anthony looked keenly at Mr Fisher's face. 'Is that where you're going? I thought you said you didn't know the way!'

'I . . .' The man's face was grim, though it was difficult to see properly in the gloom. 'What do you want wiv her?' he asked, a hostile note in his voice. 'She's all right where she is. She's safe there!'

'Safe! What do you mean, safe?' Anthony was irate. 'Do you think I mean her harm?'

'Somefink happened,' Fisher muttered. 'She's hiding from somebody. I'm taking care of her.'

'Taking care of her?' Anthony repeated. 'How? What gives you the right? Does she know?'

'I know who she really is.' Fisher dropped his voice to a whisper. 'That's why I didn't tell you where she was. Now go away. Leave her alone.'

'She's a friend of mine,' Anthony protested. 'I know who she is, and her family and friends are all anxious about her.'

'She don't want to go back,' Fisher mumbled. 'It's too much of a strain for her, singing for them society folk. She belongs here. We look after our own round here.'

Anthony shook his head. The fellow was plainly besotted by Poppy. 'Her father is worried about her,' he said quietly. 'We all are, but Miss Mazzini must make up her own mind about who she sings for. That decision is for her.'

'She's chosen already, ain't she?' Fisher sneered. 'She's come to live along of us.'

'Then she can stay, or come back if she wants to; but first I must tell her that her father and brother and friends just want to know that she's all right. Now, please excuse me.'

Fisher put his hand on Anthony's chest. 'I'm warning you,'

he said menacingly. 'If you harm her – I'll kill you.'

'I won't harm her.' Anthony shuffled back half a step. 'I've told you, I'm a friend.'

'What's your name then?' Fisher demanded. 'It ain't Martin, like you told the old man!'

'No, it isn't,' Anthony admitted. 'It's Marino. Anthony Marino.'

He saw the startled look in the man's eyes. He clearly knew his musicians. Then Fisher frowned. 'No you're not,' he said. 'Anthony Marino is out of the country.'

'I was,' Anthony declared. 'I was touring Europe. I've come back especially from Italy to look for Miss Mazzini.'

'Oh!' Fisher was clearly shaken. 'Well – well, it still stands, if she don't want to go with you and you try to force her—'

'I won't,' Anthony insisted. 'I have only her best interests at heart.'

Fisher stood back. 'Go on then.' He indicated with his head that Anthony should continue on his way. 'But I'll be waiting and watching, so don't try anything.'

'I understand. Really I do.' He felt sorry for this inadequate man with a fixation on Poppy: yet he also felt disturbed by him. How far would he go to protect her? Why did he think she was in danger, and would he take it upon himself to spirit her away so that she was hidden from everyone but himself?

'You know,' he said, 'with Miss Mazzini's talent, she doesn't belong to any one of us. She belongs to the world. But most of all she belongs to herself. She has to make the decisions about her own life. We can't make them for her.'

There was no answer from Fisher and Anthony turned away leaving him standing in the dusk, a forlorn and lonely figure.

He slipped into the Pit Stop as the customers were topping up their glasses and shuffling about on the benches, preparing themselves for the entertainment. He moved towards the crowd at the bar counter and surreptitiously placed the rose on the piano. Then without buying a drink he eased his way back to the place by the door. The landlord exhorted everyone to be quiet and then in a stentorian voice announced, 'Miss *Paula Mason*.'

Anthony saw her give a smile and glance round as if looking for someone and he pulled back into the shadows. She walked to the piano, greeting people as if she knew them, spoke a few words of welcome and prepared to sit down. He thought there was a brief shadow of distress on her face as she noticed the rose, but she picked it up, inhaled the perfume and then slowly unwrapped it.

Anthony saw her lips move as she read the words and there was a bewildered confusion on her face, but she put both the note and the rose back on the top of the piano and began to play and sing. A true professional, he thought. Give the audience what they have paid for and never mind the turmoil you are in. He listened as she sang the audience's favourite melodies and observed them as they joined in with her, and then they hushed and settled as she began a poignant melody. They were obviously aware that she was about to perform her own personal favourites. She sang 'Greensleeves', and then 'Forever True', followed by 'In the Town Where I Was Born'. Then he watched as she picked up the rose and looked round the smoky room.

'Someone has sent me a rose,' she told the audience, and asked them as a whole: 'Was it you?'

'Yers!' they all chanted.

She smiled and picking up the note, asked, 'And did you write this song for me?'

There was silence, followed by a murmuring and shaking of heads. 'We ain't clever enough fer that, Miss Mason!' a voice called.

'Well, someone did. Shall I sing it?'

'Yers,' they shouted. 'Is it a new one?'

Poppy nodded. 'Quite new, I think, but the words are long established and recognizable.'

In his corner, Anthony folded his arms over his chest as she began to sing his words and music. Would she understand that he had thought of her when he was composing, or would she think that he had just written a melody and put lyrics to it? It isn't good enough, he thought. There wasn't enough time to do justice to what I feel.

He heard the last lines – 'And come to me, for forever faithful I will be' – and slowly moved towards the piano as she rose to take her bow. He stood silently waiting, and then gave a gentle smile as she turned and saw him. He saw the relief on her face and she closed her eyes for a second, then she held out both hands to him.

'Anthony!' she breathed huskily. 'Will you take me home?'

CHAPTER FIFTY

Anthony took her first of all to his parents' house, for her clothing and trunk and personal belongings were there, and she told them tearfully and sincerely how sorry she was for having caused them distress by her disappearance. Rosina murmured and clucked, bringing her hot drinks and sweet cake as if she had been starving and lost in the desert, and although it was almost midnight Anthony took it upon himself to go to Dan's house and tell him that she was safe.

Dan arrived early the next morning and put his arms round her in a great bear hug. 'Don't think,' he whispered into her ear, 'that just because I'm an ancient old fogey I don't understand,' and she managed a laugh, for he certainly wasn't that. He looked solemnly at her and began to say something, but became overcome with emotion. 'Anthony will tell you,' he choked. 'Go home to your papa,' he advised, and blew his nose. 'I've wired him to say you're safe. Anthony will take you. And come back when you're ready. We'll be waiting for you.'

'Anthony,' she said, on the journey to King's Cross station, 'I feel terrible. I'm being such a nuisance. You're supposed to be in Italy.'

'My arrangements were fluid,' he assured her. 'I can pick up again when I know that you're safely home.'

She squeezed his hand. 'You're so good to me. I do appreciate it. I was going to move on, you know! I'd decided that that was going to be my last performance at the Pit Stop. The only thing I didn't know was where I would go. I was scared of coming back. Afraid of what you would all think of me.'

'Only good things,' he assured her. 'That's what we think of you.'

She slept for a good deal of the train journey. Her relief at being discovered and having the decision about where to go next taken from her had allowed her to relax at last, and follow the advice of those who knew what was best for her.

'Anthony!' She jerked awake, her head having rested on his shoulder. 'There was a man at the Pit Stop! He – it probably seems strange for me to say it, but I thought that he had recognized me. He was constantly watching me. He – I think it was he – he threw a flower when I performed at the Savoy. And he was waiting outside when I came out.' She took a breath. 'And when I saw the rose on the piano, I thought it was from him, and I don't know why, but I was just a bit afraid.'

'He did know you,' Anthony told her. 'I met him. He works in a music shop. His name is Fisher,' he said, and, by giving the stranger a name, diminished her fears. 'He told me that he was watching over you, making sure that you were all right. He's an admirer, that's all. He's heard you often. Your black wig didn't prevent him from recognizing you.'

She looked up at him. 'Have I been so very foolish? Such a lovesick child?'

'Not foolish at all,' he said softly, for another passenger had got into their compartment at the last station. Then he whispered. 'Are you over Charlie? Is it too soon to say?'

She gazed out of the window. A plume of smoke obscured her view of the passing countryside. 'He's going to marry someone else,' she said in a low voice. 'It didn't take him long to decide. I don't think he considered me in the least.'

'And . . .' He hesitated, for she hadn't answered the question. 'Do you think you would have married him if he'd asked you?'

'I'm not sure,' she admitted. 'He once said that if ever we were to marry, I would have to give up the stage.' She bit on her lip as she remembered. 'He was quite cross and I did worry about what my answer would be, for I could never give up singing.'

Anthony sat back and suppressed a stinging comment on the idiocy of Charles Chandler, who couldn't hear or see such prodigious talent when it was standing in front of him. Nor, he mused as the train rattled and clacked on its way towards Hull, did he appear to see her sweet innocence. She was his friend's sister and perhaps, he thought darkly, Chandler didn't want an independent though unworldly young woman in his life, but preferred a more compliant companion. But, he nodded along with the swaying and lurching of the train, I am more inclined to believe that he was jealous! Jealous of her success and of the obvious fact that one day she will be more famous than he will ever be with his fancy footwear! And as his thoughts gathered speed, he realized that he too had been guilty of jealousy, and still was. Jealousy of Charles Chandler.

Poppy's father met them at the Paragon railway station and lifted Poppy into his arms. 'You've given us some heartache, lass,' he blurted out as he hugged her. 'Whatever were you thinking of, not coming home to them that cares for you?'

'I'm sorry, Pa.' She burst into tears. 'So very sorry.'

'Well, never mind, you're safe home now, and is this the hero who rescued you?' He shook Anthony warmly by the hand. 'I'm very pleased to meet you at last, Mr Marino. Poppy has spoken of you often and of course we heard you play when you were in Hull. You are very welcome indeed and we're most grateful. Most grateful for your consideration.'

Poppy saw that her father too was becoming very emotional as he spoke, and he put his arms round both of them as they followed the porter out of the station.

'By 'look of all that luggage you've come home for a longish stay, Poppy,' he said huskily.

'Come home to lick her wounds, sir,' Anthony said in a low voice. 'She has been under considerable strain.'

'Ah!' Joshua nodded and asked no more questions as they took a cab for the short journey to Savile Street.

'We live behind and above 'shop,' he told Anthony, as they neared their destination. 'We're just simple folk, but you are very welcome to our home, Mr Marino.'

'Thank you, sir,' Anthony said. 'That's exactly the same situation as my parents. Poppy might have told you they have a small restaurant in London.'

'She did. She did.' Joshua gave his hand to Poppy to assist her down. 'And Italian too, just like us?'

He continued with small talk as he helped the driver with the luggage, and then Poppy put out her hand for Anthony to follow her inside. 'Come and meet my brother, and Mattie and – oh, Nan!' She flung her arms round Nan who stood smiling in the middle of the shop whilst Tommy and Mattie stood behind the counter. 'Oh, Nan,' she wept, 'I've missed you so!'

Anthony sidestepped them and leaned over the counter to shake hands with Tommy and then Mattie. 'How do you do?' He laughed. 'I'm Anthony Marino!'

Poppy told Nan and Mattie that Charlie was going to be married and discovered that they had already heard. He had at last written to his parents to inform them of his engagement and tell them how well his business was progressing. 'I saw his ma,' Mattie said, upstairs in Poppy's bedroom, where she was helping her unpack her trunk. 'She told me that he's making shoes for society people and stage folk too. She was quite proud of that, but sniffy about his engagement. Seemed to think that they'd never see him if he's marrying somebody out of 'top drawer.'

She must have seen Poppy's crestfallen expression, for she added, 'You're well shut of him, Poppy. I know you were fond of him, but he'd never have been faithful.'

'I expect you're right, Mattie,' Poppy said. 'But it doesn't alter the fact that I did care for him and I thought he cared for me. But as for his fiancée being top drawer, well, she's rich, or her father is, but that doesn't make them better than anyone else.'

Mattie picked up Poppy's red dancing shoes. They had worn thin on the sole and the leather had indentations where her toes had pressed. She held them up. 'Just look,' she said, dangling them by the heel. 'Worn out! Time to cast them off and get new.' She gazed at Poppy. 'He's mouth-wateringly handsome, isn't he, your Mr Marino?' She sighed. 'And those beautiful songs that he writes. How I'd love to hear him play.'

Poppy gave a surprised laugh. 'Mattie! He's not *my* Mr Marino. He's—' She swallowed. 'He's a good friend and very caring, that's true; that's why I wrote to him when I was so unhappy. I knew he would understand, and – and yes, he did come back from Italy to look for me.' Her lips parted and her eyes drifted unseeing as she pondered on that point.

'You are so naive, Poppy.' Mattie shook her head at her. 'I can't believe how innocent you are in spite of travelling abroad and working with those seasoned stage folk. Your pa was so worried that they'd corrupt you. And here you are, as green as you ever were.'

'Am I?' Poppy asked breathlessly. 'I didn't realize that I was.'

'And I suppose you can't see either that Mr Marino is besotted by you? Why, his eyes follow you everywhere! You can't fool me.' Mattie laughed. 'I know about these things.'

Poppy licked her lips. 'You're being silly, Mattie,' she said. 'And besides, being in love is far too painful. I'd be afraid of being hurt again.'

At the supper table the following evening, Joshua cleared his throat and stood up. 'We, er, we've got some news.'

Poppy looked at Tommy and Mattie and raised her eyebrows, then beamed. They must have planned a date for their wedding.

'When I say *we*, I really mean Nan and me.' Joshua glanced at Poppy, then at Tommy and Mattie, and then his eyes rested on Nan. 'Them two know already, so it'll come as no surprise. But you won't know, Poppy, that I've asked Nan to be my wife, and she's agreed.'

Poppy gasped and for a moment was lost for words. Then she started to weep great floods of tears. Anthony, who was sitting next to her, put his hand in his pocket and brought out a clean handkerchief which he silently handed to her.

The others all looked at her with various degrees of apprehension on their faces, and Nan's own eyes started to fill and her mouth to tremble. 'I know how you miss your ma, Poppy,' Joshua began, his face working with concern.

'Oh, it's not that, Pa. I'm just so happy for you both.' She couldn't see for her tears. 'I couldn't wish for anyone better for you than Nan – for all of us,' she added. 'I love Nan so much, and I love you and Tommy and Mattie.' She rose from the table and went to Nan to give her a kiss, and then her pa and then Mattie and Tommy. She stopped by Anthony, who was offering Joshua his congratulations, and put one hand on his shoulder, whilst with the other she wiped her tears. He placed his hand over hers.

'Am I the only one not to be given a kiss?' he said lightly. 'Am

I not always there with a large handkerchief at the ready to mop up the tears? Do I not deserve one on this momentous occasion, even if I am not family?'

Poppy gave a sobbing laugh and bent to touch her lips to his cheek. 'Of course you do, Anthony,' she sniffled. 'I have so much to thank you for. If it were not for you, I wouldn't be here. I'd be drifting round London, wondering what to do and where to go next.'

'And now you've the chance to decide on your future from the comfort of home,' he murmured. 'And the choice is yours.'

After supper Poppy asked Anthony if he would play the piano for them. 'It's an old one,' she explained. 'But Tommy and I could always knock out a tune on it.'

He laughed and sat down on the piano stool, and announced in a music hall manner, 'The *celebrated* Anthony Marino, knocking out a tune on the Mazzinis' old *pianner*.' Poppy screwed up her eyes and put her hand over her mouth in embarrassment, and Anthony began with a dashing flurry and a busy shower of notes from a popular song, and then another, and singing loudly, called for them to join in. This was an Anthony that she didn't know; she knew the gentle considerate one, the understanding one, but not this humorous fellow. Then, changing his style, he played simple folk songs, and with a few gentle notes began Bellini's '*La Sonnambula*'.

Poppy got up from her chair and, standing beside him, began to sing, though a single tear ran down her cheek as she remembered singing for her mother. Anthony looked up at her as they came to the end, and, beginning a selection of his own songs, said softly so that no-one else could hear, 'Sing him out of your soul, Poppy.'

She sang, for although he hadn't brought any music with him, they both knew the words and music, and the small audience sat and listened and eyed each other knowingly and tenderly.

Anthony stayed another day and then took his leave of them, as he had to travel back to Italy to continue his engagements. Tommy shook him warmly by the hand. 'Come any time you like,' he said. 'We'll be pleased to see you.' Anthony and Tommy had had several discussions about food and cooking and Anthony had told him about the food in Italy.

'If you come to London after you are married,' he told Mattie and Tommy, 'you must stay with my parents. They'd like that.' To Poppy's father and Nan he again offered his good wishes for their future together, and they both gave him their heartfelt thanks for finding Poppy.

'We would have been bereft if anything had happened to her,' Nan said, giving him a warm smile. 'And so, I suppose, would you?'

'Is it so obvious?' he asked in a low voice.

'To another woman, yes,' she answered. 'But not yet to Poppy. It's too soon,' she added, and he nodded his understanding.

'I wish,' Poppy said, as she stood with him at the railway station waiting for the train to arrive, 'I wish we'd had more time. There's so much I wanted to show you and share with you.'

She had taken him round the town of Hull, shown him the string of town docks, called in at the theatres, and walked to the pier to see the lashing waters of the Humber estuary. 'In the town where I was born there flowed a river,' he sang teasingly, his eyes gleaming.

'There's another river,' she had said, and taking his hand had led him behind the old High Street to where the river Hull ran into the Humber. 'But how did you know then how I was feeling?' she asked. 'That song could have been written for me!'

'Call it intuition,' he said softly, and tucked her arm into his.

But now he was leaving and didn't know when he would be back in England.

'I'll miss you, Anthony,' she said shyly.

'How much?' he asked, his eyes tender on her face.

She blinked. She felt vulnerable and lost. Could she ever trust again? 'A lot,' she said huskily.

The train steamed in and his parting words were lost in the noise of clanking wheels and engine, the hiss of steam, the cries of porters, engine driver and van guard, and the rush of passengers dashing to claim their seats.

'What?' she shouted, 'I didn't hear!'

'It will keep,' he said, and bent to kiss her cheek before picking up his overnight bag. 'Take care of yourself, Poppy.' He gave her a wistful smile. 'Keep on singing.'

She exhaled a breath. 'When will I see you again?'

He looked steadily at her. 'Whenever you're ready,' he said, before turning to board the train.

Poppy walked slowly back to Savile Street. She felt exhausted, and as if she was in limbo. I'll rest for a while, she thought, then play the piano and sing a little, perhaps go back to the beginning and practise, as I always used to. Her thoughts turned back to Anthony. What was it he had said as the engine blew off that screeching steam? She hunched into herself. I'm missing him already, she realized. He seemed so different, at home, away from the theatre. He's quite a different person.

She stopped at the corner of Savile Street, and on a sudden impulse turned up George Street and rang the bell of Miss Eloise's rooms.

Miss Eloise stared in amazement when she opened the door and saw Poppy standing there. 'My goodness!' she exclaimed. 'Can it be? Poppy! Come in. Come in. How lovely to see you.' They climbed the stairs to her rooms and she clapped her hands in delight. 'I never thought— Sit down, do. Tea? Yes? Well, I didn't think you would ever have the time to come and see me again,' she chatted as she brewed a pot of tea. 'I know how busy you are; that you've been travelling abroad— Oh, yes,' she said, seeing Poppy's surprised expression. 'I have followed your career avidly, as did Miss Davina, who, I'm sorry to say, has now left the area to live with her niece.'

'You must miss her,' Poppy said, knowing of their long friendship.

'I do,' Miss Eloise said. 'I feel quite lonely sometimes, but I play the piano and I sing, and music is my companion. But why are you home?' she asked. 'Are you between engagements? I read of your success in France, but nothing recently.'

'I – I have been indisposed,' Poppy murmured. 'A personal matter left me unwell.'

'Ah!' Miss Eloise said knowingly. 'A matter of the heart, perhaps?'

Poppy nodded, unwilling to say more.

'Thank goodness, I have never suffered so,' Miss Eloise poured the tea into fine china cups. 'I have never felt the thrill or loss of love for another person. My music has been my one and only love, but if I have two regrets in my life, one is that I didn't have a child, which, of course, was impossible without a husband; and the other is that I never travelled to Italy and heard opera in its rightful home.'

She clasped her hands together and lifted her eyes. 'To hear the works of Rossini in Naples or Rome. Bellini or Verdi in Milan. That is – *was* – my dream.' She lifted her shoulders. 'But, alas, it is too late now. I am too old, and I have no companion. But you, Poppy,' she shook a finger, and Poppy smiled, recalling the familiar gesture, 'that is what you must do whilst you are young. Go to Italy and hear the great composers.'

CHAPTER FIFTY-ONE

Poppy stayed with her father all summer. She slept until late in the morning and was indulged by her father and Nan. She served coffee in the coffee shop and chatted to the customers, and spent time wandering round the town, looking in the shops in Whitefriargate, strolling down to the pier and watching the ships tossing on the choppy water as they came up and down the busy estuary. She visited the theatre, sometimes taking Mattie with her. They went to variety shows at the Mechanics, which Mattie loved, especially enjoying the living tableaux and performing birds and animals.

But she went alone to the Gough and Davy promotion of a Grand Concert at the Assembly Rooms, which featured well-known singers and instrumentalists. Miss King, contralto, Miss Ribollo, soprano, and the popular tenor, Mr James Leyland. The soloist Miss Clara Asher of the London Philharmonic Orchestra played the pianoforte, and Poppy closed her eyes as she listened and thought of Anthony, and as she sat watching the performers she knew that that was where she wanted to be, up there on the stage, singing.

She wrote to Anthony, shy, halting letters, and he wrote to her. His letters were amusing as he told of the people he was meeting and the towns he was playing in. They were solicitous as he asked about her, affectionate and tender in tone.

As summer receded, Poppy visited Miss Eloise again and asked her to give her some coaching, which she did, telling her that her voice had improved and matured since she had last heard her. 'I was wrong when I said that your voice wasn't suitable for operetta,' she admitted. 'You have had a good coach. Much better than I,' and Poppy told her about Marian Bennett and of their visit to France.

'But you have also experienced life,' Miss Eloise told her. 'This is in your voice too.'

Without really intending to, Poppy confided in her about her lost love, though not Charlie's name, and about working at the Pit Stop, and her friendship with the pianist Anthony Marino.

'You must learn to love again, my dear,' Miss Eloise said kindly. 'You are only young. You are resilient, though you may not think so at the moment.'

Nan told her much the same thing, shyly adding, 'Look at your pa and me. Would you ever think that we could become fond of someone else at our age? I shall be forty-two this year.'

Poppy laughed. Nan had a pretty bloom on her, and her father seemed to be younger and merrier than he had been in a long time. 'You're in your prime, Nan,' she told her. 'I never realized you were so lovely.'

Nan patted Poppy's arm. 'Face up to life, Poppy,' she said softly. 'Wake up and look at what's in front of you. Take a chance. Don't be afraid of being hurt.' She kissed her cheek. 'Charlie wasn't meant for you. He wouldn't have made you happy. He isn't 'loving kind. But there's someone else who is.'

The following week, Poppy packed her trunk and then walked to the station to book a ticket for London for the next day. 'I'm ready to go back, Pa,' she said on her return. 'I'm ready to sing and take up my life again.'

His eyes were sad at the thought of her imminent departure, but he nodded. 'Aye,' he said gruffly. 'There are songs to sing, Poppy. We must all sing them and find that life's worthwhile after all.'

She hired a cab at King's Cross station and had her trunk delivered to the Marinos', but asked the driver to drop her off at Dan's office in St Martin's Lane. 'I need to work,' she told him after he had joyfully greeted her. She gazed steadily at him. 'But I want to go abroad. To Italy.'

'Who'll go with you?' he asked, rubbing his chin.

'Wh-what?'

'You can't go alone. You're not a music hall performer! You

have a reputation to consider. And I know that Marian can't go. Jeanette is expecting another child and she'll want to be with her.'

'Then I'll go alone,' she said firmly. She hadn't considered this aspect.

He shook his head. 'I won't book you! As your agent I must consider your safety as well as your reputation.'

She sat silently thinking as he went into the outer office to speak to Miss Battle. When he came back she had a sparkle in her eyes. 'How long will it take to make bookings, if I find someone to come with me?'

'Depends which theatre or concert hall has a vacancy. Why? What's the hurry?' he asked. 'I can get engagements in London almost immediately.'

'It has to be Italy,' she said. 'It's important.'

He gave a wide grin of comprehension. 'All right! Make your arrangements and I'll see what I can do. Florence would be a good place to start,' he added, his smile crinkling his eyes. 'A very good place indeed.'

She walked to the Marinos' where Mario greeted her like a long-lost relative. 'You must always stay with us,' he said. 'Don't think of staying anywhere else.'

'I'm going to Italy,' she told him, which silenced him for a moment, then he called to his wife.

'Rosina!' he shouted. 'Poppy! She is going to Italy!'

Poppy wrote a letter to Miss Eloise asking her if she would accompany her to Italy, and adding that she would of course pay travel expenses. A reply came back immediately to say that Miss Eloise was already packing a trunk, and that she would take care of her own expenditure, as she had a considerable fortune and nothing to spend it on.

Dan made the travel arrangements, and Miss Eloise arrived a week later. She looked exceedingly elegant, having spent a good deal of money on new clothes for the journey. Her dolman cashmere coat was trimmed with astrakhan, and her very large velvet hat supported plumes and feathers. In her hand she carried a long umbrella. 'You have no conception, my dear,' she explained to Poppy who had met her at King's Cross station to take her to the Marinos' where they were to spend the night, 'how that money has been burning in my bank account for so many years, just waiting for the opportunity to be used!'

Rosina and Dan came to see them off on the boat train, and Rosina gave her a list of things she must tell Anthony, 'if by any chance you see 'im,' she added as if it were a side issue. 'For I quite understand that you might not! Italy is a *beeg* country, but you must ask 'im for to meet my cousins and family also, if you can.'

They had smiled at each other in an implicit understanding, though Poppy was rather shy at meeting her eyes. She thinks she knows why I'm going, she thought, when I don't even know for sure if I do.

It was a long and tiring journey, but Miss Eloise was an excellent travelling companion. She organized porters and harangued station officials when trains were late or didn't arrive, and had their hotel accommodation changed if she thought it unsuitable. 'I am so enjoying myself,' she told Poppy. 'I feel as if I'm thirty-five instead of fifty-five.'

Poppy became more and more nervous and apprehensive the nearer they came to Florence. Am I being foolish again? Have I misunderstood? And perhaps Anthony might have moved on. Or he might not be pleased to see me when he's in the middle of a tour. I'm too impulsive; I should have sent a telegram to warn him. I still could, I suppose. She fiddled in her handbag to look for Anthony's address and his list of engagements in Florence, which Dan had given her. 'Just in case you should be in the vicinity,' he'd explained. 'And you must wire me as soon as you're there and I'll send details of engagements when I make them.'

They arrived in Florence at four o'clock in the afternoon. The warm October sun shone on the mellow architecture of palaces, churches and the cathedral of Santa Maria del Fiore. 'How wonderful,' Miss Eloise exclaimed, looking out of the hotel window. 'I can't believe that I'm really here. Tomorrow we must explore. Forgive me, my dear, but I cannot do more tonight than have a little supper and seek my bed. But I'm sure it will be perfectly safe for you to take a walk and view the sights, if you should wish to do so.'

'Yes,' Poppy breathed nervously. 'That is what I would like to do. I've been sitting for too long.'

She drank a cup of China tea in her room, and then bathed and changed into a gown of white spotted muslin, over an underdress of pale green silk taffeta. The sleeves were also lined in green to the elbow, and fell to a frill of white lace at the wrist. She brushed her hair and pinned it up, leaving a few tendrils around her cheeks, and put on a straw hat adorned with flowers and a short veil.

She knocked on her companion's door. 'I'll perhaps see you at supper, Miss Eloise,' she said nervously. 'Or I – I might go to a concert.'

'Of course.' Miss Eloise raised her eyebrows. 'Would you like me to come with you?'

'No, no,' Poppy hastily assured her. 'I shall be quite all right; there are so many visitors about. You have your rest,' and carrying her white parasol, she walked out of the hotel.

Miss Eloise looked out of the bedroom window and watched her; she saw heads turn and gentlemen raise their hats or give small bows. She sighed. Turning away, she slipped off her gown, took off her shoes, unhooked her stays and put on a silk robe; then she poured a glass of wine, and sitting down in a comfortable chair by the window picked up her book, *Italian for the Traveller.*

Poppy walked steadily towards the street where the concert hall stood. She had studied the map so many times that she was quite sure she knew how to find it. It was, according to the map, close by the church of Santa Croce, which she was approaching now. She stood for a moment and gazed at the poster outside the building. *Il concerto,* she read, and Antonio Marino's name was featured at the very top.

People were going in and appeared to have tickets, which they were handing in at the door. She followed them, and going to the desk asked haltingly, '*Buona sera. Per favore, vorrei un biglietto.*'

'*No, signorina,*' the booking clerk said. '*Non può entrare, lo spettacolo è iniziato.*'

Poppy put her hand to her mouth, her eyes open wide. What was he saying? That she couldn't go in?

'It ees too late. It ees starting now,' the clerk explained. 'You understand, signorina?'

'But,' Poppy pointed to the last few stragglers who had just gone in. 'They—' She put her hand to her chest. 'I'm a – *sono un' amica di* – a friend of Signor Marino.'

'Ah!' He shrugged and tore off a ticket and counted out the money she held in her hand. '*La platea!*' He pointed to a door leading into the hall and put his finger to his lips.

'*Grazie. Grazie!*' she said gratefully. 'Thank you so much.'

He nodded and smiled. '*Prego!*'

The concert hadn't started as he had said; the lights were still on, but the orchestra was tuning up and Poppy was shown to a seat on the back row. She put her parasol on the floor, removed her gloves and sat back in the chair. The hall was full; the audience was well dressed and there was a ripple of muted conversation. Then the lights were dimmed and the orchestra struck up with a medley of music from various operas. Verdi's stirring *Nabucco*, dramatic *Rigoletto* and 'Musetta's Waltz' from Puccini's *La Bohème.*

Poppy sat entranced and listened next to an elderly baritone who gave a rendition from *The Magic Flute* and *The Marriage of Figaro.* Following him, as the curtains closed, a frock-coated compère came to the front of the stage, gave a voluble speech, none of which Poppy understood, then, standing back as the curtain rose, announced, 'Signor *Antonio Marino*!'

A grand piano stood centre stage, and as the audience applauded Anthony strode on. He wore a black frock coat, narrow black trousers and a white high-collared shirt with a white tie. His sideburns were long and his hair, Poppy noticed fondly and with a skip of a heartbeat, still flopped over his forehead. He gave a bow, centre, left, then right, lifted his coat tails and sat down at the piano.

He had a vast repertoire. Poppy glanced at the programme she had bought, as Anthony played Bellini and Beethoven, and then moved into Rossini's melodic *Barber of Seville*, followed by Gounod's love-music from *Romeo et Juliette.*

She felt a tear trickle from her eyes. How was it that Anthony's playing always had the ability to make her cry? There was rousing applause after each piece and she marvelled at the Italian audience's enthusiasm. Anthony stood up finally to take a bow, and then announced something in Italian and everyone clapped and cheered.

'For the benefit of those who do not speak our beautiful Italian language,' he announced in English, 'I wish to explain that I would now like to play for you some of my own work. It is dedicated to, and was written for, a particular person. Tonight it will be played as music without words, but the words, which are love songs, are already written.'

Poppy put her hand to her cheek. Was he speaking to her? But he doesn't know I am here! Dan! Has he told him? Or is he . . . he can't be speaking of someone else? Not Jeanette? Surely not! He said he was over his love for her. She listened as with the orchestra Anthony began to play the melody from 'In the Town Where I Was Born,' which she knew he had written for her, and then he began the music from the song sheet she had bought from the costumier in London.

> Sweet eyes that smiled but not for me
> They smiled for him who was untrue . . .

and with a slight shift of improvisation he worked in the harmony of,

> If I could only love again I'd choose to love just you
> Listen and hear my silent voice, my words a muted tune
> Of some romantic melody
> Question not the but or why
> I love you now and for evermore until the day I die.

Anthony, she breathed. Why wasn't I listening?

He slipped easily and elegantly into the music he had written on the scrap of paper that had been wrapped round the rose he had placed on the piano at the Pit Stop. It was a gentle, nostalgic, evocative piece of music, new to her at the time, and which she had kept and puzzled over.

She opened up her velvet bag. Inside was the paper with the words written on it. She began to hum the refrain.

> Think no more of the lonely tears
> Mourn no more the wasted years
> Dear heart forget him, let his memory dim

And come to me
For forever faithful I will be.

Also inside the bag was the red rose, faded, yet still with its faint sweet perfume. She took it out and, rising from her seat, her green gown rustling as she moved, slowly walked towards the stage. He came to the end of the music, and lifting his head said softly, yet clearly, 'And to close the performance I would like to play the English "Greensleeves", written, it is believed, by Henry the Eighth, and introduce to you – la bella *Signorina Mazzini.*'

Poppy felt a glow of happiness spreading through her, lifting her heart and spirits. She turned to the audience and bowed, then, turning again as the audience broke into spontaneous applause at this unexpected development, she lifted the hem of her skirt and walked up the steps to the stage.

Anthony rose from the piano and went towards her, taking both of her hands in his. He kissed her on both cheeks and then tenderly on her lips, and the audience gasped and then cheered. 'I love you, is what I said, when you didn't hear,' he whispered.

She stood back, her arms outstretched, still holding his hands and gazing at him. 'And I love you,' she answered on a gentle breath. 'So very much.'

He led her towards the piano. He touched his fingers to his lips and blew her a kiss and began to play, and she, with another bow to the audience, began to sing.

'Alas my love you do me wrong
To cast me off discourtesly
For I have loved you oh so long
Delighting in your company

Greensleeves was all my joy
Greensleeves was my delight.
Greensleeves was my heart of gold
And who but my lady Greensleeves'

Poppy gave a deep curtsy to take the enthusiastic applause, but Anthony wasn't quite finished. As she raised her head, he effortlessly and gently moved into the introduction of the final lyrical piece of music, and if she needed further proof of his lasting love, here it was, for this was the music he had sent to her whilst she was singing in France, which she hadn't recognized as a love poem written for her.

The musicians, all but the violinist, laid down their instruments. The conductor raised his baton, gave a slight raise of his eyebrows to the violinist, and Poppy, glancing towards Anthony, caught his eyes and smile, and began to sing.

'My love she sits a-weeping beneath the greenwood tree
My love she sits a-weeping – but not for me.
Her tears flow for another, to me she was not true
For though I love those pale pink cheeks and starry
eyes so blue
The tender lips I fain would kiss their nectar sweet to
claim
Love only him who cares not and whisper on his name.

My love she sits a-weeping beneath the greenwood tree
My love she sits a-weeping – but not for me.

I wait for her as the year doth pass when winter turns
to spring
When fresh green grows on the greenwood tree, my
dearest love will turn to me, to bring her comfort still.
And when I look upon her face the light of love to see
And with my arms I do embrace her wounded gentle
heart
I'll claim it for my very own and tell her soft, my dearest one,
I'll never part from thee.

My love she sits a-smiling beneath the greenwood tree
My love she sits a-smiling – she smiles for me.'